THOUGH HELL
SHOULD BAR
THE WAY

THOUGH HELL
SHOULD BAR
THE WAY

THE REPUBLIC OF CINNABAR NAVY

DAVID DRAKE

TITAN BOOKS

Though Hell Should Bar the Way
Print edition ISBN: 9781785652318
E-book edition ISBN: 9781785652325

Published by Titan Books
A division of Titan Publishing Group Ltd
144 Southwark Street, London SE1 0UP

First Titan edition: June 2018
2 4 6 8 10 9 7 5 3 1

A CIP catalogue record for this title is available from the British Library.

Printed and bound in Great Britain by CPI Group UK Ltd.

To Evan Ladouceur, who already has had
not only repeated acknowledgments in this series,
but also had a superannuated light cruiser named after him.

AUTHOR'S NOTE

Classicists won't be surprised to learn that the idea for this book sprang from the events leading to the outbreak of the Second Punic War. I probably have more classicists among my readers than most other writers, but even so I doubt they're a majority.

Though that was the germ of the novel, the business of the book is more concerned with piracy. Pirates have become a big deal in recent years, but even when I was a kid there were plenty of child-accessible books about them. I particularly remember a big volume with what I now suspect were N. C. Wyeth plates. An image which is still vivid with me was of buccaneers in a small boat closing on the stern of a Spanish galleon.

As I got older, I read quite a lot more about pirates—but these were the pirates of the West Indies and the East Coast of North America. There were pirates other places too—Captain Kidd operated in the Indian Ocean—but they were pretty much the same: They captured ships and stole the cargo, behaving with greater or lesser brutality to the crews and passengers.

There were also the Barbary Pirates in the Mediterranean. I knew about them because one of the first steps the newly United States took on the international stage was to mount an expedition against them in 1801.

A catchphrase of the day was, "Millions for defense but not one cent for tribute!" Pirates from North African ports were capturing American ships and holding the crews for ransom unless the US paid tribute to Tripoli, Tunis, Algiers, and the Kingdom of Morocco, as most European nations did. Instead, the US sent a naval squadron.

Much like the 1968 Tet Offensive, the expedition had a considerable effect on public opinion back in the US, but considered simply as a military operation it was an expensive failure. There were quite a lot of heroic endeavors by American sailors—and I read about them with delight—but in fact the expedition's major success was to burn one of its own ships in Tripoli harbor after the pirates had captured it. This was truly splendid exploit, but burning your own vessels isn't a good way to force an enemy to change its ways.

The Barbary Pirates continued to operate until France conquered the region later in the nineteenth century, but that's another matter. The crucial thing, which I didn't realize until I visited Algiers in 1981, is that the Barbary Pirates weren't in the business of looting ships: They were capturing slaves.

I'm not the only one who was ignorant on the subject. A few years ago I commented to an intelligent friend that the pirates captured European slaves in numbers comparable to the numbers of African slaves shipped to the Americas. (The real figure is more like a tenth, but this is still about a million European slaves.) He accused me of getting my facts from Fox News.

Well, no. I'd noticed the wonderful tile work in many of the older buildings in Algiers (and since many such buildings have been converted to public use or into foreign missions, this isn't as hard as it may sound). When I asked about it, I learned that charitable organizations in European countries in the seventeenth and eighteenth centuries were set up to buy back enslaved sailors.

The Dutch, as one of the greatest trading nations of the period, provided a large number of both slaves and charities. Much of the ransoming was done with goods rather than gold, and the pirates turned out to be very fond of Delft tiles. The evidence is right there today for any visitor to see.

When we visited Iceland a few years later, I learned that Barbary Pirates had captured the city of Vestmannaeyjar and carried the profitable part of the population off as slaves. (Old people were burned alive in the church.) Piracy was definitely big business, in North Africa as surely as in the Antebellum South.

There's quite a lot of information about the slave-based economies of the Barbary States. I prefer to get my history from primary sources—the history really isn't as good, but it gives the reader a much better notion of how the culture *felt*, and that's important from my standpoint. There are the accounts by ransomed slaves, by free Europeans working in the Barbary Kingdoms (generally in specialist trades like medicine or gunnery), and by European officials representing citizens of their nations in the kingdoms. I found a great deal of material.

It's important to remember that slavery was a *business*. The pirate kingdoms weren't civilized by modern standards (or even by those of the Antebellum South), but there were laws, and the trade in slaves was regulated by both law and custom.

My purpose, as always, is to tell a good story. I hope I've done so here. But readers who recall that the human interactions I describe are neither invented or pre-invented (which is how I tend to think of Fox News) may learn some things they didn't previously know.

—Dave Drake

david-drake.com

...Then look for me by moonlight,
Watch for me by moonlight,
I'll come to thee by moonlight,
though hell should bar the way.

—Alfred Noyes
"The Highwayman"

Chapter One

"Now watch that you don't take this corner too short again!" Cady snarled as we approached the entrance of Bergen and Associates. "If you knock the gate post down, the repairs come straight out of your pay!"

"Yes," I said, not shouting, not mumbling, just speaking in an ordinary voice. If I didn't say anything, he'd keep shouting at me, and I was already nervous about turning into the shipyard.

I *had* clipped the corner of the Petersburg warehouse yesterday, the first time I drove the chandlery flatbed. There was no real harm done: paint smeared on the side of the truck, and wood splinters bristling on the edge of the building.

I'd sanded the corner off and repainted it on my own time; not even Cady could claim that the battered old truck was damaged so that it mattered. You could've used it for a gunnery target and it wouldn't look any worse than it did already.

Still, it saved Cady from finding something else to ride me about. Though he'd have managed regardless, of that I had no doubt. Cady didn't have any real rank at the Petersburg Chandlery, but he'd married old Fritzi's daughter. Any time Fritzi wasn't watching, Cady acted like he was the boss.

I downshifted into the creeper gear and started hauling on the big horizontal steering wheel. I was trying to watch in both side mirrors while Cady kept yammering at me. I got the nose through and stuck my head out of the cab to shout at the watchman: "Petersburg to pick up three High Drives for reconditioning?"

The watchman was missing his left ear and the sleeve on that side was pinned up. He squinted at his display and called back, "That's Bay One, to the left. Back right up to the dock. I'll let 'em know you're here."

Bergen and Associates was big for a private yard. Three four- to six-thousand-ton freighters were being serviced now, and the docks could hold vessels much bigger than them. I was facing BAY 2 in big red letters across a trackway two hundred feet wide. I turned left, keeping close to the administrative buildings along the back fence, and pulled up when I thought I'd gone far enough.

"If you'll get out and guide me," I said to Cady, "I'll back up to the loading dock."

"Who do you figure you are to give me orders, Academy boy?" Cady said, leaning against the cab door to face me. He was a big fellow and not as fat as he was going to be in a few more years of beer and fried food.

"I'm not ordering you, Cady," I said. I wished I'd come alone, but this really was a two-man job. I unlatched my door. "Look, you back her up and I'll guide you, I don't care."

"Well, *I* bloody care!" Cady said. "You don't need a guide. Just do your bloody job!"

I hopped out of the cab and walked toward the admin building. An old spacer came out the door, calling something behind him. "Hey, buddy?" I said. "I need a ground guide over to Bay One. You got a minute?"

I wasn't going to back through the shipyard without a guide. There wasn't a lot of traffic, but a lowboy was trundling past behind a tractor right now.

Besides, it'd just be stupid. I couldn't help that Cady was being a jerk, but he wasn't going to make me stupid.

"Yeah, sure," the spacer said. "You're here for those High Drives I want rebuilt?"

I opened my mouth to agree when the door opened again, and I recognized the girl who'd come out behind him.

"Roy!" she said. "Roy Olfetrie! It *is* you, isn't it?"

"Hi, Miranda," I said. "Gosh, I hadn't thought to run into you. What're you doing at Bergen's? Working in the office?"

Miranda was dressed pretty well for a clerk, but she and her mother could sew like nobody's business. She'd never looked out of place when our families got together after her father died as an RCN captain, leaving his widow and two children on a survivors' pension.

The woman in RCN utilities who followed Miranda out of the office was six and a half feet tall. Her open left palm looked like she could drive spikes with it, and the expression she gave me made me think that I'd do for a spike if I got out of line.

"Not exactly," Miranda said with the laugh I remembered

from the old days. "My husband owns the yard. I've come up in the world, Roy."

I smiled, but I guess there was something in my face because Miranda suddenly looked like I'd started sobbing. Which I hadn't done, even when it first happened.

"Ma'am?" the spacer I'd first spoken to said to Miranda. "I need to get back to the *Pocahontas*. And kid?" This to me. "I figure Chief Woetjans can guide you as well as I could."

"Look, kid!" Cady shouted from the truck. "We got work to do. Get your ass back in here!"

"In a bit!" I called over my shoulder. I felt hot because of what I'd done to Miranda, or anyway how I'd made her feel even though I hadn't meant to. "Look, Miranda, the problem was nothing to do with anybody but Dad himself. I couldn't be happier that you've been doing well. I don't know anybody who deserves it more."

"I heard about the trouble," she said, turning her eyes a little away. "I was very sorry."

Everybody on Cinnabar had heard about "the trouble," I guess, at least if they paid any attention to the news. That was just the way it was, same as if I'd been caught in the rain. Only a lot worse.

"Well, it's not so bad," I lied. "I dropped out of the Academy and got a job with a ship chandler for now. After things settle down I'll look for something—"

"Watch out!" Miranda shouted, looking past me.

I hunched over. Cady's big fist grazed my scalp, but he didn't catch me square in the temple like he'd planned to do.

I punched him twice in the gut, left and right. I'd boxed at the Academy. I didn't have the footwork to be welterweight champion, but the instructors said I had a good punch. A *bloody* good punch, and I was mad enough to give Cady all I had.

I stepped back as Cady dived forward on his nose. He'd been trying to grab me with his left hand and just overbalanced when I doubled him up. He wasn't hurt bad, but he'd remember me every time he sat up for the next few days.

Cady got his feet under him but didn't stand. "Cady!" I said. "Let's quit now and it won't go any further!"

I wasn't sure what to do next. Hitting Cady on the head wasn't going to do anything but break my knuckles, and there was no way I could keep punching him in the gut without him getting a hand on me. Then it'd be all she wrote: It's not like there was a referee to call him for fouling me, after all.

Somebody'd been opening crates at the edge of the loading dock. When Cady finally stood up, he had a crowbar in his right fist.

"Hey, kid!" called the big woman with Miranda. I let my eyes flick toward her. She tossed me the length of high-pressure tubing that she must've been holding along her right leg. I hadn't seen it behind Miranda.

"Hey!" said Cady as I caught it. I cut at his head. He got his left arm up in time to block me, but I heard a bone break when I caught him just above the wrist.

Cady swung the crowbar in a broad haymaker that would've cut me in half if it'd landed, blunt as the bar was. I stepped back and smashed his right elbow so his weapon went sailing into the trackway, sparking and bouncing on the packed gravel.

I guess I could've stopped then—yard personnel were swarming around, most of them carrying a tool or a length of pipe. I had my blood up, though. Cady'd given me a chance to get back not just at him but at the way the world had gone in the past three months.

I cracked him on the forehead with all the strength of my arm. He went down on his face, bleeding badly from the pressure cut.

I moved back and hunched to suck in all the air I could through my mouth. People were talking—shouting, some of them. I could hear them, right enough, but it was like hearing the surf: There was a lot of noise, but my brain wasn't up to making sense of it. I started to wonder if Cady had connected better with my head than I'd thought he had.

The big woman walked up beside me and shouted, "All right, spacers! Two of you get this garbage out the gate and into the gutter, all right?"

I straightened; I was all right now. "Wait!" I said. "He's been injured."

"You got that right," chuckled a man holding a ten-pound hammer. "Nice job, kid."

"Look," I said, not sure how to say what I meant. For that matter, my brain wasn't as clear as I'd like it to be. "He needs medical attention. This yard's got a medicomp, doesn't it?"

It must. Bergen and Associates were too big and successful not to.

"Yes, bring him in," Miranda said. "That's all right, isn't it, Master Mon?"

"If you say so, Mistress," said the man in a suit who'd come out after the fight started. "Tapley and Gerstall, get him into the unit."

He looked at me, friendly enough but sizing me up just the

same. He added, "It looked to me like he was getting about what he deserved, though."

"Yeah," I said, "but I don't want to kill him. I didn't even want to fight him."

I'm out of a job. The sudden realization almost made me vomit. Knocking Cady out wouldn't hurt me for getting another job particularly, but I'd had trouble enough getting in with Petersburg. Maybe being out of the news for three more months would help this time.

Men were hauling Cady inside to where the medicomp was. I started to give the length of tubing back to the woman who'd loaned it to me, then realized the tip was bloody. I wiped it on the leg of my trousers—I'd have used Cady's shirt if I'd thought about it soon enough—and handed it to her. "Thank you, ma'am," I said.

She chuckled. "I guess I'd have done more if it seemed like I needed to," she said. "Which I sure didn't."

"What's all this about?" said the fellow Miranda had called Mon. He must be the boss, because most of the folks who'd come over to watch were going back to their work.

"Sir, nothing, really," I said. "We're just here to pick up three High Drives for Petersburg Chandlery and, well, Cady took a swing at me because I was chatting with Mistress Dorst." Which she wasn't, but it was too late to change even if I'd known Miranda's married name.

"That's right, Mon," Miranda said. "Roy and I are old friends. Our mothers are cousins, you see."

Mon shrugged. "No business of mine, then." He looked at the workmen still present and added, "Raskin, get this truck to

Bay One and load it up. Weiler, Jackson, you give him a hand."

Then to me again, "You just sit for a bit, Master. Come into the office and we'll find you some cacao—or a shot of something if you'd rather. I don't want you driving until you're doing better than you are right now."

"Thank you, sir," I said. "I'll be all right by the time they've got the truck loaded, but my throat's dry, that's a fact."

"Roy, I've got to run now," Miranda said, "but drop in and see me some time soon, please. Miranda Leary at Chatsworth Minor in the Pentacrest District."

She waved and went off with the big woman—Miranda's bodyguard, obviously. She looked able to do that job, no question.

I followed Mon inside and down a short hallway to his office in back. There wasn't a clerk or receptionist. "So...?" he said, pouring cacao for both of us. "You know Mistress Leary pretty well?"

It was obvious that there was a right answer and a wrong one to that question, at least in Mon's mind. I took the mug and said, "Her twin and my older brother Dean Junior were best friends right up and through the RCN Academy. They were both killed in action. I don't think I've seen Miranda in two years."

That was the truth. What I say is generally the truth. When I was a kid I learned that I'm not a good liar, and I've never tried to get better at it.

Mon gestured me to a couch and sat behind the desk. I drank. I figured I'd finish the cacao and go out to the truck. They'd probably be finished loading it by then, and if not, it'd still give me a chance to work off some of the tremors.

"Six always had an eye for the ladies," Mon said with a nostalgic smile. "He sure picked a different one to marry, though. Mistress Leary is sharp as sharp. Not that she's not pretty too, I mean."

"I've always thought that about Miranda," I said. "At any rate..."

I look a long swallow; the cacao had been sitting awhile and wasn't over warm.

I stood and set the empty mug by the pot. "At any rate, she was too smart to let my brother get any further than good friends. A lot of girls weren't. Junior was a fine man and a fine RCN officer, but he wasn't the marrying kind."

Mon chuckled as he walked me out of the office. "To tell the truth," he said, "I'd have said the same thing about Six. But he found a good one when he changed his mind."

As I crossed the trackway, I noticed that the Bergen yard seemed a happy place as well as a busy one. I was pretty sure that if I asked Miranda to have me put on here, she'd make it happen.

I'd rather swab latrines than do that. I hadn't tried in two years to see her. I wasn't going to show up as a beggar now.

But the rent was due at the end of the week, and I wouldn't bet Fritzi was even going to pay me for time worked. He didn't treat Cady like much, but Cady was still family.

Oh, well. One thing at a time.

Chapter Two

I looked out the window of my room, holding aside the towel I'd nailed up to cover the casement. Not that anybody across the broad arterial was likely to be looking into my fourth-floor room—or that it would matter if they did.

At least I could pay for the room tomorrow. I'd told the disbursing clerk to give me my time, so I had three days wages in my pocket. Plus the florin and thirty-five pence I'd had left from last week's pay.

Pascoe, the clerk, had heard Fritzi bellowing. I'd closed the office door when I went in to explain, but that didn't help much. Pascoe hadn't asked Fritzi whether "Get out!" meant with my pay, and he'd even given me the hour I was still short of quitting time for the day. I hoped he wouldn't get in trouble for it.

I could generally pick up casual labor on the docks, though it wasn't steady enough to afford the room. I *really* didn't want to move into a flophouse, but I guessed it was going to come to that.

Tomorrow I could start walking the chandleries again. Or I could go to the shape-up at the docks and then look for something better in the afternoon if I wasn't picked. I'd sleep on it.

Somebody knocked hard on my door—on the doorframe, not the panel. I wasn't sure the panel would have taken that kind of use.

"Come in!" I said. If it was Mistress Causey, coming for her rent early because she'd heard about my job, then I wasn't going to be polite.

The door opened. In the hall were a fellow of maybe thirty in a business suit, and an older man who looked like he ought to be leaning against a barn chewing a straw.

"You're Roy Olfetrie?" the younger man said.

I swallowed. "Yes, I am," I said. "And I've seen your picture. You're Captain Daniel Leary."

God and the saints: Miranda was married to that *Leary.* The war hero.

"I know that," said Captain Leary with a friendly smile. "Now, come down to the bar and let me buy you a drink while you tell me about things I don't know. About yourself."

"I'd be honored to drink with you, sir," I said, stepping out into the hall with him. I wasn't much of a drinker, but I'd sure thought of tying one on this afternoon when I left the chandlery. "Ah, the bar on the ground floor here isn't a great place, though."

"I've drunk in worse," said Leary.

The rustic got to the stairs ahead of him but called back over his shoulder, "I've carried him out of worse, legless and singing 'I don't want to join the Army.'"

Nobody tried to come up while we were going down, but a

man was sprawled in the corner of the second-floor landing. He'd been there when I came home, too. He might as easily as not be dead, but there was nothing I could do for him.

Leary and his companion stepped over the fellow's legs just as I had, so I supposed they really did know about buildings like this one. It had been new to me when I moved in, but I'd learned fast.

The bar was pretty busy for midweek. There was a piccolo in the corner wailing that it wished Mama didn't flash her tits. There was an empty booth in back.

"What'll you have, Olfetrie?" Leary asked.

"Beer, I suppose," I said. It was less likely to poison me than spirits in a place like this, and I wanted to be awake early to make the shape-up.

"Hogg, get us a pitcher of what they have on draft," Leary said. "Bring it over to the booth."

We went to opposite sides. As I started to slide in, the bartender called, "Hey! That booth's Cabrillo's office when he comes in!"

I got out again. The rustic, Hogg, said, "Well then, we'll discuss that with Master Cabrillo if he comes in, won't we?"

He reached into a pocket of his shapeless tunic and came out with a knuckleduster. I guess he touched something because a blade shot out of the top end.

"Till then..." he said. "A pitcher and three glasses. Clean ones if you've got anything clean in here."

"Sit down, Olfetrie," Leary said. "I don't expect we'll be long enough for there to be a problem. If there is one, we'll deal with it."

"Yes sir," I said and sat down. It looked like it was my day for getting into fights. Well, I'd had a lot of new experiences since Dad shot himself.

"I looked for you at Petersburg Chandlery," Leary said mildly. "They told me you didn't work there any more?"

"The owner's son-in-law took a swing at me," I said. "I swung back. It escalated a bit, but I think the medicomp will have him fit for work in a day or two. As fit as Cady ever was."

I grimaced. "Fritzi wouldn't have cared about explanations, so I didn't give him one. Besides—"

I managed a smile. "No excuse, *sir*." The Academy answer.

Leary grinned. "Which is another thing I was wondering about," he said. "You dropped out at the start of your third year. Your grades were all right. What was the problem?"

He wasn't supposed to know my grades, but I don't guess it'd been very hard to learn.

Hogg brought a tray over to the table. He filled one of the mugs and said, "I'll stand here for a bit."

He stood at the end of the table. His right hand was in his pocket. He sipped from the mug in his left, his eyes following every movement in the bar.

Leary filled the other two mugs and slid one to me. I said, "The problem was that my father had been cheating systematically on large contracts with the Ministry of Defense. When this was uncovered, he committed suicide. All our accounts were frozen. I dropped out of the Academy because I had to earn a living."

It wasn't quite that simple. I might've been able to manage living expenses, but my dad wasn't just a crook: He'd been stealing from the RCN. I'd have been shunned in the Academy— if I'd been lucky. Chances were good that my fellow cadets would've beaten me to a pulp every night until I resigned.

"Umm," Leary said as I tasted my beer. "People have been accused of things that aren't true, you know? There was a reshuffle in the Ministry of Defense not long ago."

"Yes, sir, that's true," I said. I drank more beer, because my throat was starting to choke up and I hoped swallowing would help. "But I went over Dad's private accounts. I don't know what the inspectors will be able to prove—they won't see Dad's files, I'll tell you that. But the allegations were true."

This wasn't stuff I liked to talk about, and it wasn't any of Leary's business that I could see. Telling him to shut up was within my rights—and would've been, even if he'd been my commanding officer.

But that would look like I was afraid to talk about it. I wasn't. Talking tore me up, but better that I say things myself than that other people say them about me.

Leary refilled my mug. Hogg kept lifting his beer to his lips while he watched the door, but the level in his mug didn't seem to go down.

"What are you going to do now?" said Leary as he poured for himself.

"There's other chandleries than Petersburg," I said. That was the truth, but the confidence I tried to put in my voice was a lie. "And other work than that too, I guess."

Leary shrugged. He raised his eyes to meet mine. "All true," he said. "And you know my wife. Known her longer than I have, from what Mon says."

"Well, I've known Miranda for pretty much my whole life," I said, wondering if this was what Leary had been getting around to the whole time. All the stuff about my background didn't matter to him as far as I could see. "I don't think I've seen her since Junior, he was my older brother, got killed on New Harmony. He was Admiral Ozawa's flag lieutenant. Junior and Tim Dorst had been best friends, and the families got together even after Dad got rich and Captain Dorst had pretty much his pay to live on. And then he died."

Mom would've been happy to cut Miriam Dorst then because Miriam wasn't willing to play poor relation to her. Dad wouldn't have that. He'd been a great father and a good man—until the Navy Office looked into his accounts. Even then, thinking back, I couldn't have had a better dad.

Leary filled my mug again and said, "Hogg? We could use another pitcher."

"I shouldn't be drinking this much," I said. "I need to get up early to look for work."

"This beer isn't strong enough to hurt you," Leary said, smiling at me as he poured the rest of the pitcher into his mug.

I wasn't sure that was true—Junior'd been a hell-raiser, a proper RCN officer, but I wasn't. The beer was going to my head.

Still, chatting with somebody friendly felt awfully good. I hadn't had anybody to do that with since it came out about Dad.

"Look," I said, looking straight at Leary. "Dad probably greased the skids to get Tim Dorst into the Academy because Tim wanted it so much. Dad had a lot of influence before it hit the headlines. I remember him saying, 'Young Timothy's got what it takes. There's more about being an RCN officer than sitting on your butt in a classroom.'"

"Your father was right," Leary said as Hogg put the fresh

pitcher down. "About Midshipman Dorst and about RCN officers generally."

He looked at me and his smile was a little harder. "Did he help you get in also?" he said.

"He didn't have to," I said, maybe a little crisper also. "For me or for Junior either one. Junior wasn't much for study, but you could go a ways without finding somebody smarter."

It'd probably been the best result for Junior that he wasn't one of the handful who got out of the *Heidegger* alive after the missile hit her on lift-off. He'd been the social one of us. Having all your friends pretend they didn't see you would've been hard for him.

The gods knew it wasn't easy for me, and I didn't have any friends. Not really.

The bar was filling up, but nobody said anything more about where we were sitting. If Cabrillo had come in, he'd decided not to make an issue out of it.

"You were raised rich yourself," Leary said. "You didn't have a problem working for a ship chandler?"

I shrugged. *Bloody hell, I've drunk most of this mugful too.*

"It's honest work," I said aloud. "Cady was a prick, but I've met pricks before. I was hoping that Fritzi would let me start doing some of the inventory control—there's nobody in the office who really knows how to use a computer. Maybe the next house will."

"As it chances..." Leary said. He put his mug down with a bit of a thump. "I've got a slot for a junior officer myself. I've been asked to command a chartered transport carrying a Foreign Ministry delegation to Saguntum. Two of the officers who'd normally accompany me are staying in Xenos this time. One has a great deal of surgery and therapy yet to go before he's really fit for duty, and his fiancée has taken an appointment in Navy Office while that's happening."

"Sir?" I said. I was choking again. I put my beer down. "I'd be honored. Greatly honored. Ah—this would be on your yacht?"

The *Princess Cecile* was almost as famous as Captain Leary himself. She'd been built as a warship, a corvette. She'd punched far above her weight every time she'd been in action, according to the stories at the Academy.

"Afraid not," Leary said, smiling again. "The *Sissie*'s a little too conspicuous for this job, they tell me. Besides, there's to be twelve in the delegation, which would be a tight fit on a corvette. You'll be third officer on a standard transport, the *Sunray*. I'll be bringing some of my regular crew along, though."

"Sir, I'll serve in any fashion you and the Republic wish," I said. I was choking, I knew I was, and I rubbed my eyes to keep from embarrassing myself even worse. "Ah, I was good academically, but I wasn't at the top of my class even there."

"I know exactly where you were, Olfetrie," Leary said. "My wife asked me to do a favor if it looked reasonable, which it does to me. And Woetjans, my bosun, said she liked the way you handled yourself in a fight. She's a pretty good judge of that sort of thing."

My mug wasn't empty, but he filled it anyway. "Now drink up," he said. "You can report to the *Sunray* in Harbor Three at noon and we'll get the paperwork squared away."

I drank deeply. Tears were running down my cheeks. I decided I didn't care.

Chapter Three

Captain Leary had said "noon." I timed it to arrive at eleven in the morning. If they told me to cool my heels for an hour, that was fine. I wasn't going to take a chance on being late, though.

My room was near Harbor Two, the main harbor for Xenos. It got most of Cinnabar's commercial traffic and was the logical place for ship chandleries to cluster.

Harbor Three was the naval harbor, a long run by tram. There were water taxis too, but they wouldn't have been much quicker and they cost more than I wanted to spend anyway. I punched HARBOR THREE on the call plate—it was one of the preloaded destinations—and a tram arrived within ninety seconds. There were already two men and an old woman with a grocery bag aboard.

The woman and a man got out as we snaked along the shoreline. Seven more people got on; two stood though there were eight seats. The car passed stops from then on. It could take the weight of twelve average passengers, but eight was the normal load.

For some of the way the pylons supporting the overhead track were sunk into marsh. There might have been interesting wildlife to see if the windows hadn't been so scratched and smudged. I wasn't in a mood to sight-see anyway.

We all got out when the car arrived at Harbor Three. There were at least a dozen tram stops at Harbor Two but there was only one here, and there were armed guards besides. They didn't look too worried—they weren't even checking IDs. It had probably been different before the Treaty of Amiens and the end of the long war with the Alliance of Free Stars.

I'd been to Harbor Three a couple of times while I was at the Academy, but I didn't know the layout—let alone where the *Sunray* might be berthed. They'd have the information in Harbor Control, but before walking over there I called to the Shore Police guards, "Can any of you tell me where the *Sunray* is?"

"You want the *Sunray*?" said a voice behind me. "Thirty-seven A, but come with me 'cause I'm going there myself."

I nodded to the guards and turned. The woman who'd spoken had been on the tram with me. She was short and fit-looking and spoke with a Xenos accent.

"Thank you, mistress," I said. "I have plenty of time before I'm due, but I'd rather not spend it walking up and down the waterfront."

We started off to the right. She walked like a spacer, balancing an instant before taking the next step in case the motion of the deck had changed.

"Are you a suit?" she said, looking at me hard. "You're dressed like you belong here, but you sure don't sound like it."

She might've meant my accent, but I suspected it was the fact I was polite. Which would be regrettable, but I'd realized long before my current troubles that quite a lot of things were regrettable but true.

"I'm not a suit," I said. "Captain Leary offered me the third officer's slot on the *Sunray*."

"You know Six?" the woman said. "Well, hell, I guess you're the real thing, then. I'm Wedell; I'm a rigger in the port watch."

"I'm Roy Olfetrie," I said. I didn't offer to shake hands because I was about to become her superior officer. "Yesterday I was working for a ship chandler, but I was fired."

"Fired for what?" Wedell said, her expression getting minusculely less friendly. It was a reasonable question to ask a man who might shortly be giving you orders.

"For punching back when the owner's son-in-law swung at me," I said. "I'd do the same thing if it happened again."

Wedell laughed hard. "I shoulda figured it was something like that!" she said. "Six isn't one to screw up when he's picking officers."

"I'll hope not," I said. I smiled but I wasn't as sure of that as Wedell sounded. "If I may ask—by Six you obviously mean Captain Leary. But why?"

"Oh, it's his call sign," Wedell said. "The XO is Five. That's Lieutenant Vesey usually, but she's staying on the ground this time. Master Cazelet got his leg next thing to shot off and she's staying close. Vesey's good, a hell of an astrogator and shiphandler, but you know—when you're really in the shit and everybody's shooting at you, there's nobody like Six to have on the bridge."

From the stories at the Academy, having Captain Leary on the bridge was a pretty good way to be sure that everybody *would* be shooting at you. Still, that was the whole point of there being a Republic of Cinnabar Navy. If it was always peaceful, I'd have joined the merchant service—or maybe taken a job in one of Dad's ventures.

I'd *never* wanted to do that, which turned out to be a blessing. If I hadn't been so obviously unconnected with Dad's business, somebody—a private prosecutor if not the Solicitor of the Navy—would sure have gone after me months ago.

"Here's Thirty-seven," Wedell said, gesturing. "And that's the *Sunray* in Berth A. I can't tell you anything about her because we all just mustered aboard."

Thirty-seven was a repair dock. The slip could be drained, but it hadn't been for this job. The interior of a midsized freighter was being rebuilt extensively enough that at least three hull plates had been removed, though one of them was being welded back in place now.

"They're adding two levels of bunks to the forward hold," Wedell said. "We're boarding a crew of eighty-odd, they tell me. There's only accommodations for thirty-five normal-like. And amidships is all suites now."

Thirty-five would be ample crew for a two-ring freighter. Leary was famous for making fast passages, which worked ships and rigs hard and worked their crews even harder. The *Sunray* would look like an ordinary fast freighter, but she'd have the crew for quick runs and quick repairs.

"They expanded the arms locker too," Wedell said with a note of pride. "We've got no missiles and just the one cannon in the bow, but I guess we'll be able to take care of ourselves on the ground if it comes to that."

"I guess I'd better report aboard," I said. I was feeling a little queasy. I wasn't afraid of getting shot, but there were *so* many ways I could screw up leading ground troops. I hadn't been trained for it.

But ground combat wasn't part of the Academy curriculum, so even if I'd graduated as a midshipman it wouldn't help. Master Cazelet, the officer I was taking the place of, wouldn't have had any more training than I had. And he'd done well enough to get his leg shot off.

I grinned. Maybe I'd be luckier and take a bullet through the head. *That* would solve all my problems.

I headed for the boarding hatch but Wedell pointed to the balanced pair of freight elevators and said, "You'll need to sign in on Level One so you may as well ride since we're in dock."

I didn't want to look like a wimp, but panting after I'd climbed sixty feet of polished steel treads didn't sound like a good start for meeting my fellow officers. I took the rigger's suggestion and waved goodbye from the elevator platform. The elevators didn't have cages, just six-inch railings to keep pipes from rolling off.

I threw the lever from left to right and started trundling upward immediately, though we stopped a quarter of the way up for half a dozen workmen get onto the car balancing mine. They were going off-shift, carrying personal tools and the jackets they'd worn when they came on duty in the wee small hours. The cars began to move again; the workmen and I nodded as we passed in opposite directions.

I got to the top level and starting going back down before I realized that there wasn't an automatic stop. I threw the lever left and the car juddered to a stop. Another clump of workmen were trotting along the walkway from the ship's uppermost level. I let them get past me before going the other way.

The walk had no railings either. I'm not particularly afraid of heights, but the crew leaving work was tired and in a hurry to get other places. I didn't need to argue right-of-way with them.

Entry to bridge level was at a hatch which normally would have been torso height. The yard crew had cut it into a full-length door; the piece of hull plating lay in the rotunda beyond. They'd even attached temporary handholds to the plate, making it easier to handle.

I supposed they'd weld it back on when they were finished. I wondered if they'd fish the piece as well. In my three months at the chandlery I'd seen a lot of shortcuts to keep ships working—safely and otherwise. The "otherwise" versions made me gasp, but it was part of my education to learn that the real world wasn't always what I'd been taught that it should be.

The forward rotunda held the suit lockers, the up and down companionways, and an airlock. A corridor ran sternward to my left and to the right was an open hatch. I could see the bridge beyond. I stepped into the hatchway, rang my knuckles on the transom, and called loud enough to be heard over the sound of hammering on steel below, "Master Olfetrie reporting as ordered!"

Three or four people were on the bridge, mostly at flat-plate displays. That was a lot more instrumentation than I expected to see on a merchant ship. I figured more than bunks were being added for this mission.

The man at the console in the far bow turned on his couch and gestured me to him. He wore RCN utilities but wore the saucer hat of an officer.

A woman was at one of the stations, but she was working on a personal data unit with a holographic display; it was a blur of color to me and everybody else except the user. On a jump-seat bolted to the hull beside her was another woman with an attaché case on her lap. The man on a port-side display seemed to be running a gunnery program.

I hadn't noticed what the *Sunray*'s armament was: a single four-inch plasma cannon was more or less standard for a well-found freighter as anti-pirate defense, but I'd never been aboard a civilian ship in which anybody really cared about gunnery—until they had to use the weapon.

"I'm Cory," the officer at the command console said when I knelt beside him. "I'm second lieutenant and have the duty right now. You are?"

"Sir, I'm Roylan Olfetrie," I said. "Captain Leary visited me last night and ordered me"—that wasn't really the right word—"to report at noon today to be signed on as the *Sunray*'s third mate."

"Go sit at the striker's seat so we can hear each other over whatever the yard's doing," Cory said, gesturing me to the seat on the opposite side of the console. It was where a junior striking for a position could watch the regular officer and even control the ship if the senior spacer permitted. They were standard in naval use but much less common on civilian vessels.

I settled myself. Cory must have engaged the active

cancellation field, because the ambient noise shut off. The small flat-plate display at this position showed Cory's face. He said, "Six told me you'd be coming aboard. Welcome to the *Sunray*. You're no newer to her than all the rest of us are, but I guess we're new to you. The rest of us have been together quite a while, on various of Six's commands."

"I'll try to fit in," I said. "Anyhow, I'll do my job the best I know how to."

"You'll be covering Master Cazelet's duties," Cory said. "Do you know anything about commo?"

"What?" I said. "Well, I've had a unit on it but I don't have any experience. Was Cazelet the commo officer of, of the *Princess Cecile*?"

"No, that's Officer Mundy," Cory said with a grin that implied more than humor. "She'll have the job here too. But it's a handy skill and Rene was good at it."

He grinned more broadly. "Almost as good as I am," he said.

"I'll try to learn," I said. It was all I could figure to say.

"Astrogation?" Cory asked.

"I had two years in the Academy," I said. "I—"

"Academy?" said Cory, cutting me off. "Why did you leave?"

"Family problems," I said. I swallowed and added, "My dad was a crook. I'm not. I guess he isn't now either, because he shot himself."

Cory didn't say anything for a moment, just held my eyes. Then he said, "Well, that'll do for a reason, I guess."

"I got good grades," I said, switching back to a subject I preferred. "But I left before my senior cruise."

"Marksmanship?" Cory said.

"Personal weapons in my second year," I said. "I didn't try out for a shooting team—it seemed to me I couldn't do the practice I'd need and keep up my studies."

I thought for a moment and added, "Dad had a trap range on his estate in Oriel County. I used it the last few summers and got pretty good."

"That could be handy," Cory said, though I couldn't imagine how. I was—or anyway I wanted to be—a naval officer, not a sporting gentleman. He looked up from his display—the console was obviously transcribing the interview—and said, "Ever kill a man?"

"No, sir," I said, as though the question hadn't shocked me. "Is that a job requirement?"

"Sometimes it is, yes," Cory said. "Rene never got his… conscience, I suppose, past that, though. He was a bloody good officer and bloody good friend."

There might have been a challenge in the way he put that. I ignored the possibility and said, "I'm sorry he was injured, sir."

Cory smiled again. "Yeah," he said. "So am I, but sometimes that comes with the job too."

He stretched, spreading his arms. "I've assigned you to the port watch," Cory said. "You'll be under Lieutenant Enery for the time being, but chances are you'll take over if you work out. Six said you were to be worked like a midshipman in training, and so you shall be."

I cleared my throat. I said, "Thank you, sir. I'll fetch my baggage and report back aboard."

I didn't have to worry about housing next week after all. I think Mistress Causey would miss me: I was quiet and didn't come back drunk and singing at three in the morning. And she didn't have to worry about getting the rent on time—if I had the money, and for rooming houses like hers I wasn't the only resident who might find himself out of a job at the end of the week.

"Oh, Six also said you were to draw an advance of a hundred florins if you wanted it," Cory said, raising an eyebrow to make a question of his statement.

"Ah..." I said, thinking about what I had in pawn. Most of it I'd never need again, but—

"If I could have fifty florins," I said, "that would be useful for getting an outfit together. At the moment I've got the clothes I'm wearing, and another set like them."

Cory reached into his belt purse and placed a fifty-florin coin on top of the console. "We're not set up to run you a credit chip the normal way yet," he said. "I've got it noted on your records here and I'll get it back on payday."

"Thank you, sir," I said. It struck me that the *Sunray* operated in a very easygoing fashion, and also that Cory was a lot less concerned about fifty florins than most young lieutenants would be. I wondered if he had family money.

"Before you go, Olfetrie..." Cory said. He gestured to the woman working on her personal data unit. "Go over and talk to Officer Mundy, will you? She'll have some questions."

"The signals officer?" I said. I thought I must've misheard.

"Yeah, she's that," said Cory, "but she's a bit more than that too. Among other things, she's a good friend of Captain Leary; his best, maybe. And Olfetrie?"

"Yes," I said. Captain Leary's job offer still seemed like the best thing that'd happened to me since Dad had shot himself, but there was a lot more to it than I'd have learned in my final two years at the Academy.

"If Officer Mundy tells you to do something, do it," Cory said. "Don't worry about rank—because believe me, she doesn't. And don't argue if you think she's wrong, because I don't remember that happening. Just a friendly suggestion, of course."

"Thank you, Cory," I said and got up. This was all bloody crazy and I didn't begin to understand, but I actually believed Cory about it being friendly advice.

I walked over to the signals officer and knelt beside her station, as I'd done with Cory. "Officer Mundy?" I said in a lull in the racket of impact wrenches. "I'm Third Officer Olfetrie reporting to the *Sunray*. The OiC suggested that I speak to you."

Mundy said nothing for a moment. She was using short wands to control her data unit. I'd heard of them—they were supposed to be quicker than any other input method *if* you were good enough—but they required a delicacy of control and pressure beyond that of anybody I'd ever met.

I thought Mundy was just too busy to respond for the moment, but then the woman in the jumpseat beside her reached through the holographic display, disrupting it. Mundy looked up and focused on me with a terrifying, blank expression.

Her face relaxed, though I wouldn't call her expression welcoming. "Ah," she said, twitching her wands again.

The bridge had gone quiet again. Mundy had switched on a cancellation field. These were part of a navigation console, but I'd never heard of one being attached to a subordinate display.

"I'm glad you came over, Olfetrie," Mundy said. "I have a few background questions beyond what Cory would have asked."

"All right," I said, standing up again. I was going along with this, but I won't pretend I was happy about being questioned by a junior warrant officer.

"What are your politics?" Mundy said.

She could have asked me my favorite color and not surprised me as much. I said, "I don't have any politics. I've never voted, and I don't remember my parents ever voting, though I can't swear they didn't. We weren't a political family."

"Your father was Dean Olfetrie?" said the clerk. A *clerk*, for hell's sake! "I'd say *he* was pretty political."

I looked at her and regretted it. The clerk vanished into the background unless you focused on her. When I did that, I've seen guard dogs with warmer expressions.

"Openly political," I said, as calmly as I could manage. "My father bribed politicians, yes. I do not, nor did my brother before he was killed aboard the *Heidegger*. At present—" I fingered the coins in my pocket. "I've got eighty-two florins and change. That would probably allow me to bribe a dog warden to release my pet, but I don't think it would go much beyond that."

I glared at the clerk. To my amazement she smiled back. She said, "Good answer, kid."

Mundy, looking at her display again, said, "You mentioned family, Olfetrie. What kin have you?"

I shrugged. It was disconcerting to be interviewed by someone who didn't bother to look at me. "My mother's probably still alive," I said, "though I couldn't tell you more than that. She disappeared when the bailiffs arrived, and I haven't tried to find her. Mom . . . got very full of herself when Dad was important. I guess the scandal bothered her even more than it did me."

Though probably not for the same reasons. I'd been pretty much my dad's son.

"My brother's dead and I don't have any other siblings," I said. After thinking for a moment, I added, "Miriam Dorst is my mother's cousin. She and her daughter Miranda are probably my closest living relatives."

Mundy didn't look up or even nod. She said, "Do you have a girlfriend? Or boyfriend."

"I did, a girlfriend," I said, thinking about Rachel. "Before Dad shot himself. Pretty much everybody I knew dropped me then. Certainly she did. So no, not now."

Looking up at last, Mundy said, "The *Sunray* is carrying a diplomatic delegation, Olfetrie. That makes political neutrality for our officers more than usually important."

I smiled. "I was training to be an RCN officer," I said. "The political neutrality requirement wasn't one of those I expected to have trouble with."

"Thank you, Olfetrie," Mundy said, going back to her data unit. "I don't have any further questions. I hope our association goes well."

I left the bridge. At least I had more to think about than wondering if I'd be able to carry out the duties of a junior officer on a civilian vessel.

Chapter Four

I had a cabin on Level 1—the rebuilding had added officers' spaces as well as quarters for the crew and passengers. I had just opened the hatch to stow away the gear I'd brought, mostly retrieved from pawn, when the cabin across the corridor from mine opened.

"You're Olfetrie?" said the small woman who stuck her head out.

"Yes, ma'am," I said. "I'm the third mate."

"I'm Enery," she said. The right side of her face had a glassy perfection and moved very little when she spoke. "Come over and have a drink when you've got that"—she nodded at the bundle of my belongings—"struck down."

She gave me a smile that would've been less grisly if both sides of her face worked. She added, "Don't worry. I don't have designs on your body."

I stowed my gear in the cabinet under the bunk—which, with the small desk/chair combination on the corridor bulkhead beside the hatch, was all the furniture there was. That done, I stepped across and knocked on the first officer's hatch. She called, "It's open."

Her cabin was twice the size of mine—that didn't make it big—and there was a flat-plate display on the hull-side bulkhead. Two chairs were bolted to the deck on the corridor side and another at the display.

Enery was straddling the chair by the display. She poured whiskey into a tumbler, then handed the bottle to me. "There's another glass under the chair seat," she said, gesturing with her own drink.

I took the tumbler—it was high-density plastic—from its nest with flatware and a platter and sat down to pour. The whiskey was a Heilish County brand, a very good one that one of Dad's friends had sworn by—but it was something of an acquired taste for its heavy smokiness. It wasn't a favorite of mine, but I sipped.

I handed the bottle back and said, "Thank you, mistress."

"We're the outsiders on this run, Olfetrie," Enery said. I noticed that the back of her right hand was hairless and had the same smoothness as half her face. "I thought we ought to get to know one another."

I sipped the whiskey again to have an excuse for lowering my eyes. "Ah," I said. "You're not RCN either, then?"

"Oh, I'm RCN, all right," said Enery. Her lips worked and she took a large swallow—too large for me to equal with this stuff. If I'd tried, I'd have spewed it out my nose. "Just not one of Captain Leary's gang. I'm Admiral McKye's goddaughter, and I had a stellar career in the RCN ahead of me ten years ago."

"What happened?" I asked. I didn't want to hear the answer, I *wanted* to be back in my cabin reading—or on the bridge, practicing astrogation on one of the stations there. Enery obviously wanted to tell somebody, though, and she'd picked me for the duty. If we were going to be in the same crew, I was going to make an effort to get along. I guess I'd do that anyway.

"Lieutenant Daniel Leary happened," she said bitterly. "Oh, I don't blame him. I just happened to be in his way when he started out on the most brilliant career in the RCN. I wasn't even a bump to him."

I sipped again. I didn't want to seem ungrateful, but I *wasn't* going to have a refill of her whiskey.

"I was tipped for the command of the corvette *Princess Cecile*," Enery went on, pouring more whiskey. "She went to Leary instead. And he made her the most famous ship in the RCN."

I frowned, remembering stories that I'd heard. "I thought Captain Leary had captured the *Princess Cecile*?" I said.

"Sure, he did that right enough," Enery agreed. "But that shouldn't have mattered in the way things are done. In RCN politics, I mean. He was a new-minted lieutenant with no interest at all, and I had three admirals in my bloodline and a fleet commander as my sponsor."

Instead of slugging down the fresh drink, Enery swished the liquor around in the tumbler as she stared at it. "Leary outmaneuvered Admiral McKye," she said. "He did or his friend Mundy did. He got the ship, and I . . ."

She drank. And took a second gulp before she put the tumbler down.

She glared at me and said, "It broke me. Broke my luck, I mean. It wasn't Leary's fault any more than it was mine. I was just in the wrong place at the wrong time, and it never went right again for me."

"That was in the middle of the war," I said. "You surely weren't put on the beach because you missed that posting?"

"No," said Enery. "I was appointed first lieutenant on a destroyer commanded by a distant cousin, a very good posting for a lieutenant as junior as I was. But we were in the home fleet and saw no action. I transferred to the *Ajax* and I did well, there was never anything wrong with my work, but again we weren't in action. You don't make a name for yourself because your ship remained squared away when nothing happened. Then"—she smiled again. It was horrible to look at, but I did—"I was in line for promotion to lieutenant commander and command of a destroyer. Something finally happened on the my cruiser—a fire in a paint locker. I was head of damage control. We were in Harbor Three, so of course I didn't have a hard suit on and of course I didn't take time to put one on. The locker exploded just as I arrived."

She took more whiskey though she didn't drink immediately. The bottle was down well below half.

"I was three years in hospital," Enery said. "By the time I could return to duty, the Treaty of Amiens had been signed and Admiral McKye had retired."

"I'm very sorry," I said. *Of course* Enery hadn't thought first about protective gear in a crisis. She wouldn't have been fit to wear the uniform if she had. She'd really had bad luck for a well-connected officer. Still—

I didn't smile but I thought, *I can do you one better, honey*. Though I'm not sure Enery would have thought my situation was truly worse than hers.

"I was expecting to be beached for good and all," Enery said, looking hard at her whiskey. "But then this came up— was I willing to become first lieutenant to Captain Leary on a civilian charter? I jumped at it—of course."

"Well, it's certainly better than retirement on a lieutenant's half pay," I said. *Let alone picking up casual labor on the docks.* "I'm glad that Captain Leary gave you the opportunity."

"Him?" Enery said. "Scarcely! Navy House wished me on him. I don't doubt that he'd have put in one of his cronies if he'd been able to."

I swallowed and said, "I don't understand." I didn't see how *that* could get me into trouble, and anyway it was true.

"What do you know about Captain Leary?" Enery demanded. "As little as you seem to?"

"I know he's a hero," I said carefully. "I believe he's the son of a senator, a powerful one. And I know that he gave me an officer's slot when nobody else on Cinnabar would have."

"Leary and the crew of the *Princess Cecile*, his Sissies, are pretty much a special operations commando," Enery said. "The problem is, nobody in Navy House is quite sure *whose* commando they are. His friend Mundy, that's Lady Mundy of Chatsworth, is a spy in the intelligence network that Bernis Sand runs."

"*Our* spies?" I said. I'd never heard of Mistress Sand.

Enery shrugged. "I suppose," she said. She drank again.

"When it suits them, anyway. I've found spooks are pretty much in it for themselves when you look closely enough. Anyway, Mundy certainly isn't working for Navy House. That's why somebody at Navy House wanted me aboard the *Sunray*."

I raised my tumbler high enough for the whiskey to touch my lips, but I didn't really drink. I wondered if Enery would have been talking like this if she hadn't been punishing the bottle so hard.

Aloud I said, "You're here to spy on Captain Leary for Navy House?"

"*I'm* not a spy," Enery said. "They all know who I am. I think somebody hoped that me being aboard will put some kind of rein on Leary. That's nonsense: I can't get in Leary's way any more than I could when I was supposed to take command of the *Princess Cecile*. But it's a chance for me, anyway. A better chance than there'd be on the beach. I keep thinking, you see—"she gave me another of her terrible smiles"—that maybe my luck will change."

"Lieutenant . . ." I said. I got up and put my empty tumbler down on the seat I'd vacated. I didn't remember finishing the whiskey, but I had. That was a reason to leave if I hadn't had a better one—a desire simply to get away—before I wound up drinking more. "Lieutenant, I hope this voyage works out well for you and for all of us. Thank you for the drink."

Enery didn't speak. I glanced over my shoulder an instant before closing the hatch behind me. The first officer remained hunched over the back of her chair. The bottle was in one hand, her empty tumbler in the other.

I sat on my own bunk. I'd thought I was signing up for a charter voyage on a civilian vessel, carrying diplomats to a distant, minor posting. It sounded like it was a great deal more than that.

Regardless, it was better than casual labor.

Chapter Five

"Testing thrusters One and Six," said a raspy voice over the PA system. The *Sunray* shook and wobbled as two plasma thrusters vented into the flooded slip.

Pasternak, the Chief Engineer, was speaking. He was the old spacer I'd asked to guide me when I first arrived at Bergen and Associates a lifetime ago.

There was a brief pause. The ship still rocked as the pool settled.

"Testing thrusters Two and Five," Pasternak said, and again we roared and shook.

I was squatting on one side of the A Level corridor with other riggers, ready to go out with both watches to set sail as soon as the *Sunray* had reached orbit. There wasn't room in the rotunda for all of us, and each of the two airlocks could hold only four personnel in rigging suits at a cycle.

"Testing thrusters Three and Four," said Pasternak. This time the ship teetered slightly nose-high for a few seconds

before splashing back and lifting again for another few seconds. The central pair of thrusters weren't precisely at the *Sunray*'s balance point.

A big man—bigger yet in his rigging suit—clomped down the corridor and said to the spacer on my right, "Scoot up to the rotunda, Kellogg. I want to talk to the kid."

Kellogg, a tough-looking forty-year-old, got up with a grunt and moved forward. Barnes, the speaker, sat down beside me. He was one of the bosun's mates under Woetjans, the Chief of Rig.

"*Testing all thrusters!*" Pasternak warned. This time the *Sunray* bobbed like a cork. The leaves of the thruster nozzles were flared open, minimizing impulse, but the plasma quenched violently in the slip. The gushing steam added to lift.

"So, kid..." shouted Barnes. "Six says we're to train you like a midshipman, but this ain't the RCN. Maybe you want to tell me to bugger off because you're an officer?"

I've done my share of dumb things, but I wasn't dumb enough to take that at face value. I said, "I want you to do what Captain Leary told you to do, Barnes!"

I tried to sound authoritative, like a real officer. I don't know how well I did, but Barnes laughed and slapped my armored knee.

"*Lifting off in ten, repeat, ten seconds,*" Lieutenant Enery's voice warned as the thrusters built to full power. The *Sunray* didn't have an armored Battle Direction Center like a real warship, but the dockyard had added a full console in the stern so that she could still be directed if the bridge were destroyed.

"*Lifting off!*"

The thruster note changed as Enery closed the sphincters.

The *Sunray* shook herself free of the slip, paused a moment, then resumed her climb at an ever-increasing rate.

I was on my way to my first operational deployment as a spacer.

We began staging out through the airlocks as soon as the *Sunray* reached orbit, though by the time I'd reached the locks the High Drive motors were accelerating us. It felt to me like 1 g, comfortable for those within the hull and not particularly burdensome for the rigging watch.

No commercial vessel could accelerate much harder than that anyway, and even warships were limited because their rigging couldn't be stressed for heavy thrust and still be able to fold and telescope as it had to do for landing. Landings— and to a lesser degree lift-offs—were the real problem for a starship's rig. Atmospheric buffeting, accompanied by vibration from the thrusters running at maximum output, snapped shackles and undid any rovings that weren't snugged up tight. Microcracks, crystallized metal, frayed cables—*any* weakness was likely to be tested to destruction.

The rig was wholly automated. Gears and hydraulic motors raised and extended the antennas, rotated the spars into place, and stretched the sails in response to commands from the navigational computer. Riggers were superfluous— unless something broke or jammed.

As it always did.

The port watch was assigned to the aft ring of antennas. B Port mounted only thirty degrees and jammed, but Barnes put two other spacers to clearing it. The mainspar of B Dorsal didn't release, and that became a task for me and Wedell whom I'd met the day I reported to the *Sunray*.

The lower clamp had opened properly: It was only waist high to spacers standing flat-footed on the hull. We climbed the ratlines to the upper clamp and found it only half-open. We didn't expect to need jacks for the initial job—we wrapped our legs around the antenna, set a prybar, and put our backs into it. The clamp opened with a *clack!* just as I was about to decide I was going return for the jack after all.

I lurched backward on my perch, but my legs didn't quite lose their grip. I slid down to the hull and hit on my butt. I wasn't in real danger—I'd set my safety line before climbing— but it was a nasty feeling for a moment and a solid *thump* when I hit the steel.

I'd worn hard suits before, but I wasn't used to them. The one I'd been issued fit all right—as well as any that hadn't been personally fitted, I guess—but I knew that in the morning I was going to have worse than a rash at the points it rubbed.

Strands of monocrystal stiffened the fabric. It wasn't armor in the sense that it would stop a bullet, but it would resist a torn plate or a strand from a broken cable that would puncture an air suit. If your job was to work with torn plates and broken cables, it was definitely the garment to be wearing. It wasn't very flexible, however.

The *Sunray* entered the Matrix just after we got the spar loose. I felt my nerves tingle in a wave, starting at my toes and rolling up through my scalp. Light changed: The focused, distant glare of Cinnabar's primary vanished and the ship trembled in the glow of all universes.

The B Dorsal mainsail shook out with neat precision; the antenna rotated about fifteen degrees to impinge on Casimir radiation and propel the ship between bubble universes. Each individual spot in what looked like the starry sky above me was really a separate universe with constants of time and velocity different from those of the sidereal universe. It was by shifting from one bubble to another in the Matrix that starships were able to traverse interstellar distances in practical lengths of time.

The second part of my job and Wedell's was to fix the clamp—on the hull, if possible, but by carrying it in to the engineering shop if necessary. The driving gear in the clamp body was worn smooth, but I suspected that wouldn't have happened if the driven gear had been turning properly. We fetched a replacement clamp from an external locker, and Wedell slung the worn one to her equipment belt.

When we'd finished, our four-hour watch was pretty near over. I was looking forward to a bite to eat and my bunk. Wedell pointed back past me. I turned and found Barnes— his name was stencilled in glowpaint above the front window of his helmet—standing at my shoulder. He leaned forward slightly so that our helmets touched.

Wedell and I had been using hand signals when we needed to "speak." Rigging suits didn't have radios because the accidental use of one in the Matrix could send a ship wildly off course. I'd learned the signals in the Academy, but I wasn't very good at them yet—and Wedell and I hadn't worked together before, so we didn't know how to predict one another's actions the way an experienced team would. Still, we hadn't had real problems in such a straightforward job.

Barnes, the sound of his voice transmitted through his helmet to mine, said, "We've got a job, you and me, kid. We've got to replace the extender cable on Ventral A antenna."

I frowned. "It's broken?" I said.

"Naw," said Barnes. "It's a half millimeter undersized. Some contractor cheated, or maybe his supplier did. Who'd have thought that RCN suppliers'd be crooked, hey?"

I took a deep breath. "Then we'd better change it," I said.

I didn't bother asking why I was being held over at the end of my watch to do a lengthy, brutal job. For that matter, I didn't ask why nobody'd noticed the cable while we were in Harbor Three. That was the sort of thing that might pass unnoticed in the usual run of things, but the examination Captain Leary and his Sissies had given the *Sunray* hadn't been usual.

They had noticed it. And they'd waited until now to see how the new third officer dealt with it. I was bone tired, but I was going to be more tired before I went off watch. That was just how it was.

We trudged along the hull to the bow ring, then down to the ventral antenna. It had been raised and extended, but the spars were still locked vertical instead of being rotated ninety degrees to their set position. The sails were furled.

I'd been carrying my safety line unhooked since I left Dorsal B. I wasn't shuffling because Barnes was following me, but I made sure I set each magnetized boot sole firmly before I lifted my trailing foot. I stepped along uncomfortably fast. I'd pay for it in the morning—thigh muscles and skin abrasions both—but this was a test.

I hooked the line to one of the shackles at the base of the antenna; then I checked the raised lettering on the pulley at the foot of the mast. The nearest exterior locker was just behind Dorsal A and easily within the reach of my line. I clanked up to it, setting my feet with determination as before.

Barnes continued to shadow me. He didn't comment on what I was doing.

I opened the locker, pulling up the recessed catch before turning it. I was pleased to find a spool marked with the correct number—I hadn't been sure how far Captain Leary was willing to go in a training exercise. I'd half expected to be sent to the stern locker or to inside storage.

There was a handle on either flange of the spool. I gripped one, turned to Barnes, and mimed him taking the other one. He did—another better result than I'd feared—and we returned to Ventral A.

I could probably have handled the spool alone if I'd had to, but there was no point in making me do that—except to prove I was on the bottom of the totem pole. I already knew that.

When we got back to the antenna, I took a wrench from the satchel I was wearing and adjusted it to the nut of the hydraulic fitting that fed the pump. Barnes tapped my shoulder. I looked up and he touched helmets again.

"Six took Ventral A out of service on the main console," Barnes said. "It won't move no matter how the course changes."

"All right," I said. I finished disconnecting the hydraulic line, then took the existing cable loose from the lift spool and crimped it to the end of the fresh cable with an in-line splice. I then stuck a screwdriver through one of the holes in the take-up spool provided for the purpose and began turning it like a windlass.

Even with the cables end to end, I couldn't tell the difference in diameter by eye. I suspected that Barnes could have, however. Someday I'd have that much experience too.

The cable stuck at the first shackle. The hydraulic motor could probably have dragged it through the obstruction, but I couldn't do it by hand.

I turned to Barnes. With hand signals I asked him to keep tension on the pulley while I went up and cleared the jam. He put his hand on the screwdriver, which was all the reply I needed. He may've nodded within the rigid helmet, but I couldn't see for sure.

This was my second trip up an antenna since reporting on watch. The suit was heavy, and I wasn't used to wearing it. I fed the splice through the shackle, then climbed to the next one. Barnes resumed winding, thank goodness. Grasping the cable with my gauntlets and hauling it up by hand would have been a lot harder at best. I didn't figure I'd give up—that I could control—but I might be out here dangling from the ratlines until they hauled me in.

The splice hung at each shackle—up to the masthead and back down. I was counting them at the start—not for any reason, just for the way you do—but I lost track. I think it was seventeen.

At the bottom of the mast, I returned to where Barnes knelt. He'd coiled the original cable beside him, as neatly as the take-up spool itself could have done. I could barely see straight, but I opened the splice and hooked the new cable to the spool. I took a single turn by hand, then removed my screwdriver/handle and reconnected the hydraulic line.

It took me three tries to get the threads started so that I could snug it up with the wrench. Barnes watched impassively while I struggled, but when I rose from the job he led me to the semaphore stand by which messages were sent from the bridge to the riggers. There was also a hydromechanical override system for the rigging. Barnes unlocked it and hit three buttons in series.

We both watched as antenna Ventral A telescoped neatly, with no more than the usual jumps and catches. It remained vertical: I'd only changed the extension cable, so there was no need to test whether the antenna would hinge flat and clamp to the hull for landing.

Barnes patted me on the back and pointed to the nearer airlock. We walked to it together. I was so tired that I almost forgot to unclip my safety line from the antenna base.

Chapter Six

Barnes started taking off his helmet as soon as the outer hatch had locked closed. I knew that was usual for riggers, but I'd always been willing to wait for the pressure in the lock to build up a bit.

Still, Barnes and I were the only ones in the lock this time—we were knocking off shortly before the watch ended. I wasn't hiding in the crowd. I began to undo my catches also. The pressure had risen to ten psi by the time I had the helmet off, though.

Barnes grinned at me. "Know where the warrant officers' lounge is, kid?" he asked. "Level Two, aft of the crew's quarters?"

"I know it's there," I said. I'd never had occasion to visit it, and I hadn't imagined I ever would.

"Drop in when you've changed out of duty clothes," Barnes said. "We'll stand you a drink or three? All right?"

"I'd be honored," I said. Which was true, but it was an honor I could've done without. I'd really been looking forward to my bunk.

Barnes was out of his hard suit in half the time it took me—even with his help on the catches. I clamped the suit to its place in the locker and walked—staggered, better—to my cabin.

I'd been wearing shapeless garments, spacers' slops—brand new, bought with the fifty florin advance from Cory. The cloth was soaked with sweat, and stiff with blood at a couple of the wear points. My skin burned as I pulled them off.

My cabin didn't have a shower, but there was a tap and basin. I sponged off with a rag, then sprayed the rubbed patches with antiseptic sealant from the first aid kit. I dressed again in RCN utilities. Aboard ship they were really dress clothes for all but the commissioned officers—which I certainly was not, except in name.

I left my cabin, feeling a lot brighter than I had when I entered. Removing the hard suit had been a weight off me in more ways than one.

I took the down companionway to the second level, then walked aft through the newly built crew's quarters: bunks four high, set in alcoves partitioned by ceiling-height dividers which also provided locker space. Twenty-odd spacers were in the alcoves. Those who noticed me nodded or called, "Sir," in acknowledgement. I nodded back, surprised that anybody recognized me.

I'd heard that Leary's crew, the Sissies, considered themselves an elite and were certainly a close-knit group who'd served together for years. To my surprise, they seemed willing to treat me with more consideration than I expected most junior midshipmen got in the RCN.

There were closed compartments on either side of the

corridor when I got beyond the alcoves. The nearest one on the port side was a group shower/latrine. The hatch across from it was ajar. I tapped on the panel, then eased it open enough that I could peer through.

"Come on in, kid," Barnes called, "and shut it after you."

I entered. The cabin was twelve by eighteen. There appeared to be a full galley at the aft end, and the furniture had leather cushions. Barnes and Dasi, the other bosun's mate, sat close to one another at the round steel table in the center. On it was a tray with a bottle and tumblers, and everybody in the room was holding a drink.

Woetjans, the bosun, and Sun, who'd been acting as purser and armorer but called himself the gunner's mate, sat against the hull side of the cabin. They were all facing me.

Barnes pointed to a chair across the table from him. "Sit down and pour yourself a drink," he said. "D'ye like rum?"

"Well enough," I said, sitting as directed. "I'm not a drinking man, though, and it's been a while since I last ate."

"We've got other stuff," Sun said. "Pretty much anything you want."

He was the only ship-side warrant here; the others were riggers.

I sipped the rum. It was lightly spiced and very powerful. I didn't recognize the brand name, but it had been bottled in one of the Southern Tier counties and was *way* more expensive than anything I could've afforded on my own.

Woetjans said, "Barnes says you cut the pump line before you started working on the cable even though he'd told you Six had taken Ventral A out of the computer. That so?"

"That's so," I said calmly. I *hope* I sounded calm. "I trust Captain Leary and I trust Barnes." I nodded across the table as I spoke. "But I don't trust some dickhead not to throw a switch on the bridge while I've got my arms wrapped in cable."

I drank a bit more rum; a little more than I'd meant to, to tell the truth, and I almost snorted it out of my nose.

Oddly enough, that broke my fear. I almost started laughing at the notion. I thought, *There's never a situation so bad that it can't get worse*.

Barnes rubbed his cheek with his left hand and said, "Following procedures is all well and good, but sometimes you don't have time for it."

"I know that," I said. "In an emergency I'll do what I have to do and if I get killed, well, I wanted to join the RCN. I didn't need my brother being blown to hell on New Harmony to know that the job has risks. But today wasn't one of those times, unless you'd given me a direct order."

I met Barnes' eyes, then looked around at the others. The other members of the court-martial, it was sounding like.

"Hell, you were right," Barnes said. "I'd've pulled you up short if you'd cut corners today."

"Yeah, if we were in a rush," Dasi said, the first he'd spoken since I entered, "Six'd get us to Saguntum without a planetfall. Instead of which we're making three."

"Remember Tubby Duxford?" Woetjans said. "He was moonlighting in a dockyard when somebody reconnected the power inside. The pulley cut his hand clean off."

"He was a bloody fool to work for Sampson," Barnes growled, refilling his tumbler.

"Tubby was a bloody fool most times that I remember," Woetjans agreed. "But if he'd bothered to disconnect the gear on the take-up spool, he'd still have his left hand."

I said, "Could Captain Leary really make the voyage from Cinnabar to Saguntum without planetfall?" I said. I tried a little more rum. "It's rated as a thirty-day voyage."

"You bet your ass he could!" Sun said. He didn't sound angry, though there could've been a challenge in the words. "And it wouldn't be any thirty days, neither. He's like a wizard in the Matrix, finding routes that nobody else could."

"If we'd *really* been in a hurry," Dasi said, "we'd be aboard the *Sissie* instead of this pig. And I wish we bloody well were."

"We're keeping a low profile," Woetjans said. "Say, pass the bottle, will you?"

Barnes passed the rum back. "It's not *that* low," he said. "Six is using his own name, right? And so's the Mistress."

"Who notices the name of the signals officer?" Woetjans said as she poured. "Even the captain, that doesn't set off any bells. The *Princess Cecile*, though, everybody's heard of her. And if they haven't, she still looks like a warship. Not a transport hauling diplomats around."

"She *is* a bloody warship," Dasi said, "even if you call her a yacht."

"So she is," said Woetjans, returning the bottle to Barnes. "The kid needs some more, Barnes."

"I still don't see why they can't be Captain Smith and Signals Officer Jones," muttered Sun.

The kid *didn't* need another drink; that rum must've proofed close to the grain alcohol they used as working fluid in the

63

Power Room. Still, realization that I'd passed a test had relaxed me. I didn't object as Barnes poured me another two inches.

"Somebody who's looking already," I said to Sun, "is likely to recognize Captain Leary if they see him. And if they do that and he's pretending to be somebody else, then he *is* blown—they have to be spies. But if he's just being given a responsible job while the Republic's at peace"—I shrugged and raised my rum—"well, what's surprising about that?"

"Aw, you know they wouldn't waste Six and the Mistress like that," Sun said, but he sounded more like he was arguing than that he was sure.

I swallowed very carefully before I said, "I don't know anything of the sort. I was hired to take the place of a midshipman who'd been injured, on a charter carrying a foreign ministry delegation to Saguntum. And that's *all* I know."

"Well..." said Woetjans. "I guess I *could* get used to a quiet voyage if I had to."

"I guess," said Sun, but he didn't sound convinced.

I stayed a bit longer, but I refused another drink. Even so, I hung to the railing of the companionway when I returned to my cabin on Level One. It had been a good visit and had, I think, made me a real member of the crew.

But neither my head nor my stomach could take many repetitions.

Chapter Seven

I spent my next duty on the hull with Captain Leary as he indicated our course to me from the Dorsal A masthead platform. The captain was using a brass rod—it must have been filled with something—between our helmets so that we could talk without actually leaning into direct contact.

I listened to his descriptions of what I should be seeing as my eyes followed the sweep of his arm across the glowing Matrix. He could have been whistling to me in bird language and it would have made as much sense, or almost as much.

Apparent color indicated relative energy levels compared to the level of the bubble universe I was viewing from. That was simple enough. I didn't understand how the captain was so sure how the universes were layered, though; which one a ship should enter before it went on to the next.

I hoped that when I compared what the captain told me with the *Sunray*'s plotted course, I'd understand better. Anyway, that's what I started doing on the bridge as soon as I reentered the hull.

Cory was on duty. He let me use the command console—the only console—and took a flat-plate display himself. There was no reason he shouldn't have done that—nothing was happening or likely to happen—but it was still a kindly action.

I don't know how much it helped me, though. I felt badly out of my depth as I viewed the astrogation plot as a three-dimensional hologram and compared it with my memory of what I'd seen on the hull—and Captain Leary's commentary on it. I've got a good visual memory, but the captain had been describing subtleties which continued to escape me.

The tap on my elbow just about made me jump out of my skin. "Hellfire!" I said and turned my head.

One of the delegation stood beside the console; she'd just touched me. I'd seen her among the ministry personnel when they were boarding, but I hadn't had contact with any of them before now. There was no reason to: They had quarters separate from the officers and crew, and they messed separately also.

I'd noticed this one; she was *very* pretty. She was older than I'd thought, though; not old, but past thirty. From a distance I'd guessed she was twenty, like me.

"I'm Maeve Grimaud," she said and smiled, which made her even more attractive. "I believe you've just been out in the Matrix?"

Maeve's dark-blond hair was shoulder length. She wore a two-piece outfit of soft violet fabric which wasn't fancy but matched her eyes.

"Yes, ma'am," I said. "I'm pretty busy now."

"Well, I was hoping that you could take me out on the hull,"

Maeve said. She smiled again. "I've never seen the Matrix, and I'd like to. With a guide."

You could do better than me, I thought. Aloud I said, "Ma'am, I'm still in training. If you get permission from the captain, I suppose I can. But not now, please. I'm trying to apply what Captain Leary showed me before I forget it all."

Her face tightened a trifle, but the smile was back an instant later. "Of course," she said. "I'll hold you to that."

She turned and walked off the bridge. I followed her into the corridor with my eyes. She got into the companionway and I turned back to my exercise.

Cory was looking at me from his station. He didn't say anything, but he was smiling.

An hour later, a text crawl from Maeve appeared on the bottom of my display. It said that she had permission from Captain Leary to go onto the hull with my escort. I replied that I'd take her out at the end of my next watch.

Chapter Eight

I came in with the riggers from an uneventful watch on the hull. Starboard B hadn't rotated fully to lock during one of the course changes, though it was close enough that *I* certainly hadn't noticed the difference by eye. I suspect the experienced riggers had missed it also, because the alert came by semaphore from the bridge.

We'd examined the track and found nothing, so we walked the mast into proper registry using bars stuck into the holes in the mast. With all twelve of us tugging, we got it into place. It made me a believer in hydraulic power, though.

I started taking my suit off as the riggers around me stripped—as usual, in half the time it was taking me. When the watch had melted away to the showers and their bunks, Maeve came forward. I'd completely forgotten her.

"Are you ready to take me out?" she said. She was wearing spacers' slops, as new as mine were, but she made them look sexy. Soft, clingy fabrics were kind to her; or maybe I should say that Maeve was kind to any clothes she chose to wear.

"Yes, ma'am," I said. I didn't want to, but I'd said I would. "First we'll find a suit to fit you."

There were three spares in the end locker. The medium was probably the best bet, but when I pulled it out and compared it to Maeve it didn't look like a good one. She was the right height, but she was slim and she'd rattle around like the pea in a whistle. That would mean scrapes and bruises—at best.

"Put her in an air suit," said a voice behind me.

I turned. Officer Mundy and her clerk had come off the bridge to watch; Maeve had turned also,

"Number Seventeen should do," Mundy continued. "That's the one I wear myself."

"Ah, ma'am…?" I said, wondering how I should phrase what I was thinking. Well, I was wondering a lot of things, starting with why Mundy was speaking at all. "Mistress Grimaud doesn't have any experience outside a ship and I don't want to take chances."

"Of course," said Mundy. There was nothing in her tone—and no expression on her face at all—to make me think it, but I was sure "you dimwit" lay under in the words. "But hard suits are only safer against possible puncture. An air suit is more comfortable and less clumsy, which makes it safer generally for a novice. Or an incompetent like me. We're less likely to drift off the hull."

I opened my mouth to say, "She'll be attached both to me and the ship with safety lines!" but Mundy probably knew that. And being jerked up short by a safety line wouldn't be very comfortable anyway.

"Ah, Mistress?" I said to Maeve. "Are you willing to wear an air suit?"

"Yes, if you think it's all right," Maeve said, glancing at Mundy and then back at me. I wasn't sure what I'd seen in the look she gave the signals officer, but it certainly wasn't friendly.

"We'll try you in an air suit, then," I said, turning to the lockers on the other side of the rotunda.

"While you're at it," said Mundy's clerk, "why don't you take one of Six's communication rods? I'm sure he'll be willing to help young love along."

I felt myself blushing. I started to turn, then decided I'd be better off ignoring it than shouting at Officer Mundy's clerk. That'd make me look like an idiot.

I remembered the warning Cory had given me the day I reported aboard. I didn't believe all the rumors I'd been hearing about Lady Mundy; but she was sure Captain Leary's friend, and that too was a good enough reason to let her clerk's comment go.

"Yes, that's a good idea," Mundy said. "Tovera, there's one in the captain's cruising cabin. Fetch it for Officer Olfetrie, if you please."

I was ready to help Maeve into the air suit, but she had no trouble with it. Either she was familiar with suits, or she was an extremely quick study. Given the suppleness with which she moved, I was willing to believe this was not her first experience. She was fully dressed before I'd gotten my torso section back on.

Mundy watched but didn't speak except to hand me the communication rod when her clerk came back with it a moment later. I checked Maeve's seals—all as should be—

and gestured her to the open airlock. Turning, I nodded to Mundy—I hadn't put on my helmet—and said, "Thank you, mistress." Then I followed Maeve into the airlock.

As soon as the inner door had dogged shut, Maeve let out a deep breath and said, "Thank heavens! Doesn't that Tovera give you the creeps?"

I'd started to put my helmet on, but I paused as pumps drew out the air. "Mundy's clerk?" I said. "No, not particularly. She's got something of an attitude; but if it doesn't bother her mistress, I can live with it."

"Clerk?" Maeve said in amazement that I thought was at least a bit put on. "I should offer to sell you the Pentacrest! Prime Xenos real estate!"

She closed her faceplate. I put my helmet on and latched it in place.

I clipped the free end of a safety line to Maeve's equipment belt, then led her onto the hull when the telltale over the outer hatch went green. I watched carefully as Maeve followed until I was sure that she understood the need to set the magnetic soles of her boots firmly on the steel hull.

I hooked another line for each of us to one of the attachment points near the hatch, then led Maeve into the bow. We weren't in anybody's way there and the sails didn't block our view of the Matrix. The dorsal and ventral masts rotated while we were moving, but that didn't affect us except to wait while Maeve stared at the movement.

When we were well forward, I stopped and took her arm. I gestured to the Matrix, then linked us with the communications rod. "This is the Matrix which joins every universe in the cosmos," I said. "This is everything there is; all existence."

Maeve looked across the horizon in front of her. The rod rattled against her helmet as she moved, so I lowered it. She reached down and brought one end firmly back into contact. "What am I supposed to be seeing?" she said.

"Well," I said, "if you're like me, you see dots of color across the whole sky. They're not stars, they're not even galaxies; they're whole universes. The ship travels from one to another, according to the course programmed into its computer."

"So it's like looking through the window of an aircar in flight?" Maeve said.

"For me, yes," I said. "There's some people who see god in the Matrix. Maybe they're right. I haven't found god there. Or anywhere else."

I shrugged, which she couldn't see in my hard suit.

"There's a few people can actually see a course through the Matrix better than what the astrogation computer can plot," I said. "Captain Leary's famous for it. He judges energy gradients by the colors and picks a route with fewer translations than a computer would. Or the Academy solution, either one. I suppose that's why Navy House picked him for this mission."

Maeve turned to face me, then clamped the rod to her again. "Do you really think that's why Captain Leary was given this mission?" she said.

"Yes, ma'am, I do," I said, trying not to sound defensive. "He's just as good an astrogator as the stories about him say. He's trying to teach me. The heavens know I'm trying to learn, but I'm not sure I'm even on the right page yet."

"You see that Daniel Leary is too senior an officer for what this mission is supposed to be, do you not?" Maeve said. She was still staring at my helmet, but I didn't turn to face her.

"Yes, ma'am," I said. "But it's a diplomatic mission, and the Republic is at peace."

I couldn't be sure of the sound Maeve made, but I think it was an audible sneer. "Relations between us and Saguntum could scarcely be of less importance," she said. "As for peace, though, there you've put your finger on it."

"I have?" I said.

"Roy, a powerful cabal of bureaucrats, unelected bureaucrats," Maeve said, "have repeatedly sent their preferred tool, Lady Mundy, and her assassin Tovera, to worlds they've decided to subvert. You can check this easily enough, though probably not on the *Sunray*—unless you're willing to look at material which I can provide you with."

She stopped there. I'd as soon not have replied, but it seemed that I had to. I said, "Ma'am, I know Captain Leary was a war hero, and I believe what you say about Officer Mundy not being just a signals officer."

That's basically what Barnes and his fellows had been saying last night. They'd served with Captain Leary—and with Lady Mundy—for long enough to know.

"But it's no business of mine. I've never been interested in spying—or politics, or *anything* like that. I just want to do my job and to learn to be a better astrogator."

"It could be—" she started to say.

I didn't let her go on. "Ma'am!" I said. "I don't want to talk about this. Right now I think we'd better go inside, because I want to learn more about Hansen's World. We'll be landing there in a few hours, I think."

I started back to the airlock. Maeve came along, which was good. I was feeling prickly enough that I'd have dragged her if she'd forced me.

Chapter Nine

I was using one of the displays on the bridge to read what the *Sailing Directions* had to say about Hansen's World. I wanted to learn as much as I could, but mainly I was focusing on something other than the fact that my guts had been turning somersaults ever since we extracted from the Matrix. We were in freefall orbit around the planet. I was hoping that I'd feel better as soon as we landed; it wouldn't be hard for however I felt to be better.

I'd been told that every time you extracted it felt different; and that every time was bad; and that you never, ever, got used to the experience. This was the first time I'd gone through an extraction, but at least the part about it being bad was true.

The PA system said, *"Lieutenant Enery, come to the command console and take the conn for landing."*

There was a pause; I wasn't really paying attention. Then the speaker added, *"Officer Olfetrie, come to the command console and echo the landing from the striker's station."*

I was reading about vegetable exports from Hansen's

World. If it hadn't been my name—that kinda cuts through everything, at least with me—I probably wouldn't have heard a word of the announcement.

Even so, I was half convinced I'd imagined it, until I turned my head. Captain Leary was looking at me; he smiled and pointed to the seat on the back of the console. Cory had been sitting there, but he was heading off the bridge with quick hand pats against the corridor walls. If Enery was coming forward, then Cory was probably heading back to man the back-up position in the stern.

The striker's station had a saddle, not a couch. I climbed onto it, noticing that my stomach had settled down the instant I registered the command.

The display could be run separate from that of the primary station or it could echo the primary. Cory had been using it separately—some sort of communications program, as best I could tell. I switched it to echo the primary, a view of the planet we were orbiting, plus some smaller insets.

The continent we were over had broad margins of green and dark green, and a gray-brown interior. Some of the darker green patches had straight margins. They must have been enormous to be so clear from orbit. I remembered what I'd just read about the sorghum fodder which, with meat and dairy products, Hansen's World exported to the whole region.

Enery was on the couch across the console from me, though I hadn't seen her arrive. The display shifted to bring up the power controls, thruster and High Drive both.

A schematic of the planet—the same continent—appeared above the controls on the display. Enery highlighted

Breckinridge—the planetary capital and largest city—on the east coast. A series of numbers appeared in a sidebar beside the schematic.

"Braking to land," Enery announced. She highlighted the second set of numbers from the top—they were time calculations. The High Drive vibrated; the *Sunray* began to fall out of orbit against 1 g of thrust.

To my surprise, Enery disconnected the automatic landing program. She lighted the plasma thrusters, adding their impulse to that of the more efficient High Drives, balanced them—and cut the High Drives completely, though we were still in hard vacuum.

We continued to drop, but against the roar of thrusters instead of the high frequency buzz of matter/antimatter recombination. As we entered the atmosphere, buffeting quickly built along with rattles and clangs.

My hand was poised above the Override button and the automated landing controls. If something happened to Enery, it would be my job to land the *Sunray*. At my level of skill, the best option would be to let the computer do it.

The *Sunray* slowed noticeably; we were actually braking harder than we had been under computer control. Enery had rotated the ship on her axis as we slowed. At an altitude of three thousand feet we were parallel to the surface according to the reading on my display. We were still moving forward and dropping, but we were in the realm of aircar velocities now.

Inset in the display's upper left quadrant of the forward view, land swelled from the ocean. Enery brought the *Sunray* into a near hover, then reduced flow to the bow pair of thrusters by two percent. We set us down in a concrete slip. The berth to port was empty; that to our starboard held two skeletal ships intended to haul containers of bulk produce which would be hooked onto the frames.

Enery shut down the thrusters though the water in the slip continued to boil for nearly a minute as the *Sunray*'s underside cooled. We rocked side to side, and steam continued to shroud the sensors in the visible range. I heard hatches opening, though that let in not only warm air but steam and whiffs of ozone—unquenched reminders of the thrusters' plasma exhaust.

"Lieutenant Enery?" I said, opening a two-way link through the console. Ambient noise was still too loud to imagine speaking to anyone without electronic aid. "May I ask you a question, over?"

"*Go ahead, Olfetrie,*" Enery said. "*Over.*"

I couldn't tell whether she was irritated or just surprised that I'd spoken. Her immediate duties were complete, and it'd be another ten minutes or more before the exterior cooled enough for people to leave the ship.

"Ma'am?" I said. "Is there a problem with the automated system that you chose to land us manually? Over."

There was no response for a moment. Then Enery gave a tiny chuckle and said, "*Well, that's a fair question, Olfetrie. Since you're an outsider like me, you don't know that Captain Leary makes a fetish of manual landings and shiphandling generally. I was just demonstrating that he and the people he trains aren't the only ones able to bring a ship in, over.*"

"I see," I said. "Ma'am, why did you switch to thrusters so quickly, over?"

"*We have plenty of reaction mass now,*" Enery said, "*and we're about to land in an ocean harbor. Our thrusters and High Drives are both in good shape, but thrusters can be repaired while High Drives have to be replaced.*"

For a moment I thought that Enery had finished without closing. Then she burst out, "*I'm not incompetent and I'm not a cipher. I'm the bloody first lieutenant of this ship! Over!*"

"Yes, ma'am," I said. "Olfetrie out."

"*Olfetrie, this is Six,*" the console said in Captain Leary's voice. "*Woetjans and Pasternak have put together a list of stores and equipment we need to pick up here. I want you and Woetjans to take care of that. Then you can go on liberty until 0600 hours. Over.*"

"Yes, *sir!*" I said. "Olfetrie out."

I knew that this was the first time Barnes and Dasi had landed on Hansen's World, so probably the captain hadn't either. At any rate, he hadn't directed me to a particular outfitter.

Cory might want his place back now that we'd landed. Rather than contact Mundy electronically, I walked over to the station where she was working with her personal data unit.

Tovera moved as though she intended to block me when she saw what I was doing, but I thrust my arm out in front of her. I *was* a ship's officer. I had no desire to throw my—minuscule—weight around, but I wasn't going to let a clerk stop me from carrying out the captain's orders.

"Officer Mundy?" I said.

For a moment she didn't respond. I remembered Tovera had thrust a hand through Mundy's display to get her attention.

I was about to try that technique, but before I could Mundy turned and looked up.

"Yes, Master Olfetrie?" she said.

Well, I'd never heard her put any emotion in her words, so I don't know why I found the polite words, well, scary now. I said, "I'm hoping that as communications officer you can help me. I want to find a chandlery that will be able to provide the ship's requirements at the best prices, but I don't even know if Breckinridge has a data net."

"It does," Mundy said. "And I've just connected us with it. Here"—schematic map and list of names appeared before me, projected by her personal unit. The resolution was remarkably high—"are the businesses who offer to outfit starships, though of course the list may not be complete."

Well, *that* startled me. I was glad, of course, but that was a lot of information for somebody just landed on a new planet.

I looked at the list and the map. Not surprisingly, the establishments were all on the harbor front.

"Is there anything else you need?" Mundy asked.

"Well, we don't need it, exactly," I said, "but what I'd like would be a list of their holdings to compare with the list that Woetjans will be bringing me. I guess we can just hoof it along the harbor road."

Mundy got up from her station. "Sit here," she said. "I'll queue up the inventories so that you can go through them."

"Ma'am?" I said. I'd heard what she'd said, but I couldn't fathom it.

Mundy moved to the adjacent station which Sun had just vacated. "Let me know if you need more," she said as she resumed whatever she'd been doing before I'd interrupted her.

Tovera moved over with her, grinning at me. She reminded me of a lizard, and I was suddenly glad that it was a happy lizard.

Using the station's built-in light pen, I started scrolling through the first of the businesses on the list—the one to the left of our berth; the other seven were spaced to starboard along Water Boulevard. Woetjans entered the bridge with a piece of flimsy in her hand. I motioned her over and took the list.

I was viewing not only the inventory of Agnelli Outfitters but also the wholesale price of each item. I checked the next business on the list—Kropatschek and Sons—and found the same thing. And rather wider margins on items with the same wholesale prices as Agnelli.

I looked over at Mundy, who was lost in her own business again. I had nothing to say to her; *she* already knew that she'd given me access to the companies' internal records.

"Sir?" said Woetjans. She was polite, but she didn't sound best pleased. "I think we ought to be going. I've got a dinner with Six this evening, and I don't know how long it's going to take us to find all the items."

"Officer Mundy has provided us with full inventories and prices for all the ship chandlers in Breckinridge," I said. "So if you'll just sit for a few minutes and jot down notes, the actual work is going to be relatively simple."

"Oh!" said Woetjans, flipping down the jump seat Tovera had vacated. "Well, if you're working with the Mistress, that's fine."

Apparently it would be. It was still a long list and a lot of choices, but I was already getting a feel for where we'd be going. I called off numbers to the bosun and she jotted them down on another sheet of flimsy.

About an hour later, I stretched and stood up. I grinned and Woetjans and said, "Ready for a trip to Apex Outfitters, Chief?"

"Yessir!" said Woetjans, getting up from the chair like a crane extending to tower over me. "But sir? These numbers don't mean anything to me. Are you going to do the talking?"

I frowned. I was pretty sure that wasn't the way Captain Leary had seen the business going—send the kid out with the bosun to get a little experience in the way things were really done—but thanks to Officer Mundy's data and my own experience, that was the best way.

"Right, Woetjans," I said. "I'll do the talking."

We stopped at my cabin so that I could change from the slops I was wearing into utilities. I'd expected to go on liberty immediately on landing, but if Captain Leary tapped me for the anchor watch, the slops were fine. What I hadn't expected was to be sent to represent the *Sunray* on shore.

The boarding hold was still steamy and with sharp touches of ozone when Woetjans and I reached it. Any organic matter floating in the slip during landing had been incinerated also, so the atmosphere stank.

The processed air of a starship underway was clean, perfectly balanced—and dead. I wasn't surprised that the crew had begun opening hatches high in the hull as soon as we were safely on the surface. It was good to have something real after a period of manufactured air.

"Hey, kid?" Sun called as we started toward the ramp. The purser's shop was a small compartment in the aft corridor, just off the hold; he was standing in the hatchway.

"Yes?" I said. Woetjans had already stopped.

"You'll want a saucer hat," Sun said, "since you're going off to be an officer. I already put this on your account."

He held out a flat-topped visored hat with a modest knot of gold braid on the front. The fabric was white in contrast to my dark-gray utilities.

I traded my soft cap for the saucer hat. "Thank you, Sun," I said. "I'm too new to this business to keep everything straight."

There were rails the length of the quay. On them ran a truck with a boarding extension which could align with the ramp of a ship regardless of where it lay within the slip. We crossed it to the quay and walked down to the street proper. It was a sunny day but brisk.

Woetjans kneaded her pectoral muscles with her fingers and looked sideways at me. "Sorry," she muttered in apparent embarrassment. "I took some slugs a couple years ago and they tighten up when they get cold."

I said, "I'd been thinking that a jacket might have been a good plan. We could go back?"

"Bloody hell, *no*," the bosun said.

The chandleries along Water Boulevard were separated from one another by bars and brothels. We'd left the ship long enough behind the main liberty group that the prostitutes were back out on the sidewalk in strength.

Woetjans moved slightly ahead of me and cleared a path— less brutally than I'd feared, but thoroughly nonetheless. "Move along, girls," she said, though none that I saw were girls and not all were even female. "We're on business now, maybe later."

She paused in front of the next chandlery where the walk

was clear and said, "Unless you'd like to stop in, sir? I didn't mean to—"

"Good heavens, *no*," I said, genuinely shocked at the notion. The whores here were the equivalent of the air above the slip when we'd just landed: real beyond question, but with no other virtues that I could see.

"I think Apex is the next one," I said and moved up beside Woetjans again. We entered the business together.

I felt at home. Dad had worked his way up through chandleries; some of my earliest memories were of riding on my dad's shoulder through places like Apex Outfitters.

The clerk behind the counter was reading an illustrated paper. He looked up, eyed us, and went back to his paper. He was about my age, but possibly younger.

"Good afternoon," I said. No one else was in the store that I could see, though someone could be walking among the racks of goods. "We need to speak with the person in charge."

"That's me," said the youth. He put his paper down but eyed us without enthusiasm. "What d'ye need?"

I thought for a moment, then said, "Come along, Woetjans. If this person is in charge, we need to go elsewhere. Blakesley Brothers was the next firm on my list."

I wasn't shouting, but I pitched my voice to be heard in the office to the right behind the counter. Its door was ajar and a light was on inside.

Woetjans turned to go, but I put a hand on her shoulder. As I expected, the office door opened and a man of fifty-odd came out. His hairline was receding, making him look older than he was.

"Sir?" he called to me. "Can I help you?" To the clerk he added, "I'll handle this, Amos."

"But you *said* ..." the youth whined.

Both the older man and I ignored him. I said, "I have a list of purchases to bring our ship up to RCN spec. I'd like to discuss quantities and pricing with you."

"I'm Artur Ferrante," the older man said, opening a gate in the counter. "If you'll come this way, we can discuss it in my office."

There were two straight chairs before the cluttered desk. One had a caddie of electronic files on it, but I lifted them off and put them on the floor behind me. That left the other chair open for Woetjans, but she stood by a file cabinet instead.

Ferrante latched the door firmly and sat down behind the desk. "My wife's nephew," he said in a low voice. "I was hoping that he'd come along a little faster than he has."

"He won't unless he changes his attitude," I said, "but that's not my problem. We're here to outfit the *Sunray* properly. We're an RCN crew carrying a Cinnabar trade delegation to Saguntum in a chartered vessel. This is the first leg, and there are significant deficiencies to correct."

Ferrante brought up the workstation at his desk. "What in particular are you looking for?" he said. "I think we'll be able to handle your requests."

I know you will, I thought. *But you may not like the price I'm offering.*

I read off the items on the list which the Chief of Rig and Chief of Ship—Woetjans and Pasternak—had prepared. Ferrante entered the items and quantities.

When I got to the end of the list, I said, "I mentioned that we were on a trade mission. If it's as successful as I expect it to be, there will be much more commercial traffic between Cinnabar and Saguntum than there is at present. There will also be increased RCN traffic, though of course that depends on many factors."

Ferrante smiled and nodded. "Apex Outfitters will be delighted to serve their needs with high-quality merchandise," he said.

He cleared his throat and looked down at his display. "I find the total of your current order to be—"

He paused and looked up. "Would you like the figure in florins or would you prefer another currency?"

"Florins are fine," I said. "If I may ask you a question, Master Ferrante? Are you the owner or the manager of Apex?"

"I'm the sole owner," Ferrante said. His eyes had narrowed slightly. "I married the founder's daughter, but I've built the business up considerably since then."

"Excellent," I said. "Go on."

"As I was saying," Ferrante said, "in florins, the total is eighty-seven hundred and I'll knock off a hundred for the new relationship."

I nodded and said, "I'm offering sixty-one hundred."

"What!"

"Incidentally, this will be in the form of a draft of the Shippers' and Merchants' Treasury"—I'd checked while I was putting together the proposal—"rather than RCN scrip. It allows you a fair profit on every item, and I've included the ten percent surcharge that I would have paid to a manager as an expediter's fee."

"You were planning to *bribe* me?" Ferrante said.

"I was prepared to bribe a manager," I said. "I'm glad I didn't have to. And I point out, not only is the price fair, it really will lead to increased business for you when I make my report in Cinnabar."

"*I'll* decide if the price is fair," Ferrante muttered as he went over the figures on his display. I glanced at Woetjans, who looked stunned. She didn't even meet my eyes.

After a moment Ferrante looked up. "Maybe that's what they call fair on Cinnabar," he growled. "But I suppose I can live with it."

He suddenly laughed. "Say, you wouldn't like to jump ship and come work for me, would you?"

I smiled back as I got to my feet. "Thank you, sir, but no," I said. "There'll be a credit chip in the full amount waiting at the *Sunray* when the order is delivered."

The sun was low as Woetjans and I returned to the boulevard. I was feeling extremely good for the first time in a long while.

The first time since Dad shot himself.

Chapter Ten

By the time Woetjans and I got back to the *Sunray*, Captain Leary and the senior personnel who'd served with him on the *Princess Cecile*—the former Sissies—had gone off to dinner. Woetjans went to her cabin to change before joining them.

Lieutenant Enery was the duty officer. When I entered the bridge, she asked, "Were you able to get most of what we needed?"

"Yes, ma'am," I said. "All of it."

I checked for incoming messages on Officer Mundy's station since it was the one I'd used in the past. The minute of agreement from Apex Outfitters had arrived, along with a delivery schedule beginning at 0900 hours and concluding at 1800 when the last items arrived from a warehouse west of Breckinridge proper.

I forwarded the file to the command console, addressed to All Personnel, though the common spacers didn't have access to it except for the stations on the bridge, stern, and Power

Room. "They had everything and in the quantities we needed."

"And quality?" Enery said as she brought up the file.

"See you at 0600!" Woetjans called from the corridor as she entered the down companionway. Her boots crashed on the metal treads as she jumped down the helical stairway.

"Well, we won't be able to tell that till the lots are delivered," I said. "They can be rejected for quality, of course; we won't pay until you accept the goods. The samples in the showroom were satisfactory to Chief Woetjans."

Enery rotated her couch and looked at me. "Olfetrie, these prices are very good. *Very* good," she said.

"Thank you, ma'am," I said. "I, well, my father was a chandler before his business expanded. And the other things that I'm sure you heard about. But he really was a good businessman."

Enery smiled at me. The stiffness of the right side of her face distorted the expression, but I'm pretty sure it was meant to be wry regardless.

"Captain Leary has the devil's own luck," she said. "No two ways about that. And it looks like he's been lucky again when he signed you on, Olfetrie."

"Ah, thank you, ma'am," I said. Glad of an excuse to change the subject, I said, "Lieutenant, do you know what restaurant Captain Leary is going to? I didn't think to ask Woetjans."

"He's at Rustermann's," Enery said. "I know in case there's an emergency." After a pause, she said, "You're joining them, Olfetrie?"

"Good heavens, no!" I said, more forcefully than I would've spoken if I hadn't just understood why her tone had suddenly frozen. "I just figured that where he is, there'll be other decent restaurants around. I didn't want to eat on the Strip if there's a reasonable choice in walking distance."

"Ah," said Enery. "Yes, I see. I believe Rustermann's might be on the pricey side; but yes, the district should be far enough away from the harbor to have restaurants that don't cater to spacers."

"I don't have a lot to spend my pay on," I said, smiling. "I just thought I'd treat myself to a decent meal."

The first one since Dad's death.

I went back to my cabin and changed into a set of the civilian clothes that I'd gotten out of pawn: tailored slacks and a jacket of hard fabric with a patterned weave. I'd kept them because they'd be proper office wear if I were ever promoted to an office job at Petersburg Chandlery. They weren't fancy, but they were too good for the scut work I'd been doing there.

As I dressed, I thought about Ferrante's offer. He'd been joking, of course, but it wouldn't have been a joke if I'd showed interest. If he'd offered the opening on the afternoon before Captain Leary knocked on my door, I'd have taken him up like a shot.

"Good night, Lieutenant," I called to Enery through the bridge hatch.

"Good luck to you finding dinner, Olfetrie," she said.

I thought I heard something wistful in her voice, so I paused at the head of the companionway, looking toward her. The ship was nearly deserted. Besides us, there were guards in the boarding hold, and a few personnel in the stern and the Power Room.

"I don't grudge Captain Leary his good luck," Enery said musingly. "It's what he's done with it that made his career, not the luck itself. But"—She gave me her awful smile again—

"sometimes I wonder if there's just so much luck in the universe, and he's gotten all of my share too."

"I hope not, ma'am," I said and escaped down the companionway.

In the boarding hold, Jablonsky—playing cards with Merritt, his fellow guard—said, "You're getting a late start, sir. Want to catch up with some spirits?"

He offered a clear flask. It appeared to be working fluid cut—slightly—with grape juice.

"You're confusing me with my brother, Josip," I said. "He was the drinker of the family."

I walked to the quay and up it, thinking about Junior. Everybody'd liked him. He was always the life of the party and went off, not necessarily home, with the prettiest girl. He'd had a brilliant career ahead, if the partying hadn't caught up with him in a few years.

And of course, if a missile hadn't gutted the *Heidegger* when she was a hundred feet in the air. I thought about what Enery had said about luck.

Rustermann's was on Third Street, but the first of the two blocks was a long one because Harbor Street followed the shoreline. I had the chance to buy pretty much anything the locals thought a spacer might want, including some that I hoped to heaven no spacer on any ship I was aboard *did* want.

Third Street straight back from the water was apartments, shops and bars that catered to locals. It wasn't fancy, but I didn't see any dives as bad as the one I'd lived above in Xenos. I turned left and found, as I'd hoped, that the neighborhood was becoming increasingly respectable.

I saw Rustermann's just ahead across the street and signs for other restaurants on both sides beyond. Rustermann's had a narrow patio in front, set off from the right-of-way by a low stone wall.

To my surprise, Woetjans was on the sidewalk, arguing with the two waiters who were barring her from the patio. Another waiter and a busboy came out of the restaurant proper, moving fast. They didn't jump in immediately, but they were obviously ready to lend a hand if required.

I started over. As I approached I heard a waiter snarling, "Look! I don't care if the Admiral of Known Space asked you to dinner, you don't eat *here*. Rustermann's doesn't serve spacers!"

Woetjans was wearing her Liberty Suit: a set of utilities tailored to fit her perfectly and decorated with ribbons with the names of every ship she'd served on, and the fabric embroidered with patches from every planet she'd landed on. Liberty Suits were both labors of love—spacers generally did all the tailoring themselves—and proof of their seniority.

They were also flamboyant proof that the wearer was a spacer.

Instead of getting involved at the entrance, I slipped past Woetjans and the first two waiters. The late-coming staff noted my civilian garments—a very high-quality suit, though I'm not sure their taste was that refined—and let me enter the restaurant without hesitation.

I'd intended to find Captain Leary, but at a good table near the staircase leading to the upper level Artur Ferrante sat with a woman of his own age—or possibly a few years more. That was even better.

"Master Ferrante!" I shouted. Diners had turned toward the voices raised outside the restaurant; I drew their attention to me.

"Will you please find Captain Leary and inform him that the proprietors here feel that his Chief of Rig is an unfit customer for their establishment? He's probably in a private room."

A man in dress clothes at the head of the staircase started down. I heard motion at the door, but before I could turn, men seized both my arms from behind. Diners were getting up, and I saw several duck under their tables, or as nearly as their dress clothes would allow.

"*Let him go!*" somebody shouted. I thought I'd been loud, but Woetjans was in a different league altogether. The waiter released my left arm instantly. The busboy gaped in indecision, but I could turn now.

Woetjans stood with her back to the wall beside the door. She'd gathered up two chairs by the backs on her way through the patio. She held one out in front of her like a shield—or a four-shafted lance, depending on what she decided to do with it. The other was vertical in her right hand, the feet jabbing the ceiling.

I'd known she was big. Now, though, she looked like an avenging goddess. Diners scuttled away like roaches when the pantry light goes on.

The manager reached the bottom of the stairs, but he didn't seem sure what to do. I detached the busboy's hand finger by finger; he seemed unwilling to move even that much on his own.

From the head of the stairs Captain Leary called, "Come on up, Woetjans! We've saved some of the liquor for you."

I could see Barnes, Dasi and Sun behind the captain, but to

my surprise Hogg and Tovera were shoulder to shoulder with him. Hogg had his hands in his tunic pockets, and the clerk held an attaché case half-open in front of her.

"Yes, of course," the manager said. "Mistress, allow me to escort you to your party."

It was a moment before Woetjans lowered the chairs and allowed the manager to take her arm. Her face was as white as chipped stone when she passed me.

I took a deep breath and bowed to Ferrante. "Thank you for your help, Master Ferrante," I said. "I'm glad no more than your presence was needed."

Everybody kept out of my way as I left Rustermann's. I walked across the street to Gino's, which turned out to be steak house.

I was most of the way through a rare rib eye and contemplating a second glass of the red wine the waiter had recommended. It was strong flavored, but it complemented the meat—from real Earth cows—perfectly.

I was beginning to relax. It'd been a hell of a day.

A tubby man came over to the table where I sat alone. He wore an open-necked shirt and loose trousers, but he didn't need dress clothes or a uniform to project authority.

"The meal has been to your taste, sir?" he asked.

"Perfectly," I said. "I'm never sure what I'm going to get when I order 'rare,' but here it's rare."

"If I may ask, sir?"

I nodded, wondering what was going to come next. I took

the last sip from my glass, holding the man's eyes.

"My head waiter tells me that you were ejected from Rustermann's," the man said. "Was that the case?"

I put my glass down. "Not exactly," I said. "I had no intention of eating there, but I saw some flunkies barring a shipmate whom I knew to have been invited to a dinner there with our captain. It was a dress-code violation."

I felt my lips purse as I wondered how to put the next part. I said, "I intervened to bring the matter to the manager's attention. It, ah, got heated for a moment at the end. If that's a problem, I'll pay and leave immediately."

"Is no problem," the man said. He set my bill on the table—a trifle early, I thought, but nobody wants brawlers in his business.

I reached for the bill, but the man scrawled something across the face of it with a stylus. He turned and walked off, but I'm sure the words he muttered were "Snooty bastards!"

I looked at the bill. The price was as bad as I'd expected it to be. Over it was written *Paid in Full/Gino*.

I left a full tip on the table when I left, after another glass of wine.

Chapter Eleven

Barnes had warned me that the two of us would be dry-lubing Antenna Dorsal A on our next watch. Though I'd never done it, I knew that applying graphite to all the joints was a miserable, filthy job. Well, I wanted to be a spacer.

Very few people had dry-lubed an antenna in space. It's never necessary to do. Not doing it just means the antenna moves a little more stiffly than it ought to and puts a little more strain on the machinery. Commercial ships don't have the sail area to take an antenna out of service for most of a day, and even naval vessels preferred to leave the job to shipyards where the dust could be washed off instead of being brought into the ship's interior.

The coming job was hanging over me, but I still had a couple hours of my own time. Our next landfall was Santiago. I'd read what I could find about the place, but it occurred to me that Officer Mundy might have information beyond the official bare bones.

I'd heard more things about Mundy by now. I was sure that they weren't all true—they couldn't be if she was human—but I was willing to accept that she was a spy and that she was a skilled librarian. Her spying was no business of mine, but someone who had the skill of researching and organizing information was exactly what I needed now.

At the moment she was lost in the world formed by her dancing control wands. Instead of breaking in, I walked to her servant, seated beside Mundy at her station and said, "Mistress Tovera, I would like to ask Officer Mundy about information on Santiago. Background beyond the *Sailing Directions* for when we touch down. Would you pass that request to her when she becomes free, please?"

Tovera grinned at me. I'd heard more about her too. Now that I'd known Tovera for a little while, Maeve's statement that she was a sociopathic killer didn't seem as ridiculous as it had at the time.

"I'll let her know," Tovera said. "I expect that she'll have a file ready for you when you come off watch."

"Thank you, mistress," I said. I made a slight bow and headed to my cabin to catch an hour of sleep before I went on watch.

I wasn't sure how to deal with Tovera; she certainly wasn't just the clerk of a junior warrant officer, whom I as an officer ranked. On the other hand, simple courtesy generally struck me as the best choice, unless there was a good reason for something else. And maybe even then.

* * *

Barnes and I fed graphite into the antenna's topmast joint. I didn't bother disconnecting the pump because we wouldn't have body parts in the way at this stage. It was a dirty job, but it wasn't a particularly tough one.

Barnes sent me to the emergency controls. I selected the topmast and held my gauntleted thumb on the Down button. The mast began to telescope, but very slowly. Barnes signalled me to stop and rejoin him. I locked the controls closed before I obeyed.

He'd already started opening the gearbox when I got there. He put his helmet to mine and said, "I should've checked this first. It wasn't the tubes binding, they were fine. The drive gear's worn!"

He pointed his finger. The pulley was pinned to a gear, which in turn was driven by a gear in the transmission. The alignment hadn't been perfect; the drive gear had been running on the outer edge of the driven gear and had worn it almost smooth.

I bent to read the inventory number. Barnes lifted my head and said, "For now we're not going to bother with replacing the set and restringing the cable. I'll show you a trick."

He disconnected the hydraulic line—I'd have done it myself if he hadn't—and took a chisel and heavy hammer from his pouch. He placed the chisel edge on the side of the driven gear and struck a hard blow, shearing off the rivet head. He set the chisel again and pointed to the gear; I held it by the gear teeth, keeping my fingers out of Barnes way. He struck again and the gear came loose in my hand. I cupped it in my palms while the bosun's mate knocked the shafts of the beheaded rivets out of the pulley.

Barnes thrust cotter pins through both rivet holes, then set the driven gear over them—with the other face upward. He peened over the legs of the cotter pins, then touched helmets with me. "Hook the motor back up, kid," he said. "I think that'll hold till we're on the ground again."

The antenna ran up and down slickly. Lubricating the joint no doubt helped, but not enough to mention. The problem had been the worn gear.

Barnes and I locked through at the end of watch with Bondurant and Cerne, who were arguing about the relative merits of the prostitutes to be had on Bryce and Pleasaunce. Garden-variety streetwalkers, I gathered; neither man sounded as though he had refined tastes.

Bryce and Pleasaunce were powerful members of the Alliance of Free Stars and not common destinations for Cinnabar citizens. Very few people on Xenos could have joined in the discussion. It demonstrated that experience didn't equate with culture.

To Barnes as the lock filled, I said, "Will those cotter pins hold up?"

"Long enough," he said, shrugging in his hard suit. "I didn't feel like swapping out the pulley in the Matrix when we'll be on the surface in a couple watches."

He grinned broadly. "You already proved you could string a cable," he said, "and that's what it'd take to replace the whole set."

The lock opened. In the rotunda I began undoing my suit.

Barnes, Bondurant and Cerne got theirs off quickly. The common spacers were arguing fine points that I couldn't even understand. I was all right with my ignorance.

Woetjans came out of the companionway, saw me, and braced my shoulder as I got my legs clear. "Hey, kid?" she said. "We oughta be on Santiago in a couple hours. Got any plans for there?"

"No, ma'am," I said over my shoulder as I hung up my suit. "Do you want me to swap watches with somebody?"

"Not that," said the bosun. She looked away. "Look, kid? Would you let me take you to dinner? I'll pay, only you gotta pick the place."

I guess my face went blank. The gods know my mind did.

"Oh, bloody hell, not that!" Woetjans said. I swear to heaven she was blushing. "Look, not that you're not cute, but I like 'em a little better growed. Naw, I just want to talk with you where we can. I owe you for Breckinridge, you know."

"You don't owe me anything!" I said. "We're shipmates. But I'm not proud—I'll let you buy me dinner. Or whatever it is when we land."

"Thanks, kid," she said as she strode to the companionways again. "Remember, you pick the place!"

I went onto the bridge to see what Officer Mundy had for me. I hoped that she'd found information on restaurants not too far from the harbor. That hadn't been one of the things I'd been worried about.

Chapter Twelve

Captain Leary brought us down in the harbor at Santiago, the capital of the planet of the same name. He put me in the striker's seat, just as he had when Lieutenant Enery landed on Hansen's World.

I'd thought Enery's landing was flawless. I thought the same of the Captain's. I was no expert, but both were a lot smoother than the computer landings I'd experienced in jaunts to orbit and back in training. Seeing it done right made me even more determined to leave the job to the computer, at least until I'd had several more years of training on simulators.

After landing I went to my cabin to change for liberty. The boarding hold was already full of spacers going on leave, but they'd be wearing utilities. I was changing out of uniform. The *Sunray* was a commercial vessel, but she was run on RCN lines by RCN personnel, and I didn't intend to give myself any breaks.

I decided to wear an outfit different from what I'd worn on Hansen's World: dark brown slacks and a matching jacket, over a bright yellow tunic. As I sealed the shirt seam, someone knocked on the door panel.

"Just a second!" I called, tucking in the shirt tail. I strolled to the panel.

I figured that Woetjans had gotten through with the docking procedures more quickly than she'd expected to. There was no reason for the bosun to superintend rolling out the extension bridge with a crew as experienced as this one. She and both her mates had been present to check me out in the lounge; a senior rigger was probably in charge on the hull, but they were *all* senior riggers. Woetjans liked to do it, though.

I opened the panel. Maeve smiled at me. She said, "I decided that the hull wasn't the best place for us to get acquainted. Would you like to go to dinner tonight? I hear that Santiago has some nice places."

She was wearing a body suit, black with sudden silvery highlights. It wasn't at all tight, but the ways it clung and slipped would've gotten any man's attention. It sure got mine.

"I'm very sorry, Maeve," I said. "I've already made a dinner engagement for tonight."

Maeve looked startled, then smiled warmly. "Well, there'll be another time," she said. "I hope so, anyway."

Her eyes narrowed slightly and she added, "With Lieutenant Enery, I suppose? She's had some bad luck and certainly deserves some fun in her life."

I thought I heard condescension in Maeve's voice. I found the first officer unsettling to be around, but the sneer—maybe I imagined it, *maybe*—made me angry on Enery's account even though she wasn't present to hear it.

"No, mistress," I said as calmly as I could. "I'm having dinner with the Chief of Rig tonight. Bosun Woetjans, you know."

It suddenly struck me that I didn't know Woetjans' first name. *I'll ask her tonight, though I don't suppose it really matters.*

"I don't think I know..." Maeve said. Her smile slipped. "Oh. *Oh.*"

When the smile returned, it was as false as a politician's. "Well, another time, as I said."

She turned and strode very quickly to the companionway. I couldn't have offended her so badly if I'd slapped her face.

But you shouldn't treat people that way, even if you're pretty and they never were, even before they got burned. I put on the jacket I'd laid on the bed; then I went to the bridge and chatted with Cory while I waited for Woetjans to get off duty.

According to the information from Mundy, there was a Museum of the Settlement in Santiago. It didn't sound like much, but I'd try it tomorrow if I had time to. Far planets were a new experience to me. I might get blasé about them, but I didn't think so.

Woetjans stuck her head onto the bridge and said that she was going to change and would be back in a jiff. "No rush," I called to her back. I didn't expect to make a long night of it.

Cory was telling me about visiting public works departments when they landed on new planets, the ones organized enough to have such things. His father was a paving contractor on their homeworld of Florentine, and it gave Cory a feeling of comfort to talk shop.

I thought about the sudden wash of homesickness when I'd walked into Apex Outfitters. I wondered if I could arrange to negotiate with all suppliers, as long as I was aboard the *Sunray*.

"Okay, kid," Woetjans called from the hatchway. "Where're we going to dinner?"

I looked at her. "A place called the Plumb Bob," I said. "But what happened to your liberty suit?"

She was wearing new utilities, tailored but otherwise unadorned.

Woetjans looked away. "Well," she said, "you know...I appreciate what you did in Breckinridge, but I don't want to embarrass you."

"Woetjans!" I said. "Put your bloody liberty suit on! I'm not taking us anywhere they won't serve spacers, and if I've figured wrong we'll bloody well go somewhere else!"

Woetjans looked blank for a moment. "Yessir!" she said and trotted for her cabin.

When she was out of sight, Cory chuckled slightly. "You know, Roy," he said, "I wasn't sure you were really cut out to be an officer. Guess I was wrong to wonder."

Woetjans was back in a moment, bright and fluttering. We headed down to the boarding hold and out. I turned left at the street along the harbor, saying, "It's about six blocks. Mostly west, but a block in from the harbor, that's north."

"Then let's take the block inland first," Woetjans said. "Along the street by the harbor, it runs to warehouses and factories even beyond where it's dives. Most of the places I've been, I mean."

"That's better than what I've got," I said, changing direction to cross the street. "All I have is a map."

We crossed as a couple of heavy trucks rolled past—one in

either direction. They weren't moving fast.

"The information I've got is about three years old," I said. "The place I'm looking for may not be around."

"Kid, I don't care," Woetjans said. "Not a scrap. I just wanted it to be you picking, not me."

The traffic along the street we were following was steady but not fast. The standard local vehicle had four tall wheels and a squarish box on top of them. It seemed to me that if one hit us, the car would be worse off than we were—though they were probably sturdier than they looked.

Woetjans shook herself. She kneaded her pectoral muscles with both hands.

I could loan her my jacket as a drape over her shoulders; it wouldn't fit, of course. I was finding the evening a little nippy myself.

Woetjans saw me looking at her and said, "It's just the muscles still tighten up when it gets cold. I'm fine, the weather here's warmer than lots of places I've been."

"Ah," I said. "You were shot several times in the chest and returned to duty?"

"You're bloody right I did!" Woetjans said. "It was just a dumb mistake, I wasn't fast enough getting through a doorway. There was a medicomp in the next bloody room!"

"Right!" I said, nodding in fierce agreement. You don't suggest to anybody that they can't do their job, and suggesting that to somebody like Woetjans could be, well, dangerous.

And I hadn't meant to do that, but it'd come out that way to her just because it *was* such a hot button. I chuckled. To explain it I said aloud, "Bloody hell, woman, who'd be dumb enough to say that *you* couldn't do your job?"

What I'd *really* been thinking was that I'd known being an RCN officer was dangerous. I hadn't guessed that asking a simple question about information a shipmate had volunteered might be one of those dangers.

"Nobody who didn't want to learn how far I could throw them through the nearest wall," Woetjans said. She laughed as well, but I was pretty sure that it was also the cold truth. I'd gotten a break because she liked me and she was sure I hadn't meant anything by it.

The sign of the place where the Plumb Bob was supposed to be now read CATCH OF THE DAY, with a leaping fish which seemed to have fins sticking out in four directions. "Are you up for seafood?" I said. "I guess they changed their menu since Officer Mundy got her information."

"Sure, that's fine," Woetjans said. "Say, that fish looks just like a ship, don't it?"

The fins really did stick out from the fish's body the way antennas did from a starship's hull in the Matrix. It wasn't a connection I'd have made, but I hadn't spent my working life as a rigger.

The doors pulled open; the headwaiter's station was set just back from the entrance. It could have been in Xenos— or in Breckinridge or I suspect anywhere people weren't too close to the edge. A city with a busy starport has at least modest comforts for the locals—as well as with the sort of establishments that serve spacers.

"A table for two," I said to the dapper little man who turned a professional smile on us. More than half the seats were filled, but the place wasn't packed yet. "A booth if that's possible."

"And I get the bill!" said Woetjans. She didn't exactly shout, but her voice from just behind—and above—me made me jump.

"Lucinda will seat you, madame and master," said the headwaiter. His smile was a little wider; and I thought it had become real.

He thinks I'm Woetjans' gigolo, I realized.

We followed a pert young woman—a slightly younger, female edition of the headwaiter—to a booth at the back. "Sorry, kid," Woetjans muttered. "Hope I didn't embarrass you. I just didn't want you to forget what I said."

"Of course you didn't embarrass me," I lied. "But I've looked at the prices, and I guarantee I could handle it."

"Yeah, well, you're not going to," Woetjans said, taking the opposite side of the booth after I slid onto a bench. "I've made plenty in prizes, serving as bosun to Six. And I pissed away some of it, sure—I've got three sisters, all of 'em married and none of the husbands worth the powder to blow 'em away."

She grinned. "I kept some for myself, though. You bet your ass I did."

The server made the usual offers. I didn't know enough about local food to make a competent choice, so I chose the peppered ragfish special—it sounded interesting, so why not?—and a glass of the house white.

Woetjans ordered the same, only she'd drink gin with a peppermint candy. To my amazement the server was no more surprised by that than she had been by my wine. I was broadening my horizons, though Woetjans' choice wasn't a taste I expected to cultivate myself.

"Two questions, Woetjans," I said as we waited for our drinks. I was raising my voice a little to be heard over the other diners and the bustle of servers. The bar on one side of the building was already crowded.

"Shoot," she said.

"What's your first name?" I said. "I'm Roy, but 'kid' works fine."

"I guess you're going to stay 'kid,'" Woetjans said. "That's just how you come through. I'm sorry, I guess, but you just do."

"That's the breaks," I said. "There's worse. But your name?"

"I'm Ellie," Woetjans said, "but nobody but my family calls me that. Blood family, I mean. With the Sissies, I'm 'Chief.'"

She threw her shoulders back on the bench. "Two questions, you said. What's the other?"

"What the bloody hell do you want from me?" I said, not letting my voice change from when I asked her name.

Woetjans looked blank for a moment; then she began laughing. Her laughter was loud enough—and harsh enough—that people were turning to look at our booth.

The drinks came. Woetjans downed half her gin, then smiled at me.

"Okay, kid," she said. "I want to know what you're doing here. You're not like anybody I've seen before. Just tell me what you're up to."

"You want it straight?" I said. "I was in the Academy, but my dad was Dean Olfetrie. He was bribing politicians and Navy House bureaucrats to rob the RCN blind. So I dropped out of the Academy, did some scut work, and took the first decent job I was offered. Which was by Captain Leary, who brought me here."

I sucked my lips in, then said, "Are you shocked? Want me to buy my own dinner now?"

"I guess your old man isn't the first crooked outfitter I've heard of," Woetjans said. "The cable you replaced the first day out was from a reel marked with the right size, but there was a ring around the hub to make up for the cable's smaller diameter."

She drank again, then thought about it and emptied the glass. She held it high, which I took as a silent request for a refill. "Go on, kid," she said.

"Maybe it was Dad doing so much work with the RCN," I said. "I don't know. Both Junior and I wanted to be RCN officers, though. He was killed at New Harmony."

I frowned as I tried to focus my mind on a past that had changed completely since my father's death. "Look," I said. "I know I don't seem like an RCN officer, but I could've been one."

I was trying to put words to things I'd thought for years but hadn't been willing to say even to myself—because it'd seem like whining. "My brother had the look, I know what you mean," I said. "He partied and he was everybody's drinking buddy—and if you passed out trying to drink along with him, he'd pull your girlfriend sure as lead sinks. But my navigation was better than Junior's and I could take him apart on the tactical simulator, even when I was twelve and he was an Academy graduate!"

The server did indeed arrive with a gin, and a peppermint candy that Woetjans cracked with the back of a spoon. The bosun put half in her cheek and sipped at her drink. She said, "Barnes said you did a good job rerigging Dorsal B."

I shrugged. "Barnes and Dasi could've done the job in half

the time," I said. "I've watched them work."

Woetjans smiled broadly. The server, arriving with our meals, shied back, though I'm not sure she had anything to do with Woetjans' expression.

"Barnes and Dasi've been working rigging for a long time," Woetjans said. "Either one could be bosun on a cruiser if he wanted to. Besides, Barnes was laying back to see how you'd handle the job."

"You could be on a battleship, Ellie," I said. "Why aren't you?"

Woetjans laughed again. "I been on a battleship," she said. She cut a big bite of fish, guiding it to her mouth with both fork and the tip of her knife. "My first tour as an able spacer was on the *Renown*. Didn't like it worth a damn—seemed like the admiral was always looking over my shoulder. Transferred to destroyers, then got a slot as bosun's mate on a courier ship—the *Aglaia*. Best luck I ever hope to have."

The ragfish was pretty good, though bland to my taste. The peppers were strands of bell pepper, not the hot pepper I'd expected.

"You liked the courier ship that much?" I said to keep the conversation going.

"It was bloody awful," Woetjans said, shoveling the rest of her fish into her mouth. "You not only have extra ship's officers, you got the passengers like as not nosing into your business. But that's where I met Six, and I been with him ever since."

I was taking longer to finish my meal than Woetjans had. For that matter, I still had half a glass of wine and she was ordering her third gin. I said, "Because of the prizes?" I said. "I guess all the crew who've served with Captain Leary are pretty rich by now."

Woetjans laughed, but without the enthusiasm that'd rattled the windows before. "Most of the Sissies, they've got maybe a pot to piss in, kid," she said. "They're spacers. The ones who've got more—Pasternak's got a regular manor back in Wassail County where he grew up—it don't do them no good. It don't do *me* no good, except if I want to take a kid to dinner to learn what makes him tick, I don't worry what the tab's going to be."

She paused and pursed her lips. "We Sissies are all spacers," she said. "Every single soul who stuck with Six is that, and you don't need money to be a spacer. If you signed with Six to get rich, you're a bloody fool. You're more likely to lose your arm or your ass than to get rich."

"I joined to be a spacer," I said. "I'm learning to do that. I'll never be the astrogator that Captain Leary and even Cory are, but I'll be better than I am now. And eventually I'll be pretty good."

I shrugged. My glass was empty, so I held it up the way Woetjans had hers. "I know there's risks," I said. "They told us not to open the coffin when they shipped Junior back for burial. Mom thought that meant his body'd been torn up and maybe Dad thought that too, but I heard the gravel rattle when I shifted the coffin a little. Junior'd been burned so bad they had to ballast the coffin before they sent it back. But he'd been a spacer, and I'm going to be a spacer."

My wine came. I took a deep draft, I guess to cool myself off. I'd gotten pretty hot talking like that.

"That stuff any good?" Woetjans said.

"It's all right for me," I said. "I'm not much of a drinker. But I can tell you, my fiancée's father wouldn't use it to clean drains. Ex-fiancée."

"Toss it down and let's get out of here," Woetjans said. "We'll find a place near the harbor and really tie one on if you like."

I didn't—I peeled off when the bosun stopped at a place on the harborfront. But I went back aboard the *Sunray*, feeling that it'd been a good evening. My astrogation was improving faster than it ever would have if I'd stayed in the Academy, and I'd gotten through another test.

I guess the tests would keep coming till I died. Well, that was all right.

Chapter Thirteen

My last watch before Saguntum was in the Power Room. Captain Leary believed that an officer had to know the whole ship, not just the rigging and how to astrogate. One of the things Pasternak's list had directed me to buy on Hansen's World was a flow pump. This wasn't the big unit which sucked water into the reaction mass tanks; it was a relatively small pump submerged in the tank to feed the fluid to the plasma thrusters or to the antimatter converters for the High Drive, depending on which we were using at the time.

"Got a job for you, kid," said Pasternak when I reported. "You and Gamba are going to be replacing the flow pump, and I don't mind telling you that it'll be a bitch of a job."

It was that in truth. Pasternak had run the tank down lower than he said he liked, but me and Gamba, a Tech 4, had to wear air suits working inside in four feet of water to remove frozen bolts.

Some time in the last few years, the *Sunray* had filled its tanks with water which was either contaminated with something more corrosive than salt, or which perhaps wasn't water at all. Any fluid which would feed through the lines became reaction mass so far as the propulsion units were concerned.

The pump was supposed to be a sealed unit, but Pasternak said it had been running hot ever since we lifted from Xenos because of a corroded rotor shaft. The lock nuts (the bolts were welded to the tank) had long given up any pretence of having corrosion-resistant coatings.

When we got the pump loose, I released the short line that clamped me to the inflow grating in the tank floor. Without those tethers, we'd have been bobbing like corks in our air suits. I opened the faceplate and called, "We got it loose! We're ready to haul it out!"

I expected somebody to bring a chain hoist above the open lid of the tank. Instead, a tech named Evans leaned over the side and gripped the output pipe. It had been unhooked from the manifold.

"Keep outa the way," Evans said. He tilted the pipe to make sure the pump really was free of all the bolts, then slid it toward him in the tank. Finally he lifted the pump hand over hand until he could rest it on the lip.

"Now, you boys just sit there and you can put the new one back on," Evans grunted. He swung the pump to the deck and disappeared for a moment.

"Bloody hell," I said to Gamba, who'd also opened his helmet. "I *know* what that thing weighs!"

"Yeah, Evans is showing off for the new officer," Gamba said. He was as overqualified for this job as Barnes had been to act as my helper in restringing a cable; his ears were the smallest I'd ever seen on an adult man. "Mind, he's got a lot to show off. He's thick as a brick, though."

"With Captain Leary on the bridge," I said, "the rest of us don't need to be brilliant."

Shuffling and heavy thumps indicated that something was happening on the deck above us; then I heard the squeals and bangs of a crate being broken up. Beaumont, a Tech 3, leaned over and called, "Just a second more. We gotta hook up the exit pipe."

"We're not going anywhere," I said. I wondered if Gamba and me would even be able to get out by ourselves. Maybe if I was strong enough to haul myself up from Gamba's shoulders and then strong enough to pull him up in turn . . . but I'd use a rope or a length of cable for that, not just reaching down and grabbing him by the hand.

"Stand clear!" somebody shouted. Then a new pump appeared over the rim and descended into the tank—faster than the old one had risen but still under control. It hit the water with enough of a splash that I was glad I'd closed up my helmet again.

There'd been several techs skidding the new unit along the decking, but Evans had apparently decided to lower it alone. *I* wouldn't get in his way about any bloody thing he wanted to do.

Gamba and I walked the new unit over the to the mounting plate on its edge. The trick then was to align it with the bolts.

Gamba grinned at me. "It's on you now, kid," he said.

"Right," I said. "But look, you get over against the side, okay? I'll come up and ask for help if I have to"—I couldn't honestly think of anything a second man could do that would be useful—"but I *don't* want to lose a hand if the pump moves while I'm between it and the bottom."

"Right, kid," Gamba said with a serious expression. He at least knew to look like he was as concerned as I was. The corner of his mouth quirked. "Besides..." he said, "I think Woetjans'd pull my arms off if anything like that happened."

"I'll be done as quick as I can," I said and closed my face shield. Mostly to get on with the job, but I didn't want to talk about me and Woetjans either. Mind, there was nothing to talk about anyway.

I hooked to the grating again. My helmet still bobbed, but I could keep my arms and torso under water. I rotated the pump so that the flange was up on one of the four bolts, then used a screwdriver through another hole to crab the unit onto the remaining three bolts.

Now was when I really could have used some help, but only if we could've communicated. I grabbed the outflow pipe with both hands and turned it carefully, like it was an analog clock. This would've been a lot easier if I were strong as Evans was, but I'm not sure I'd ever met anybody else that strong. I heard a *click!* and felt the pipe wobble.

I straightened and opened my face shield. "Okay, Gamba," I said. "I got it balanced here. Now we just need to line it up with the bolts and let it fall home."

Gamba grinned at me. "Keep your hands on the pipe, kid," he said, "but you just feel. And make sure your boots aren't in the way. Right?"

"Right," I said and shuffled back a boot's length. I'd asked for help, not to have Gamba to take over. On the other hand, I was so exhausted that I didn't really care.

The pipe tilted one way and another, turning by equally tiny bits under my gloves. It suddenly gave and clanged to its seat. Gamba stepped back; he was breathing hard, so it hadn't really been as easy as he'd made it seem.

"Got the old nuts, kid?" he asked.

"Sure," I said. I reached for them. "Right here in my pouch."

"Leave 'em and throw 'em away when we're out of this," Gamba said. He held up a little net bag with four bright-finished nuts. "We'll use these instead because we can. That'll make it easier for the next couple bastards. Who won't be us, I hope to hell."

It was a lot easier to snug the nuts up than it had been to crack them loose to begin with. That would've been true even if Gamba hadn't given me a power wrench small enough to hold in my hand, instead of using the box wrench I'd taken them off with. As a matter of fact, the biggest problem screwing the nuts on was keeping hold of the wrench against the torque.

Beaumont hooked a tubular ladder over the side. I climbed up behind Gamba. It was long past the end of the watch. I was wrung out, as I generally was since I joined the *Sunray*. I wasn't complaining, but I'd never have worked this hard at a regular civilian job.

I walked to the entrance of the Power Room and started to take off my air suit near the lockers there. The bulkhead was armored, like that of the bridge. It wouldn't exactly withstand the blast of a ruptured fusion bottle, but it should redirect the fireball through the deliberately weakened vent plates in the exterior hull.

Pasternak gestured me to come over to his enclosed office across from the lockers. I closed the hatch behind me because of the racket. Four techs were guiding the lid back over the tank—using the travelling hoist. The Power Room was noisy enough at any time, but the clanking and shouts made it something out of Hell.

"Six wants to see you on the bridge, kid," Pasternak said.

"Thanks, Chief," I said. What I was really thinking was, "*No bloody way!*"

I chuckled as I finished removing the air suit. I couldn't even complain about it not being fair. I was a volunteer.

"There you are, Olfetrie," Captain Leary said, rotating his couch at the console to face me as I entered the bridge. "Say, you've got a nice suit, right?"

"Well, I've got a suit," I said. "Several of them. But I left all my dress clothes in pawn in Xenos."

By now they'd probably have been sold. Well, I couldn't imagine I'd ever again have entre to society in which they'd be required. I might've gotten a few extra florins if I'd flat sold them instead of pawning them, but at the time I did it I hadn't really internalized how complete my disaster was.

"They're civilian," the captain said, smiling. "And I suspect anybody else aboard would call them dress clothes." He frowned across at the commo station and added, "Well, maybe not Adele."

Looking at me again, he said, "Anyway, the delegation needs an escort of five spacers when they present their credentials in Saguntum, and I need an officer to command the escort. You're what I've got with civilian clothes."

"Ah..." I said. I had nowhere to go with the thought, so I said, "Yes, sir!" and shut my mouth.

"I don't believe you've met our passengers," Captain Leary said. He grinned. "Except for the pretty one, right?"

"Mistress Grimaud," I said, nodding vigorously. "Though I don't know precisely what her position is."

"If she'd told you..." the captain said, "she'd probably have lied. We'll go down now—no, clean up and put on a suit before we do that. When you're presentable, I'll introduce you to the delegation. Director Jimenez seemed to be concerned that his escort would be a bunch of roughs who'd embarrass the dignity of the Foreign Ministry."

His smile wasn't altogether warm. "Personally," he went on, "I don't believe anything the RCN did could possibly lower it to the level of the Foreign Ministry, but I figure your experience will put his mind at rest."

I thought of just changing clothes, but I knew I looked like something the cat had dragged in. Five hours working—and I mean *work*ing—in an air suit really takes it out of you. I showered before changing. It made me feel more human as well as cleaner, though I was still very tired.

I came back, wearing my dull green jacket over gray tunic and slacks. "I knew you'd clean up nice," Captain Leary said. "Doesn't he, Hogg?"

"Pretty as a picture," his servant said, rising from the

striker's seat to take a good look at me. "I hope he can take care of himself."

"Now, Hogg," the captain said. "It's not going to be that kind of escort. They won't be carrying weapons."

"I *can* take care of myself, Hogg," I said. If he'd been a gentleman, I'd have said, "Master Hogg," but he wasn't. "But your servant raises a good point, sir: Who have you chosen for the escort?"

The captain shrugged. "I figured I'd leave that to you, Olfetrie," he said. "Pick any five you'd be comfortable leading on this business."

I started to protest, then caught myself. I wanted to be an officer; this was my job. "Yes, sir," I said. "I suppose any of the crew, at least of the former Sissies, would stay solid if something went unexpectedly wrong."

"They're all former Sissies," the captain said. "Except for you, that is."

He was watching me. There might be a touch of amusement in his eyes. I was pretty sure that he wouldn't let me go *too* far wrong, though he'd said it was my decision.

"The main thing we have to worry about is keeping Director Jimenez happy," I said. "We'll want clean-cut personnel, and people who won't scare the civilians. Also with a bias toward smart rather than, say, *quick*. So—"

I took a couple seconds to go over my choices one last time. "Sun and Barnes," I said. "I say Barnes instead of Dasi, because I know him better and because Dasi's nose is crooked from where it was broken. Wedell and Gamba, in both cases because I've worked with them and trust their judgment."

"And Woetjans?" the captain said.

"Even if Jimenez is as slow as the mid-level Foreign Ministry staffers I've met have been," I said, "Ellie would scare him to death. But I would like Tovera, because she wouldn't scare anybody."

Captain Leary's face went very still. "Have you looked Tovera in the eyes?" he said.

"Yes," I said. Tovera and her mistress were in earshot, but I didn't turn my head. "But Jimenez won't. Most people won't. They won't notice her at all."

I wouldn't have either, except that Maeve had told me that Mundy's clerk was an assassin. Since then I'd been watching her; I had no *proof* that Tovera was what Maeve called her, but the feeling I got from her was certainly that.

"Tovera isn't under my command," the captain said, "so I can't—"

"*I can*," said Mundy's voice from the speaker on the command console. "*Tovera is welcome to join Master Olfetrie if he wants to have her. And she's amenable, of course.*"

"Sure," said Tovera. Mundy was still looking down at her data unit, but Tovera—as always—was scanning the room with an alert expression, like a lizard looking for a meal. "I don't expect there'll be any fun, but I never lose hope."

The grin that followed the comment would've convinced me that Maeve was right even if I hadn't already been sure.

"All right, then," Captain Leary said. "Tovera, you'll have to leave your briefcase behind; Sun will find you a set of utilities so that you fit in. Olfetrie, let's you and I visit our betters."

I matched his grin with an equally broad one.

* * *

The passengers' accommodations on Level 3 probably didn't seem palatial to the civilians, but for somebody who'd gotten used to a cabin barely big enough for its bunk and desk, they certainly seemed so. The captain—or more likely, Officer Mundy—must have alerted the delegation that we were coming, because a female servant held open the hatch to what turned out to be a lounge when we came out of the companionway.

She bowed as we approached, then closed the panel behind us. Inside were cushioned seats—rather than pressed steel like elsewhere on the ship—and tables with floral designs on the upper surfaces. The only person standing was another servant, this one male. Like the woman at the door, he wore a uniform of brown fabric with a slick finish.

"Captain Leary," said the man in the chair facing the hatch. The words were an acknowledgement rather than a greeting. He was alone at a table for four.

Captain Leary nodded to the seated man. "Director Jimenez, I've come to introduce the officer who'll command your escort to the Councillor's Residence in Jacquerie. This is Lieutenant Olfetrie."

I stepped forward and bowed. "Sir," I said as I straightened, "I'm greatly honored to be chosen for this duty. I served an internship in the Bureau of Friendship Affairs. I've always felt that the Foreign Ministry does more to preserve the Republic than any other branch of government."

It was true about the internship: Mother had thought the diplomatic service was more refined than the RCN and had pushed to get both her sons into it. Junior had flat refused, but I'd given it a try.

It hadn't worked out well. I was quieter than Junior, but I hadn't been willing to solemnly nod when a fool talked nonsense to me, and there were other things. At the time, of course, I'd been a rich man's son looking for a profession rather than a job.

"You do?" Jimenez said, clearly startled. He was a trim little man, perfectly groomed the way you get only if you spend more time on it than a man ought to spend. "Then why are you here? What are you doing here?"

I shook my head with a sad expression. "I couldn't fool myself, sir," I said. "I knew within a week that I wasn't fit for the work. I was unwilling to drag down the fine people around me in the department. I was on the Kostroma desk under Director Kwalit."

I shrugged. "I still wanted to serve the Republic, so I joined the Navy," I said, deliberately using the civilian term for the RCN. "It was a surprise, a wonderful surprise, to learn that I was posted here."

"Well . . ." Jimenez said. "You're confident that your guards won't embarrass us? You see, Saguntum has no relations whatever with the Republic. Any sort of high-handed behavior or even the sort of normal loutishness to be expected of spacers—it might absolutely scuttle our mission."

"Sir," I said, with more truth than most of what I'd been saying. "I can honestly tell you that I've hand picked each person with an eye to intelligence and proper decorum."

I regretted that Captain Leary was listening to this. Heaven be thanked that Woetjans wasn't. She'd take it as a betrayal, and I had a good notion of how she'd deal with a traitor.

"Well," said Jimenez. He put a slight emphasis on the word to make it approving. "Here on my right is Master Han"—thin, bald man of uncertain age. His face showed no more expression than an insect's does—"who's our finance expert, and on my left Master Banta, whose specialty is agriculture."

I exchanged nods with both men. Banta was round, very pale, and gave the impression of having the intelligence of a cabbage...which to a degree he resembled.

My eyes followed Jimenez's. For the first time since I'd entered, they rested on Maeve. She was in ochre tonight. Smiling, she nodded to me.

"And this is Mistress Grimaud, my secretary," Jimenez said.

I nodded to her, then returned my gaze to the Director.

"Well, I must say," Jimenez said, "this is much better news than I was expecting. Captain Leary, I congratulate you. I'll make sure my superiors learn how well you've executed their instructions."

Captain Leary bowed, just as I had when I greeted the Director. He said, "Thank you, sir. We of the RCN set great store on the faithful execution of our orders."

We nodded again to the delegates, then left the lounge promptly to go back to where we belonged. I'd have been on the edge of laughter except for one thing: the look in Maeve's eyes as she smiled at me.

Maeve moved like a cat. For a moment she'd made me feel like a mouse.

Chapter Fourteen

The captain and I went from the companionway to the bridge: he to his console, me to stand at parade rest in front of Officer Mundy. She sat as usual with her back to the flat-plate display and her attention on the data unit in her lap.

Tovera watched me from the jump seat beside her mistress. I was reading amusement into Tovera's expression, but I knew that was me. I wasn't sure that Mundy's servant had feelings.

"Officer Mundy," I said. "To prepare for my escort duties, I would like to see pictures of the members of the Councillor's court whom I may be meeting. Can you provide me with such imagery?"

"Yes," said Mundy. I hadn't been sure she was listening to me, but as an afterthought she looked up at me. "Would you like dossiers on them as well?"

"Ah, yes, very much," I said. "That would be ..."

"Take the striker's position," Mundy said. Her hands did something with the control wands. "Hogg has no reason to be there."

Her eyes lifted and held mine for a moment. "From your performance before Director Jimenez," she said, "I'm surprised that you didn't continue with the foreign ministry. You would seem to have a natural aptitude for the work."

I swallowed. Captain Leary hadn't said anything to her; we'd returned to the bridge together. Mundy must have eavesdropping apparatus in the passenger lounge...and very possibly in every other compartment in the *Sunray*. I thought of Enery's concern to keep our conversation private.

I smiled. I didn't think I'd said anything I shouldn't have, but there wasn't much I could do about it now anyway. Aloud I said, "Officer Mundy, I left shortly after telling Director Kwalit that if he didn't take his hand off my thigh, I was going to rip it off and return it through his arsehole. I don't think diplomacy is really one of my strengths."

"I see," Mundy said. Her eyes returned to her holographic display. "Perhaps you're correct, then."

"Ma'am," I said. "I could be more helpful if I knew what I was really supposed to be doing."

I suppose the tiny movement of Mundy's lips was a smile. She looked at me again. She appeared to be a middle-aged woman without any distinguishing features, but every atom of her being was precise. She reminded me of a chronometer; or a target pistol.

"What you're supposed to do, Olfetrie..." she said. "Is to be yourself. To behave as you would normally behave. That's all."

I wanted to shout, "I don't understand!" which would have been just as pointless as it was true. Instead I nodded and said, "Thank you, Officer Mundy," and took the saddle at the back of the console. Hogg had moved to an open seat across the bridge from Tovera.

The data Mundy had offered waited for me as a glowing icon on the striker's display. I began sifting through it. There were about forty personnel all told, including members of the Saguntine government, the members of the bureaucracy who would be negotiating with our passengers, prominent business people—and to my surprise, members of the Karst Observation Mission to Saguntum.

I should have expected that. I knew that though Saguntum was independent in most realms, her foreign policy was wholly under the control of Karst.

The chief executive of Saguntum was called the Councillor. He was elected for life from the Board of Advisors, of whom he had to be a male member. The Councillor for the past fifteen years was Israel Perez; he'd succeeded his uncle, and before that the Councillor had been his grandfather. Israel was forty, intellectual looking, and had a receding forehead. There was nothing surprising about any of that.

The surprise came with the second person, Colonel Eugene Foliot, the Director of Public Safety. Foliot's picture showed a man of over fifty, clean shaven and hard. He wore a civilian suit of thin blue stripes, but he'd have looked more at home in uniform.

Before coming to Saguntum fifteen years ago and allying himself with the new Councillor Perez, Foliot had been Chief of the Governing Board—ruler—of Garofolo. He left Garofolo after a coup.

"Officer Mundy," I said, opening a link to her position,

"this is Olfetrie. I have a question about the information you sent me, over."

"*Go ahead, Olfetrie,*" Mundy said through the console. "*You want to know why Perez trusts Foliot, I suppose?*"

She didn't close the statement, but I could see that she'd stopped talking. I said, "Well, yes, ma'am. Why anybody would trust Foliot, I guess. If he was ousted by a coup himself, surely it'd be natural for him to at least consider returning to power the same way."

"*Quite reasonable, granting the initial premise,*" Mundy said. "*Which is incorrect. Foliot wasn't ousted by his chancellor's coup. He survived the bomb explosion which killed his wife, and he carried out a purge of the plotters with a thoroughness that Speaker Leary would have approved. It's reported that he personally executed several of the leading plotters—and also the technician who placed the bomb. Foliot was quite attached to his wife.*"

If I hadn't made a point of keeping my mouth closed, I'd have been gaping. When I decided that Mundy had finished speaking, I said, "Ma'am, if he'd won, why did Foliot leave Garofolo? Was he afraid there'd be another coup?"

Mundy shrugged where she sat, though she didn't look up at me. "*You'll have to ask him yourself when you see him,*" she said. "*If I were speculating, I would suspect that he felt uncomfortable about doing what he felt necessary after the coup he'd survived.*"

Suddenly she did look at me. "*There's no evidence that Speaker Leary regretted his similar actions, however.*"

"I see," I said. "Thank you, Officer Mundy. Olfetrie out."

There was more to what Mundy had said than was in her words, but I didn't know what it was. She had to be referring to the Three Circles Conspiracy, but that had taken place before I was born.

I could look it up on the console's database, but I might as well ask Mundy directly since certainly she would learn about any search I made on the *Sunray*. It sounded like a minefield, and it seemed a much better idea for me to leave it alone.

I resumed reading about the Saguntine government.

"Saguntum Orbital Control, we are preparing to land," Cory announced. Orbital Control was a tug with no interstellar capacity and additional sensors and communications gear added. *"Break. Ship, prepare for landing. Braking for landing…now!"*

Cory slammed the High Drive on hard. I had an image of Jacquerie Harbor set at the center bottom of my display. It began to swell, though that was a computer effect in between samples of real imagery from the sensors when the orbit permitted it.

I was in the stern station, seated at the flat-plate display alongside Lieutenant Enery. My hand was poised over the switch that would return our landing to computer control if Cory and Enery were simultaneously struck dead. Even a disaster of vanishingly small likelihood wasn't going to make me capable of a manual landing in crisis conditions.

For several seconds the thrusters added their braking effort to that of the High Drives. Then the High Drive buzzing vanished and even the roar of the thrusters became lost in the shaking and rattling of the atmospheric buffeting as the *Sunray* plunged deeper toward the surface.

Beside me, Enery had her fingers on the virtual throttles at the base of her display. She was prepared to take over manually if something happened to Cory. I'd seen how skillful she was when she landed on Hansen's World so I didn't doubt that she could do it...and yet, and yet—

It was just a form of bragging. There was no point in it, and no point in Cory choosing to make a manual landing to begin with. There were circumstances where a manual landing was a good idea—when the landing had to be made on a hard surface, a skilled human could ease the ship in more gently than a computer would when billowing steam didn't swaddle the hull in the final approach. Jacquerie had a well-appointed harbor, and at present it wasn't even crowded.

Maybe Cory felt that practice made perfect. More likely, he was bragging—and Enery was ready to play the same game.

And why had I decided to join the RCN? Sure, now it was a job with a real chance of advancement, but at the time I decided to enter the Academy I was the son of a wealthy entrepreneur who moved at the highest levels of the Republic. I could have spent my life in study and leisure activities—or in drunken debauchery, like the sons of most of Dad's intimates.

Cory brought the *Sunray* into balance with gravity at two hundred feet, then eased her to the surface. For a moment I thought we were drifting; then I realized that Cory had hovered us to the mouth of the slip and was slanting us in bow foremost. As the thruster exhaust licked the harbor, steam shrouded the

Sunray and hid our surroundings in the optical range. I manually switched to active imaging—microwave—as we slid neatly into our berth. It had been a lovely piece of work.

The thrusters shut down, though the slap of water between the walls of the slip continued to buffet us as the environment cooled.

I took my fingers from the controls and let out a deep breath. I was where I wanted to be.

If choosing to be a member of the RCN was a form of bragging, so be it. It was something worth bragging about.

Chapter Fifteen

The cabin of the limousine which the Saguntines provided for the officials had room for six; I waited while they entered. Maeve Grimaud sat primly with her back to the driver, facing the three men from the Foreign Ministry. The vehicle was old—probably of off-planet manufacture—but it had been lovingly maintained (or possibly restored).

The locals had provided an armored personnel carrier for me and the escort. It moved on wheels like the limousine, but it was much newer and was locally built. Sun chatted with the vehicle commander in the cupola about the APC's automatic impeller.

I watched the limousine following us through the armored glass (I'd opened the steel shutter) in the rear gate. I didn't know what I could do if something had happened to the limousine, but I guess I had to worry about something.

The APC had ports in the sides through which I got glimpses of Jacquerie, sepia toned by the thick glass. It looked pretty ordinary. Along our route it had been mostly one- and two-story structures with businesses on the ground floor and apartments on the higher level. There'd been a handful which were tall enough that I couldn't see the tops through the windows, but I was pretty sure four stories was as high as anything got here.

We drove past a stone-faced building set back behind a plaza; our APC slowed to a halt. There were full-height pilasters set into the facade, and a pair of ornamental-looking guards at the entrances. Civilians on the plaza lounged in the shade of trees in big pots.

I fumbled to open the gate, but Sun reached past me and dropped the ramp with a clang of steel on stone. We trotted out and were standing beside the limo before the Saguntine staff—a driver and his assistant—got the passenger doors open.

Sun grinned at me and said, "That was a combat release. The hydraulics would've taken forever, and I didn't think you wanted to wait."

"Too bloody right," I muttered as Director Jimenez got out gracefully. He had experience doing that sort of thing.

The driver's assistant whispered to me, "I'll guide you if you like, sir."

I nodded, because I certainly would like. With Sun beside me and the four ministry people strung out behind us, we walked to the entrance. The rest of my spacers brought up the rear.

Maeve was in a black suit whose flowing trouser legs could have been a skirt to look at. The tailored jacket she wore over the dark-gray tunic was completely demure—but a prostitute on the strip outside Harbor Three couldn't have looked more alluring.

"Wait here one moment, please," my guide said. He spoke

to a civilian just inside the entrance. The guards' weapons were chromed. That didn't mean they wouldn't work, but neither of the men in green and gold uniforms struck me as the sort I wanted behind me if things got rough. I guess Sun thought the same, because he muttered in my ear, "Pretty little fellers, aren't they?"

"What's going on?" Jimenez demanded in a peevish voice.

Our guide returned and said—to me and the Director both, "It'll be just a moment, and—"

From inside but clearly audible boomed the loudest unamplified voice I'd ever heard, "Your grace, allow me to introduce Director Oleg Jimenez of the Republic of Cinnabar, and the members of his honorable delegation!"

Sun and I moved fast to lead Jimenez inside. Beyond the anteroom was a large hall in which about forty people stood in small clumps. At the front were two desks, one facing the entrance and the other at right angles where two female clerks worked.

Councillor Perez—I recognized him from his picture—stood up behind the desk facing us. He was wearing a business suit.

"Greetings, Director Jimenez," Perez said. "You are welcome on your own behalf and in the name of the great republic you represent. Please come forward."

The Director and his two male associates walked through the assembly; in the big room it was too sparse to be called a crowd. I gestured to my spacers to stop. Until I was told otherwise, we were going to wait at the back of the hall and remain unobtrusive.

Jimenez and Perez spoke when they met beside the desk. After a moment, Perez turned to the general audience and said,

"My friends? Director Jimenez and his companions are going to join me briefly in my private office. I'll return shortly."

"What's that about?" Sun whispered to me as Perez let the delegates through a door in the wall behind his desk.

I started to shrug, then really thought about the question. "More bloody nonsense," I whispered back. "But they're dressing it up to look like something. I don't know how much trade there even *could* be between us and Saguntum, but Cinnabar is big and Perez wants to be polite."

When the door to the private office closed, there was motion and a louder buzz of conversation in the hall. A table with glasses and pitchers stood in a corner. The pitchers probably held water, but Sun and the other spacers drifted hopefully in that direction anyway.

I stayed where I was, but the fact that other people were moving allowed me to see faces where there'd been only the backs of heads before. I saw several people whom Mundy's dossiers described as business leaders, and against the back wall, on the side opposite the door to the private office, was Colonel Foliot in civilian clothes. He was talking to a younger man in uniform. The uniform wasn't quite battledress, but neither was it a comic opera outfit like those of the guards at the entrance.

I felt motion in the corner of my eye. I glanced left. Representative McKinnon, the head of the Karst Observation Mission, was smiling at my side. I didn't like the smile; nor the pudgy man with thinning, sandy hair if it came to that.

"So..." McKinnon said. He was holding a glass, about half-full of water. "What are you really here for, then?"

"Sir?" I said. "Oh, we're spacers from the *Sunray*. We're

escorting those diplomats who just went in with the boss here. I guess we'll escort 'em back to the ship when they're done talking."

"Yes, but what is the *Sunray* really doing on Saguntum?" McKinnon said. "You surely don't think I'm fool enough to believe your story about a trade delegation!"

It wasn't hard for me to act like an ignorant spacer. I wasn't *quite* ignorant enough not to know McKinnon was trying to pump me, but it was simpler to pretend to be.

I said, "Sir, I don't know you well enough to think anything about you." I offered my right hand to shake and added, "I'm Roy Olfetrie, third officer on the *Sunray*. And you?"

McKinnon made a noise in his throat and turned on his heel. I'd thought for an instant that he was going to slap my hand away. If he'd done that, I was going to give him my left in the pit of his stomach.

That might've caused trouble when Director Jimenez learned about it, which didn't concern me; or when I reported it to Captain Leary, whose opinion did matter. But I'd asked Officer Mundy how I was supposed to behave, and she'd said clearly that I was supposed to be myself. If you hit me, you'd better expect to be hit back.

Besides, I didn't think an RCN officer was required to let himself be assaulted by foreigners. If I was wrong about that, it was a good thing that I'd dropped out of the Academy.

Maeve had remained in the rear of the hall when her colleagues went into conference with Councillor Perez. She'd been watching with a smile. Now she came over and said, "You don't seem to have hit it off with the gentleman from Karst, Master Olfetrie."

"He wanted me to talk about things I don't know about," I said, my eyes on McKinnon's back. "And were none of his business anyway."

Maeve chuckled. "Well, I wouldn't bet about it being none of his business," she said. "He's Karst's chief spy on Saguntum. But it's certainly not your business to answer him."

She cocked her head. She said, "You know, Roy...it's still all right to call you Roy, isn't it?"

I remembered the way we'd last parted. "Sure," I said. "And me to call you Maeve, I hope."

"Of course," she said warmly. "I was wondering if you had plans for after this levee?" she added, gesturing around the room with her left hand.

"Well, I'm still on duty after I get my people back to the ship..." I said.

"Can you get off?" Maeve said. "I'd like to have dinner with a pleasant companion for a change."

"Well, I probably can," I said. "I don't know anything about restaurants in Jacquerie, though."

Maeve laughed again. "No matter," she said. "I have quite a number of contacts here. I think the best choice would be to eat in my hotel and then decide what to do afterward."

I started to ask what she meant by "my hotel" but the door to the private office opened. Councillor Perez came out and spoke to one of the clerks at the other desk while the three Cinnabar delegates filed past him and returned to where I waited. I'd formed up my five spacers.

"Han will be going back to the ship with you, Olfetrie," Jimenez said. "He'll arrange the transport of the delegation's baggage here. The delegation is moving to the palace for the duration of our stay."

"Ah," I said. "Sir, what shall I tell Captain Leary?"

"Tell him?" said the Director. "I don't see that you need to tell him anything. His orders are to transport me and to provide any assistance I require. I assure you that when I require something, I'll let Leary know."

"Thank you, sir," I said, bowing. "Were you told what vehicle we were to return in?"

"That's really none of my concern, Lieutenant," Jimenez said and led Master Banta to the pair of clerks in the front of the room. Not a man I warmed to.

I looked at Master Han, who had no expression at all. "Sir," I said, "let's go outside and I'll see if I can raise a vehicle."

Han bowed to me. "I will be glad to travel with you, Lieutenant," he said.

I was struck that Han had been given the job of getting the baggage together, rather than Maeve. It seemed more like a secretary's job, but she was seeming less and less like a secretary.

With Han and my spacers in tow, I went back onto the plaza. Our guide waited there. The limo had vanished, but the armored vehicle remained.

"Sir?" I said. "Can the APC run us back to the ship? And we've got one of the delegation too, but there's room for him in the box if it isn't a problem with you."

"No problem, sir," said the guide. I'd thought of him as the assistant driver, but he seemed to be the senior man in the limo, my counterpart of head of the Saguntine escort.

"Roy, I wonder if I could come back to the port with you?"

Maeve said, smiling toward the local as she spoke to me. "The restaurant is in walking distance, so we can leave from there when you've gotten approval from your captain."

The guide met my eyes. "Of course," he said. Then he winked.

I hadn't noticed the noise on the way to the palace. I did on the ride back—the engine was loud, the hard tires drummed the pavement, and the armored body rang at a thousand points of contact with its own elements. I was glad of that, because it was an excuse not to talk with Maeve in front of the spacers I commanded.

I wasn't sure what she might say. And I was even less sure of what I *wanted* her to say.

Captain Leary was absent. Lieutenant Enery checked the log and said, "Once your escort duties are finished, you're all off-duty till 0600. Isn't that what Captain Leary told you?"

"Yes, ma'am," I said and went down to the crew's quarters to relay the news. The enlisted spacers were already heading out; they'd been told the same thing I had, and they believed it. Well, why shouldn't they?

I changed into a different suit—brown with russet patches—and met Maeve on the bridge. She'd changed also, into a tan suit that matched mine rather nicely. I wondered if that was chance—it just about had to be chance, because I'd made my choice when I returned to my cabin—but I didn't say anything.

As we started across the boarding bridge—even the extension was wide enough for two abreast, if they were careful—Maeve said, "How many different suits did you bring, Roy?"

"It was bring them or let them be sold out of pawn," I said, knowing I sounded defensive. Then, because I hadn't answered the question, I said, "There's six of them, I guess. They were comfortable, so why not?"

"No reason whatever," Maeve said. I may have been inventing the laughter I thought I heard under the words. She made me uncomfortable, and I was pretty sure that she was doing that deliberately. I thought of Rachel, my fiancée until the bottom dropped out of my prospects. I wondered what Rachel was doing now, and I hated myself for caring.

"Here's the place," Maeve said as we crossed the second street up from the harbor. The building ahead of us was four stories. The bar on the corner was THE FOUNTAIN with a neon sign on which a blue fountain mounted to the top of a green frame before sinking back to the base. In the middle of the block was a separate entrance with a doorman. The bronze letters above that door were externally lighted and read, THE SAINT JAMES.

"The restaurant is through here," Maeve said, angling toward the bar. "Though we could reach it through the hotel also." She glanced up at me and said, "But I thought we'd eat first?"

"Yes," I said, determinedly not meeting her eyes.

We entered; it seemed a decent place with half a dozen customers at present. The barman caught our eyes but Maeve waved cheerfully to him and started up the staircase in the back. She certainly did have contacts in Jacquerie.

"Two, please, Jean," she said to the greeter. "A quiet booth, if we could."

"It's a quiet night, Mistress Grimaud," the greeter said. "But we'd find something for you regardless. Come with me, please."

The greeter bowed Maeve into a banquette seat. "Have you been here many times?" I asked as I slid into the other side.

"Well, no, I've never been on Saguntum before this mission," Maeve said. "But when I learned I'd be living in this hotel, I made a point of introducing myself to the staff I'd be dealing with."

And feeing them very heavily ahead of time, I realized, though I didn't say that aloud. I didn't care about that—it was Foreign Ministry money; if they were wasting it, that was their business.

But it did make me wonder what Maeve expected to get for her money. She didn't strike me like the sort who would be *that* concerned about a good table in a restaurant.

"The chicken here is supposed to be very good," Maeve volunteered when the waiter arrived to take our order; but she let me make my choice first and then got the same thing, a house specialty.

Maeve asked for the wine list. Though I said I wasn't much of a drinker, she ordered a bottle rather than individual glasses.

As we waited for our entrees, Maeve smiled in the dim light and said, "You know, you're really quite a handsome young fellow, Roy. I hope you don't mind my saying that."

"I don't mind," I said, sipping my wine. I'd let her fill the goblet. "I think you're wrong, though."

Maeve laughed. In the same voice as before, as though she weren't changing the subject, she said, "What do you think of the Navy and politics, Roy?"

I didn't choke on the wine, but I put the goblet down before

I said, "Ma'am, I'm glad the RCN isn't *in* politics."

"That's not true, you know," Maeve said calmly. "Even the way you mean it. There isn't a Navy Party, but you know that Minister Forbes wouldn't have come out of the political wilderness if she hadn't joined with Captain Leary."

"Ma'am, I *don't* know that," I said. "I don't say you're wrong, because I don't know anything about it. I don't care about it. It's none of my business."

I was trying to keep my voice calm. It was true as true that I didn't care, and I *really* didn't want to talk about it.

"Well, I can't speak to the rest of what you say ..." Maeve said over the rim of her wine glass. "But it certainly *is* your business. It was because Elisabeth Forbes became Minister of Defense and needed to make her mark quickly that your father was driven to ruin and suicide."

"Dad shot himself because he got unmasked as a crook," I said. My mouth was dry, even after I took a gulp of wine. "Mistress Forbes may have had private reasons for doing that, I don't know. But it was her bloody job to do regardless!"

Maeve looked at me steadily. She smiled again and said, "You're a very sensible young man. And you're really quite smart, aren't you."

"That's not what my professors at the Academy would tell you," I said, more embarrassed than I'd been when she called me handsome.

The food arrived then, which I was glad of. Maeve took my lapse in attention to refill my glass. There was also a fresh bottle on the serving table beside her, without me hearing her order it.

The special turned out to be thin slices of chicken breast cooked between equally thin slices of bacon like a layer cake. There were vegetables with it, and a spicy sauce.

Mom would've been able to tell what went into the sauce just by sniffing, like enough. She could've discussed the wine, too. When we'd come into money, she'd gone whole hog into what to eat, drink, and wear. She said Dad had low tastes, which was true enough. Junior had no taste at all, though Mom would never have said anything that could be taken as a criticism of Dean Junior. Dad used to say that Mom thought the sun shone out of Junior's backside.

Mom and Dad didn't talk about me. There wasn't anything really to talk about. I did my schoolwork and played sports without making waves. I wasn't bad or even mediocre, but I wasn't right at the top either. There just wasn't much to say.

Maeve started asking me about working in the Matrix, then. I guess I babbled to her because it was all new to me too. I hadn't gotten far enough in the Academy to have real experience on the hull after insertion. Astrogation was more important to a career as an officer than being able to scramble up antennas to free a joint or unkink a cable, but I'd *done* astrogation. Not a lot and not enough to stand out at it, but enough to see the principles and be able to apply them.

I guess I was beginning to see why it had such an appeal to Captain Leary, too. Heaven knows, Barnes and the other riggers I was training with never talked about that part of what I was seeing, but the realization that I was in midst of all there was, of *All*, seeped deeper into my marrow with every watch I spent on the hull.

I was seeing the Matrix as a series of pathways instead of just being blurs of light which suggested energy gradients. I'd never be as good an astrogator as Captain Leary, but I was certainly becoming better than I had been.

"I'm getting to be a better astrogator than the Academy would ever have made me!" I said to Maeve.

I heard the words when they came out of my mouth. For a moment I was shocked, but what I'd said was the truth and nothing to be ashamed of. Even so I raised my goblet. To my surprise, it was empty. I remembered Maeve refilling it several times as I talked, and I was pretty sure that the server had brought more than one additional bottle during the evening.

"Oh!" I said.

"We could have more," Maeve said. "It's good wine. But I think I'd rather go up to my room."

I got up—lurched, rather; it was a banquette, so I didn't knock my chair over.

I was pleased to be able to step to Maeve's seat and offer my arm. Apparently my experience in the rigging had given me the ability to walk upright even when I was drunk.

I was certainly drunk.

Maeve laid her fingers on my forearm and rose to her feet with the liquid grace of a fountain. I was pretty sure she'd have grabbed and supported me if she'd needed to, but I was perfectly steady.

We walked through the restaurant. I heard Maeve call, "On the room, Jean," but I was concentrating on walking toward the doorway. Everything outside that rectangle was a gray blur.

An elevator opened beside me. Maeve directed me in. I didn't recall an elevator before. We'd come up to the restaurant by stairs.

The door opened again. We walked into a hallway. I must have been sobering, because I could see in color again. Everything was still fuzzy, though.

We entered Maeve's room. I heard the door close; I turned her toward me and kissed her. She responded with an enthusiasm that startled me. I cupped her breasts within the garment. The fabric must have been even thinner than it seemed to look at. It had been a very long time since I'd last been with Rachel.

Maeve kissed me again but broke away. "Now let me talk for just a moment, Roy," she said, "because I want this as much as you do. Now, just sit down."

She patted to the bed. I sat beside her and tried to embrace her again. She squirmed away and kept hold of both my hands.

"You joined the Navy to protect Cinnabar," Maeve said, her eyes holding mine. "Protect the Republic against *all* her enemies."

"All right," I said. I didn't know why she was talking about that. I wasn't sure what she'd just said was true. I'd entered the Academy basically as a matter of inertia: I didn't want to think about my future, so when Junior joined the RCN, I decided I would too.

"There are people who use Cinnabar as a tool to make themselves important," Maeve said. "The worst of these is Bernis Sand, who has a private apparatus outside the Foreign Ministry. She has the ear of very important politicians and we're sure she's getting money from the Republic even when she's working against its best interests."

I shook my head to clear it. Maeve put my hands back in my lap and let them go.

"What Sand is doing now," Maeve said, "is trying to stir up war between Cinnabar and Karst. Which will be a disaster."

"Karst isn't such a big deal," I said. My voice sounded like a growl even in my own ears.

"No," Maeve said. "But that will breach the treaty, and we'll be back at war with the Alliance."

I was staring at her bosom. She covered my right hand with her left and raised it to her breast. She giggled. I was so startled that by the time I reacted by shifting forward, Maeve had risen to her feet and walked around my outstretched legs to sit on my other side.

"Now just listen for another moment," she said. "I know you respect Captain Leary, and perhaps you respect Lady Mundy too. You *should*. But they're acting as tools of Bernis Sand, and they'll destroy the Republic unless they're stopped. Our economy and our society will break under the strain of resumed all-out war with the Alliance."

Maeve leaned forward and kissed me again as hard as she had when we first came through the door. She said, "You'll help me save Cinnabar, won't you Roy? You're a patriot, not one of Captain Leary's retainers!"

She lifted my hands to her breasts again.

I pulled away and stood. I couldn't claim to be sober, but my mind was as cold as the hull in space.

"I'll be leaving now," I said. "We'll work out what I owe you for dinner, but not just now."

I walked to the door like I was a puppet on a string, opened it, and went out into the hall. I half expected Maeve to come out of the room after me, but the door remained as I'd shut it.

Instead of riding the elevator, I took the stairs at the other end of the hall. I think it sobered me up some; my legs worked, and my brain was starting to work again.

And the anger helped a lot too. They—Maeve and whoever she worked for—were treating me like I was dishonest. They hadn't offered me money, they'd offered me Maeve's body. I wondered if Dad had used whores to bribe people too.

The door at the ground floor opened into the street. I was about to cross, heading back for the *Sunray* and wondering what I was going to say about what'd just happened. Probably nothing, but I wasn't in any shape to decide tonight.

THE FOUNTAIN bubbled to the top again. I turned and went into the bar. I was sober again and I didn't want to be.

"A double of your house whiskey," I said. I thought for a moment. "You do have whiskey on Saguntum, don't you?"

"We've got whiskey," the bartender said. He turned up a glass and began to fill it from a bottle fitted with a pour spout. I wondered how much money I had with me. Enough to tie one on properly, I was sure. I'd probably have to borrow against my salary to cover tonight's dinner, but I was *damned* if I was going to feel that I'd taken any money from Maeve and the people behind her.

A man came in from the street and took a place at the bar to my left. "Say," he said. "You're Tommy Reisberg from Xenos, aren't you? Have a drink on me, Tommy."

"I've never met Tommy Reisberg," I said, "but I am from Xenos and I'll cheerfully take your drink. If you'll have one on me next."

Another man got up from the table and moved to my other

side. "Say, I thought you were Tommy too," he said. "What you doing in Jacquerie, Tommy?"

The barman put my drink before me as I turned to look at the new man. I'd never seen him before. I'd never seen either of them before.

"I'm still not anybody named Reisberg," I said.

The man on my right had brought his drink with him from the table. "Well, we'll straighten things out over a few more of these," he said. He polished off the clear liquid and set his glass down.

I drank also. The local whiskey seemed to be a rye, but there was an odd undertaste to it.

My knees gave way. The man on my right caught me as I fell into him.

A coin rang on the counter. I heard the other man say, "Tommy never did have a good head. I think this'll take care of everything. We'll take Tommy home."

About that time the gray fog filling my head dimmed to black.

Chapter Sixteen

I didn't exactly wake up, but I came around enough to realize that somebody was shaking me and shouting, "Get up, numbnuts!"

The High Drive was on. The buzz made my brain tremble. I didn't know where I was; I wasn't sure *who* I was. It occurred to me that I might be dead and in Hell.

"*Get up, you little shit!*"

Water splashed in my face. A second voice said, "Hey, watch the bunk, Wellesley."

There was a rope tethering my thighs to the bunk. My eyes didn't work right; I saw a blur lean close and move back, but I wasn't sure anything moved except in my mind.

The water on my lips tasted good. I licked them and sat up.

"About bloody time," the voice said. I threw up.

I wasn't aiming at the speaker—I wasn't awake enough to do anything that organized—but I was looking toward the blur that spoke. I guess that was good enough to get the same result.

The voice roared, "You little *shit*!" and something slugged me. I went back into blackness.

When I finally came around the ship was under way in the Matrix. I felt as if there was a membrane shrunk over my skin, moving when I did. It didn't get in my way—but it was there.

I opened my eyes. I was on the bottom bunk of a tier. The two higher bunks were raised against the bulkhead, which is how I'd been able to sit up before.

The side of my jaw hurt. *One thing at a time*. First I had to learn where I was.

The man at the console heard the bunk springs squeal and turned to look at me. "Bloody well about time," he said. "I was beginning to think we'd paid good money for a deader. Not a lot of money, though."

I recognized the voice of the man who'd waked me the first time—and who'd then slugged me when I threw up. He was big and broad, though short legged as best I could tell in a seated figure. The right half of his skull was bald and he was missing the top of his right ear. I didn't see any scar tissue on his scalp.

He had a nasty voice, but I was already sure we weren't going to be friends. If I remembered correctly from when I was still under the drug, his name was Wellesley.

"Where am I?" I said. I was glad to learn that my voice worked. I didn't try to shout, partly because I didn't have the energy. I felt like a dishrag.

I'd heard the outer airlock close as I came around, but I

wasn't sure whether it was for people going out on the hull or coming back in. Now the dogs of the inner lock drew back in a series of small clicks and the hatch opened. Three spacers entered the cabin, two in hard suits and the third in an air suit.

They'd already taken their helmets off. One was a hatchet-faced spacer who must be seventy; the other two were as pale as anyone I'd ever seen.

"Where you are," Wellesley said, "is aboard the *Martinique*, on the way to Blanchard. And you're a landsman."

"I rated able spacer in the RCN," I lied. I didn't know exactly what the situation was, but I didn't see any advantage to blurting that I could astrogate. I wasn't great, but I was probably as good as any of this lot.

"I'm still captain of the *Martinique*, Wellesley," the old man said as he continued to strip off his suit. He turned to me and said, "I'm Captain Langland. What's your name, spacer?"

The captain's hard suit looked like a piece of junk, but it was better than the suit the crewman behind him was taking off. The air suit that the other spacer was getting out of was visibly patched with cargo tape.

"I'm Roy Olfetrie, crew on the *Sunray* till you drugged and kidnapped me," I said. "Where are we headed?"

"That's a bloody lie!" Wellesley said. "Two of your friends brought you aboard!"

"We're headed for Blanchard," Langland said. "We're twelve days out."

I sat up carefully. My arms were ready to support me but they didn't need to; I'd slept off whatever it was that they'd drugged me with, though I still felt weak.

I stank. I guess somebody'd cleaned the deck, but the front of my tunic was soaked with my own vomit. "Bloody hell," I muttered. "Where do I clean up, Langland? And I need a change of clothes, at least a tunic. I'm not going to wait twelve bloody days."

"There's the head," Langland said, gesturing to the corner with the rear bulkhead. The screen there was the same grease-dulled color as the deck and bulkheads; with my current fuzzy vision I hadn't noticed it. "And I guess a set of my slops'll fit you."

I got up with only a momentary rush of dizziness and started for the head. "Look, Olfetrie?" Langland said. "You're not raising hell about this?"

I looked at him over my shoulder. "That wouldn't do much good, would it?" I said. "You going to turn around and put me back on Saguntum?"

"Like hell we will!" Wellesley said.

"Yeah, that's what I figured," I said. I walked into the head and stripped off my tunic. "I've never been on Blanchard, but I guess it's got bars. That makes it pretty much all same-same as Saguntum so far as I care."

"Well, you're a cool little bastard," said Langland.

I ran water into the basin and rinsed out my tunic. Then I used the wet garment to wipe my face and torso before rinsing it again. One thing about a starship is that there's always water from the tanks of reaction mass.

I wasn't looking forward to being a crewman on the *Martinique*, but after Dad shot himself I'd given up expecting things to be the way I wanted. This wasn't going to be fun, but I guessed it'd be livable. If I was wrong about that, well, then I didn't have any problems at all.

The *Martinique* didn't have proper watches, but when we'd dropped into normal space so that Langland could fix our position, he swore and said, "Wellesley, we've got to get the starboard antenna back in service. It'll be a month before we make Blanchard at this rate, and we don't have food for that long."

"All right," Wellesley said. "I'll take the landsman out and we'll free the cable."

We were all more or less average size, though Wellesley probably strained the expansion seams of the hard suits. I went to the less-good hard suit, though that was a toss-up: The cushion lining was almost completely gone from this one, but it looked to me like the interior flex at the joints was maybe in a little better shape than on the other.

Wellesley cuffed me away. "Who told you to take a hard suit?" he snarled. "Put on one of the air suits until I decide you're ready for a good one!"

"I won't wear one of those air suits," I said. "Especially if I'm going out with you."

"You'll do what I bloody say!" said Wellesley. "I'm the mate!"

He cocked his fist. I set my feet and said, "I'm not drugged now!"

Wellesley didn't swing. I was about to start things myself, moving in and hitting him as many times as I could in the pit of his stomach. I wasn't as strong as Wellesley and he had

DAVID DRAKE

forty pounds on me besides, but I hit hard and I didn't figure he was used to taking punishment.

"Oh, back off, Wellesley," the captain said. "I'll take Olfetrie out. You recalibrate us for Blanchard with starboard in service again."

When the hatch had closed behind me and Langland in the airlock, I said, "What's the story about the other two?"

He frowned. "Glance and Bodo, no story," he said. "They don't speak much Standard, but they're good spacers. I'm not sure where they come from. Never much cared, to tell the truth."

I wondered what he paid them. As little as he could, and that was probably less than a spacer with a better grasp of Standard would've gotten. I wouldn't have called them "good spacers," but I was comparing them against the *Sunray*'s crew. Chances were the run of RCN ships wouldn't have measured up to that standard.

The cable that extended and furled the starboard sails was jammed at the masthead. I climbed up to it and found the reason: The cable had been spliced into a rat's nest about four times the diameter of the line proper. Apparently it'd worked for a while, but when it finally jammed, the cable guide had buggered it hopelessly.

I came back down, put my helmet against Langland's, and said, "I guess we can resplice this, but it isn't going to be easy. Do you have a spare cable?"

I could resplice it, anyway. I figured that whoever'd made the botch that I'd seen there now wasn't going to do any better a second time.

"Well, nothing of the weight," Langland said. "That's why

I had Bodo and Glance splice it."

He led me to the outside supply locker. There was indeed a spool in it—marked #8, which meant it was exactly half the diameter of the cable on the antenna at present. This was the cable that'd usually be used to raise yards, not to extend the antenna itself. On the other hand...

"Okay, we'll swap it out," I told Langland. I wasn't acting like a junior spacer, but they hadn't recruited me in the proper way either. I hadn't liked the notion of running out of food on the way to Blanchard.

"But that's not heavy enough," Langland said.

"It doesn't have to serve for long," I said. "We'll take the old cable aboard and I'll splice it in the cabin. If I try to do it out here, I'm likely to butcher it as badly as the first guy did."

That wasn't true. It was, however, true that I didn't want to do a major splice in a hard suit that I didn't trust not to fall apart even without being poked by a frayed cable.

I disconnected the hydraulic line, then went up the antenna again, carrying the new spool. It was a lot easier this time than it'd been on the *Sunray*. Not only was the antenna not extended—that was the problem, after all—but I cut the original cable and used it as a traveller after I'd reconnected hydraulic line.

It was easier also because I'd done it before—and because I'd done a lot of other things as well since Barnes first ran me through my paces on the *Sunray*. I was confident, because I'd managed to hold my own in a picked crew under a famous captain. There were plenty of better spacers, but none of them were on the *Martinique*.

We hauled the old cable in together, loosely gathered since there was no point in rolling it properly. I wasn't looking forward to making a proper splice, but that was the job.

Wellesley complained that the cable took up most of the cabin, which it did. I didn't bother explaining why I was doing the job inside rather than on the antenna. That was obvious if you accepted that I didn't want to die because I'd ripped the suit open. Wellesley probably *didn't* accept that, but even he wasn't willing to push the business too hard.

I'd squared the ends on either side of the previous splice. That was a bad enough job in itself as the *Martinique*'s saw was on its last legs. The power supply didn't hold a charge—I had to recharge it three times on each cut—and the diamonds of the blade were worn almost smooth with the steel disk they were set into.

I thought about the tools I'd seen by the scores in the chandleries that Dad supplied. It hadn't crossed my mind that there were a lot of ship masters who couldn't afford to replace basic equipment when it was worn out.

Splicing was a simple job. Wearing gauntlets I spread both ends of the cable a foot back from the cut, using the handle of a pair of pliers since the ship didn't have the hardened spike intended for the job, then laboriously braided each matching pair of filament bundles with the same pliers.

Using hand tools I couldn't possibly join the ends tightly enough to take the strain of extending the antenna, but the interior supply locker had a can of vacuum adhesive. It wasn't full, but I was pretty sure there was enough to lock the pairs together until we got to the ground.

What happened then was no concern of mine. Blanchard was a civilized world, and I was pretty sure that the local authorities wouldn't be willing to forcibly return a jumped spacer to his ship if he insisted he was a Cinnabar citizen. Cinnabar was a long way away, but the Republic made rather a thing about the rights of her citizens.

Even if there wasn't a Cinnabar consul, on something like this I could probably get help from the Alliance embassy. Neither of the great powers had any use for dirtball worlds giving themselves airs.

I kept working my watch. I'd thought of telling the others to cover for me while I focused on the splice. They'd gotten along without me before they landed on Saguntum, after all, though the rigging's wretched condition showed that they'd gotten along very poorly.

But so long as the #8 cable continued to work, there wasn't a crisis. I didn't want to provoke a fight unless I had to. It wasn't as though I had anything better to do with my time than work on the rigging.

Splicing gave me a lot of time to think. Mostly what I thought about was why I'd been drugged and sold to a short-crewed ship that was lifting immediately.

It had to have been at Maeve's orders. It can't have been because she was angry about me turning her down, because there had to have been a lot of preplanning.

The only thing that made sense to me was that Maeve was afraid I'd warn Captain Leary that she was planning something—she was or the Foreign Ministry was.

I probably wouldn't have said anything anyway, mostly because I was embarrassed about the whole business. "Sir, a woman came on to me and I ran away."

But what was Maeve—or maybe what was the Foreign Ministry—planning? She had some sort of gang working for her, but I didn't see how they could accomplish anything serious against the *Sunray*'s crew. A couple thugs could easy enough nobble a young fool like me, but it wouldn't have worked with an experienced spacer.

Lady Mundy, whom Maeve had said was the leader of the conspiracy to start a war, would never have been caught by such local talent. The stories I'd heard from spacers from the *Princess Cecile* made "the Mistress" out to be a demon from Hell, and she was always with Tovera, who was even worse.

Anyway, that's how it stood until the *Martinique* reached Blanchard orbit with food still in her lockers.

Then the undersized cable on the starboard antenna snapped when Captain Langland started to retract it.

Chapter Seventeen

"So what're we supposed to do now?" Wellesley said. "We can't enter the atmosphere with an antenna up or the stresses'll tear the ship apart!"

He sounded like he meant the question rather than just faking stupid to be nasty, though "being nasty" was generally a good bet with Wellesley. I said, "We put the original cable back on the antenna. I've completed the splice except for spraying the adhesive, and we'd need to do that in vacuum anyway."

I started putting a suit on. Wellesley said, "Well, if you hadn't done such a half-assed job the first time—"

But Captain Langland, suiting up beside me, said, "Wellesley, belt up. Take the console. Bodo and Glance, you come out too. We'll need both of you to hold the line for spraying the adhesive."

With the loosely bunched cable it took two cycles of the airlock: me, Langland and the cable through first, then Bodo and Glance when we were clear. While we waited for them to arrive, I looked down on Blanchard. The continent we were passing over was mostly beige, running into orange. There were two green streaks running toward the east coast, so it wasn't completely arid.

I didn't suppose it mattered. I wasn't going to be on Blanchard long enough to care.

With the two spacers to either side holding the cable up and the captain with his gauntlets gripping either side of the splice, I applied the adhesive. I didn't trust any of the others to do it, and it could be that they felt the same way. Anyhow, none of the others argued that he ought to be the one to do it.

I got the two sides, then had the crew rotate the cable on its axis and got what had been the top and bottom of the seam. The sprayer worked best when I could hold it level, so it was worth the effort of explaining what I wanted to Bodo and Glance.

I'd just hooked the spliced cable to one end of the broken #8 when the hull vibrated and the two antennas I could see— dorsal and ventral—telescoped. I knew that the take-up reel of starboard would be spinning also if I hadn't disconnected the hydraulics before I started work. It wouldn't have done anything to the antenna; but when the line with the bight in it whirled through my hands it might have taken them off.

Langland gestured to me and trotted toward the lock as quickly as anybody could move in a hard suit. I was up in the rigging, so I just stayed there. Bodo and Glance followed the captain, which I'm pretty sure he hadn't meant them to do. It didn't matter, though; there was nothing more for them to do on the hull.

I was looking down at Blanchard again—we'd proceeded west over an ocean and were over another continent, when something blocked my view: Another spaceship had just slid within a hundred feet of us. I jumped in my suit. The ship must have some sort of propulsion other than plasma thrusters, because otherwise they wouldn't have sufficiently delicate control.

I felt a loud *clang!* through my boots; my antenna swayed noticeably. My first thought was that the *Martinique* was falling apart, perhaps because of something the strange ship had done. Then as our orbit continued, sunlight caught the line which now connected our ship to the other: The stranger had sent across a magnetic grapple. We were being captured by a pirate ship.

The pirate puffed exhaust—steam, I figured, from the glitter of ice crystals that formed on the hull near the nozzles. The stranger halted at about fifty feet; maybe it even started to edge away.

Several figures stood near an airlock open on the pirate's hull. As I watched, they jumped in turn along the grappling line.

From where I stood they seemed to be holding on to the cable, but they probably were using rings of some sort pre-looped over the line. You could expect at least one fiber of a cable to fray in ordinary use, and it might easily find a seam in a gauntlet. Certainly I wouldn't trust the *Martinique*'s equipment to protect my hands or my life.

The first pirate reached the hull with an impact I could barely feel. They couldn't enter the airlock if those inside kept the inner hatch open, but I doubted Langland and the others would try to do that.

On the pirate ship's bow was a set of four bombardment rockets pivoted toward the *Martinique*. They were probably six or eight inches in diameter—I couldn't tell which from where I was; both sizes were standard—and carried enough explosive to dish in a starship's hull plating.

They were standard chandler's stores. Bigger, better-found ships like the *Sunray* generally mounted a plasma cannon, but a basket of rockets was a cheaper defensive fitment. At the bottom end, there were many tramps like the *Martinique* with nothing at all.

Pirates used rockets also. From the stories, when a ship got far enough out from civilized worlds, whether it was a pirate or a trader depended on its immediate circumstances.

I was pretty sure pirates would be willing to blow an airlock open with explosives if a crew kept the inner hatch door open so that the interlock would prevent the outer door from opening normally. I wouldn't have let anybody try that trick if I'd been in the cabin.

The third pirate was sailing toward the *Martinique* when the line twitched. The two ships had been drawing apart ever since the final braking puff of steam. The cable went taut as it snubbed up the pirate vessel.

The shock was really very slight—I doubt the relative movement can have been as much as a mile an hour—but it flung the pirate loose from his hold. Instead of landing softly, using both his grip and his flexed knees to brake him, he hit hard, fell full length on the hull, and bounced away.

I didn't think; there wasn't time to. I knew my safety line was anchored, because I never worked on the hull without my line. I judged the pirate's trajectory—at the moment he was just a spacer who was about to carom off into vacuum—and jumped for where he'd be when I reached the same point. It was as if we were gymnasts executing a trick we hadn't practiced.

The thing I didn't know was whether my safety line was long enough to allow me to reach him. The one I was using was a standard length—ten meters, I thought. It'd either work or it wouldn't.

I caught the pirate around the waist. We slammed the hull together, him underneath. We started to slide off again, but I got the soles of both my magnetic boots flat against the steel. Between them and the safety line reaching the end of its play, we stopped.

The pirate had been flailing his arms. Now he went rigid and allowed me to set him down firmly on the hull in front of me. Only one of his boots took hold; the magnets in the sole of the other were missing.

The pirate turned and faced me. He looked terrified, which was a pretty reasonable reaction.

I walked us to the open airlock where the other two pirates waited. I sure didn't want to stay out here, though I wasn't looking forward to what happened next in the cabin either.

I unhooked my safety line from the ring at the airlock coaming.

The pirates started taking their helmets off in the airlock in usual fashion. I hesitated to do that, but I decided that regardless of what my shipmates in the cabin were going to do I was better off doing exactly what the pirates did. The leader—he had a pair of red-dyed bird plumes glued to his helmet—wore a holstered pistol, and knives dangled from the bandoliers of the other two.

The leader had a goatee. I smiled at him and said, "I'm Roy Olfetrie. What happens next?"

The pirate glared at me. The four of us were crammed pretty tight in the airlock. A crappy hard suit (and all of these were) took up just as much room as a good one.

The man I'd saved was only a few years older than I was. He said, "We take you to Salaam on ben Yusuf and sell you. Unless your world has a treaty with us?"

"I'm a Cinnabar citizen," I said.

"It doesn't matter, Lal," the leader said. "He's crew, not a passenger, so he goes with the ship's registry."

He drew his pistol and opened the inner airlock. He gestured me out first.

My shipmates stood on the far side of the cabin. Bodo and Glance were blank-faced—as usual; Captain Langland looked downcast. Wellesley seemed furious, but that wasn't different enough from his usual expression for me to make anything of it.

Lal—the man I'd saved—went over to the console. He checked readings, then called the pirate ship.

"I'm Captain Hakim," the leader said, looking across me and my shipmates. "Now, which of you wants to join my crew on shares? Otherwise you'll be sold in Salaam and take your chances."

"It was pirates like you that killed my brother," Wellesley said. The words came out slowly, as though he were carving them individually out of wood.

A light tap on the hull was followed by three ringing notes. The pirate ship must've cut power to the grapnel, because Lal lit the High Drives. We began to accelerate at the *Martinique*'s modest best.

"I'll help you work ship," I said. "I won't join your crew, but I'll help you get the *Martinique* into harbor."

"You little turd," Wellesley said, glaring at me. "They're pirates. No decent man could join them!"

I met his eyes. "You shanghaied me," I said. "By my books, you're as much a pirate as they are. Besides which, you tried to drop out of orbit when you spotted the pirates. You'd have killed all of us on the hull if you'd been able to lower the starboard antenna so that it wouldn't set you spinning when you hit the atmosphere."

Wellesley shouted something about my mother and swung for my face. I was wearing a hard suit, so that was the only target he had. The fiberglass-stiffened sleeve kept me from moving as quickly as I usually could have. I was holding the helmet in my right gauntlet, though, and I got it in the way of Wellesley's fist.

He shouted again, grabbing his broken knuckles with his free hand. I straightened my arm, still holding the helmet, in a punch to Wellesley's head. The weight and stiff suit slowed me down, but it was still enough to bounce the mate's skull against the steel bulkhead. He collapsed onto the deck.

I backed away, weak from the adrenalin pumping through me. I started to wonder how the pirates were going to react, though there was nothing else I could've done.

I needn't have worried. Hakim started laughing; the pirate

beside him sheathed the curved knife he'd drawn, and Lal grinned as he turned back to the console display.

"Sure you don't want to join my crew?" Hakim said. "I could use you."

"I'm sure," I said. "But I'll go out now and finish connecting the starboard antenna. As soon as I've changed my air bottle, I mean."

"I'll go with you," said Lal, getting up from the console. "It's a two-man job."

Lal was good to work with—as good as Langland, and sure a lot better than Bodo or Glance. We rerigged the antenna, then matched course with the pirate ship again. I'd thought that Blanchard might have some kind of patrol, but there wasn't one.

Hakim said that occasionally there'd be a well-armed freighter in harbor and the Blanchard authorities would hire it to chase pirates away, but that didn't happen very often. He said they kept a careful watch while they were in Blanchard orbit, but they were in no real danger.

With both ships coasting outward in free fall, the pirate vessel reattached the grapple. Hakim went back aboard his own vessel, taking with him Langland, Bodo and Glance. Two more pirates came across to join me, Lal, and Stephanos with the curved knife, giving the *Martinique* as full a crew as before to work her to ben Yusuf.

The new men brought with them a net bag holding containers. I assumed they were additional food—the *Martinique*'s larder was down to boring if not dangerous levels.

As it turned out, the new stores were entirely wine—a harsh red vintage, very strong. A mouthful was enough for me. The only use I could imagine for it was as paint stripper, but the pirates went through it at a rate that astounded me.

Wellesley stayed aboard the *Martinique*, in the shower. His limbs were bound with cargo tape, and he was gagged between feedings. I hosed him off when he fouled himself, which the situation forced him to do.

I didn't ungag him, though, let alone consider loosing his limbs. I wished that Hakim had taken Wellesley aboard his ship, but I wasn't going to endanger myself in order to ease the situation for a bastard who'd tried to kill me when he tried to enter the atmosphere when I was on the hull.

I thought that Lal had been appointed captain, but within a day I realized that there was no captain. The pirates acted as equals, cooperating pretty well. Lal happened to be the only one aboard—besides me—who could do even basic programming on the astrogation console.

How basic I realized on the second day out from Blanchard. Tarek was fooling with the console. He suddenly gave a cry of horror—the display had gone pearly blank the way it did if you tried to access a sensor input while the ship was in the Matrix.

I didn't think anything of it until Lal took over at the console and began attempting more and more frantic commands. He began to pray aloud in a rising voice.

I joined Lal at the console. Actually, everybody was standing around it. Lal's panic had already started to affect them.

"Here, let me," I said. "Now back away, for heaven's sake."

Lal gave up the seat. The crowding and chattering I simply had to work with.

It didn't take long to find the problem. Tarek had switched the display to remote input—and there were no remotes attached to this console.

When I returned to an ordinary navigation display, I said, "All right, from now on only Lal touches the console, okay? *I* don't want to starve to death in the Matrix. Do you all agree?"

They did, or anyway they muttered things that I took as agreement.

In another day and a half, the *Martinique* was in ben Yusuf orbit. Lal let the console land her.

Chapter Eighteen

From my bunk I'd watched the display over Lal's shoulder as the *Martinique* landed at Salaam. We were coming down in a wide bay fringed by what looked during the approach like sandy beaches. A town sprawled away from the water in a relatively narrow band. There was at least one missile installation near the shoreline. It was raised enough for the afternoon sun to cast a long shadow onto the land.

I didn't see any sign of harbor improvements.

We landed in the usual rush of steam with sparkles of unquenched plasma. Tarek got out of his bunk and threw a lever on the other side from the airlock; there was a splash and a loud rattling. Lal got up from the console.

"What was that?" I asked as I got up also. The *Martinique* pitched, though at a longer period than I expected; the chop in an ordinary slip was quick though relatively mild.

"If we didn't anchor," Lal said, looking at me in surprise, "we'd drift."

"Aren't there docks to tie up to?" I said, surprised in my turn.

"Well, not most harbors," Lal said. "Blanchard City has one, and I'm told Jacquerie Haven on Saguntum does."

"Yeah, it does," I said. I had more to learn about the universe than I'd ever dreamed in Xenos. I thought about Maeve. I had more to learn about life, too.

"Should we send up a flare?" Tarek said to Lal.

Lal shrugged. "No need," he said. "They'll be waiting for us. Hakim will have beaten us here."

"The *Martinique* doesn't carry flares," I said. "There's a box in the stores locker, but it's empty."

"It's all right," said Lal. "There's a boat on its way already."

He touched a console control. At first I thought something had gone wrong—the ship rang with repeated hammerblows. I realized that I'd never before heard the *Martinique*'s hatch lower.

Ali and Tarek looked worried also, but Lal merely waved his hand. "No problem," he said. "The extension gear is missing some teeth. I've seen that before. Heard it."

A breeze carried hot air and a tang of ozone, but it wasn't as bad as I'd expected for the ship to have been opened as soon after landing as this one had been. The fact that the *Martinique* floated free in a wind-swept bay seemed to have dissipated exhaust residues faster than I was used to.

There were a fair number of starships in the bay, twenty or thirty of them. Most were either in the shallows or actually drawn up on shore. With only a few exceptions, all were extremely small, five hundred tons or less. I couldn't tell which was Captain Hakim's ship, but it had been pretty much the same as the others in harbor.

Lal and Tarek walked out into the cargo compartment to meet the motor launch which was coming from the shore. I joined them to see something of ben Yusuf, and the other three crew followed.

We were about two hundred feet off the shore. The current was strong enough to swing the ship clockwise to the end of the play of the anchor line; that was probably why the water was clear also. In many ways this was an idyllic setting, the sort of place I'd daydreamed about when I was growing up.

I just hadn't expected to be visiting places like this as a slave. *I could die here and nobody would have any idea of what had happened to me....*

The launch curved up to the end of the ramp. Tarek said, "I'll go fetch the captain. All right?"

"Go ahead," Lal said. He gestured back into the ship with his thumb. "But take the tied one with you. He stinks."

"We'll all go," said Ali. "No reason to stay aboard now."

"Roy and me will wait for Hakim," Lal said. "But take the prisoner."

Tarek and Ali dragged Wellesley instead of carrying him, but the deck and ramp were smooth enough that it wasn't torture. I hadn't cleaned him for twelve hours or so, which gave me a twinge of conscience. I'd preferred not to think about the mate. I hadn't felt any duty toward him except what was owed to another human being...but that should've counted for more than it had.

The launch headed back to the shore with our shipmates. I said to Lal, "What happens now to me?"

Lal shrugged. "Hakim will sell you with the other prisoners,"

171

he said. "You're healthy and good-looking—you'll get a decent spot, servant in one of the merchants' households, maybe."

He looked sidelong at me. "There's still time to join Hakim's crew," he said. "It's not a bad life."

I hadn't liked the comment about me being "good-looking," but I said, "No, I don't think so. I swore I'd stay honest after my father died. Aren't there any regular spacers on ben Yusuf? Not pirates, I mean?"

Lal nodded respectfully though he'd probably misunderstood what I was saying about Dad. "There's no trade here but what they bring in by force," he said. "I was a crewman on a ship from Pride when Hakim captured us five years ago. I joined him. I don't like it, but what was a poor man like me to do?"

Then he said, "The wine is awful, but that's why the others were in such a hurry to get to Salaam. We'd drunk all we brought and they wanted more."

"You're from Pride?" I said. The boat that had carried the others to shore was coming back to us. There were two passengers besides the boatman.

"I am from Kashgar," Lal said with an unexpected dignity. "I am of a very low caste on Kashgar, though."

I'd never heard of either Kashgar or Pride. The *Martinique* had no reference materials aboard, just destinations preloaded into the astrogational computer with minimal data. Looking up the names wouldn't tell me anything if they were even included.

The launch bumped at the end of the ramp. Captain Hakim stood amidships with a bulky stranger wearing red pantaloons and a gold-embroidered vest over his loose white tunic. Hakim and the boatman caught rings on the edge of the ramp and tied the boat up. Hakim hopped aboard and offered the stranger his hand to mount.

The man in red hung back; Hakim instead stepped up to me. He said, "So, Olfetrie. Tarek says you know how to fix a console?"

"I had a little training on Cinnabar," I said, wondering what under heaven I'd been volunteered for. "I'm not a technician or any kind of expert, though."

Hakim looked over his shoulder at the stranger. That fellow muttered, "I need *somebody*." Then to me he said, "You— Olfetrie? You're from Cinnabar?"

"Right," I said. "From Xenos."

At least if they were talking about my computer skills, I wasn't going to be sold as somebody's bum-boy. I didn't know for sure what I'd do if that happened, but I didn't figure it'd be survivable.

"He'll do," the stranger said to Hakim. "He'll have to, I need somebody *now*."

"All right, Olfetrie," Hakim said. "You're a lucky boy. Instead of being auctioned the usual way, you're been bought by Master Giorgios, the Admiral's own chamberlain. You'll be living in the palace."

A large boat, a barge or a lighter, had put out from the shore and seemed to be heading toward us. Giorgios turned toward the launch, but Hakim put a hand on his arm and said, "If you're taking him now, you need to pay now. Otherwise he'll go to auction."

"You'll get your money!" the chamberlain said.

"Yes," said Hakim. "Now."

Giorgios untied the mouth of his belt purse and rooted inside. He came out with a gold piece, but he hesitated and said, "It's too much!"

Hakim shrugged and said, "You set the price. If you'd rather wait for the auction...?"

Giorgios swore under his breath and pressed the coin into the captain's hand. "Get into the boat!" he snarled at me.

Hakim grinned down at me and he and I cast the boat loose. "Good luck, Olfetrie," he called. "Let me know how you're doing if you get a chance."

"You're part of the Admiral's household now," Giorgios said to me. "You don't have any business with lone captains."

I laughed as our launch pulled away from the ramp. The barge nosed in behind us. There were no seats on the launch so we had to stand, holding the high railing. I didn't like that, even as calm as the bay seemed.

"You're a member of the Admiral's household, aren't you?" I said. "And you're dealing with Hakim, right?"

Giorgios spun to face me, clenching his fists. I was afraid that I might have pushed too hard, but when he spoke it was to say, "For god's sake, do you want to get us both hanged? Keep quiet about this!"

"I don't want anybody to be hanged," I said. "If you'll tell me what's going on instead of ordering me around, we'll do a lot better."

Giorgios was on the good side—barely—of fifty, and he was soft to the point of being fat. He sighed and I realized that the main reason for the bluster was that he was so frightened.

In a low voice—though I doubt the boatman would've

heard a shout over the keen of his electric motor—Giorgios said, "I order all the goods the Admiral's household needs and pay the suppliers. The divisions send me their requirements on the household network, and I send the orders to suppliers. The ordering network has stopped working. I need you to fix it."

"Don't you have a technician who can do that?" I said, frowning. If this required any real expertise, Giorgios was going to be disappointed, and heaven knew what would happen to me.

"It's never failed!" the chamberlain said. "Guido never had any trouble in the five years I was his assistant, so I told the Admiral I knew how to run the system when he promoted me."

"Umm," I said. "Where's Guido now?"

"The Admiral had him hanged last month," Giorgios said miserably. "He was taking too big a cut from the suppliers. Or anyway, the Admiral thought he was."

Very possibly the Admiral thought that because Guido's assistant had told him so, I thought. And then the assistant turned out not to be able to do the job after all. That would explain why Giorgios had been in such a hurry, and also why he was so frightened.

"And who's this Admiral who I work for?" I said.

"He runs Salaam," Giorgios said. "And you don't work for him; he *owns* you."

We grounded on the beach. The closest approach to port facilities was a parking area where three self-propelled lowboys were forming up. One had backed down to a hardstand at the edge of the shore. The barge which had gone out to the *Martinique* would be able to land here and offload

DAVID DRAKE

cargo, using the shearlegs in the bow. We were carrying milled cotton from Saguntum.

I didn't respond to the chamberlain's comment. I was thinking about being a slave. It didn't seem possible—a Cinnabar citizen who a year ago had been a cadet in the RCN Academy. But I was many days' sail from Cinnabar, and I might never again meet a Cinnabar citizen.

I felt sick to my stomach. I could vanish as though I'd never existed . . . and just possibly, I'd already done that.

Giorgios paid off the boatman. There were dozens of similar craft on the beach. Some were fishermen, judging from nets drying on racks behind lean-tos farther back on the sand, but boats were also the only way to reach the starships moored in the bay.

The brick fortress nearby on the shore was forty feet high. I knew from seeing it from above as the *Martinique* landed that it held three antistarship missiles, lowered for the time being. I wondered how serviceable they were.

Half a dozen vehicles sat at the back of the parking area. Most were motorized platforms with small wheels, though I saw a front-pedaled tricycle with a wicker bench over the back wheels. Drivers squatted in the shade of native trees with foliage that stuck out in all directions like fright wigs.

Wellesley lay on the ground nearby, bound and motionless.

"Hey!" I said, walking over to the spacer. He'd probably been in the shade when Tarek and his fellows came ashore, but by now he'd be baking until sunset.

"What are you doing?" Giorgios said. He'd mounted one of the low platforms. It had a high handrail like the launch and a control column with a T-bar in front. "Come on, we've got to get to the palace."

"He'll die if we don't get him to shelter!" I said, wondering if Wellesley was alive even now. I touched his throat and felt the pulse of his heart, though he didn't appear to feel the contact.

"What of it?" Giorgios said. "You don't have a share in his sale, do you?"

"Look, we move him or I don't go with you," I said. "Can we take him to the palace?"

A voice at the back of my mind wondered why I cared. Maybe I didn't, except that Wellesley was a human being. Not one I'd ever warm to, but I wasn't going to leave him to die in the sun.

"You're a bloody fool," Giorgios muttered, a statement I more or less agreed with. "We'll drop him off at the slave pen. *Bloody* fool."

I couldn't put one of Wellesley's arms over my shoulders because his wrists were taped together, but I gripped him below the rib cage and managed to haul him with only his heels dragging.

I dropped him on the back of Giorgios' vehicle. One of his boots had scraped off, but I didn't care about that. I was breathing hard.

The chamberlain started up the street running inland from the bay. All buildings were set back within compounds. The greenery I'd seen from the air was foliage hanging over the walls of gardens on both sides of the street. Gates to the interior were closed and two or three guards diced or played cards in each archway.

Our vehicle moved at a walking pace; the road was paved with irregular blocks which would have jarred our kidneys out if we'd gone any faster. I got a good look at the guards, who didn't seem any more impressive than their equipment. They'd leaned their weapons against the walls nearby. They were in poor condition; some didn't even have ammunition tubes attached.

"Why is Salaam so long and thin?" I said, raising my voice to be heard above the wheels on stone.

"The water," said Giorgios. He pointed ahead of us. "There's a river underground here from the mountains fifty miles south. If you build too far away to sink a well, you depend on cisterns or the kindness of your neighbors."

I snorted. I'd learned about the kindness of neighbors when Dad was disgraced. I could have been diagnosed with leprosy and been less of a pariah in the place I'd lived for a decade. From the chamberlain's tone, things weren't much different on ben Yusuf.

The walls bordering the street were eight or ten feet tall. The buildings I could see within the courtyards were two or three stories. The roofs were flat, and frequently foliage stuck over the top of them.

Giorgios turned left and snaked through an alley which was barely wide enough for the narrow vehicle. Some shops displayed their wares—electronics, garments, pots—on trays sticking out in front. The clatter of our wheels on the pavement was as good a warning as a horn would have been; shop boys snatched the trays inside.

Pedestrians and customers squeezed in also or found crannies for shelter. Giorgios showed no sign of caring whether he ran into someone or not.

We drew up at the east edge of town. We were high enough that I could look over the roofs of some of the structures farther down the swale.

"Here's the slave pen," said Giorgios. All I could see was a mud hut and half a dozen sheds of plastic sheeting on brushwood frames. A man lounging there walked over to us, leaving his carbine in the shade with his fellows.

"I've got a slave," Giorgios said. He turned and raised an eyebrow to me. "He goes on Hakim's account, I suppose?"

I said, "Yes, Hakim captured us. But where are the prisoners kept?"

The guard laughed. "Come and see," he said. To the men in the sheds he called, "One more for Hakim! Come give me a hand."

Two guards took Wellesley by the arms and dragged him toward the yard where several other guards were doing something on the ground; the leader and I followed. Beyond was a pit covered with an iron grating. The guards were lifting a hinged trap at one end.

I leaned forward to look in, holding my breath. The pit was ten feet deep; the fifty or so men inside didn't crowd it.

"Here, some of you take him," a guard called. Three of them fed Wellesley feet first through the trap, into a clot of men below.

"Olfetrie!" someone called from the pit. I couldn't make out individuals in the gloom. Then a different voice, Langland's, called, "Hey, Olfetrie? Can you get me out of here?"

"Come along, now," Giorgios said. "We've wasted enough time."

I paused. To the chamberlain I said, "How long will they stay in this prison?"

"A few days," Giorgios said. "A week at most. They're just useless mouths until they're sold."

"You'll be out in a week or less," I shouted into the pit. Then I turned and walked quickly back to the vehicle. I couldn't do anything more for Langland, and it wasn't as though I owed him. He hadn't been a bad shipmate, but I wouldn't have been here myself if he hadn't bought me from kidnappers.

"Who buys the slaves?" I asked as the chamberlain turned us around.

"Sometimes there's foreigners," he said. "People with a plantation or a factory on another planet they need staff for. And there's ships from charities in big places that buy back their own spacers even if there isn't a treaty with Salaam. If there's a treaty, the ships're exempt, but citizens who're crew on other ships can still be captured."

"Can't anybody stop it?" I said. I guess I sounded pretty angry, because Giorgios turned and looked at me with a frown.

"Why?" he said. "Slavery's legal many places besides ben Yusuf. And a lot of slaves, they're bought by locals and work on farms right alongside their owners. It's not so bad. Look at you, you're fine. If you play your cards right, you could wind up in charge of one of the Admiral's own ships."

I thought of telling him that I'd refused to join a pirate crew already, and I certainly wasn't going to be running one. It wouldn't do any good, though. Nothing would do any good but an RCN squadron...but maybe someday I could help make that happen.

It struck me that though Cinnabar didn't have a presence on ben Yusuf, Saguntum might. I said, "Giorgios, if I were a citizen of Saguntum, what would happen to me?"

The chamberlain shrugged. "You were crew on a ship from Masque, and Masque doesn't have a treaty with us. Saguntum has a treaty but there's no consul. Their treaty rights are handled by the Karst consul."

I remembered Lady Mundy telling me that Karst controlled Saguntum's foreign policy. Karst really would be powerful in this region.

"How would I be able to talk to the Karst consul?" I asked.

"You wouldn't!" Giorgios said. He was too forceful for me to believe him. "You've got no business with him and he wouldn't see a slave anyway."

He turned and glared. "You're a member of the Admiral's household!" he said. "Be thankful for it!"

I nodded. I wasn't thankful to be a slave.

We reached the street that had brought us from the bay and turned up it. Giorgios pointed at the massive building just ahead to the right and said, "There's the palace."

"Giorgios?" I said, because my mind was still back on something else. "Have there been escapes from the slave pen?"

There were enough prisoners in the pit to form a pyramid from which half a dozen men could work on the grating. That was massive but it hadn't looked particularly sturdy. I was pretty sure I could crack some of welds myself, given time—and the guards didn't seem to pay much attention.

The chamberlain laughed. "If there's a lot of noise from the pen," he said, "they toss a grenade at where the noise is loudest. The last time it happened, they used white phosphorus—an incendiary grenade."

I didn't say anything. I was going to get out of this place one way or another.

The front of the palace was three stories tall, and the arched gateway in front rose two of them. The gate leaves were split in half vertically though, and the guards pushed the right portion open as soon as they saw us approaching.

We jolted through a tunnel and into a courtyard which was smaller than I'd expected. It was more like a light well; the hollow walls on both sides were twenty feet thick. The upper stories had windows and balconies. Poles protruded with clothes drying and hanging plant baskets. Children were playing noisily and women chatted as they watched.

Directly in front of us was a blank curtain wall. Spikes glittered on top. It wasn't an outside wall; there was clearly a higher wing beyond it. What I could see merely divided the courtyard into the larger portion that we'd driven into and a smaller section on the other side.

Giorgios parked by an interior doorway. Three attendants wearing sandals and pantaloons wheeled the vehicle away, pushing it instead of driving. The chamberlain saw me studying the curtain wall and said, "Better keep away from that, Olfetrie. That's the wives' quarter. If you're caught trying to look in, you'll be gelded and become an attendant."

I turned my head. There were better and worse places to be a slave on Salaam.

People stood on both sides of the passage we'd entered, talking and dozing as best I could tell. The passage was shaded and there was a slight breeze through it, so it was a reasonable place to be if you had nothing better to do. That seemed to be the case for plenty of people in the Admiral's palace.

We went up a set of wooden stairs in a stone well. Instead of curling like the companionways on a ship, these made right angles every six treads or so. The whole rig seemed flimsy, and it'd be a chimney packed with kindling if it ever caught fire.

A couple people vanished onto upper stories when they saw the chamberlain coming, but there wasn't a crowd on the stairs like I'd half expected after the entrance passage. Maybe more people than me thought the stairs were an accident waiting to happen.

When we reached the third floor, Giorgios was puffing. He threw open the door and announced proudly, "The entire top floor of this wing is for me and my household! You'll have a room in my private suite, where the computer is."

"At least the stairs'll keep me in good condition," I said. If the palace caught fire, I'd have to learn to fly very fast; but maybe that wouldn't happen.

We were in the left wing. A gallery ran the length of it on the outside. Most of the doorways opening off it were long, narrow rooms running toward another gallery at the courtyard end. Faces peered out of curtained alcoves, then ducked away.

There were electrical lights of various sorts—mostly glowstrips, but fluorescent, incandescent, and diode fixtures as well. I didn't see any two of the same sort.

Also I didn't see any open flames, which was a mercy. At this time of afternoon there was still a lot of daylight coming through the galleries, anyway.

Giorgios' suite turned out to be the last quarter of the corridor. He walked me past a pair of attendants—guards, I suppose, though I saw only one carbine—and into the far end where an astrogation console from a starship sat in an alcove.

Giorgios pulled curtains to shield us and switched it on. "See?" he said when the stand-by display, an opalescent globe, appeared. "It doesn't work."

I used the keyboard to get to the sidebar, where I switched the holographic display from astrogation to what I hoped was the local area. The unit was of Karst manufacture, but the hollow square looked like a good bet for my first try. A list of proper names came up with no other information.

"How did you do that?" Giorgios shouted. "Is all the information still there?"

I had no idea what "information" there might have been, so I called up one of the names—Petruschka. It expanded into a list of foodstuffs, as best I could tell. It was so long a list that it spread into a second screen when I expanded the typeface to a readable size.

"Is this what you're looking for?" I said.

"Oh, thank the Great God!" Giorgios said. "I'm saved! No wonder he was complaining that if the deliveries didn't come in, we'd run out of food!"

Giorgios disappeared into another alcove for a moment, then returned with a stylus and a notebook. "Here," he said, thrusting them at me. "Write down all the orders and I'll send out messengers at once. Oh, the Great God is good to me!"

I got to work. Among other things, *I* was feeling hungry. I decided that would be my second item of business.

Chapter Nineteen

That was my introduction to my duties as the chamberlain's assistant. I copied out the food orders and gave them to Giorgios. He would have gone off with them, leaving me on my own, if I hadn't followed him out of the alcove and caught him by the flowing sleeve.

"Sir!" I said. "I need somebody to guide me around. Where do I get food? For that matter, where's the latrine?"

Giorgios glared at me, but he couldn't pull his tunic away without tearing the fabric. We had an audience, at least a dozen people, watching more or less openly. The chamberlain pointed at one of them, a boy of fifteen or so, and said, "Abram, this is Olfetrie. Do whatever he tells you."

Abram said, "Suits me," without enthusiasm. He continued to squat on his heels as Giorgios swept into the gallery and out of sight.

"I want some food," I said to the boy. "While we're eating, I'll have some more questions for you."

"Would the food include wine for me?" Abram said, raising an eyebrow.

"It could," I agreed.

He bounded upright as though he were a toy driven by a spring. His grin was not only alert but friendly. "Willing to take a bit of a walk?" Abram said.

"Yes, if there's a reason to," I said, wondering what this was about.

"I won't say old Martial has better food than the refectory here in Giorgios' suite," the boy said, "but Martial's wine is a *lot* better. He taps the Admiral's own casks, right? Now, it'll cost a bit."

"I don't have any money," I said.

"Well, I'll front you till you start making your own graft," Abram said. "And you're in a bloody good place to do that, it seems to me."

We went down a different set of stairs. If anything, they were flimsier than the ones Giorgios had led me up. At the bottom, we went left and through a door that led outdoors rather than into the courtyard. Thirty-odd people, men and women both, stood near a kiosk built against the outside wall. We were on the north side of the palace, so there was a strip of shade even now in early afternoon.

Abram squeezed up to the counter. There were two servers—both middle-aged women—but Abram shouted, "Hey, Martial! I want you to meet a friend of mine. Olfetrie runs the chamberlain's computer!"

The cook turned around. "No fooling?" he said. He was a fat man of fifty, bald on top but sporting a magnificent moustache and sideburns. His terry cloth singlet was soaked with sweat but without any other stains that I could see. "Hey, Ayesha? I'm going to take a break. Come on back, Abram."

One of the servers took over at the grill. Abram led me under the end of the counter—we ducked; it didn't have a gate to lift—and into a door in the palace wall. It seemed to have been enlarged from a ventilator. The interior was a large storeroom.

Martial twisted two bare wires together; fluorescents flickered on. He gestured to the low stools along the interior wall. "Will you have wine?"

"Do fish piss in the sea?" Abram said. "I'm paying for my friend Olfetrie until he gets something going."

I took the glass of red wine and tasted it with my tongue. It was good, good enough that my mother would have approved. Well, she would have approved if anybody but Dad had offered it; nothing Dad did was good enough. Or anything I did, come to think.

"So..." Martial said, settling onto another stool. "Do you think you'll be able to earn some money, Olfetrie?"

"Yes," I said. "And if we're going to be friends, I go by Roy. As for the details, I won't know exactly how until I learn the system here, but"—I shrugged and turned my free hand up—"I can think of half a dozen ways off the top of my head. It shouldn't be hard."

I'd told Captain Leary that I wasn't a crook like my dad, and I wasn't. That didn't mean I didn't know how a system *could* be fiddled. There was nothing about Giorgios or his master the Admiral that made me imagine that I owed them loyal service.

"I can find anything you want, Roy," Abram said. "Say, are you looking for girl?"

"Maybe later," I said. I didn't say that I'd rather meet somebody on my own. "I told you, I need to learn the system."

"That's smart," said Martial. "Jumping in too quick, you're likely to get trapped." He snorted. "Or clapped."

"*Hey*, Martial," Abram said. "You know I wouldn't let him get burned!"

To me, in a wheedling tone, he said, "Boys, maybe?"

"No," I said. "Abram, if I need something, I'll let you know."

Someone knocked on the outside door. Abram hopped up and opened it, then returned to us carrying a tray of hot pasties. He held out the tray to me, but he'd taken one himself with his free hand.

"Which division do you eat in, Roy?" Martial said. "The chamberlain's, I suppose?"

"I suppose," I said. "Giorgios didn't say, but he said I'm his slave."

Martial's mouth worked as though he were going to spit in disgust, but what came out was only the words, "Gardane's the cheapest bastard in the palace. I'd as soon drink lamp oil as the wine he serves."

I took a careful nibble off the end of a pasty. It was a green vegetable, probably spinach, and very good. It was hot enough that I was glad not to have taken a larger bite, but it made me realize how hungry I was.

"Can I transfer from his division to yours, Martial?" I asked around another mouthful. "I'm not really enrolled yet, after all."

"Naw, the bastard won't let you go," the cook said glumly. "The losing division has to agree, and Gardane won't. He screws half the per-person allowance in straight profit, and he won't let a soul off his books."

"Oh," I said. "If it's just a matter of getting Master Gardane's agreement, then I can talk to him. I think he'll be reasonable if I ask him the right way."

"Dream on, buddy," Martial said. "Here, though, another glassful on me."

"I'll take the wine," I said. "But Abram, you and I need to get going soon. I have a lot of work to do. A *lot* of work."

I'd decided that my first priority was to prepare for my interview with Gardane. I already had some ideas about that.

I wasn't a computer expert, but the palace's systems were so unsophisticated that I was sure within a few hours that my only problems were going to be with preexisting input errors. Nothing was encrypted, but a number of the files were corrupt beyond my ability to clarify.

There were areas which had been mechanically blocked. They would require chipped inserts, in the unit's present configuration. I figured I had an answer to that, but it could wait until I had the leisure.

I found the refectory accounts easily, but it took me and Abram two hours to compile the list I wanted. The boy knew more than half the names, but the rest took research. I found a few by searching the computer, but mostly "research" meant Abram running off and talking to friends. He knew a lot of people in the palace, which didn't surprise me; and at least at the bottom end, people seemed to like him—which didn't surprise me either.

When I decided I was ready, I had a much longer list than I'd expected at the start. "Now..." I said to Abram. "Lead me to Gardane. Then go do something else. This will work best if it's just me and the cook in private. It shouldn't be a big deal."

The chamberlain's refectory was five bays in the south wing of the third floor, just around the corner from Giorgios' staff quarters. The first two bays off the gallery were given over to tables; a third was the kitchen itself. The remaining two were housing and offices.

Abram brought me to the last of these and said to the guard, "This is the chamberlain's personal assistant. He needs to talk to Gardane."

"It isn't time yet for Gardane to see people," the guard said stolidly.

"Giorgios told me that Olfetrie goes everywhere!" Abram said, which wasn't quite true. "Do you want to spend the short rest of your life on a stake because you didn't obey the chamberlain? This is important!"

I kept my mouth shut and looked stern. Maybe I could get a uniform. I was wearing spacers' slops, comfortable but not very imposing. The palace seemed to be big on appearances.

Well, bigger on appearances than society generally. And as I thought about it some more, maybe not that much bigger.

"Look," said the guard, "don't try to put me in the middle of this. It's between the chamberlain and my boss. Nothing to do with me at all!"

He stepped out of the way and I walked in, through strings of metal beads hanging down like a curtain. Three women were in the anteroom, whispering together in a corner. They sprang apart, one of them with an audible, "*Eep!*"

I pointed to that one. "I need to speak with Master Gardane, *now*," I said. "In private. You go fetch him, all right? In one minute I'll come back and find him if he hasn't made it out here before then."

The woman scampered off. All three were dressed as maids: young enough to be more than that, but too plain for that to seem probable.

The two who remained clutched one another's hands and stared at me with a frightened expression. I smiled at them with what I hoped was a friendly face and said, "I'm new here, but your master and I are going to be great friends shortly. I've just come by to get acquainted."

They continued to stare like bunnies in the headlights. At least they weren't screaming.

It had been long enough that I was just about to go deeper into the bay, when a man in his forties came out of the back, still tying a blue gauze sash around his waist. He glared at me and said, "If Giorgios thinks he's got to see me, he can make an appointment!"

Which meant that the girl I'd sent as a messenger had reported the exchange between Abram and the guard as well as what I'd said. That was a degree of initiative that I hadn't expected.

"I don't think either one of us want to see Giorgios," I said. "And *certainly* not the Admiral. Is there some place we can talk in private?"

The girl who'd eeped was peering out through the bead screen to the back of the suite. I already knew that she was smart enough to be dangerous.

Gardane hesitated a moment. Then he said, "Come on. We'll go up to the roof."

We went deeper into the bay, then up a circular metal staircase set into an alcove. I suspected the stairs had been salvaged from a starship's companionway. The trap door at the top was open, but Gardane clanged it closed when we stepped out onto a roof of tiles set in cement. Trees with short fuzzy trunks and broad foliage sat in pots in a rough circle around the trap so that shade fell on the wicker couches and table regardless of the time of day or year.

"Go away," Gardane said to the pair of attendants who'd been lounging in the shade. He made shooing notions with his hands. They obediently sauntered toward the nearest of the five other potted oases visible.

The fourth wing of the palace was a story higher than the front and sides, and it had a real wall around it instead of just curbing. I remembered Giorgios' warning about the wives' section and quickly looked at a tree.

"Say what you want to say," Gardane snapped.

I handed over my list, three sheets which I had been carrying rolled in my left hand. "Before we talk," I said, "I'd like you to read this."

The cook scanned the first sheet, turned to the second, and finally the third. He looked at me. He must go to some effort to keep himself in shape, but he liked food too well to be completely successful at that.

"It's a list of names," he said, working to stay calm. "What do they mean to you?"

Keeping my voice emotionless so that the words wouldn't sound like a threat, I said, "It's a list of people who are assigned to the chamberlain's refectory but who are also drawing rations from other divisions. And of people who are not members of the palace complement at all, but who are assigned to the chamberlain's refectory. And of people who aren't people; non-existent people who are assigned to the chamberlain's refectory."

"I see," Gardane said. His eyes flicked in the direction of the guards whom he'd sent away. "What do you propose to do with this list?"

"Absolutely nothing," I said. "I came to see you because I've been told that you have the authority to transfer my meal allowance to another palace division. In this case, I'd like you to transfer me and the boy Abram, and also the last four names on the list"—people who didn't exist for any purpose except to draw rations—"to the division of Chef Martial. I believe his division generally handles gardeners and other outside workers; day laborers, many of them."

Gardane's eyes went to the guards again. If he called to them, I was going to punch him in the stomach and fling open the trap door, hoping to get down the stairs before reinforcements arrived to throw me off the roof.

"If I do that," Gardane said carefully, "what other business will you and I have? In particular, what will the chamberlain himself have to say about it?"

"Giorgios will say nothing because he will know nothing,"

I said. "I am responsible for all data entry."

"Agreed, then," Gardane said. He smiled. "I suggest we go down and seal the bargain with a glass of wine."

The wine wasn't bad. Abram had been right, though: Martial's seemed better.

I was organizing the accounts, division by division. I hadn't thought of the Petersburg Chandlery as being very organized, but if I ever found myself back there I would apologize for my previous sneers.

The sneers hadn't reached my lips, and there was vanishingly small chance of me revisiting Petersburg Chandlery. For that matter, at the moment things weren't looking good for me ever seeing Cinnabar again.

I left the curtain open while I was working. There was a little air circulation that way, and the gang of household residents watching me weren't a problem after I'd gotten used to them.

If they pushed too close, Abram chased them away with threats of what the Admiral's guards would do if they disturbed me. Initially I thought the threats were just over-the-top hyperbole, but after a few days in the palace I'd seen enough casual cruelty to fear that they were literally true.

There was a thrumming bustle behind me, the way birds scatter when a hawk appears. The noise wasn't frightening, but the sudden silence that followed worried me. I turned to ask Abram what was going on.

Abram wasn't there, but a pudgy man with a red turban,

a cloth-of-gold tunic, and an entourage of three guards was. I'd never seen the Admiral, but I was pretty sure who this fellow was.

I got up from the console, uncertain whether I was supposed to bow or maybe even throw myself on the floor. Sure, I'm a Cinnabar citizen and proud of it, but I'd already watched two people—a guy about my age and a kid of ten or so—be impaled on stakes. I'm willing to die rather than do some things, but I'm not willing to die *that* way unless there really isn't a choice.

"Get out of here, you fool!" a guard growled, jabbing his impeller at me. I jumped clear and whisked around the partition into Giorgios' bedroom. There'd usually have been an attendant there to keep underlings out, but that fellow had vanished when the Admiral arrived.

The chamberlain was alone in his big bed. He'd awakened, probably when his attendants fled. He swung his legs out—he was wearing a paisley shift—and gestured me to the back of the suite. We went out onto the gallery and Giorgios closed the door behind us. There was no one in sight.

"Did he say what he was looking for?" Giorgios whispered.

"He didn't say anything," I whispered back. "A guard told me to get out. Does this happen often?"

"Not often," Giorgios said. "He doesn't usually leave the Wives' Wing except on court days. And this is early!"

Then he gasped and said, "The computer was working, wasn't it? It wasn't a blank screen?"

"The console was fine," I said soothingly. It was nearly midday—which might have been early for the Admiral, come to think, as well as for his chamberlain. "I was going over the Treasury Division accounts."

That led to an obvious segue and I said, "What does the Admiral do at the console?"

If he was checking the treasury accounts, there were going to be more people on stakes shortly. I wasn't doing an audit—and I'd just started on the division anyway—but the corruption I'd found in household expenses was subtle compared to what I'd seen at a glance in the Chancellor's department.

"I don't know," Giorgios said miserably. "Do you suppose he's checking on me?"

I started to say, "Well, I'll tell you as soon as I look at the console history," but I decided to keep quiet about that. The chamberlain certainly didn't know that the console logged usage, and I realized that the Admiral himself probably didn't.

"I guess we'd better hope not," I said instead. Then, because Giorgios was so rattled, I said, "I think that for safety's sake, I'd better start contacting the vendors myself instead of you sending the orders by messengers. Heavens only knows what some of them would say under a little pressure."

"Oh, Great God," Giorgios said. "Do you really think so? Oh Great God."

I patted him on the shoulder. "It's going to be fine," I said. "I'll take care of it and we'll both be safe."

I wouldn't be safe until I was gone from ben Yusuf. I was pretty sure this would be a step toward getting me there.

Chapter Twenty

I'd thought my first order of business would be to find Abram, but I heard his laugh—a cheerful bray—coming up from below several times while Giorgios and I were chatting. I leaned over the gallery railing and saw the boy among the customers at Martial's diner.

I could have shouted to him, but walking down the stairs didn't arouse general notice. That didn't necessarily make me safe, but keeping a low profile struck me as the better option.

People who randomly whack the heads off flowers start with the tallest stems. There were plenty of randomly violent people in the Admiral's palace.

When Abram saw me walking toward the diner, he waved and trotted to meet me. "Hey, boss," he said. "Glad you don't need a stake to stay upright. How's Giorgios?"

"The same when I left him," I said. "He may need to change his trousers. Though come to think, he was still in his nightshirt. Still, it seemed like a good time to get out into the town. Take me to Balian's, to begin with."

"We have an order for Balian?" Abram said. "He usually gives me a glass of wine when I bring him an order."

"I'll talk with Balian," I said. "There'll be others today, and more later too."

I planned to come away with more than a glass of wine. Martial had kept me supplied with as much as I needed in piaster coins—he'd still be making a nice profit on the six "mouths" I'd transferred to his roster—but I thought it was time that I started making my own way.

Abram led. I made an effort to recall the turns, but I wasn't very concerned about it. I'd be just as happy to have a companion every time I wandered the city.

I could get Giorgios to assign armed guards, I suppose, but I trusted Abram and his wits to stand me in as good stead as any of the guards I'd seen thus far. They seemed to be village boys who'd been handed a weapon. They might be brave enough, but they had the intelligence of the goats they'd been herding before they entered Salaam.

Abram turned into a plaza around a sprawling building with white walls. The walls were less than ten feet tall, but I could see that the roof was covered by a series of vaults. As soon as we stepped inside, keepers of the shops inside greeted us with noisy enthusiasm.

They came from behind their counters, often with a selection of their wares hanging from one outstretched arm. Those in this neighborhood seemed to be jewelers, offering chains and bangles hanging from chains.

"We want hardware," Abram explained to me in a dismissive

tone. "That is"—his expression grew cunning—"unless you've changed your mind about a girl? Murid in the last shop down is my friend and he can give you a good price."

"I haven't changed my mind," I said, keeping my eyes straight ahead despite the fingers plucking my sleeves. Did they treat everybody this way? Because Abram and I certainly weren't dressed to impress people with our wealth.

We continued through to a cross bay and turned right. This time the shops sold low-end clothing, the local equivalent of the spacers' slops I was wearing. I could use more garments, but not now.

For that matter, my inclination was to let Abram shop for my personal needs. I preferred to bargain at a higher level.

Beyond the clothing was a hardware market. The shopkeepers were mostly male as they had been in the jewelry bay, but they were less boisterously enthusiastic. The garment sellers had been women.

Balian was an old man seated at the back of the shop. At the counter were two younger men; one wasn't much older than Abram. They cheerfully greeted him, taking him by the arms and drawing him past the counters of pipe fittings and into the racks of tools.

I'd intended to have lists with me when I began visiting shopkeepers, but the Admiral's arrival hadn't given me time to plan. I'd recently gone over hardware purchases, though, so I figured I was current enough for the present purposes.

"And this one...?" said the older of the youths, eying me without pleasure. "You're training to be the new messenger?"

The words were harmless. The insult was in the tone.

"Not exactly," I said. The acoustics in this large hall were designed for drinking clatter rather than for transmitting speech clearly, but I could see that the old man in back was listening intently. I pitched my voice for him: "I'm the chamberlain's assistant and have sole control of the console. I'm here to discuss future orders rather than to place one today."

The younger clerk sniffed. "Well, I guess we can stand a second glass of wine," he said loudly.

I looked over his head at Balian and smiled. It wasn't a good-humored smile. I didn't speak, which seemed to put the boy off his stride.

The old man got up and said, "Mehmet, why don't you and Suleiman attend our friend Abram. I will take the new gentleman—your name, sir?"

"Roy Olfetrie," I said, nodding slightly.

"Our new friend Roy into my office," Balian said. To me he added, "It's quieter, and perhaps I could find a better bottle of wine?"

"I'm not here for wine," I said as I followed him toward the back of the shop.

"No, no, I didn't think you were," Balian said sadly. He opened a door to which a rack of small metal fittings hung. They tinkled when the panel moved. "Well, what can a poor man do?"

The office was small but antiseptically clean: one small desk, two straight chairs, and a four-drawer file cabinet. The old man opened the bottom drawer of the cabinet and came out holding an earthenware bottle and two shapely tulip glasses.

He looked up and paused. "Unless perchance you'd like something stronger?"

"Ben Yusuf wine is quite strong enough for me," I said.

Balian handed me a glass and closed the bottle with a plug of waxed wood. When he'd settled into his chair with the second glass, he eyed me and said, "Not bad, don't you think?"

"Yes," I agreed after a taste. "But as I said, I'm not here for the refreshment."

"Of course," Balian said. "What proposition do you have for me, Roy Olfetrie?"

"For every twenty items ordered for the palace," I said, "you invoice twenty-one as delivered. I enter the twenty-one, and you and I split the billed amount of the twenty-first. You pay over my share in cash the next time I come by."

"Indeed," said the old man, speaking with no inflection. "And what would you do, Roy Olfetrie, if I reported this conversation the Giorgios, your master?"

I shrugged. "I think he'd be pleased," I said. "At least when I explain that your pique is natural, given that I moved all the hardware purchases to Ajah. He agreed to pay a twenty-five percent commission to the chamberlain instead of twenty, you see."

"Ajah won't pay twenty-five percent!" Balian snarled, the first time his mask had slipped.

I shrugged again. "I suspect he will if I double his volume," I said.

For a moment, Balian stared at me with an expression as blank as a pearl. Then he chuckled and said, "You know, you might be right about that. But"—his eyes hard-focused again—"you haven't actually done that yet?"

"You were my first stop," I said truthfully. "As best as I

could tell, your prices are better than Ajah's. While the well-being of my employer—my owner, I suppose I should say—isn't my only consideration, I did take it into account."

Balian chuckled again. He set his glass down on the desk and laughed harder.

It didn't hurt me, but neither did the business seem to me such a funny joke. I said, "Where do you get your supplies? Are there factories elsewhere on ben Yusuf? Because I haven't seen much sign of them in Salaam."

"Pipe and fittings are mostly made on planet," the old man said, sobering. "There's an extrusion plant in the west suburbs here. Hand tools, some on ben Yusuf; there's a couple factories in Eski Marakech. Power tools, they're all from off planet."

I thought of what Giorgios had said when he brought me to the palace. I said, "I didn't realize ben Yusuf had off-planet trade."

"Charities on other planets buy back their citizens under truce," Balian explained. "That's mostly done in Eski Marakech, but my agent there buys on my orders and ships them to me."

He lifted the wine bottle. "Another?" he said.

"Not for me," I said, getting to my feet. "But I'll be sending Abram with a formal order in a few days, once I've checked my records on the console."

That wasn't all I'd be checking on the console. I hoped the Admiral was finished by now. I was looking forward to learning what he'd been doing.

I let Abram check about on the Admiral's whereabouts. I didn't want to be seen asking about him or about much of anything. That was largely my plan of keeping a low profile, but I'd seen from our first meeting that Abram would get better information than I could. He knew so much that his quick brain could cross-check whatever people told him, and nobody was going to ask why he wanted to know something.

Abram was always working an angle. If you stayed on his good side, you wouldn't find that angle jabbing you in the dark some night.

The Admiral had only stayed twenty minutes before going back to the women's wing with his entourage of guards and toadies. None of them were permitted to watch what he was doing at the console.

As before, I had Abram shoo the spectators off to a distance, though there hadn't been any reason for that except that I didn't want to be jostled. Less than half of the palace staff were even literate, and all I was doing at the computer was my job as the chamberlain's assistant. I didn't intend to discuss with the chamberlain what I was doing, sure; but he was probably happier not to know.

I checked the usage log and found that all the Admiral's activity had been in areas accessed after insertion of a chip key. That disassociated them from the console's normal routines.

The only way around that was to create an identical key—impossible for me and probably impossible for anybody else unless they had the original to copy—or to reset the console itself and to wipe all security formatting. That too was impossible unless you had the console's password, which could be set to fourteen digits of letters, numbers, and symbols.

In the RCN, every console was given a password generated

by cosmic ray impacts; I'm sure the Alliance used a similar system. As consoles came from the manufacturer, though, the normal default was the last three digits of the unit's serial number. The palace console was ex-commercial; as I expected, keying in A3* opened all sectors of the console to me.

There were document files which could be updated by information transferred when the key was inserted. That had been done regularly, but there'd been no changes in the past month. Each was a personnel file, so to speak: the name of a woman; particulars of height, weight, and identifying characteristics; and where applicable the name of her father and her birth village, with the bride price.

In five cases the file gave the woman's name and planet of origin, with no mention of bride price. Four of those women did have prices listed, but with the name of a captain rather than a father; they'd been bought at slave auctions.

The unique item on the list was Monica Smith, a blonde from Saguntum. She was the most recent arrival, from three months back. No source or price appeared. That was a puzzle with no obvious means of solution.

The sectors which the Admiral had been checking a few minutes ago were displays for observation cameras in the Wives' Wing, though I had to check the sources to be sure of that.

I blanked the display in sudden terror, then turned on the couch. The console was in an alcove. Ten or a dozen palace servants sat in a loose semicircle out in the gallery. They were staring at my back. They didn't seem concerned or even interested when I looked at them.

Between me and them squatted Abram, with a double-edged dagger in his lap. Nobody was close enough for the point of the dagger to reach—quite—if Abram suddenly started swiping at spectators. I made sure the focus of my holographic display was set so that the images cohered only from within sixteen centimeters—the unit was of Karst manufacture—of where my eyes were when I sat at the console.

I took a deep breath and opened one of the camera feeds.

I was looking at a woman with lovely blond hair, about as old as I am. She was staring at a window covered by a carved wooden screen. The screen was a marvel of workmanship; the craftsman who'd made it could have earned a fortune on Cinnabar, turning out one-off masterpieces for newly rich gentlemen in Xenos.

People like my dad had been.

The blond was in a corner room; I judged that she was looking over the alley on the south side of the palace. I doubted whether she could see the pavement, and I wasn't sure that she could even see the tops of the two-story buildings across the way; the screen was finger thick, and the openings were narrow swirls an inch or two long.

The blond got up from the window ledge. Her expression was the only part of her that wasn't lovely. It was as cold as polished granite, not ugly but inhuman. There was only one blond in the Admiral's records, so this was Monica Smith.

Monica picked up a long-necked stringed instrument and walked to the door. I lost her when she went out, but there were more than twenty other feeds. I cycled through them until one gave me a large bay, probably the central half of the wing.

Eight women lounged there. Two were playing a game with

cards and tiles; three sat at another table and drank small cupfuls from an urn; and the final three read or stared at wood-screened windows, much as Monica had been doing in her room.

The camera installation had been expert. It covered the entire top floor of the wing and showed the interiors of every chamber. The feeds must have come from extreme fish-eye lenses, but there was no distortion in what I saw because the console's enormous capacity easily corrected the images.

I wondered who had installed and connected the equipment; and I wondered also if they had long survived the task. It was possible that the work had been done by women or by eunuchs. My suspicion after my past experience with the palace was that the Admiral had bought slaves with the necessary expertise and then had executed them.

The women were all dressed in loose garments and slippers. Monica wore a shift much like the one Giorgios slept in, though hers was white instead of patterned. Most of the others were in similar garments or skirts and blouses, though one of the game players wore only a bandeau above the waist.

Monica walked to a woman reading. They moved to a bench without back or arms and sat. Monica began to play while the other woman watched her fingering intently.

Another woman entered the hall from a door which had been closed until then. The observation cameras didn't have sound—and I wouldn't have dared use it anyway—but the roomful of women started as suddenly as birds raised by a gun dog.

The newcomer was older than most of the others—midforties I would guess—but in very good condition. She was plumper than my taste, but that seemed to be the norm for ben Yusuf. The only slim adult woman whom I'd seen here was Monica.

The woman who'd been sitting with Monica disappeared into one of the rooms. She left behind the book she'd been reading. Monica stood also, but she didn't back away.

The Admiral's chief wife was Azul, fifty years old and born on ben Yusuf. I was certain now that I was watching her, though she wore her age well. I couldn't hear the words the two women exchanged, but I could read them easily enough in the postures and expressions.

Azul advanced. Instead of backing away, Monica picked up a lamp of turned brass from the table where her instructor had been reading. Azul halted.

The older woman was dressed with greater formality than the other wives. Her long, pale-blue dress was cinched at the waist with a broad belt of leather dyed a darker blue which matched the material of her cut-work slippers. Her hair fell loose on the right side but was gathered by a gaudy barrette on the left.

Azul looked over her shoulder. A moment later, two men wearing pantaloons and loose blouses joined her. They were thick bodied and soft looking, but they were also big. One spoke to Azul; then they moved on Monica from either side.

For a moment I thought the girl was going to fight them. Then she hurled the lamp to the floor and handed the musical instrument to the man—the eunuch, obviously—on her right.

That servant carried the instrument to Azul, bowed, and handed it over. The other eunuch shifted slightly so that he was directly between the women. He continued to watch Monica.

Azul examined the instrument. The sound box was very small compared to the long neck. She walked to the outside wall where Monica could see her clearly. Raising the instrument in both hands as though she were using an axe, she swung it against the masonry. It shattered into scraps of light wood and the sturdier neck from which the four strings dangled.

Azul tossed the neck to the floor. She turned and walked back into the room she had appeared from.

Monica said nothing. She too returned to her room. She closed her door with a controlled motion instead of banging it.

I blanked my display. I was trembling inside. Then after a moment I reopened the feed I had started with, the interior of Monica's room. It was the last one the Admiral had been watching.

Monica lay on her bed, her face buried into the bedclothes. Judging from the way her body shook, she was sobbing.

I turned off the console. I wasn't sure what I wanted to do just now, but I knew I didn't want to see more of the internal politics of the Wives' Wing.

I was at work on the dry goods accounts, as best as I could. It was a tangled mess, with minimal data entered—usually a gross amount—and uncertain dates. At least a third of the entries were identical to the sou to one or more other entries. That didn't necessarily mean they were false, however, because it was the nature of housekeeping expenses to be repetitive.

I'd have been right more often than not to say an account was false, though. It's not just that ben Yusuf existed by piracy. Its society was corrupt from bottom to top. I wasn't taking a moral stance to think that it should be remade; that was just a pragmatic assessment.

Abram rang a brass triangle right behind me. I jumped, but it'd been my idea. When I was working, I tuned out my surroundings. That was fine for most things, but if I ignored the Admiral when he visited I was likely to be alerted by a guard using the butt of his impeller.

I blanked the display before I turned around. There was nothing wrong with me going over household accounts, but I might have been viewing the Wives' Wing. I was training myself to react the safe way, every time. I didn't want either gelding or impaling to become part of my work history.

Abram stood with Lal, my shipmate from Captain Hakim's crew. I surprised myself with how glad I was to see him. Lal and Abram were the closest thing to friends I'd made since I was shanghaied on Saguntum.

"Say, spacer!" I said, getting up from the console. My eyes had to adjust before I could see him properly. "What're you doing here?"

"Well, when we landed at Salaam, I thought I'd see how you were getting on," Lal said, looking around. "I thought you'd be all right, but I'm still surprised that you're doing *this* well. From what I hear, you're running things in the palace."

"No, not that," I said truthfully. I didn't add, "And if it were true I wouldn't say it. Even Giorgios doesn't find me so indispensable that he wouldn't have somebody knife me if he decided I was a danger to him."

Aloud I went on, "Have you had lunch? Let me buy you lunch!"

"I wouldn't mind," Lal said. "We made a couple decent captures this time, but Captain Hakim won't be paying off till the auction in a week or so."

I looked at Abram and made a quick calculation. "Abram," I said, "let's you and I find a place we can have lunch with my old shipmate. Some place the food's as good as Martial's but where we don't have to stand outside."

"Right," said Abram. "I really like Etzil's down by the harbor, if you don't mind a bit of a walk?"

We didn't mind. Of course.

I've heard people say, "You've got to trust somebody!" and I've also heard them say, "You can't trust anybody!" Neither of those things is true; both are just words that people shout when a plan or a relationship goes belly-up.

I've known people who didn't seem to trust anybody. My dad was one of them. Certainly neither my brother nor I had any notion of how he was getting his contracts. As for Mom, I don't doubt that she was just as shocked as she seemed when the investigators and the bailiffs descended on us.

But by the same token, none of Dad's business associates betrayed him. He was unmasked when a new Minister of Defense took over and for her own political purposes forced a really serious audit.

But that was the thing: Dad had lost—I don't know a better word for what had happened—despite not trusting anyone. And I simply didn't want to live that way.

Sure, I could go off with Lal on my own without arousing suspicion in anybody but Abram himself (and maybe not even in him). He might be able to help, though; and anyway I just wanted to let him know what I was thinking.

Etzil's was a narrow frontage between a pair of large shops catering to spacers with clothing, cheap jewelry, and personal weapons. Etzil had a satellite location, though, a combination of marquee and shed on an outcrop closer to the water. A sheet of structural plastic formed a floor flat enough for chairs, but because of the rock, nobody came ashore there.

We took a table and were waited on by a boy younger than Abram. When he had scampered back to the main building to fetch our wine and food, I first nodded to Abram, then said to Lal, "I want to get off planet."

"I'd say you were sitting pretty," Lal said. "Why would you want to leave?"

"He doesn't belong here," said Abram unexpectedly. "There's some from the big worlds that really take to it—Guido, the War Chief, he's from Pantellaria, and the vizier of Eski Marakech is from Pleasaunce itself. But Roy here"—he nodded to me—"is scheming to get away. And some other stuff too, I shouldn't wonder. He'll lose his wedding tackle if he's not lucky."

I didn't say anything, but my heart was a block of ice.

"Well, you're out of luck if you think one of the captains is going to sign you on," Lal said to me. "Even Hakim. He'd have been glad to have you before, but now that you're the Admiral's slave he won't touch you. He wouldn't be able to come back to Salaam if he did, and even if he was willing to lift out of some place else it wouldn't do you any good. The admirals all stick together that much—they won't harbor each other's run slaves."

"What about other planets?" I said. My hopes were melting. "I could pay well."

"Where do you suppose a ship from ben Yusuf could land and not everybody aboard be hanged?" Lal said. "*I* don't know of anyplace."

Our orders came. The food was a thick fish stew spread on a trencher of barley bread. We ate with spoons and our hands. It was the best meal I'd had on ben Yusuf, and I'm not complaining about Martial's food.

"If you had enough money..." Abram said, wiping his mouth with the back of his hand. "You could buy a ship."

"And then what?" said Lal. "Oh, sure, Roy could captain it and maybe work it alone—I don't believe that, but maybe he could. But where's he going then? To Blanchard or St. Julien? They'd more likely shoot him when he opened the airlock than they'd start cheering about his escape. If it's a bigger place that has a guard ship, you won't get out of orbit."

"Yeah," said Abram without the animation of a moment before. "Anybody arriving on a cutter from ben Yusuf is a pirate when he reaches anywhere else."

"That's not what I wanted to hear," I said, scraping a spoonful of sopped bread from my trencher. I think I sounded calm. I sounded calmer than I felt anyway.

"Look..." said Lal. "If I knew a way, I'd tell you. You saved my life, Roy. I'll do anything I can for you."

"Boss, I don't want you to leave Salaam, believe me," Abram said earnestly. "But you'll die if you stay here. I won't turn you in but somebody will. So you better get out or quit looking at the wives.... And I don't know how you can get out."

Etzil's wine wasn't very good, but we drank a lot more of it before Lal went off to his room and Abram led me to the palace. On the way back I said, "Abram, why do you think I've been looking at the place you said?"

I didn't want to use the words. I didn't think anybody passing in the street would hear enough to be a problem, but I'd been *sure* that nobody could see the display when I was using it.

Abram looked at me. "Look, boss, I didn't know what you were doing and I figured I ought to," he said. "The way you were acting, there was more than just money."

He grinned. "You don't care about money," he said. "You could make a lot more easy, but you don't bother."

"I suppose that's true," I said. "But how did you see a display that was focused just for me?"

"I rigged a mirror on the pillar in front of me," Abram said. "I watched your fingers move. I can't read, but I'm good on motion. And when you were asleep, I did what you'd been doing. If anybody'd asked, I'd have said I was doing it for you—but nobody asked. But when I got the place you mostly went to—"

He put his hand on my arm and stopped me where we were, twenty feet from the gate of the palace. In an even softer voice than before, he continued, "I glanced at it and then I shut down. I never want to see that again. No matter how bad Giorgios needs you, he'll have you impaled and probably me too if he ever gets a whiff of what you're doing."

I took a deep breath. "I'm sorry, Abram," I said. "If you want to get a long way away from me before anything happens, I won't blame you. But I'm not going to quit. And I'm going to get her away with me. Somehow."

Chapter Twenty-one

I'd say that the lunch with Lal had changed my life, but it really didn't. It just sort of reinforced my plan to keep on doing things the way I was.

Particularly about trusting Abram. The worst Giorgios and the Admiral would do if Abram told them I was planning to escape would be to put me in shackles, but if Abram had told them what he'd figured out on his own—that I was spying on the wives—my punishment wouldn't have stopped till I was dead.

I kept watching the wives, but mostly I kept watching Monica. She didn't belong as the Admiral's wife, any more than I belonged as his slave. Maybe that was part of what was eating at me about Monica, the fact we were unfairly in the same boat, but I don't kid myself that I'd have thought about her so much if she'd been old and ugly. I try to be a person I can smile at when I look in the mirror, but I never wanted to be a saint.

There was plenty of work to do. I was combining the week's

food order—I wouldn't put it all with the same broker, but bulk still gave me more leverage than I'd have had otherwise—when Abram brought me into the present by ringing the triangle.

I shut down and turned as the chamberlain entered the gallery. I didn't see Giorgios very often except when he was passing through, to and from his own apartments. He was so willing to leave the console to me that he didn't seem to look at it.

"We've bought a lemon tree," he said, sounding flustered. "It's being delivered this afternoon,"

I'd gotten up, clearing the couch for Giorgios. "Yes, sir?" I said politely. I couldn't imagine why he was upset by a purchase which didn't sound particularly major. Nobody'd submitted an invoice yet, so I couldn't be quite sure of that.

"It's for the wives' garden!" Giorgios said. "The Admiral will be here shortly to unlock the alley entrance! Is the console working properly?"

"It's working perfectly," I said. "I was just checking the food orders, but there's no rush on that."

"Oh, thank the Great God," said Giorgios. "I'm always afraid that it will fail again and I'll be blamed!"

"I'll keep out of the way, then," I said calmly. "I didn't know there was an alley entrance."

I bowed to Giorgios, then slipped through what was left of the usual gathering of spectators. Most of them had disappeared as soon as they'd heard that the Admiral was coming.

Abram followed without me needing to call him. I'm not sure whether he was coming with me or just dodging the Admiral.

"Let's see Martial," I said, though what I really meant was "Let's go outside."

When we got through the main entrance, Abram gestured to the left. Martial's diner would have been to the right.

"I figured you wanted to know about the alley entrance," Abram said. "There's a bit of a plaza at this end of the alley—there's a common well. That'll let us watch without, you know, getting caught up in it."

"I'm glad you're on my side," I said. That was the truth if I'd ever spoken it.

There were lots of people in the plaza, which was a flagstoned triangle with a street on one side and the sides of buildings built askew on the other two. There wasn't any furniture, but a pair of local trees grew in terracotta pots which were as sturdy as the dry stone well curb.

We sat on the edge of a pot, and Abram began trimming the callus on his left heel with his long knife. The three men who'd been standing nearby moved away.

"They're house slaves," he said. "They're just here with the women—"

He nodded in the direction of the well where heavily bundled-up women stood gossiping.

"Down the alley there is where they'll be bringing in the tree."

Six guards with impellers and wearing edged weapons stood in the middle of the narrow passage. They were led by an officer wearing a fur cap above which nodded a long feather dyed bright blue.

"There's a tunnel through the wing and into the little garden just for the wives," Abram said. "There's no door through the wall between the courtyard and the wives' garden. Food and stuff you can bring into the wing through the regular passages, but this is a tree."

A pair of motorized platforms came up the street from the direction of the bay. They looked like the one Giorgios used when he went out, but they were linked back to back. A tree with a cloth-wrapped root ball rode the join. Men stood on either side, bracing the trunk with their hands.

"I wonder why the Admiral uses the cameras to watch what he could be right there in person watching," I said. I *had* wondered, and this was a chance to discuss it with the one person on ben Yusuf I could do that with.

Abram snorted. "Hey, he's getting on," he said. "He's fat, he drinks, and he's bored. I don't guess the wives get much personal attention, though you'd know that better'n me. If he can't do it himself, he can still get a kick out of peeping at what the women get up to on their own."

I thought about it. "I suppose," I said.

Certainly the Admiral didn't visit any of his wives' rooms often. I didn't watch what happened during those visits, but from the determination with which several of the women tried to entice him, he wasn't terribly interested in sex.

Giorgios arrived from the other end of the alley. When he gave an order, a guard grasped the door handle—it was a U of reinforcing rod welded onto the metal door—and tugged. Another guard joined him before the panel started to open, but it took a third man to actually haul it fully back.

The crew who'd arrived with the tree lifted it down on its wooden framework, then carried it into the passage. There were half a dozen of them, but two carried shovels and a pick from the vehicle.

"There's another door on the garden end," Abram said. "Boutros, he's one of the geldings, he told me. There's no key lock, just the console that only the Admiral can work."

He looked at me and raised an eyebrow. "Except maybe you can too, can you?" he added.

I shrugged. "I ought to be able to," I said. "I haven't looked for a lock control on the console, though."

The guards and workmen finally came out of the passage. The last one was Giorgios. I turned my head away, but Abram didn't bother to. The chamberlain seemed to have paid attention only to the door as the guards forced it shut with a loud clang.

The workmen rode off on their vehicle. Giorgios and most of the guards waited near the closed door, but one man scampered past us and continued up the street toward the front of the palace.

"They've gotta tell the Admiral to lock it again," Abram said. "I hear that some places, they got radios to do that from a ways away. Is that true?"

"That's true," I agreed. Then I said, "Abram, would you be able to find me some penetrating oil and a pry bar?"

"Yeah," he said. "If you were crazy enough to want them."

I heard another clang from down the alley, sharper and lighter than that of the door itself being closed. This must have been the electronic bolt being shot home by the console. Giorgios and the remainder of the guards walked off, going in the other direction.

"I'm that crazy," I said.

* * *

I wasn't going to do anything until I saw a way of doing everything I needed. It was a case of one step at a time, but most steps had to be in different directions rather than marching straight toward a goal.

I daubed the three massive hinges of the alley door with penetrating oil, but then I reentered the palace and hid the remainder of the can of penetrating oil in the framework from which Giorgios' bed curtains hung. I could retrieve it easily there, but even if it were found it didn't point to me.

When Giorgios next came past my alcove, I stopped him. "Sir?" I said. "Was the Admiral pleased with the way I've kept the console in operating condition?"

"Yes, everything went well," the chamberlain said. He looked a little worried, which is what I intended when I brought up the console and the fact it depended on me.

"Good," I said. "Good. I want to attend the sale of slaves this afternoon, sir."

"You do?" Giorgios said. His mild worry had risen to alarm. "Ah. I suppose you're planning to buy a slave of your own. Slaves, perhaps?"

"I'm just considering possibilities, sir," I said. It was normal for slaves of some rank to own slaves themselves. Generally it was a mark of status, though I'd run into cases where a slave official's slaves did all the official's work.

To make sure Giorgios was getting the point, I said, "I think I'll have to continue doing all the computer work, though. This console is remarkably finicky, and I regularly have to reset it when it locks up. I could never train somebody who could keep it going."

"Well, there's no reason you shouldn't buy a slave," Giorgios said. "Ah, and you can come to me if you need someone to guarantee your credit with the auctioneer."

He strode quickly into his bedroom. I bowed respectfully to his back, then said to Abram, "Let's go watch an auction."

"Suits me," Abram said. "Though I don't know what you want a slave for."

I didn't. What I wanted was a look at—and just possibly a meeting with—the Karst consul.

Slaves were sold at the top of the swale near the underground prison. There were stone seats and a permanent roof of structural plastic for spectators.

There was nothing for the prisoners, unless you counted the tower which mounted an automatic impeller. It was sited on the back side of the bleachers, which struck me as odd until I realized that from this location the muzzle couldn't be lowered enough to bear on the customers. Given the quality of the guards I'd seen in Salaam, that was a wise precaution.

They'd started to bring out the prisoners by the time we arrived. They were in groups of five roped together at the right ankle. Guards were linking them as they climbed a ladder from the pit. None of them looked in great shape even without bonds, but I suppose the Admiral saw no reason to take chances.

We climbed four levels of seats, above the audience already in place. Those seated on the bottom row had come with cushions. Two of the four principals had brought attendants.

"The high mucky-mucks down there're the consuls," Abram whispered. "That's Platt from Karst on the right and the woman on the left's Kimber or Kimley, something like that, from the Alliance. The two in the middle are the Solitan League and the Sworn Brotherhood. They're each three worlds, but they don't count for much."

The Alliance consul was the only woman visible. Platt was taller than me but he looked worn. His curly hair was obviously dyed and had receded high up his forehead. My first glance wasn't encouraging, but it seemed that he might be what I had to work with.

I looked at the woman from the Alliance. There was no legal connection there, but maybe her gender would help? The thing was, I'd met plenty of women doing jobs that mostly were handled by men. From what I'd seen—and I was an outsider, I know—most of them were harder on other women than a man would have been. I guess they were just proving they weren't soft.

The first gang of slaves shuffled in front of the stands. They were looking down and sometimes shielding their eyes with their hands: The roof didn't cover them.

"Five spacers from the ship *Hentzau*," the auctioneer called. He was in the chancellor's division, a man named Albert. I knew him slightly because he chose to buy meals from Martial instead of eating with his own division. "All sound in limb."

Two men in the second row bid against one another without enthusiasm. The lot was sold at 120 piasters per person. Guards shuffled the slaves off to the other end, where groups of attendants waited. An aide to the successful bidder jotted notes, as did Albert's assistant.

"They're both off-planet labor contractors," Abram explained. "They're putting together gangs to ship out of Eski Marakech."

Another group was offered. This time an old man seated just below us with a grandson asked for a closer examination. He looked at the spacers—also from the *Hentzau*—individually, demanding they open their mouths. He finally offered 200 piasters on the second man in line. No one bid against him, though the other labor contractor bought the remainder of the coffle at 110 apiece.

These were men just like me. It bothered me a little that I was thinking of them as items of trade—as I would think of shovels or bags of barley being bought for the palace. I don't suppose it mattered. I *wasn't* buying them, even buying them for the palace.

Giorgios had an assistant to purchase labor. That fellow, Ali son of Ali, wasn't present today.

I said to Abram, "How about me? I wasn't paraded like those fellows."

"Oh, I heard about that," he said. "That was really hush-hush, you know? Giorgios did a deal with the cutter's captain who took you, cash under the table. The chancellor didn't get his cut, but maybe Giorgios squared him."

Abram looked at me and grinned. "I guess he had to pay pretty well to get an expert on the console like you, huh?" he said.

"I don't know what he paid," I said. "It was off-book like you figure, so I haven't found it in the records. I think he paid in Alliance thalers."

I didn't argue about being called an expert on the console. In Salaam, that's what I was.

The third group came up to bid. Albert hadn't more than stated, "Five spacers from the *S611* out of Rupert's Planet," when the tall man at the head of the line put his arms akimbo.

"I am a citizen of Bryce!" he called, looking from one consul to the other. "I'm being improperly held!"

Albert turned to the woman. "Mistress Kimber?" he said. "This spacer was a member of the crew of *S611*, which is registered on Rupert's Planet. Salaam has no treaty with Rupert's Planet."

"That's a lie!" said the spacer. "I'm Gus Andre and I was a passenger on *S611*, not crew!"

"Master Albert?" said the woman. Two of her aides were whispering together as one consulted his personal data unit. "What evidence do you have that this man was crew and not a passenger?"

"The *S611* didn't have facilities for passengers," said Albert, pulling a hardcopy document from his scrip. "Just bunks for the crew."

"I slept in a bunk," Andre said, "but I wasn't crew!"

"Do you have the ship's log showing that Andre was enrolled in the crew?" Kimber demanded.

"I don't have record of that, no," Albert said. Before the consul could speak again, Albert gestured to one of the escorting guards. "Release this man to the care of the Alliance consul."

An attendant separated the freed man from the rest of the coffle by using shears to snip the light rope which attached his ankle to a heavy hawser. He tried to run over to the consul with his arms outstretched, but one of her aides intercepted him and led him off to the side where attendants waited.

Bidding began on the remainder of the coffle.

"Are there any women?" I asked Abram.

"They're sold separately," he said. "They're kept in that building with the yellow window frames."

He gestured back toward the town proper. The barred windows didn't set it off from other houses.

"And the really pretty ones don't come to public auction anyway," Abram continued. "The chancellor holds a private sale for high rollers. But say, look—if you want a woman, I can find you plenty of stuff that's just as good as what comes off captured ships. Except maybe hair color—real blond is hard, but I could keep an eye out."

"Thank you, Abram," I said, "but it was just curiosity. I like to know things, but I'm not looking for a woman."

"If you've got problems with buying one, there's a lot of fathers I could introduce you to," Abram said. "You're a big man, Roy, even though you don't put on side. There's a lot of girls who'd really like to be your woman."

Arguing with him didn't do any good, so I concentrated on the new line of prisoners shuffling in. The man in the middle was arguing with the guards. When he reached the display area he called to the consuls, "I'm from Andover and I was a passenger on the *Regenswelt*! A passenger!"

"This man is Thom Burris, crewman on the *Regenswelt* out of Grantholm," Albert said, reading from his hardcopy. "He has spacers' tattoos."

"Those aren't spacers' tattoos!" Burris shouted. "Ariel is my girlfriend, not a ship! Well, she was. I've never been in space except as a passenger, and I was on my way back home

224

when you bastards caught the *Regenswelt* in orbit!"

The consul for the Sworn Brotherhood got to his feet and said, "Master Albert, tattoos are common on Andover. There's nothing about Master Burris' tattoo to suggest he's anything but a healthy young man with a girlfriend."

Albert glanced at his hardcopy again, then looked up and said, "Appeal denied. Five spacers, one missing three fingers of his left hand. What am I offered?"

"I protest!" the consul shouted.

"You can't do this!" said Burris.

Albert said nothing to the consul. To the nearest guard he said, "Silence the prisoner so that I can get on with the auction."

The guard had a thick-bladed cutlass instead of an impeller. He chopped at Burris' head with the flat. The prisoner got his hands up, but the edge scraped his forearm. He staggered back and fell.

The guard moved forward, but Albert said, "That's enough." To the consul he added, "You can make a protest to your government if you like. When the auction closes, I'll give you a note as to where the man has been sold for you to pursue it if you like."

The sale proceeded. I said to Abram, "I don't see how Albert could be so certain. A tattoo doesn't seem much evidence the fellow was a crewman."

Abram shrugged and said, "The Sworn Brotherhood has maybe three gunboats and a very old destroyer if they get everything together. The consul would have to send the message off through Eski Marakech, which would take a good month. Whereas the Alliance could have a standby squadron here in six weeks and stay long enough to screw everybody on ben Yusuf's life up. They wouldn't land troops themself, but they might make it hot enough for the other admirals to make a change in who was running Salaam."

"I see," I said.

As the next coffle was arriving, I tapped Abram on the arm. "I guess I've seen enough," I said.

We got up and headed back for the palace. The delivery from Roussel should be made this afternoon. I wanted to see Monica unwrap the sauces she'd ordered

Chapter Twenty-two

Abram and I stopped at Martial's for a meal and a chat with laborers at the bottom echelon of the palace. I had a pasty and wine watered at my request; Abram drank his wine straight and had a second glass besides. I'd have needed help getting up the stairs if I'd done that.

The wine Martial served us was quite strong. I don't know what the rest of his customers ate, but there was meat in my pasty. I'm pretty sure the other diners got a filling of lentils and rice; which, with the sauce it was cooked with, would have been very good.

Two of those eating turned out to be gardeners who'd helped plant the new lemon tree. I treated them to an extra glass each and said, "Do you fellows have to tend the tree now that it's in the ground?"

"Naw," said Omar, the senior man. "The girls're going to do that, Setne says."

The other man, Carlo, said, "Setne's our foreman. Which

means he sits on his butt in the shade and watches us work."

Omar said, "Well, I guess they can pour a bucket of water on it every day. And when it sets fruit, they can pick it."

We chatted a little longer, then went upstairs. Abram hadn't said anything during the meal, but his very silence showed that he was worried. Normally after a couple glasses of wine, he'd be chattering like a magpie.

When I got to the console, the first thing I did was enter the day's invoices. They included the order from Roussel, who specialized in exotic items. These generally had to be ordered and bought from off planet and imported through Eski Marakech, which added several levels of delay and expense to the process.

I'd noticed a repeated order for Saguntine pepper sauce for the Wives' Wing. The only person from Saguntum in that wing was Monica Smith. Supposedly Saguntum was covered by treaty with ben Yusuf, so there shouldn't have been any Saguntines in the palace except by their own will.

Monica was certainly not here by her own will.

I checked the camera in her room. She wasn't present, but in the corner of her bed was the box which had contained the sauces. It sat upended to display the bottom. On the fiberboard was printed the word YES in large black letters. As best as I could tell on the screen, she'd written with kohl eyeliner and a brush.

I switched to one of the pair of cameras on the wives' garden. Three of the wives sat on the shaded side. A pair of female servants served them cool drinks, and a eunuch waved a feather fan without enthusiasm in front of Derega—a local wife, but very delicate in her tastes.

Monica sat against the opposite wall, reading. She was backed deep into the plantings there, though they included hollies with prickly leaves. The foliage protected all but her lower legs from the sun; she was wearing loose trousers and slippers with long stockings.

Her head was within six inches of the door to the tunnel by which the tree had been brought in.

I took a deep breath. This might work or it might not, but it was as good a time as any. I unlocked the electronic bolts, then got up and said to Abram, "You might want to stay here. Or go someplace else with lots of witnesses."

"I'll come along," he said with a sour expression. "For a smart man, Roy, you act like a bloody fool sometimes."

I didn't argue with him.

I took the pry bar, which I didn't expect to need, and a screwdriver which I did. I don't know what Abram had besides the knife, but he laid that open in his lap as he squatted beside the alley door.

"I'll tap when I'm ready to come out," I said with my hand on the strap handle. "If somebody's in the alley, you ring something metal on the panel and I wait."

"What if it's the Admiral's soldiers and they want in?" Abram said. I don't think he was really worried about that, but he was in a sour mood and determined to put a dark wash on everything.

"Let them try," I said, shrugging. "There's a sliding bolt on my side."

Of course, in that case I'd have to leave through the Wives' Wing. I just might be able to make it alive, but I had no way of getting out of Salaam, let alone off planet.

There was no one in the alley. I pulled the door open with my left hand. It was a strain, but the penetrating oil had worked. The bar was in my right hand, but that was partly in case somebody was waiting in the passage—which of course there wasn't. I closed the massive panel behind me; and because Abram had made a point about it, I shot the sliding bolt.

The passage was unlighted. I hadn't brought a light with me because the passage was straight and the walls were smooth. I shuffled ahead with my left fingertips on the wall and the bar outstretched in front of me like a steel cane. It touched the interior door with a faint *chink*.

I set the bar down and felt for the view panel, suddenly wishing I'd brought a light after all. There was a slot-head screw in each corner of the cover plate. I'd lubed each of them on my first visit to the passage, but I hadn't come back to open them.

I fitted the screwdriver, gripped the handle with both hands, and leaned against the butt to keep it in contact. To my great relief, the first three cracked free when I turned them out.

When I started to turn the last one, the plate itself swung down as the screwhead loosened. The screech of rusted metal probably wasn't loud anywhere but in the sealed passage, but despite my startlement I was also relieved that I'd been able to open the thing. I hadn't really been sure until it happened.

"Are you there?" a girl asked from the other side of the heavy screen. "Can you get me out of here? I can pay well!"

"I'm here," I said, looking out at the back of a blond head.

"But getting you out is going to take a while. I plan to do it."

"Can you watch for anyone coming up behind me?" the woman said. She got up and turned her wicker chair around, then sat down again facing where I stood. Her lips were farther away, but I could see them—which really would help me understand her words.

"Who are you?" Monica said. "And how were you able to send me a message in the package of hot sauce?"

"Look, I'm a friend," I said. "And I want to get you out of here, but it takes planning."

I was afraid to tell her my name. I didn't know whether she was the sort to blurt things to friends or scream threats to an enemy; and anyway, it wouldn't help her to know.

From what I'd seen from the cameras, Monica was about as solid as I could wish for. I was still afraid.

The note was simple enough. I had gone to Roussel with the latest specialty order and told him to place it under the four bottles of Saguntine pepper sauce. If he did so without opening it, there would be a hundred piasters cash as soon as I was sure.

The note said:

> If you want to get out, write YES on a card and place it where the camera in your room can see it. Then sit in the garden near the door through which the lemon tree came in. It may take some days for me to respond.
>
> If this note has been opened, write NO. I'll find another way.

"All right," said Monica. She swallowed. "How can I help?"

I could see to the cross wall past her blond head, but the opening was fairly narrow. It was possible that someone could approach from the side without me seeing them. That would require walking in the direct sun, but I still worried.

Monica may have thought the same thing. She grinned and raised her open book slightly. "I've begun mumbling the words when I read," she said. "It won't surprise anyone. Only three of the other wives can read at all."

"Getting us off planet is going to be very hard," I said. "You're a Saguntine citizen, though, so you're covered by treaty. I could get you to the Karst consul, and he could get you back to Saguntum."

"No!" Monica said, loud enough that she started herself. She turned her head to see if anybody else had heard her. Apparently not, because she faced me again and said, "He already knows I'm here. He won't help. He doesn't dare help!"

"All right," I said. That wasn't what I'd wanted to hear but I'd have to take her word for it. "I'll work something else out."

"Marc is coming over with a glass of sherbet!" Monica said, her voice dropping to a hiss. "When can we talk again?"

"Keep coming here," I said. "I don't know how long it'll take."

I swung the plate up over the screen. I fitted in a second screw with my fingers because I didn't want to touch metal to metal while a eunuch might be right outside.

Back to square one. Well, I'd get there.

We'd get there.

* * *

On the way around toward the palace entrance, I said to Abram, "Do you know anything about the Karst consul?"

"Platt?" He snorted. "Nothing that makes me want to know him better. What are you after?"

"Anything you can get," I said. "Everything."

Despite Monica's violent response, it seemed to me that Platt was the best place to start. All I could find on the console about him was his rank, where he lived, and how many soldiers—six—were assigned for his protection.

Foreigners generally had official guards with them when they went out. Most of Salaam was what would be called a slum on any civilized world, and the locals were likely to blame foreigners rather than accept the responsibility themselves. I'd been told there'd been riots in the past, but all that I'd heard of during my weeks on ben Yusuf were cases of stone throwing directed at merchants from off planet.

I wore the feathered red cap of the palace, and mostly I was with Abram. I hadn't had any trouble.

I'd switched to going over the food deliveries, figuring my portion. It was about time for me to canvas the suppliers to pick up the cash I was owed. As a result I'd forgotten about Platt when Abram reappeared at my side.

"Want to meet a couple guys?" he said when I'd paused and looked at him.

"Sure," I said. "Where and when?"

"Right now," Abram said. "And down to Etzil's, if that's all right."

"Sure," I said, rising from the console.

"Ah, this might cost something, you know," Abram added with a frown.

"That's all right too," I said as we headed for the stairs.

I was carrying several thousand piasters in my money belt. Ben Yusuf didn't have scrip or a real credit-banking system, but I was going to have to find something to do with my earnings pretty soon or I'd weigh too much to move around. Abram would probably have a suggestion.

I'd just started my graft to give me pocket money, but it'd taken off almost by itself. I wondered what my dad would have thought?

What *I* thought was that I ought to be ashamed of myself. I was stealing candy from babies, it was so easy. But I *had* to have money to get off planet, and this was the only way a slave could get it.

The cafe was more crowded than it had been the first time I'd visited, but Etzil had moved other tables to a distance from the one the boy led us to. One of the two men already sitting there looked enough like Abram that they could have been related; the other was a foreigner whom I recalled sitting beside Platt during the slave auction.

They already had wine in front of them. I waited till the boy served me and Abram, then said, "I'm hoping you gentlemen can give me information about Consul Platt. Can you?"

"I guess we can," said the local. "Whether we will or not, that's something else."

"Yeah," said the other man. "We work for the Karst consul so the Admiral doesn't have any authority over us."

"You'd be compensated for anything you told me," I said, giving them a friendly smile. "And so long as you never leave the consulate, you're absolutely correct about the Admiral's authority."

I paused and added, "His *legal* authority."

"Look, what is it you want to know?" the local said.

I shrugged. "Start with the house," I said. "How's it arranged?"

I didn't see how that could help me, but it was all grist for the mill. Besides, it got them talking and allowed me to pay them for something that looked harmless. That would lubricate the process.

"Well, it's split in half," the local said. "Half is consulate, but the other half's where Platt lives with his family. They got a separate entrance."

"Family?" I said. I hadn't thought of that.

"Wife and three kids," the local said. "She's from Karst too, and a nastier bitch I don't want to meet."

"He deserves her," said the other man. "He figures he can treat me any bloody way he pleases because I can't get off planet without him."

"I suppose that'd take a lot of money?" I said.

"Too bloody right!" he said. "Over a thousand pi, to get to Eski Marakech and buy passage on a freighter there."

"Platt has a local squeeze on the official side," the local said. "He changes her every six months or so."

"I suppose the wife knows?" I said. "Servants talk, I mean."

"Hell yes, they talk!" the other man said. "Besides, she's having it off with the chauffeur, so it's not like she's got a complaint."

I put a hundred-piaster coin in the middle of the table, then thought for a moment and slid it in front of the local man and brought a similar coin out. That one I put in front of the other man.

"Go on," I said. "They're yours."

Their hands swept up the coins like lizards snapping flies. They looked at me. The local said, "That's all you wanted to know?"

"No," I said, smiling again. "I believe that the consulate has a master computer. Is that so?"

The local said, "Yeah, Abram said you'd probably want to know about that. That's why I brought Ajax here."

The other man swallowed. "I run the console," he said.

"Can you give me electronic access to it?" I said. "Passwords, encryption—whatever I need to make full use of it?"

The two men looked at one another. "For how much?" the local said.

"Five hundred to Ajax right here," I said. "After I've entered successfully, another fifteen hundred piasters to Ajax and"—I grinned at the local—"a thousand for you as a finder's fee."

"Bloody hell," Ajax murmured.

"He's a genius with the console!" Abram said, sounding like he meant it. If I'd really been a computer genius, I wouldn't need the information I was buying. On the other hand, I had a good idea of what money could buy and how to buy those things.

"How quickly can you get me the information?" I asked, taking coins out of my belt. I had them in pockets of five hundred piasters each.

"How quick can you pay us?" the local said.

"I'll give you both your money," I said, "as soon as I've entered Platt's computer successfully."

I set the stack of five hundred-piaster coins in front of Ajax, but I kept my finger on top of it. "So," I said, meeting his eyes. "Do we have a deal?"

Ajax licked his lips and said, "Yeah, we got a deal. I'll go back and get the codes. I can't do it off the toppa my head. And look, I can't get you into the consulate anyway!"

"No problem," I said, taking my finger off the coins and making a brushing motion with my hand toward Ajax. "You can give the information to Abram to bring back to me. I'll give him the money for you as soon as it's worked."

"I don't want him to have our money!" the local man said.

I shrugged. "All right, I'll come down and pay you myself in the alley behind the palace," I said. "Or you can come up to the chamberlain's suite if you like. Abram can get you in, I'm sure."

I crooked an eyebrow. Abram nodded solemnly.

Ajax swallowed. "Okay," he said, sweeping up the money. "Abram can come with me now. I'll write the codes down and come back with him. I'll wait in the alley while he runs it up to you."

"*We'll* wait in the alley," the local man said. "And don't screw around! Come right back with the money!"

Or what? I thought, but I had no intention of stiffing them. "As soon as the codes work," I said, nodding.

I went back to the palace and got to work. I liked to be seen at the console when Giorgios made one of his occasional passes through, though after my first few days on the job he'd never spoken to me about what I was doing.

Orders were entered, directed to the proper vendors, marked as delivered, and paid as quickly as an invoice could work its way through the chancellor's office. Which wasn't very quickly, but that was outside my department.

It seemed that so long as the job was getting done, the chamberlain didn't care how that was happening. I'd been cheerful the few times he came by, but I wasn't exactly welcoming. He was free to do anything he could on the console, but that was bloody little; and I didn't set out to train him to do additional things.

I was lost in maintenance accounts when Abram reappeared. He got my attention by stepping so close that he was almost leaning into the projected image. I raised a finger for attention, shut down what I was doing, and said, "What do you have?"

He handed me a piece of paper, the inside of a wrapper from a container of toiletries from Karst. "They're in a hurry," he said.

"They'll wait," I said as I began the process of connecting with the computer in the Karst consulate.

Salaam didn't really have an internet, but there were wired connections from the four off-planet consulates to the palace, as well as a connection between the palace and the Admiralty, which was the headquarters of the War Leader who would command the community's ships in event of open warfare.

That would only come about if another planet attacked ben Yusuf, which hadn't happened in living memory. It was less expensive to make treaties with the pirate cities and pay tribute—it was called "indemnities"—for the privilege of placing consuls to safeguard captured citizens.

I had my own opinion of that, but it was a political question and the Olfetries weren't politicians. I'd joined—tried to join—the RCN, though, which I guess was my answer to the question.

I reached the Karst computer, which I hadn't been sure of

doing, and keyed in the initial password—Demetrian. The site responded, albeit slowly.

"I wonder why Demetrian?" I muttered, mostly to myself.

Abram was standing close. He said, "That's Ajax's name, his last name. Why?"

I looked at him. "It's the password," I said. "Can you read, Abram?"

"Naw, it didn't seem worth the effort," he said. He tried not to sound defensive, but he turned his face away as he spoke.

"It's the main password for the computer," I said. "I don't think being able to read gains anybody much on ben Yusuf, no."

If I were going to stay, I'd see to it that somebody taught Abram to read. I looked at the computer directory, then opened the subdirectory marked CONSULATE. It required the second of three numerical passwords which Ajax had written under Demetrian.

It was an inventory of consulate equipment. It included a ship, the *Alfraz*.

I got up. "Let's go give our friends their pay, Abram," I said. "They've earned it."

Chapter Twenty-three

My money belt was a lot lighter as Ajax and his buddy walked out of the alley, but that didn't matter. I had no use for ben Yusuf money except to get off ben Yusuf, and I still had this week's round of the suppliers to make.

We were alone in the alley, so it was a good place to talk. "Abram," I said. "There's a ship in the harbor named the *Alfraz*. I want to know what its status is, what crew; everything you can about it."

"I don't know nuffing about ships," Abram said, frowning.

I grimaced, but it was the truth. Asking a layman to investigate a specialized subject wasn't a good way to learn things.

"Find out what you can," I said. "They main thing I want to know is how much it'd take to get the ship ready to lift. And say—is Lal still around?"

"I can ask," Abram said. "He was in a spacers' hostel because he doesn't have family in Salaam."

"I'd like to see him," I said. "Ah, Abram? Would it be possible for me to get a pistol here? I don't want one right now, but could I?"

"I guess," said Abram. He looked like I'd told him to smother his pet dog. "It'll cost you something, but I guess you don't care about that."

"No, I don't," I said calmly. Abram sounded bitter. I could imagine several reasons, but frankly they didn't matter. I wasn't behaving the way he wanted me to, and he wasn't willing to accept that it was none of his business.

"Hey boss?" he said, looking up suddenly. "How many men does it take to crew a spaceship?"

"It depends," I said, "but half a dozen would be an ordinary short crew for a civilian ship. The one I was captured on had a crew of five."

"Well, I'll see if I can turn up Lal," Abram said. "Since that's what you want."

When I didn't walk with him toward the alley mouth, he stopped and said, "You're not coming?"

"Not just yet," I said.

"You're a *bloody* fool," he said and went off.

I opened the alley door and slipped into the passage. I'd seen Monica through the garden camera when Abram called me down to meet Platt's servants. I'd stuck the screwdriver in my pocket then.

I removed the upper screw—I'd only put one back of the three I'd taken off originally—and the cover plate rotated clear. The sound was part squeal, part scrape.

"Oh, thank the heavens!" Monica said, jolted alert in her chair. She was facing the opening when I peered through. "Where have you been?"

"Working to get you free, mistress," I said, polite but feeling a little miffed. It seemed to me obvious that this was a major job and that I had better things to do than chat with her.

Though I'd really been looking forward to chatting with her again. And now I was doing that, and she was snarling at me.

"Look, I've just spent thirty-two hundred piasters toward getting you free," I said. "I don't care about the money, but that ought to show you that it's taking a lot of effort to get there. It's going to take a good deal more time, too. If I try to cut corners, I'm going to get caught. Then you'll be here until you rot, and I'll be screaming my lungs out as they slide me down on a stake. Okay?"

"Oh, I'm sorry," the girl said. "I can make up the money to you if we just get to a civilized planet. I'm just—oh, it's awful and I'm losing my *mind*!"

"If you throw a hissie now, you're going to get noticed," I said, as calm as I could. Her nervousness was getting me wound up. "Just keep calm and we'll get out of here. It'll just take a while."

"All right," she said, her face lowered. She looked up again. "I'll be all right now. I'm sorry."

"Well, I just wanted you to know that things are moving even if you don't see anything for a while," I said. "Ah...look. I take your word that Platt isn't going to do his job, but I think he'd do pretty much anything for money. I'd really like to approach him with that in mind."

Monica looked straight at my grating but didn't speak for a moment. Then she said, quietly but very distinctly, "Platt raped me when I was brought here. He and the Admiral together. That's why I'm sure that Platt will do anything to stop me from getting back to my father."

Ah. I swallowed. "Yes, I see," I said.

Before I could figure out what to say next, Monica said, "You've been watching me on the cameras, haven't you?"

"I've watched you, yes," I said. That was obvious, after all. "I'm sorry. I'll stop doing it."

She sounded calm. I hope I did too. She said, "Tell me about yourself. I can't see anything of you."

Since there were no lights in the passage, she wouldn't have been able to see my face even if the grating hadn't been there.

I said, "I'm a slave. I'm twenty."

I swallowed again and said, "My name's Roylan Olfetrie and I'm from Cinnabar. The chamberlain bought me to run the palace computer."

There was no point in hiding my name when she could find out who I was easy enough from what I'd told her already. Things could go wrong, but I no longer imagined that she might blurt my name by accident.

"I'm going back upstairs now," I said. "There's other ways to get us off planet, but I've got a lot of work to do."

Monica nodded. She said, "Thank you, Roy. And I'd like you to continue watching my room. It's the only way I can let you know if an emergency occurs."

She looked like a queen. I said, "All right," and raised the cover plate again.

* * *

I spent the next several hours investigating the Karst computer. With the exception of Ajax and Madame Platt's maid, all the personnel were locals.

Their vehicle was a six-place ground car, manufactured on Pleasaunce twenty years ago. I learned that from the parts orders—parts were a huge problem. The chauffeur seemed to be the mechanic also. He regularly put in reimbursement requests for locally made alternatives to the Pleasaunce originals.

There was almost nothing about the *Alfraz*, however. It could be that there was a computer sector I couldn't find or even a separate computer dealing with the ship. More likely, the *Alfraz* was simply rusting somewhere in the harbor.

When I originally thought of bribing Platt to get me and Monica off planet, I'd thought it would be expensive. That was all right—I could make a one-time theft of at least twenty thousand piasters.

The amounts I was getting at present could never be discovered with the palace records in such a jumble. Nothing recorded was actually going into my pocket, and an inventory of purchased goods would be wildly off, as much through incompetence as embezzlement and sales by divisional officers. Nobody but the suppliers knew that I was getting a small rake-off, and they had no reason to complain.

A big chunk would mean writing a series of large false invoices, which associates of Abram would present. Even here that wouldn't go unnoticed, but I hadn't worried about anybody uncovering the theft in anything less than a month. By that time I'd be off planet, or I'd have worse problems than being uncovered as a thief.

Platt was running so close to the edge, however, that I'm pretty sure I could have bought him for less than I'd paid his employees to betray him. Platt couldn't be any part of the escape plan now, though; or at any rate, he couldn't be aware of the part he'd be playing.

Abram's reappearance startled me as it always did when I was concentrating. Which, come to think, was most of the time I was alone.

"A good time for a break at Etzil's?" he said.

I shut down the console. "A really good time," I said.

We walked down to the seafront in silence, as usual. I think it would've been safe to talk. We weren't going to say anything that two or three words would've gotten us attention, and nobody would hear more as we passed them, but Abram was busy watching our surroundings and neighbors as though he expected an ambush.

There were certainly places in Salaam that a stranger shouldn't enter, especially after dark, but broad daylight on the central boulevard wasn't one of them. Still, if it made Abram more comfortable to do it his way, that didn't hurt me.

We got a table, as usual. "Lal's going to meet us here soonest," Abram said. He grimaced and added, "Say, that other thing we were talking about? You still want it?"

I nodded. "You have it?"

"I can get it," he said. "But it's three hundred pi."

I drew the money out of my belt. I didn't know what I might need a pistol for, and I hoped I wouldn't need one at all. I certainly wouldn't need three hundred ben Yusuf piasters if I got off planet.

Lal joined us as Abram wrapped the money into his tight-wound turban. The boy set wine around and left. I said, "What can you two tell me about the *Alfraz*?"

"Me, nothing, so I looked up Lal," Abram said. "I'm a slave and none of the boatmen will take me out to a ship. They lose both hands if they help a slave escape."

Lal looked at the glass of wine with a sour expression. "Abram got me a bottle to carry out with me," he said. "That was the ticket with the watchman, Ahmed, but I had to drink with him."

He shook his head. "It's awful stuff, just awful," he said. "I'd give a lot for a drink of fresh palm sap from Kashgar … but it has to be fresh, or it'd be worse than this,"

He tapped the glass.

"What about the *Alfraz*?" I said. I didn't disagree about the wine in places like Etzil's, but it didn't matter.

Lal shrugged. "Two thousand tonnes," he said. "One antenna ring. In bad shape on the outside, worse on the inside."

He grinned at me. "About the same as the *Martinique*. Maybe even a little worse. There's electric cables running over the cabin floor, I guess because the console's been rewired."

"Can it lift?" I said.

"I guess," Lal said. "Platt put a watchman aboard, so I guess he thought so, at least. I didn't touch the console, let alone light the thrusters."

"How did you get aboard with the watchman?" Abram said. "Just trying to figure it out in case I need to do something like that myself."

"I told Ahmed I'd been a crewman on the ship who just

wanted another look for old times," Lal said, grinning. "But mostly, I waved the bottle when I'd banged on the float so he stuck his head out the hatch. That did the talking for me."

"Is Ahmed a spacer?" I said.

"I don't think so," Lal said. "Also from the way he talked, he'd been a doorkeeper before Platt hired him to live on board the ship. He's got a little skiff to paddle himself to shore for supplies."

Lal grinned again. "From the way Ahmed talked," he said, "he hasn't been paid in near six months. He's sold everything loose in the cabin for his upkeep, and if he knows about the outside tool lockers, he's cleaned them out too."

I took a deep breath and asked the big question. "How large a crew would the *Alfraz* need?" I said. "Could we work her with two? That's you and me?"

Lal's expression was a lot like the one Abram got when I insisted on interfering in the Wives' Wing. "It'll be slow," he said. "You know the rig isn't going to work worth a damn, and that means recalculating every course. We'll be hopping all over the cosmos to get where we're trying to go."

I nodded. "I agree," I said. "I think I can plot us a better course than the console alone can, but that's not going to help the ship hold that course if the rig won't go into place."

"I guess we could do it," Lal said. He gave me his grin again, this time with a very sad tinge. "You saved my life, Roy. There's ways I'd rather spend it than dicking around the Matrix in a tramp spaceship—but that's still better than floating the rest of my life in a crap air suit."

"Deal," I said, offering him my hand. We shook.

"If you're not going to drink this," said Abram, picking up Lal's untouched wine, "I guess I am."

He tossed it down.

Abram and I spent the afternoon on our rounds of the suppliers. Not only would an influx of cash feel good—I wasn't short, but there'd been enough outgo to make me uneasy—but it was important not to change my regular behavior now. Anything that made people wonder about me was dangerous, because they might start looking more closely.

By now, the suppliers smiled when we came in. Balian even took me into his office while his nephews drank with Abram.

"You know, Roy..." Balian said as he poured the wine. "I was worried when you showed up. The palace, they think they can squeeze and squeeze and little businessmen like me, we've got to pay. But if they squeeze too hard, they'll kill us. They wouldn't like that, and I really wouldn't like it."

"There's plenty to go around," I said between sips, "if everybody's reasonable."

"I appreciate how you took care of Mehmet when he got drafted," Balian said.

"One of Bashir's sergeants had decided to go into business for himself," I said. "I explained to Bashir that if Mehmet"—one of the nephews in the front of the shop—"wasn't released from conscription immediately, the Admiral was going to muster the entire army as listed on the pay records. It turned out that wasn't something Bashir wanted to have happen."

Bashir collected the pay of nearly twice as many soldiers as were actually in the palace. That was in addition to what he stole on equipment.

"Could you have done that?" Balian said.

I shrugged. "Bashir thought I could," I said. "I'd never want to swear to what the Admiral was going to do."

Balian began to laugh. "Myself, I would not bet against you, Roy," he said. "It is much better to be your friend."

We chatted a little longer. Then I left with Abram, on the way to the next vendor on my list. The nephews had put the week's payment into the satchel over Abram's shoulder. Its thin fabric was woven from the roots of a local plant and would turn a knife slash.

I thought of what my disappearance would mean for Balian and the other suppliers. They didn't all like me—Ali son of Ali, the main local wine supplier, didn't like anyone, as best I could tell—but they were all better off for my presence in the equation, and I think they'd all admit it. Their lives were going to get worse when I was gone, whether that meant off planet or dead.

I liked them, mostly. Even Ali son of Ali kept his word. To me, that is; his invoices to the palace were as false as everybody else's.

I would feel sorry for people who were harmed by my leaving, but my duty lay elsewhere: to the Republic of Cinnabar; to Captain Leary, who'd given me a chance when nobody else had been willing to. And just maybe to Roylan Olfetrie, a kid who'd never consciously done anybody harm.

Our way out of the market took us to a coffee bar at the intersection of the aisle we were following with a cross aisle. I gestured to it and said, "I want some coffee. And I want to talk."

My drink at home was beer or the bitter chocolate beverage

that was more popular on Alliance worlds than in Cinnabar space, but I thought the coffee might clear my head. Balian hadn't been the only supplier who'd chosen to be hospitable while paying over my commission.

We moved cushions to an open space and the proprietor brought a little three-legged table to set beside us. The coffee came in tiny glasses. You had to drink it carefully or you'd choke on the grounds that half-filled each container.

"So," I said to Abram. The racket in the covered market hid our words from anybody who wasn't seated with us. "Are you coming with me?"

"I don't know anything about spaceships," Abram said sullenly. He wasn't meeting my eyes.

"I didn't ask if you'd join the crew," I said. "Frankly, I don't have time to train you, so you'd be more trouble than you were worth. But"—I carefully tasted my coffee. This wasn't going to change my opinion of the beverage—"though there won't be anything from me linking you to what's going to happen, I don't have to tell you that if I'm not around to talk to, they'll be talking to the folks who knew me best."

I smiled, because I'd thought of something funny. I said, "You know, Giorgios is going to be lucky if he just loses his job. Well, he chose his side when he bought me."

"I got family in the Kabylia," Abram muttered. "They don't like me much, but if somebody from the city comes out to the farm, they'll be lucky to get farther than the bottom of the cesspool."

"You'll have plenty of warning," I said, taking another taste. "But I wanted you to know that you've got a choice."

"I came here from the farm," Abram said. His hands began to shake and he put his cup down. "I never been anywhere else. Not even Eski Marakech."

He swallowed. "Look," he said to his cup on the table, "I've talked to spacers plenty. I'm not yellow, I'll fight anybody, I *will*. But it scares me, all that nothing. It scares me and I'm sorry but it does."

Abram's eyes were tight shut, but tears were leaking out of them. I put down my coffee and leaned forward to hold his shoulders. "Hey, buddy," I said. "No sweat. Look, I've been in space myself and I don't disagree with you."

I held Abram until his body stopped shaking. When I released him, he blew his nose violently on his sleeve and looked up at me.

"The thing is," I said, "you know the things I've been doing. How much longer do you think I'm going to get away with it?"

"Yeah," Abram said. "Well, let's get your ass off planet before you wind up with a stake up it, hey?"

When we got back to the palace, I found the Admiral at the console again. I swallowed and went down to the main courtyard where I played a game of checkers with one of the regulars there.

I desperately wanted to get off ben Yusuf.

But my stomach turned every time I thought of the Admiral and Monica. I wanted her out of this place even more than I wanted to be out myself.

251

Chapter Twenty-four

When I was sure that the Admiral had gone back to the Wives' Wing, I checked the cameras myself. Monica was in the garden. I thought twice about what I was going to do next, but I really wanted to talk to her. I headed down for the alley door.

Abram had gone off "on business," without telling me what that was. He carried the satchel. We'd transferred the takings from it to my money belt.

I brought a heavy broom, as I'd taken to doing. At Martial's at lunch one day, a yard man who'd seen me leaving the palace with it asked what the broom was for. I told him Giorgios had told me to sweep the alley, I guessed because the Admiral had said something. Did he want me to tell Giorgios that the yard man was wondering about what was going on?

The yard man didn't, and that ended the discussion for good. I thought of Giorgios as a pompous joke, but he frightened people on the bottom rung of the palace. He made a point of bullying those whom he could, and the fact he reported directly to the Admiral gave him a certain amount of real authority.

Mind, what I'd told Balian was true: You could never count on the direction the Admiral's whim was going to take him. I couldn't think of any situation in which I didn't believe I'd be better off going unnoticed than I would be for enlisting the Admiral's help.

I walked into the alley whistling. There were two men farther down. I began to sweep enthusiastically, keeping my eyes on the job. The men moved off in the other direction. There was nothing they could do about my plans, but I didn't want spectators.

I pulled the door open and slipped inside. It was getting easier to swing the door every time I used it. The electronic locks remained in place until the moment I was ready to leave the console. It was likely enough that somebody passing through the alley would tug at the handle in a vague hope of finding something to steal inside.

I walked quickly to the inner end of the passage. I realized that I'd better have a light with me when I fetched Monica. Somebody who didn't trust that the tunnel was clear wasn't likely to stride along in the dark at the speed I wanted us to be showing then.

I'd picked up a fist-sized lamp from Bryce that glowed when I twisted the top. Balian hadn't been sure how long it would stay lit, but the two of us plus Abram and the nephews couldn't find any way to change batteries. I might get a nasty surprise, but it was still a better choice than bringing along an oil lamp.

I opened the grating cover. "Thank heaven," Monica said. "Thank *heaven*."

"Things are moving along," I said. "I think it may be very soon."

"It can't be too soon," she said fiercely. "I think I'm going to go mad if I have to stay one more day!"

I grimaced, an expression which she couldn't see. "Look," I said, "this is really dangerous. I mean, there's a lot of stuff I can't check ahead of time."

I tapped lightly on the grating.

"Even opening this door," I said. "I've been oiling the hinges but I don't dare risk opening it before we're really going."

"Roy," Monica said, leaning forward in her seat. "You're not guaranteeing me a happy future. You're just making it possible for me to have a future that I'll want to live."

I swallowed. "Yeah, well, I'll try," I said. "Ah, Monica, could you be ready to go tonight? To be out at this door at eleven thirty?"

"Yes," she said. "Can we go then?"

I'd considered the possibilities. I didn't see any reason not to do it immediately, though it scared the crap out of me.

"We'll go tonight unless something comes up, and then I'll try to tell you," I said. There wasn't any way to tell her anything except by coming to the grate. What if something happened to me? Maybe Abram would be willing to take a message?

"Look, I'll go off now," I said. "There's stuff I need to set up. But we'll try tonight."

I closed the grate, running through the number of people I had to see immediately.

I grinned. If I waited another month it'd still scare the crap out of me. This way, I didn't have as long to worry.

* * *

I knew the day Monica had entered the Wives' Wing. Through that date I'd found the Admiral's first approach to Platt. I crafted my own to echo it:

> *Most excellent colleague and friend!*
>
> *I have been fortunate in finding another quantity of fine Saguntine vintage—equal and perhaps superior in quality to that which we shared six months ago. This has a beauty which blazes like the very sun, and I am convinced it has never been uncorked.*
>
> *If at midnight tonight you will appear at the alley entrance as before, a trusted servant will conduct you to where I wait with the vintage. We will throw dice, you and I, for the privilege of the first sip from the bottle. Then, man and man, we will take turns throughout the night.*
>
> *Yours in truest fellowship*
Mustapha Reis

I sent the message off, then leaned back and let out my breath. I must have closed my eyes.

Abram jolted me alert by saying, "Did you just bloody die?"

I jumped upright. He was standing beside me, looking disgusted and angry. The satchel was over his shoulder. He glanced down at it and said, "I got something for you."

"Let's go down to Martial's," I said. It struck me that there were a lot of people on Salaam whom I was going to miss, which I never would have believed when I arrived here.

Martial's was busy. Abram and I picked up pasties and wine and carried them farther up the side of the palace to where we were alone. We squatted with our backs leaned against the stone. I wasn't in the mood to eat, but I needed to get something in my stomach. The next few hours were just going to make me more nervous.

Abram set the satchel between us. He took a deep draft of his wine and said, "This is yours."

I set my glass down on the other side to free a hand, then with one finger lifted the length of finely woven goat's wool to see the pistol beneath it. It was standard Alliance military issue and looked brand new.

There was a loading tube in place, though I didn't know how many rounds were in it. I wasn't going to take the weapon out and look it over until I knew I was alone—probably tonight in the passage—but for now it looked like a very functional pistol.

"Thank you," I said. I took a bite of pasty, then opened a pocket of my money belt. "I've got some money for you."

"What's that for?" Abram said. He covered the coins with his hand as I opened a second pocket.

"For your family," I said, handing over more coins. "This is a good time to visit them. I mean right now."

I opened a third pocket and emptied it also. I'd still have thirty-five Alliance thalers and forty Karst sequins, both of which could be negotiated on most planets of the region. I hadn't dared to collect more off-world currency for fear of raising questions, but I'd happily accepted it in place of piasters when a supplier had offered it.

"Look," Abram said angrily. "I'm not working for you any

more. That's what you're saying, right?"

I didn't understand his tone, but I nodded as I continued to hand over all my local money. "If you want to put it that way, yes."

"Then you don't have any right to tell me where to go!" Abram said. "I'll go where I bloody well want to go whenever I want to do it!"

I started to say that I hadn't been trying to give him orders, but he knew that. I nodded and took another bite of my pasty. It was extremely good.

Abram crammed the rest of his into his mouth, chewed and swallowed. Then, still around a normal mouthful, said, "I'm going to get another glass of wine, and then I've got business to tend to."

He stood and added, "Business of my own!"

"I hope it goes well," I said to his back as he stalked off.

I thought of taking a nap—I had a little room off Giorgios' entrance hall. I didn't bother, because I couldn't have slept; much as I knew I'd need it later. Besides, somebody likely would've come in and waked me up for some favor or other if I'd tried to sleep in the daytime.

If Abram had been here, he'd have guarded the door curtain. I hoped that, despite his bravado about not getting out of Salaam, he'd had sense enough to leave at least until people had forgotten about me.

I didn't doubt his courage, but he had a good mind too. When he cooled off, he could see that him staying around to be caught wouldn't help anybody.

An hour before midnight, I hung the satchel over my right shoulder, picked up my broom, and made my way down to the front entrance. There were a lot of folks in the plaza, chatting with friends and passing bottles around.

At least two people within earshot were playing stringed instruments and singing. They were different songs, and at least the nearer singer was so drunk that he was repeating the same line: "...*we will miss your bright eyes and sweet smile* ..."

I could hear people in the alley as I reached it from the side street. I was having to deal with something I hadn't thought of even sooner than I'd thought I would. Mind, this was something I *should* have thought of.

One choice was simply to ignore the people whispering and to go past them to the door. Instead I reached into the satchel and brought out the lamp in my left hand. Holding it up and out, I loudly said, "Hoy! What're you playing at?"

The light worked fine. It wasn't bright but in the close darkness it was as good as a spotlight. I saw three forms, all men as best I could tell in the swirl of loose garments, as they ran the other way down the alley.

That wasn't the only thing that could've happened, but my right hand was inside the hanging satchel. I hadn't had to test the pistol also, thank heavens.

I entered the passage and closed the door after me. I was breathing hard. I set down the satchel. It was heavy enough to unbalance me with the weight of both the pistol and the pry bar. I hoped I wouldn't have to use either one, but who knew?

The light was still on. I started to turn it off to conserve power, then worried that I wouldn't be able to turn it back on. Finally I left it on just for the company the light would give me for the next twenty minutes.

I'd shot the hand bolt on the alley door. There was one on the garden door also, but I left it. I wasn't worried about somebody trying to enter from the Wives' Wing. At 11:27 p.m. I dropped the cover plate. Through the grating I heard a woman say, "What's that light!"

The voice wasn't Monica's. I'd forgotten that at night, any light in the passage would be visible in the garden.

I heard a *thunk*. "Quick!" Monica said. "Open the door!"

I pulled it open. The hinges were stiff, but the oil had done its job. My blood was jumping with so much adrenaline that I felt like I could've ripped the door off, let alone opening it.

Azul lay in front of the doorway. Monica was bending over her. She'd dropped the unlit brass lamp that she seemed to have used as a club. She removed a glittery barrette from the fallen woman's hair.

"Get her inside," Monica said. Then she said, almost the same breath, "Oh, thank the heavens you're here!"

I dragged Azul into the passage. Her head was bleeding; that must've been a hell of a clout.

As soon as Azul's feet were out of the way, Monica tried to close the door. It was far too heavy for her. I reached past her and shoved it shut, then shot the interior bolt.

I bent at the waist so that I could suck in more air. All my muscles were wobbling. I pointed a finger at Azul and said, "What was *she* doing here?"

Monica settled the barrette in her own hair and straightened.

"I told her that I'd found something that frightened me and I needed her to take it to the Admiral," she said. "We slipped out secretly."

"But *why?*" I said.

"She saw this in my hair the first day I arrived..." Monica said, touching the barrette. "And took it. I think just because I had it, not that she particularly wanted it. And she kept wearing it so that I'd see it every day."

"Look, she's a nasty person"—or anyway, she used to be a nasty person. Her breathing was loud and very slow—"but she might not have come alone."

"She did, though," Monica said, drawing herself up straight. "And I wasn't going to let the bitch rob me."

I'd have bought you ten baubles just as nice as that one, the first time we got to a civilized planet, I thought. The trick was that we had to get off ben Yusuf first. Complaining would be as pointless as what Monica had done.

"Come on," I said aloud. "Our ride is going to be here at any time now."

We left Azul snoring on the ground and walked briskly to the alley end of the passage. I said, "I'm going to switch off the light now," and did so. The sudden darkness helped me relax.

Monica was wearing loose trousers and tunic, all the clothing any of the wives had. It wasn't ideal for anything but the Wives' Wing, but she wouldn't have had a choice.

"Why did you turn the light out?" she asked.

"I'm waiting for somebody to come with a car," I said. "I don't want him to get a good view of us until, well, until I'm ready for him to."

She didn't respond. There was nothing to say, but I still expected her to say something. Monica was a real person, not an image in a camera, and I was starting to get a view of what was below that surface.

Someone knocked at the alley door.

I was expecting that, but I still jumped nearly out of my skin. They were using their knuckles, not something hard.

I slid back the bolt. There wasn't a view slit on this door, so I had to assume that Platt had arrived. Idlers in the alley might've tried the door, but they wouldn't have knocked. I shoved it open and whispered, "Come in quick!"

Somebody squeezed through the crack in the door. "Can't we have a light?" the man said.

I pulled the door shut behind him. I got the pistol out of my cargo pocket, then turned the light on.

"Master Platt," I said, quietly but not whispering any longer. "You're to do exactly what I tell you. If you don't, I'll shoot you dead. Do you understand?"

Platt's throat worked as he swallowed. His eyes were wide and his mouth fell open.

"*Do* you understand?" I repeated.

"I do . . ." he said. Then he said, "Who are you?"

"A distressed spacer, whom you're going to help get off planet," I said. That was more or less his job, after all. "Do you have a gun?"

"No," he said. "No." He swallowed again and added, "My driver has a gun."

"Then I'd like you to go to the door and call him in here," I said. I was impressed at how calm I sounded. "Monica, keep hold of the back of his tunic but try not to be seen. If he makes a break I'll have to kill him, and I don't want to do that."

Platt hesitated; the door was closed, after all. I smiled at him, keeping the pistol aimed at his belly but my bent arm withdrawn a little. I didn't want him to grab for it.

"Just call him calmly," I said. "He needs to give me his gun, but nobody's going to be hurt if he does."

I pushed the door open enough that Platt could put his head out. "Hiram?" he said. There was a squeakiness to his voice, but I didn't suppose he could help that. "Come in with me."

The driver replied something but I couldn't make out the words. Platt was wearing a loose brown tunic, a local garment; Monica had gathered a double fistful of the material into her hands, but she was bending down to stay hidden by the door panel.

Platt snarled, "Just leave the bloody car! Leave it!"

I heard the car door open and thunk shut. I could drive, but the alley was so narrow that getting down it with enough room to open a door was an expert job. If I'd backed out, I'd have had to navigate by the sound of fenders rubbing.

"Sir?" said a voice outside.

I pushed the door farther open, straining not to seem to be straining. I said, "Come on in. Just stay calm and everything's going to be fine."

"Wha wha wha...?" the driver said. He was about forty and sturdy looking, but his face was unmarked. I didn't have the impression of a brawler.

"Platt, back up," I said. "Let Hiram come in."

The consul jerked backward with a squawk. Monica was a

strong lady, and a very determined one.

"Come in, Hiram," I repeated, "and put your hands on the wall while I take your gun."

The driver squeezed through the opening, moving as far to the right as he could. My pistol was aimed at his left eye. He whispered, "Don't shoot me...."

"Just lean on the wall," I said. "I'm not going to hurt you."

The driver was wearing a blue jacket, maybe from a uniform of some sort, but his pistol was loose in the side pocket instead of being holstered. I withdrew it and dropped it into my left cargo pocket.

Stepping back but keeping my eyes on our two prisoners, I said, "Now, we're getting back into the car and Hiram will drive to the harbor. Monica, take the pistol I just put in my pocket and go out first. Walk to the ride so that you're not in the way if one of them does something dumb."

"Where are we going?" Platt said. He kept swallowing and his voice was ragged.

I felt Monica take the gun and slip out behind me. When she'd reached the alley, I said, "We're just going to the harbor, like I said. I'll leave the two of you there. You've got nothing to worry about."

"I'm ready!" Monica called.

"You next, Hiram," I said. "Don't get into the car until the rest of us are out, though. But no problems, okay? I'm a very good shot."

I wasn't, not with a pistol anyway. I hoped I wouldn't need to prove that.

The driver left the passage, then Platt himself when I nodded to him. I followed them, still holding the light.

I left the door open. Azul had been a thorough bitch from everything I'd seen through the cameras—and particularly a bitch to the blond, young Monica. I still didn't want to leave her to die in a dark tunnel. If it was open at the alley end, somebody was going to venture in soon. They might even do something for the injured woman.

Monica held her pistol concealed under a fold of her loose sleeve. It was aimed at the driver.

"Do I get in or are you leaving me?" Platt said.

"Hiram, open the trunk," I said. "Get in the trunk, Master Platt. You're going along, but I don't need you until you tell your watchman that it's all right for us to come aboard."

"You can't do that!" Platt said.

The driver leaned through his open window and touched a control. The trunk lid popped open.

"Get in," I said, "or I'll leave you here in the tunnel, dead. And I'll figure to bribe the watchman. Your choice."

Platt climbed carefully into the trunk. He was trying to find a comfortable spot to lie down when Monica slammed the lid onto him. He shouted angrily, but when she slammed it again he'd flattened out of the way.

"Monica, get in back," I said. "Keep your gun on Hiram as he gets in. And then I'll go around to the other side and get in beside him."

When she was inside with her pistol touching the back of the driver's neck, I walked around to the passenger door and got in beside him. "Now just drive down to the harbor and park where the boats are pulled up on shore," I said. "No need for a hurry. As soon as we're gone, you and your boss can go do anything you please."

The driver was as rigid as a statue behind the steering yoke, but he drove precisely. He didn't look over at me or the pistol in my lap.

We drove to the end of the alley without touching a wall. A step encroached from the left near the far end, but we rocked over it without difficulty; the driver fed in just enough power to get us up and then down with minimum disruption.

We turned left at the street and continued toward the water at the same sedate pace as we'd navigated the alley. The pavement was wide enough, but there were scores of idlers out on the hot night. They moved out of the way, but occasionally somebody shouted an insult.

Monica slid across the back seat and put her lips close to my right ear, the one away from the driver. "This pistol," she whispered. "It isn't loaded. The tube fell out."

"All right," I said. I suspected that the driver hadn't known that the pistol he carried was empty; certainly he'd acted as though Monica was holding a loaded gun. It wasn't exactly a complication, since I hadn't planned on getting a second pistol from our prisoners. I'd *thought* we might, though.

We drove toward the harbor, rocking on the irregular pavers. We reached the parking area where Giorgios had brought me. The sand beyond that point was too soft for normal tires. There were no other vehicles, but some of the watermen's huts were lighted by small fires or lamps like the one I'd used in the passage.

"Now Hiram," I said. "We're all going to get out. Then you're going to reach in through the window again and open the trunk so that the consul can join us."

Monica continued to point her pistol at the driver from under the fabric so that he couldn't see that there wasn't a loading tube. I wondered if it'd fallen out unnoticed in his pocket when he'd bumped something or if he simply hadn't realized it was missing to begin with. The amount of technical ignorance on ben Yusuf went beyond making me a wizard for being able to give a computer basic commands.

The trunk popped open. "Out," I said.

Platt carefully straightened, then clambered out as quickly as he could. I guess he was afraid that Monica would slam the lid on him again. We were far enough from the huts that the watermen couldn't be sure of what was going on at the car.

"Now," I said to him, "we're going over to the shelters and find a boatman to take us to the *Alfraz*. She's your ship, so there shouldn't be any—"

"*Roy*," Monica said, not loud but urgently. I broke off and followed her eyes. Somebody was coming toward us from the huts.

The trunk lid was still up. I shifted to the side so that I was sure the newcomer couldn't see my pistol.

"Hey, boss," Abram called. "I figured you'd come here looking for a boat, but I didn't realize you were coming in style. That's the Karst consul's car, isn't it?"

"Yes, and this is the Karst consul," I said. "You might want to go somewhere else, stranger."

"I'll take my chances," Abram said, nonchalant as always. "Anyway, I already got a boat laid on for you. Come on down to the freight landing."

"Hang on," I said and did some quick figuring. "Hiram,

you get into the trunk now. I still need your boss to board the *Alfraz*, but I don't want to have to watch you too."

The driver bowed and said, "Yes, lord." He got into the trunk quickly and made himself as low as he could. Monica closed the lid over him.

I nodded to Abram. "We're ready," I said.

A cargo lighter of some size was drawn up at the landing stage. I heard a *thrum* rather than the sound of a reciprocating engine; it was probably the flywheel of some sort of electrical drive. The water alongside the hull quivered in the starlight. A mound of supplies filled the central portion of the vessel.

Abram hopped on. "You next, consul," I said. I was holding the pistol close to my chest. It was possible that the two boatmen in the stern couldn't see it in this light, but they could probably guess that something off-kilter was going on.

I trusted Abram to fix any problem that this caused. I was out of my depth.

We boarded. Abram cast off the line looped around a concrete bollard. Without verbal commands, the lighter backed into the bay, coasted for a moment with the drive grunting, and then proceeded forward in a curve that took us to the ship moored five hundred feet off shore. Even in the darkness I could see that the hull was bigger than those of the pirate cutters that made up most of the port's traffic.

The boatman cut the drive when we were fifty feet short of the nearer outrigger on a parallel line. We closed on momentum; then the boatman switched to reverse. Our bow dipped, but only momentarily. The lighter's side swung against the outrigger with a *clang* that could've waked the dead, but

267

our speed was so slight that we didn't even rebound.

Abram hopped onto the outrigger and looped the hawser around one of the struts. When he tossed the free end back, I hitched it to a cleat on the lighter's side.

The small hatch into the cabin started to open. I turned to Platt and said, "Stand up—you're on now. Tell him we're boarding for an inspection."

The consul stood up shakily. "Ahmed, it's your master!" he called. "We're coming aboard!"

Lal stood in the hatchway. "Welcome, Captain Roy," he said. "I've just been having a drink with my friend Ahmed. Do you want to board by the way of the strut or should I lower the main hatch?"

"We've got a load of stores," Abram said. "Lower the hatch and you come help us get it aboard, too."

The cabin hatch was an airlock and not ordinarily used while a ship was on a planet. A spacer could easily mount the forward strut which attached the outrigger to the hull. The struts were extended now but would draw in close when the ship reached orbit. When fully lowered, the main hatch became a ramp resting on the port outrigger and giving general access to the ship.

I wasn't sure Monica could board by the strut, so I'd have asked Lal to lower the main hatch anyway. But I was frowning as I looked at Abram and said, "What supplies?"

Bolts released. The hatch began squealing down slowly.

"That," Abram said, nodding toward cargo amidships. "Look, I talked more to Lal. The watchman'd sold every bloody thing he could get hold of. You'd have been eating your boots till you got to the next landfall, and those"—he glanced down at my feet and grinned—"are plastic, right?"

"Synthetic, yeah," I said, "but—look, Abram, what'd all this cost?"

"Not a bloody thing so far as you're concerned!" he said.

"I meant that money for you!" I said.

"Well, then, I spent it on what I wanted, didn't I?" Abram said. "Look, how much do you think my family eats? Or what d'ye think there is to buy in the hills?"

The hatch, now a ramp, clanged onto the outrigger. I squeezed Abram's shoulder and looked away from him. "All right," I said. "Platt, get aboard, go into the cabin. Monica, go with him."

"You said you'd let me go," the consul said in a wobbly voice.

"You'll go back with the lighter!" I said. "But I'm getting you out of my way for now."

Platt turned and began trudging up the ramp. Monica looked sharply at me before following. I gave her my pistol, butt first. I was going to need both my hands for shifting the stores.

Chapter Twenty-five

The boatmen—they may have been two brothers, both of about forty—helped us unload the lighter. When I made my first trip up the ramp carrying a case of dehydrated food—it had been manufactured on Pleasaunce, almost certainly from the stores of a ship captured by pirates—I got my first view of the interior of the *Alfraz*. I hadn't expected much, but it was worse than that.

A replacement fusion bottle had been placed in the hold in a corner with the bulkhead separating the cabin from the hold. It was a large unit, probably out of a major warship. A freighter's Power Room wouldn't have been able to hold it, so a dockyard had dispensed with the usual containment bulkheads and just put the bottle where it would fit.

Heavy conduits ran from the bottle in several directions. One of them entered the cabin through a U-shaped cut in the pressure hatch from the hold. The hole had been packed with some gummy material which I hoped was air tight. In theory the cargo hold should hold an atmosphere so long as the main hatch was closed, but there was always leakage on older ships. I was afraid that on the *Alfraz* there would be a lot of leakage.

I set my load down and clamped it with one of the hold's internal tie-downs. Half of them were missing, but because they were part of the ship's fabric the watchman hadn't sold them, the way he apparently had everything loose.

I said to Abram, coming in with a similar load, "I'm going to check the console." I walked into the cabin.

The bunks in two stacks, three and three, stood on either side of the communicating hatch. They were slotted metal sheets, four of them still folded against the bulkhead. Their padding was gone.

A local man, presumably the watchman, lay on his back on one, snoring. Platt sat on the other lowered bunk looking frightened and uncomfortable. Monica had rotated the console's seat so that she could keep the pistol aimed at Platt's belly.

"I need to check the controls," I said. Monica got up without speaking and stood against the starboard bulkhead. Her eyes and the gun muzzle remained fixed on Platt.

The console came up promptly. The holographic display had good definition, much better than that of the *Martinique*. Like the fusion bottle, it had been salvaged from a naval vessel.

I checked the read-outs. The bottle was running in the green, which was a blessing because I was pretty sure that Lal wasn't a competent tech. Neither was I, but I was probably up to the average of engineers in this region of the galaxy.

The reaction mass tanks were very low. There was no excuse for that, since the ship floated in a bay which could have topped them off in a few hours. I didn't have time to take care of it now, but it would be my first priority on our next landing.

I checked the astrogation data. There was full information with way points for a run back to Karst, but except for that it was spotty. Planets had only cursory legends—Air, Water—or none at all. I hadn't expected much, but again reality was at least as bad as I'd feared.

I started the internal pumps to circulate reaction mass to the propulsion system, the plasma thrusters and the antimatter converters which fed the High Drive motors. The system worked to eighty percent of original specifications, which was quite good. If the drive units were in comparable shape, we'd be all right.

"We'll lift as soon as we finish loading," I explained to Monica as I left the cabin. She nodded but didn't speak.

It took a full half hour for the five of us to empty the lighter. I didn't even consider asking Ahmed to help. Even if he hadn't been drunk he was too frail to add much to the process.

We got the job done, though. I went into the cabin to get Ahmed. "We're just about done," I said to Monica.

I bent to pick up the watchman, since he obviously wasn't up to leaving on his own. I suddenly had another thought. "Platt," I said. "Where's your purse?"

"You're going to rob me now?" he snapped.

"Don't push your luck," I said. I lifted his tunic and opened the belt purse I found under it. It was heavy, but there were only twenty-two Karst sequins and about a hundred piasters in local coins. I put the sequins in my own purse and transferred the piasters to Ahmed's; it was the only way he was going to collect any of his back pay.

"Up you go, buddy," I said to the watchman, lifting him with his right arm over my shoulders. I used my right hand to keep his face turned away from me in case he vomited.

As we shuffled off the ship, I called over my shoulder, "As soon as we've got him aboard, you can let Platt go too."

Lal and Abram were in the hold. Both came to help me with the watchman, but Abram got to him first. The boatmen had gone back to their vessel; the stern was starting to swing away from the *Alfraz*'s outrigger because they'd loosed the aft mooring line.

"Thanks," I said across the lolling drunk between us. "I put some money in his purse. Can he shelter in a hut down here?"

"I'll fix it," Abram said. "He'll probably get robbed, but the sun'll probably rise in the east too."

We laid the watchman in the lighter with his head lifted slightly on the tarpaulin that had covered the stores.

"Abram," I said as I straightened. "If you're ever in a place that I can help you, let me know. I've owed you from the first day I arrived on ben Yusuf."

He looked away. "Yeah, well," he said. "You treated me square."

He looked up again and met my eyes. "You trusted me, boss. Nobody *ever* trusted me before."

"Then they're fools," I said. I don't know what I might've said next, but the shots inside the ship stopped me.

There were two—*Whack! Whack!* They were louder but not as sharp as a pistol usually sounds. With the second shot I heard the slug ricocheting off the steel bulkheads.

"Prepare to cast off!" I shouted to Abram as I sprinted up the ramp. I didn't want Abram to be caught in this, whatever the hell had happened.

Lal was at the internal hatchway, looking into the cabin. I brushed past him and ran inside.

Monica stood, holding the pistol. The heated barrel glowed slightly and the vaporized aluminum driving bands shimmered above the weapon.

Platt quivered facedown on the deck. There was a splash of blood on the bulkhead behind where he'd been sitting. I didn't know where the first slug had gone until I rolled the body over; it had broken his shoulder but hadn't penetrated the bone. His eyes were open, but glazing.

I looked up at Monica. "What happened?" I said.

She thrust the pistol at me muzzle first. Her face was wild. "Take it!" she said. "*Take* it!"

I did, if only to get it out of Monica's hands. I grabbed it by the receiver, but I managed to touch the hot tip of the barrel to the inside of my wrist. I shouted and jerked away. I was lucky not to fling the weapon into the overhead.

"What happened?" I repeated as I took the pistol by the grip and put it on Safe. I was working to sound calm, both for Monica's sake and my own.

"He smiled at me," she said.

Her voice was clear, but I thought I must've misunderstood. "What?"

"When he thought he was going to be released . . ." she said, swallowing. "He smiled. Just the way he did before he raped me. I shot him; I didn't know I was going to shoot him."

She swallowed again and said, "Then I shot him again."

"Well, no loss," I said, though my stomach was roiling. That was partly the smell; Platt's bowels had released when he died.

I walked back into the hold and stood in the hatchway. The lighter still floated alongside, though Abram held the bow hawser in both hands.

"Everything's fine!" I called. "Platt's going off with us. Don't forget to let the driver go from the car trunk, all right?"

I returned to the cabin and set the main hatch closing. Over the squeal I said, "Prepare for lift-off, both of you. Monica, we've got cushions and bedding in the hold. See if you can get that struck down while Lal and I are busy."

The external sensors had *terrible* optics, but the lighter was big enough that I could follow its wake to the dark, shapeless blob of the vessel itself. It was far enough out that I figured it was safe to light our thrusters at low output.

I wished there was somebody in the Power Room, but I suspect the *Alfraz* had operated without an engineer for her whole active life. "Lighting One and Six," I said.

The PA speaker in the cabin had so much distortion that I couldn't have understood the words myself. The one in the hold seemed a little clearer, though I couldn't be sure over the interference from the nearer unit.

The thrusters lighted properly. Feed pressure didn't drop.

I shut down the first pair and said, "Lighting Two and Five."

The second pair ran smoothly also. I hadn't been able to check them externally, but the instruments seemed happy.

When I heard the hatch close, I turned and shouted to Lal,

"Get the body into the hold. We'll dump him when we enter the Matrix!"

I pointed and made arm gestures to show him what I wanted. Lal hesitated at the order, which I didn't blame him for. Worst case I'd take care of Platt myself when we reached orbit, but I'd really have liked to get rid of the smell and also the lump in the corner of my eye.

Monica got up from where she was attaching the cushions to the bunks. She grabbed Platt by the wrists and dragged him toward the hatch. When she got there, Lal came and lifted the body by the ankles until they had it over the coaming. They dumped it in the hold and together pulled the connecting hatch to.

I shut down Two and Five, then called, "Lighting Three and Four!"

As I ran up the middle pair of thrusters, I switched my short-wave transmitter to twenty meters and called, "Karst Transport *Alfraz* to Salaam control. We are preparing for immediate lift-off."

There was no response, as I'd expected. Lal was on the striker's seat; Monica lay down on a bunk—not the one beneath the splash of the consul's blood on the bulkhead. That was probably the best choice for lift-off, though I doubted whether the *Alfraz* could accelerate hard enough to worry about.

As my last act as a resident of ben Yusuf, I opened a link to the palace console. I'd set it up two days ago, when I'd begun to firm up my plan for escape. Through it I locked out the antiship batteries on the jaws of the harbor. They would continue to function normally—except that they wouldn't accept a launch signal.

It would be easy to reverse my program edit—as soon as somebody noticed it. I was pretty sure that would be long after the *Alfraz* had left the region of ben Yusuf. It was likely enough that the crews would *never* realize that their batteries weren't functional. That was pretty much the norm for governmental departments in Salaam.

"Lighting all thrusters!" I said. With all six venting plasma into the harbor, the *Alfraz* rocked and pitched. Mostly that was the water boiling under our outriggers, because with the nozzles flared the thrusters provided very little impulse.

"Lifting in five seconds!" I said. I was shouting, but I doubt my companions could hear me. It was what they must have expected though, even Monica.

I ran the thrusters up to full output, checked briefly that there were no instrument anomalies, and said, "Lifting off!" I sphinctered the thruster leaves to minimum.

We rose more smoothly than I'd feared. The *Alfraz* was taking on a list to port, but that was alignment; output on all six thrusters was within a two percent range, but either port or starboard was misaligned. They were all supposed to be set at ninety degrees.

I adjusted the port set five degrees inward, choosing by guess. I was ready to reverse the controls if we started toward a roll, but in fact the hull shifted properly upright. The maneuver had been dangerous—we'd probably have reached orbit if I'd done nothing—but because the thruster output was marginal for our weight I'd been sure that I'd have enough time to correct the mistake if I'd guessed wrong.

We'd reached the upper levels of ben Yusuf's atmosphere.

"Switching to High Drive," I said and cut them in. The *Alfraz* had only four motors, so our acceleration until we inserted into the Matrix would be painfully slight, but beggars can't be choosers.

The High Drive made a nasty buzz as matter and antimatter recombined. This was a much more efficient way to accelerate us, but it got on my nerves the way the steady roaring of the thrusters did not.

I began calculating a course as the ship drove outward. There was no reason to pause in orbit; we all wanted to be away from ben Yusuf, and straight out was as efficient a method as there was.

Monica unstrapped herself from her bunk and walked over to the console. Our acceleration was below 1.5 gs, so it wasn't a remarkable feat. It must've been work, though.

"We're off ben Yusuf, aren't we?" she shouted in my ear.

"Yeah," I said. "Twenty miles above the surface is the legal definition, and we're above all but traces of atmosphere."

I looked at her. "We're a long way short of getting where we want to go, though," I said.

"Where I wanted to go was off that horrible planet," Monica said. Then she kissed me.

Monica went back to the bunk. It took me a while to get back to my course calculations, but eventually I did.

I hadn't had time to check the suit locker. When I thought of it I was momentarily dizzy with fear. If the watchman had been able to get into it, he would've sold the suits as he had everything else.

My only choice then would've been to land at another harbor on ben Yusuf and purchase at least one suit there—hoping that the news from Salaam wouldn't arrive before I'd been able to do that. That was unlikely, since I'd have to earn money for the suit. I didn't have a clue as to how to do that.

I grinned. Perhaps Lal and I could rob a pirate cutter. If it had been Abram with me, I might've thought I had a chance.

The suit locker was secure storage, opened by the console. That was common on freighters on the fringes. Weapons and liquor would be similarly secured, though the *Alfraz* carried neither.

I opened the locker and stood. "Let's go take a look," I shouted to Lal, but Monica joined us as well.

I breathed out in relief as I saw suits. I was glad to have anything, though the reality wasn't great. The only hard suit was missing the left lower leg. The four air suits had all their limbs, but I could see gaps at the joints of one when I manipulated them.

I could have repaired that well enough for the purpose with a roll of cargo tape, the sturdy material designed to keep cargo from shifting in the hold under sideways acceleration. Unfortunately, any cargo tape aboard the *Alfraz* had been sold for Ahmed's upkeep.

"Well, I figure two of them will work," I said to Lal, hoping that I sounded cheerful. "That's an advantage of being short-crewed, right?"

"And perhaps the rigging won't need much help," Lal said, showing that he was trying to keep up spirits as well.

Our sensors didn't show any other ship above ben Yusuf.

I didn't trust the *Alfraz*'s electronics, but I hoped they were good enough to warn me at least if there were another ship closing with ours.

"I'm going to raise the rig," I shouted to my companions over the discharge of the High Drive. As soon as I thought we had time, I was going to swap the speaker in the hold for the useless one here in the cabin.

I set the rig to deploy in stand-by condition, sails furled and yards remaining vertical against the antennas. The bolts and clamps withdrew like a badly performed version of the "Anvil Chorus". Whines and squeals followed as hydraulic motors began to lift the antennas.

"Captain?" said Lal. "Do you want me to go out and see how the equipment is working?"

I shook my head and shouted, "No. Neither of us go out until we can go out together. I won't trust the suits until we've tried them. We'll each be ready to get the other back to the airlock if something goes wrong."

If they both failed at the same time, we were screwed. So, for that matter, was Monica.

I smiled reassuringly toward her. It was the only thing I could do. Her expression didn't change, but she nodded in acknowledgement.

When the sound of the rig ceased, I took a deep breath and shut off the High Drive. I said in a loud, clear voice, "We will enter the Matrix in five seconds. Entering the Matrix . . . *now*."

I pressed the EXECUTE button with the heel of my palm. The *Alfraz* entered the Matrix as smoothly as a fish leaps back into the sea. In that aspect at least, our ship was exceptionally good. I could only hope that she would extract as easily when the time came.

I queued up the course data, then pressed EXECUTE again. Rising from the console, I said to Lal, "Let's get suits on and inspect the ship, shall we?"

So far, so good.

The air suits didn't fall apart when we pulled them on. Monica hovered close, but she didn't get in the way or ask questions. She was obviously nervous, but she kept it controlled.

I set the pistol on the floor of the locker, just to get it out of my pocket. There wasn't room inside the suit anyway. It was possible we'd need it again—I *had* needed it to cow Platt and his driver—but I sure didn't like having it on me.

There turned out to be tools in the locker: a kit attached to the belt of the hard suit and a separate kit with only an adjustable wrench and combination screwdriver/pry bar. I suspect the tools with the hard suit had been forgotten when the leg was removed and the suit became unserviceable.

The airlock was beside the console. We entered and I immediately locked down my helmet. I began turning and moving my limbs as pumps evacuated the lock. If something was going to let go, I'd rather that it happened while I was still aboard.

Lal watched me impassively. I suppose he was used to equipment of this quality. The suit he'd been wearing when I grabbed him as he floated away from the *Martinique* was worse than the one he'd taken from the locker. We'd checked the magnets in the boot soles before we got into the airlock.

When the pump stopped, I unlocked the outer hatch and led Lal onto the hull.

The Matrix surrounded us in pastel glory. Captain Leary had told me he was in the presence of God every time he stood in the Matrix. I wasn't spiritual, but it was a magnificent thing even to me.

Our family had never been religious, though Mom had made of point of attending fashionable temples when money had lifted us into higher society. When I stood in the Matrix, I could imagine that the god-bothering types might be right... but *might* be, that was all.

With a single ring of antennas, it was easy to make a circuit of inspection. Proper safety lines had gone down the watchman's belly if there'd been any aboard, but I'd cut two fifty-foot lengths from the coil of rope Abram had provided. It was woven from the leaf spines of a desert tree and was good enough for the purpose. I'd have preferred RCN-standard beryllium monocrystal, but something around my waist was better than something better in a warehouse on Cinnabar.

The ventral antenna hadn't rotated properly, though the yards were extended and had shaken the sails out. They were blocking Casimir Radiation to drive us off course, unfortunately.

I opened the cover of the gearbox at the base of the antenna. A tower gear spun determinedly, but it wasn't turning the cog which should have driven the antenna.

I removed the hydraulic line. When the gear stopped, we could see that the lower half the beveled side had been worn smooth; it was misaligned, so a portion of the teeth had been having to do the work of the whole length.

Remembering Barnes' lesson, I unlocked the tower gear from its retaining clip, turned it upside down, and reclipped it. When I reconnected the hydraulic line, the antenna started rotating properly.

I was grinning as I stood and gestured Lal back to the airlock. This had been a good watch.

"Give me a moment," I said to Monica as we entered. "I'll tell you what's going on after I've reset this."

I didn't bother taking off the air suit before I sat down at the console, though I had removed the helmet. I recomputed our course to correct for the time the antenna failed to turn. When I sent that command to the rig, I stood up, stretched, and walked over to the locker to change.

Lal had removed his suit while I was busy. He wore shorts and a sleeveless tunic and was barefoot as he'd been even on the ground. That wasn't uncommon in Salaam, though at least half the men had sandals.

The boots that Captain Hakim had worn when he captured the *Martinique* were unique in my experience. He probably wore them as a mark of rank.

"The rig is working now," I said as I stripped off the leggings. "We repaired a gear. It ought to be replaced but it seems to be working now."

"The captain repaired the motor," Lal said to Monica. "I could not have."

"You can now," I said. "You hadn't been trained, is all. If

283

we get to a civilized planet, maybe we can buy a replacement. Though I don't know what we'd use for money."

I hung up the air suit. Thinking about it, I might be able to trade my skill at a computer for a used tower gear. Ben Yusuf might be unusually ignorant, but I suspect in this arm of the galaxy my level of expertise would have been a boon to most chandleries or scrap yards. Even on Xenos, I'd have been more use to Petersburg in the office than I was as a flunky.

"When we get to Saguntum," Monica said from where she sat, "I can get as much money as we need."

"Well, for now we're heading in the other direction," I said, sitting on the bottom bunk of the other stack. "We need reaction mass, and such navigational data as we have indicates there's a water world almost as close in the other direction as there would be if we'd headed for Saguntum. There may not be anybody chasing us from ben Yusuf, but I *really* don't want to be recaptured."

"I'm in your hands," Monica said simply.

The bulkhead behind me was wet. While Lal and I were on the hull, Monica must have washed Platt's remains off the steel.

I remembered that I'd meant to put the body out when we entered the Matrix. Well, so long as we got rid of it before we were next in contact with anybody,

I let out my breath again, feeling more relaxed than I had since I'd been shanghaied aboard the *Martinique*. Aloud I said, "We're on our way!"

Chapter Twenty-six

We extracted from the Matrix about the right distance from the unnamed planet's primary. We were on the wrong side of the primary though, where the world we wanted would be in another half circuit.

I felt too awful to even pretend to be pleased with my astrogation. I'd had a reasonably easy time with extractions before now. Even veteran spacers talked about how bad they felt after an extraction, so I'd been congratulating myself for being one of the lucky ones.

I'd *been* one of the lucky ones. This time I felt as though my flesh had been replaced with half-melted ice cubes which then had been poured back inside my skin. I was shivering so badly that I had difficulty entering the new course data.

"Inserting into the Matrix," I said. "Now."

I closed my eyes as I pressed EXECUTE this time, because I didn't want to think about what I was doing. Entering the Matrix meant that I'd have to extract again, and right at this moment I'd almost rather have died than do that.

If other people feel this way, how do they manage to keep on doing it? I thought.

We shuddered into the Matrix. It was a short hop, crossing the orbit; probably less than three hundred million miles. We could even have managed it using the High Drive in the sidereal universe. I didn't feel quite miserable enough to start the calculations for that, because I knew it would be a matter of weeks or even months; but I was almost that miserable.

"I feel awful," Monica said. "Someone is chopping on my head with an axe."

Lal sat with his head in his hands, saying nothing. I guess it was all of us. Maybe it had just been an unusually bad extraction.

A telltale on the display winked at me. "Extracting," I said and threw the toggle.

It was as gentle as sliding into warm cream. I muttered a prayer. I hadn't prayed before the extraction because I didn't in my heart of hearts believe in divine powers. I was willing to thank powers that might not be, though, rather than not be courteous in case they were real.

We were above our destination at about a hundred thousand miles. I made quick calculations and entered a High Drive burn of just under three minutes to kick us into orbit so that we could pick a landing spot. Lal was on the striker's seat but Monica came and stood beside me, gripping the back of my couch when we entered free fall.

The world below was half deep ocean, but the other half was a shallow sea with thousands of islands. Mostly the islands were arrayed in strings and circles. Even where the land didn't break surface I could see patterning on the bottom.

There were no signs of human involvement, but many of the islands were green, especially around the fringes. The ship's optics weren't good enough for me to make out details.

"I guess it doesn't matter where I land," I said. "We'll have water regardless."

"Land in a lagoon," Monica said. "We may not be able to go ashore, but we'll have some protection if there's a storm. And if we can go ashore, I'd like that."

"We'll do that," I said. I located a spot on the surface, marked it on the display, and set the console to calculate the landing.

"Better take your bunk," I said to Monica. "I'm using the automatic landing program, so I don't know when or how long we'll be braking—"

The thrusters kicked in, starting us down toward the surface. It caught Monica by surprise, but her two-handed grip on my couch kept her from falling. She returned to her bunk with two quick strides which were just short of leaps, then strapped herself in.

I kept my hands on the controls, but though the descent was rough I didn't even consider making a manual landing. I practiced constantly with the console, but lives depended now on the landing.

I could probably have brought us in safely, but the console certainly could. I had a lot to learn and nothing at all to prove.

I expected the banging in the lower atmosphere to become violently worse when a rigging clamp failed and some major assembly tore off—or possibly tore the ship apart instead.

That didn't happen, and the buffeting reduced. The image on the display had degraded with the vibration, but it sharpened as our speed dropped. I saw that we were heading for the center of an atoll.

This console didn't pause to hover as some programs did. Instead we plunged toward the water swiftly until the pressure of steam and reflected thrust brought us into dynamic balance for a moment.

The thrusters shut off and dropped the *Alfraz* the remaining distance to the surface of the lagoon. It was probably no more than a few inches, but it was enough to shake me. Monica yelped and Lal fell off the striker's seat to sprawl on the deck.

Next time I'd bring us down the last ten feet myself. Though we were safe, as best I could tell.

I unhooked my restraint harness. "All right," I said. "We can't open the ship up yet, but we can start filling the reaction mass tanks."

The pump was in the main hold. I opened the fairing and lowered the intake pipe, but the pump icon on the console display was yellowed out.

"It's not recognizing the pump?" I said aloud, hoping that when I heard the words, an obvious answer would occur to me.

"It's been rewired when the new bottle was put in," Lal called from the hold. "Would you like me to throw it?"

"Wait!" I said, because I wasn't about to agree to something that I didn't understand. I walked into the hold and saw Lal with his hand on a knife switch projecting from a control box beside the main hatch. A heavy lead entered from the fusion bottle; another ran to the intake pump on the other side.

"Why is it like this?" I said.

Lal shrugged. "They didn't want to reprogram the console," he said, "so they left the control circuit in place but put in a separate power switch. I've seen it before, or setups like it."

I took in what Lal had said. "All right," I said. He threw the switch in a sudden spurt of blue sparks.

I walked back to the console. The pump icon was live again. I switched it on and was gratified by the heavy vibration as the pump began sucking the lagoon's contents into the tanks.

When I first boarded the *Alfraz*, I'd noticed the octopus of armored conduits leading from the fusion bottle. They'd been clamped to the deck and to bulkheads rather than being buried within the ship's fabric as the originals had been. I'd been disgusted, but in a detached fashion; I hadn't made a detailed study on the new routings. If I'd had a thought, it was to hope I'd soon return to civilized planets on which even tramp freighters had to meet higher standards if they were to lift off after inspection.

I suppose I was better off to remain in ignorance as long as I could. I'd just added to my list of necessary repairs—once we'd reached a repair yard—to put a cage over the knife switch. It wouldn't be possible to rewire the pump without a full rebuild, but it wasn't necessary to leave high-amperage connectors open to the air.

"Let's take a look at our new world," I said to Monica, speaking as cheerfully as I could. No reason to tell her that we were riding in a deathtrap. "Want to name it?"

I started the hatch to open. Thank goodness it hadn't needed rewiring also.

"No," Monica said. "I just want to get home. I really want to get home."

"Don't we all, my dear," I said, but as the words came out I wondered what my home was now. Xenos three years ago, I suppose. Simply going back to a cheap apartment on Cinnabar wouldn't take me home.

When the hatch opened, the local atmosphere rushed in with the residues of our exhaust. I sneezed from the ozone, but the usual stench of garbage incinerated by our thruster exhaust was absent.

I smiled. We weren't in a regular harbor into which ships and often the community itself dumped waste. This was a barren island without civilized amenities.

We were in the middle of the lagoon. On the blue-green water around us floated the bodies of worms from six inches to a foot long, probably boiled by our exhaust. Winged creatures about two feet long made short hops from the low islands around us, hovered momentarily above the water, and stabbed down with long tongues.

Most of them concentrated on the worms we'd killed, but other flyers were plucking similar worms from the lagoon's fringes beyond the range the plasma had heated.

"I think they have exoskeletons!" Monica said, walking out on the ramp. "I wonder if we could catch one?"

"Like insects, you mean?" I said. I joined her, though I'd just as soon *not* get too close, myself. The creatures' long noses uncoiled at least six inches to spike the worms. Even if they weren't poisonous, I didn't want anything six inches long driven into my body.

"Well, like insects—or lobsters," Monica said. "But they must have real lungs to fly like that."

The creatures had thin bodies with four slender limbs. The wings were translucent fabric stretching between the pair of limbs on each side. I didn't know if the creatures could walk on the ground. They landed with their prey only momentarily, then spat off the worm's shrunken husk and hopped into the air again.

They clicked as they flew. I wasn't sure where the sound came from—the wingtips touching at the bottom of each stroke, I suspected—but the air was alive with it.

The pump started to labor. I wanted to believe that I was imagining the change in note, but walked back into the hold. It seemed to me that the water wasn't humping as actively as it had been along the side of our hull above where the intake was.

The pump began shaking angrily in its housing. I didn't take the time to check flow rate on the console. I lifted the knife switch and the pump shut off.

"What's the matter with it?" Lal asked as I headed for the console.

"I hope it's just sucked up some mud," I said, though that didn't seem likely. The water was so clear that I could see the sand bottom.

According to the console display, the reaction mass tank had come up enough to notice but was nowhere near full. I guess at the back of my mind, I'd hoped that the antibackflow switch hadn't shut the pump off when the tank had filled.

I went back to the pump itself and laid a hand on the housing. It was cool to the touch so at least an internal problem hadn't burned it up.

"Okay," I said to Lal. "We'll go down and see what's in the screen. First, though, we're going to disconnect the top end of the intake pipe."

"Can I help?" said Monica, who'd come in with us.

"I guess you can hand us tools," I said. "It's going to be tight even for two in the housing, though."

We got to work. The eight-inch pipe was dense plastic rather than the steel I'd expected, so at least we didn't have to worry about corrosion. Structural plastic was better in a nonstressed application like this, but it really couldn't be repaired. Even on a world as benighted as ben Yusuf, you could find somebody who could weld steel.

We took the bottom flange loose first, handing the nuts and bolts to Monica as we removed them. "Why are you doing that?" she asked. "Can you reach the blockage that way?"

"No," I said as I stood and stretched before we started work on the upper flange of the elbow. "This is just so that if the pump turns on while we're at the intake opening, we don't get sucked up the pipe."

"But that can't happen, can it?" Monica said, frowning.

"It can't if we take a three-foot section out of the pipe," I said, handing her the next nut and then knocking the bolt clear to give her also.

I couldn't imagine Monica throwing the big switch while we were down there, and I'd taken the pump off-line at the console as well. Regardless, we had time to do this job safely. I didn't see any reason to take risks to save half an hour that we wouldn't miss.

Lal and I put on air suits but left the helmets off. I had no idea what was in the water beside the worms.

As I started toward the hold, I heard a splash. I ran through the connecting hatch a good deal faster than I'd planned.

Monica was standing out on the ramp. It was only after I'd gotten to the main hatch that I saw what had made the splash: Platt's body floated in the lagoon.

At least she tossed it over the end of the ramp. There it floated on the other side of the outrigger from where Lal and I would be working on the pipe.

I didn't say anything, but Monica raised her jaw as she looked at me. She said, "It was about time we got rid of that! It was just covered with a tarp."

"Time and past," I agreed, walking to the outrigger and out on it. I looped a line over a top cleat. "I kept meaning to put him out every time we inserted, but I kept forgetting."

I sat and dangled my legs in the water, wishing we had a proper ladder. Gripping the rope, I let my body down and paddled over to the intake. The magnetic soles kept my feet down and the laden tool kit at my waist gave me almost perfect neutral buoyancy. I could have adjusted that by adding or removing tools, but I was glad not to have to.

I found the underwater intake easily because the open cover plate stood at ninety degrees from the hull. Even without a light, I could see that the grating looked fuzzy instead of a sharp-edged grid of heavy wire. It was *moving*, like a dog's fur in a breeze.

"The worms are trying to get in," Lal said from the other side of the opening. "Why are they doing that, do you think?"

"They probably got sucked in," I said, thinking about it. "There must be a mother-huge lot of them in this lagoon. Do you suppose they hatched here?"

Lal didn't answer, but it didn't matter. They were soft bodied and shouldn't be a problem if their pureed flesh went into the reaction mass tanks. We'd have picked up worse in most harbors on developed worlds.

"Okay," I said. "We'll take the grate off, fill the tank, and then put the grate back on before we lift. Otherwise it'll just jam again as soon as we start the pump."

"Yes, Captain," Lal said. He was a skilled and experienced spacer, but anything out of his experience was an impenetrable problem to him. He didn't even begin to think about it; his mind just switched off.

That was better than getting a lot of backchat from a subordinate, I suppose, but I'd have been glad to get a second opinion on some of this business. It was all new to me too.

There were twelve bolts, threaded into the hull itself. I put them down the throats of our suits rather than chancing trying to put them into the tool kit and maybe losing one. The grate didn't get a lot of stress when the cover plate was closed, but I didn't fully trust the cover plate either. I didn't trust any part of the structure of the *Alfraz*.

When we got the grating off, I said to Lal, "Get back on the ramp and I'll hand this up to you. We'll get the pump running again, then clean this before we put it back on."

Lal splashed over to the outrigger where he could get onto the ship again. I worked my way along the side with care, using my magnetic boots to grip where there was nothing for my hands.

The grating was in the crook of my right arm, and I held the safety line in my left hand. I couldn't swim with the weight of the grating, let alone swim with one hand. Keeping my head above water with my feet on the curving hull was like holding a sit-up midway.

Lal reached the midpoint on the ramp when I did. By lying on his belly and reaching down, he managed to take the grating, which allowed me to relax and let my legs drop.

Inside the ship Monica screamed, then shouted, "Help! Help me!"

Lal dropped the grating with a clang and ran into the hold. I tried to lift myself directly onto the ramp, which was stupid. I could've done it in shorts and a jersey, but not with the suit and the weight of the tool kit.

Using the rope and all the strength of my arms, I hauled myself to the outrigger and climbed out. Monica called something, but her voice was distorted. I heard the sounds as, "I can't hold it!"

I ran up the ramp. I couldn't see Monica, but Lal was using a wrench as a club to pound the yellow-white form that hunched up at the internal hatch. It was a worm like the thousands of worms in the lagoon, but this was the size of a cow.

The cabin hatch burst open—Monica hadn't gotten to it in time to dog it shut. She shouted a despairing curse. Lal's blows weren't even leaving marks on the creature's hide.

"Don't touch metal!" I said, pulling the prybar from its loop on my toolbelt.

The worm extended into the cabin like a stream of pus. Its foreparts twisted to the right, probably following Monica whom I couldn't see. The creature had crawled up the eight-inch pipe and into the hold where I'd taken the section out—for safety, I had thought.

"Don't touch metal!" I repeated and laid the bar between the live contact of the knife switch and the bulkhead, shorting the load into the steel fabric of the ship.

Metal exploded. Blue coruscance momentarily sprang from every surface. The bar jerked in my gloved hand. It would have thrown me onto my back except for my deathgrip. The current had welded both ends in the microsecond before the circuit breaker flipped.

"Are you all right!" I called. I stepped back from the switch and took off my right glove. The bar was glowing red and had started to burn me. "Monica, are you all right?"

"Yes," she called. "Is it dead?"

Her voice wavered, but mine too sounded tinny in my own ears. The short circuit had been as loud as lightning striking a power pole twenty feet away.

"It's dead," I said, leaning over the worm's smoking corpse so that I could look around the bulkhead. Monica sat on her mattress, her legs drawn up to her chest and her arms hugging them tightly. Her eyes held mine.

The worm's head had reached the edge of the bunk when I electrocuted it. Now the body was shrivelling. A pool of liquid continued to spread beneath the charred skin.

"You can touch metal again," I said. I suddenly realized that until I'd removed the pry bar there was a dead short if I closed the circuit breaker. I stepped back and kicked the middle of the bar with my boot heel, cracking both welds. The bar fell to the deck.

Monica got off the bunk. "Can we get this thing off the ship?" she said, looking down at the worm. She moved sideways as the leaking fluids approached her soft boots.

"I sure hope so," I said. "Lal, grab this with me and let's see if we can get it through the main hatch while the skin's still holding together."

It smelled awful. A few years ago a fish thirty feet long— I'd never learned what it had been when it was alive—had washed up on the shore of the island where we had a vacation home. It had been dead at least a month and most of the skin had sloughed off. I hadn't imagined that I would ever smell anything that bad again.

"Let me put a suit on and I'll help push," Monica said, trotting over to the suit locker. "I would have gotten the gun from there if there'd been time, but after the thing pushed the door open it was between me and the locker."

I didn't blame her for wanting to wear protective gear before she touched the worm. This was one of those awful jobs that you did and did your best to forget about afterward.

With Lal holding two handsful of the skin on one side and me doing the same on the other, we were able to get the front of the body over the hatch coaming. It was easy then to slide it across the deck and onto the boarding ramp. By then Monica was ready to help us dump it into the lagoon.

We rolled the worm off the edge of the ramp. At least half its original mass was a tacky smear on the deck.

"I'll start washing the ship out," Monica said. "I don't suppose there's anything like a mop aboard?"

"Look," said Lal, pointing into the lagoon.

Platt's body floated near the ramp. It was wrigglingly fuzzy, much as the grating had been. The birds—the big insects, I guess—were diving down and spearing some of the worms which were burrowing into the floating corpse. They collided with one another in the air, making a louder version of the clattering we'd heard before.

"My God," Monica said softly. It sounded like a real prayer.

"I'll see about getting the ship ready to lift," I said. "I don't know how much damage the short circuit did."

"The gun wouldn't have stopped it, would it?" Monica said.

"I'll see how much damage I did," I repeated. "Then I'll help you and Lal clean."

I spent nearly an hour with the circuitry. The console was unharmed—it was completely shielded from the hull.

Most of the time I took involved me poking about in the switch box, where a small circuit board had fed the console's commands to the pump. It had disintegrated. I literally wasn't sure what the components had been, let alone being able to replace or bypass them.

Staring at the ruin didn't make it less complete. I finally gave up and joined my shipmates. They'd made scrubbing pads from rope and garments—a breechclout and a gauzy underlayer of Monica's shift. Food boxes served as buckets.

"If I'd known we were going to do this," Monica said brightly as I approached, "I'd have saved Platt's clothing before I put him over the side."

"I'm not going to fight the worms for it," I said, squatting down. The job was almost done, at least as much as it could be with what we had. It would take lye and a good airing to really clean the *Alfraz*.

"I think the mother must breed in this lagoon to protect the eggs and hatchlings from predators in the open sea. All but the flying ones, of course."

I nodded, but I wasn't really paying attention. I'd smiled to my shipmates' hopeful faces, but I let my expression settle back into the resignation which I felt.

"Look," I said, "we're not going to be able to head straight for Saguntum as I'd hoped. The pump switch can't be repaired, and we don't have enough reaction mass to make the whole voyage. We have to replace the switch."

"What does that mean?" Monica asked with an appearance of calm. Lal simply watched me, much the way a rabbit might watch a snake.

"Plaquemines is within the amount of reaction mass we've got aboard," I said, hoping that I sounded more confident that I felt. "It's a developed world, enough that I'd even heard of it on Cinnabar. We'll be able to replace the switch circuitry there."

I cleared my throat. "The thing is, the parts and probably labor aren't going to be really expensive, but they'll cost more than I've got in coins. I'll need to get a job and raise some money. I don't think that'll be hard, but don't know how long it'll take. Two, three weeks, I'd guess."

"You say, 'not really expensive,'" Monica said. "How expensive is that?"

I was a little disturbed by the intensity with which she looked at me. I shrugged and said, "On Xenos I'd guess about three hundred florins. I don't know prices on Plaquemines, of course."

Not for the first time, I regretted that the *Alfraz* didn't have a set of *Sailing Directions* for the region. I'm not sure there was one, but the Fleet had probably compiled a similar set.

"That would be about five hundred Alliance thalers, wouldn't it?" Monica said.

"About," I agreed, more than a little surprised that she was familiar with the conversion rate. Cinnabar currency had been unknown on ben Yusuf, and it must be rare even on Saguntum. "I've got twenty-two at the moment."

Monica lifted her hands to her hair and brought down the jeweled barrette she'd taken—back—from Azul the night we escaped. It opened when she squeezed a hidden catch.

A credit chip popped out. She handed it to me and said, "Here. This is good for ten thousand thalers at the Central Bank of Pleasaunce."

I took it, then raised my eyes to meet hers. *Who is she?*

"In that case," I said aloud, "the only trick is getting to Plaquemines. That's my job."

I rose from my squat. "I'll start plotting the course right now." I walked to the console. *Who the hell is she?*

Chapter Twenty-seven

"Karst Registry freighter *Alfraz* requests landing permission for St. Marie's Port," I said on the twenty-meter band. "*Alfraz* requests to land, over."

The *Alfraz* had a microwave suite, but I was a little surprised to hear it chirp, "*Plaquemines Control to Alfraz. What is your cargo, Alfraz, over?*"

I'd noticed a second ship in orbit a little below us as we approached, but I hadn't expected it to be a customs vessel. Saguntum had one, but the briefing materials I'd read before the voyage had suggested such formalities were rare in the region. Plaquemines might be a more significant place than I'd expected.

"Plaquemines, this is Captain Olfetrie of the *Alfraz*," I said. "We're landing for minor repairs. We have no cargo, over."

I hoped that the microwave antenna was self-aiming; that is, that it responded on a reciprocal of the signal it had received. I hadn't been sure that the microwave worked at all, and I certainly didn't fancy my chances of manually aiming a tight-beam antenna.

"*Proceed to St. Marie Port,* Alfraz," the voice responded. "*Do not leave your ship before you've been inspected by port officials. Plaquemines Control out.*"

"Thank you, Plaquemines Control," I said. "*Alfraz* out."

I looked at my shipmates and said, "They've marked a berth for us. Just so you know, I'm going to let the console bring us in down to the last ten feet. I'll take over there and complete the landing."

I grinned, but I was pretty nervous about it in truth. "If that turns out to be a bad idea," I said, "I'll let the machine do the whole job the next time. Now that we know to brace ourselves good for the last bit."

I was tired and I hurt all over. Lal and I had been doing the work of six; though the ordinary crew of a tramp in this region would have been three or four rather than six. An air suit didn't rub as badly as a hard suit did, but it was a protective garment and as rugged to the wearer's skin as it was to the conditions outside.

The High Drive engaged. When the thrusters took over, the atmosphere began to bounce us around. I don't suppose I'd ever trust the rig of the *Alfraz*, but the clamps had been working as well as anyone could ask.

We came low enough to land on our second circuit within the atmosphere. The *Alfraz* was underpowered—certainly compared to a warship—but her weak acceleration and braking meant that sloppy control linkages didn't get her into trouble quickly.

I guess I was coming to like the old girl. She was, after all, my first command.

The console guided us toward the berth the port authorities had chosen. St. Marie Port was on a mile-wide river fifty miles up from the coast. The surrounding continent had been a surface of yellow-green vegetation with occasional rectangles of different colors, plantations cut by human settlers.

A red telltale alerted me that the ship's sensors thought we were twenty feet above the surface. I took manual control and locked the thruster output at the current level. We continued to descend on the programmed course, entering the quay from the open mouth. As we slid toward the far end, I adjusted the thruster angle five degrees forward and with my other hand flared the sphincter petals gradually.

The usual gush of steam warned me we were about to touch down. The outriggers hit with solid splashes, the port one an instant before the starboard.

I chopped the throttles and leaned back. It hadn't been perfect, but it was pretty bloody good. The hours I'd been spending on the simulator had been worth it.

"What do we do now?" Monica said.

"Now, we wait for the local inspectors to clear us," I said without getting up. I was worse wrung out by the landing than I'd been by the days of doing two men's work in the rigging. "Same as always."

I thought for a moment and added, "Except I think I'll open the ship up a little quicker than I'd do if that worm hadn't melted the way it did."

Ozone and garbage burned by the thrusters didn't seem too bad as an alternative to the present on-board atmosphere.

* * *

"Good heavens," the inspector said as he stepped into the main hatch. He backed away, then turned and stared at me. "Good *heavens*!" he said.

"A wild animal got aboard while we were taking on water," I said. We'd met the official at the foot of the boarding ramp. I'd walked him up while Monica and Lal waited below. "We had to kill it, but the reaction mass pump was damaged. We need to repair that, but we're also going to pick up cleaning supplies."

"I should think so!" the inspector said. He craned his neck and looked around the nearly empty hold.

"You're welcome to search us," I said. "We recaptured the ship from pirates, and it'd been completely stripped. We just want to get home to Saguntum."

That was as much fancy as truth, but the official didn't need details which would just confuse him. He could see we didn't have any dutiable goods aboard.

"I don't see any reason to waste more time here," the inspector said. He jotted on his metal-backed pad, then tore off and handed me one end of the form. He kept the counterfoil.

"Carry the inspection report to the port office," he said as we walked back to my shipmates. "You'll still have to pay landing fees but that will be hull only, forty thalers."

"I suppose the chandleries are on Water Street?" I said.

"St. Marie Street we call it," the man said. "But yes. I recommend the Trident House, myself."

"We'll try it," I agreed.

* * *

The inspector got onto the saddle of his jitney and rode off. I said to Monica, "We'll try the Trident House. His recommendation."

She frowned. "He's probably been paid to say that," she said.

"Of course," I said. "He wasn't a prick, the way petty officials always can be. Even if his brother owns the place, that's still a good reason to do business there if they're halfway reasonable."

Lal didn't say anything. I'm not sure he'd even heard the exchange. He figured it was none of his business, I suppose. That was how I figured too, if it came to that.

Trident House was the furthest of the three ship chandlers facing the harbor and was a little more imposing than the others. The doorway was framed by bright yellow pillars running up to roof height; the counter in back was painted a matching color.

I walked up the central aisle and said to the middle-aged man behind the counter, "I need an electrician and a switch circuit for the reaction mass pump."

"And we need bleach and mops," said Monica. She remained slightly behind me, but she was fully part of the discussion.

"Of course," said the counterman. "We normally use Ricardo; I'll give you directions to his shop."

He coughed into his hand and said, "Do you have an account here, Captain?"

"We're good for the cost," I said, smiling. I handed over the credit chip.

I hadn't given it back to Monica. I'd seen that at any distance from Cinnabar and the core worlds of the Alliance, women tended to be taken less seriously than men. To tell the truth, even in Xenos—especially as you went down the social scale—there were plenty of situations in which I figured I'd get a better deal than Monica would have.

The counterman inserted the card into his reader, then looked up at me with sudden respect. "I *see*, sir."

"Before you find the electrician," Monica said, "I want mops and five gallons of bleach. Lal and I can get started on the cleanup."

She pursed her lips and added, "And clothing. Ordinary spacer's clothes, but clean. Several changes."

"And for me also," I added. "Lal?"

"If the captain is willing, a set of slops would be welcome," he said.

"And two hundred thalers cash," I said to the counterman. "If you're willing to be our bank."

"Of course, Captain," he said. He opened a cash drawer.

I wondered what he made of us. We were an odd-looking trio, certainly. Remembering what I'd told the customs inspector, I said, "We escaped from pirates, but we don't have much besides money and the ship."

"That's quite sufficient for me," said the counterman with a grin.

Monica, Lal, and a boy with the Trident handcart returned to the *Alfraz*. Monica had a hundred and fifty thalers—of her own money, of course.

I found Ricardo's shop easily—halfway down the nearest cross street—but the woman there explained he was out on a job. She sent me with their ten-year-old son as a guide to find him.

We did, but the job was on the opposite side of St. Marie. Ricardo made a good impression and agreed to come out to the *Alfraz* in the morning to spec the job—but he wouldn't leave this afternoon, even if I doubled the extra ten thalers I'd offered him to slip our job in before he finished wiring the new construction he was working on.

It was nearing evening by the time the boy led me back to the port office and left me. The clerks had already gone home, so I wearily trudged to the quay and down it, looking for the *Alfraz*. What was left of the preserved food we'd brought from ben Yusuf wasn't very exciting, but I was looking forward to a quiet meal and then sleep.

Sleep out on the outrigger. I'd gotten used to the stench of the ship's interior, but sleeping in an atmosphere of chlorine bleach would be dangerous instead of merely uncomfortable.

The lights of the *Alfraz* shone in the dusk. Every hatch was open. Monica and Lal were at the bottom on the boarding ramp. She sat cross-legged, he squatted. They rose as they heard me approach.

"I thought we'd make up shake-downs on the outriggers tonight," I said. I didn't see the piles of bedding that I hoped had been removed before they doused the ship's interior with bleach.

"I've taken care of that," Monica said calmly. "Roy, what's the correct pay for a spacer?"

"On Cinnabar?" I said. "A florin a day for a landsman. One and a half for an ordinary spacer, two for an able spacer."

Monica sat again and began counting coins onto the ramp

where the ship's running lights fell on them. She said, "Lal, we're paying you as an able spacer. Is that acceptable to you?"

"Lady, that is very generous," Lal said. He bowed to her before he scooped the coins into a purse which hung under his breechclout.

Lal probably wasn't qualified as "able" but he still wasn't being overpaid. He'd worked like two men on this voyage.

"I suggest you find a meal and accommodations on your own," Monica said. "You're dismissed until noon tomorrow."

He bowed again. "Thank you, Lady," he said and disappeared up the quay.

Ordinarily pay—and duty schedules—were the business of the captain alone. I suspected that Monica already knew that; I didn't feel any desire to raise the matter aloud.

"I rented a houseboat," Monica said to me. "I thought we could spend the night there. It didn't look like rain, but I wouldn't feel comfortable simply lying out in the open on a strange planet."

She looked away and added, "Also, I bought fresh food which we can heat now that you've arrived. On the boat, that is."

"Great idea," I said honestly. I was confused by all this. Everything Monica had arranged was good, but it was different from the very simple one-foot-in-front-of-the-other evening I'd planned. I was physically and mentally tired, and I resented even good changes that made me think.

I hadn't noticed the houseboat floating between the starboard outrigger and the hull of the *Alfraz*. It was about twenty feet long with most of the length covered by a curved roof. We stepped easily from the boarding ramp to the short deck in the bow.

I sat on a cushion while Monica heated the meal she'd

bought—a stew of meat and vegetables. The stove was a can half filled with sand into which she'd poured diesel which wicked up to burn safely at the surface.

"I didn't really make it myself," she said. "I bought it from a restaurant on shore and brought it back to heat when you got here. The food we've been eating is so bland and I wanted something different."

"This is much better," I agreed, though it was really a little too spicy for me. She must have bought the bowls and spoons also. "Ah—if I can ask you a personal question?"

"You can," Monica said, looking up. "You haven't asked me anything all the time we've been together."

There were a couple reasons for that, and I didn't plan to go into them now. I said, "You have money. Why weren't you ransomed instead of being stuck in the Admiral's harem?"

"Well, I couldn't buy myself free," she said. "They'd have just stolen the credit chip if they'd known about it. The way Azul did the barrette. And the Karst consul couldn't allow me to be freed after he'd helped rape me instead of doing his duty to me as a Saguntine citizen."

She swallowed and put her spoon down beside her bowl. Staring at them she said, "Maybe if I'd screamed at the beginning that I was important, it would have been better. But I was from Saguntum and I thought I'd be all right if I just kept in the background and it'd all be over...."

"That was what I'd have done too," I said, though I really didn't have any idea what I'd have done in her situation. Because of our different genders, there was no real comparison in the ways the pirates had treated us.

Monica started to cry.

I don't know what I'd been expecting, but it wasn't that. It had gotten really dark while we ate. I'd thought of bringing out the little light I'd bought in Salaam, but I hadn't gotten around to it. Pretty clearly this wasn't the time to climb up to the hold of the Alfraz and go rummaging around, though I've got to admit the thought crossed my mind.

I put my hand on Monica's shoulder. I didn't say anything. I'd set my bowl to the side, but she knocked hers aside as she threw her arms around my neck and drew herself against me. I patted her on the back, wondering what the hell to do.

Suddenly Monica straightened. I wished there'd been some light so that I could see her face.

"What's the matter?" she said. "Don't you like me? Why don't you kiss me?"

I kissed her, but withdrew a little and said, "I like you very much, but I didn't want to…"

I didn't want to have her scream, "You raped me!" at me some time in the future.

"I don't want to take advantage of you," I said. I didn't know where her head was right this instant, and she obviously wasn't in the best shape.

"Is it because I was raped?" she said. Her voice rose. "Do you think I'm *dirty*?"

"No!" I said. "Monica, you're wonderful and—"

She kissed me hard. "Then come," she said. "I want to make love, and I want to make love with you."

And so we did.

Chapter Twenty-eight

I was still making my first survey of the interior of the *Alfraz* when Ricardo arrived, pedaling a large-wheeled tricycle. There was a cage of woven-wire fencing, empty at the moment, over the back wheels. When I heard Monica greet him, I stepped onto the ramp.

"Come on up," I called. "It's not too bad."

The pong of the dead worm was gone. I was still aware of the bleach, but leaving the ship open overnight with the ventilator circulating kept it from being a problem.

I thought about the night for just an instant before my mind shied away. It had been a really long time since I'd been with Rachel. A lifetime.

I didn't know what the future was going to be like. I suppose I should have been thankful for what had happened instead of worried about losing it again, but that wasn't how I felt.

Ricardo took a look at the open knife switch and whistled. "Hey," he said. "That's bloody dangerous. You know, you ought to have the whole rig rewired rather than just replace the control circuit."

"I do know that," I said, "and I will as soon as it's practical. For now, though, I just want to be able to fill with reaction mass and get home to Saguntum. There the new owners can upgrade the *Alfraz*."

I didn't own the ship, after all. I wasn't even sure who did. Platt wouldn't dispute my title, but perhaps the Hegemony of Karst could.

"Well, if that's what you want..." Ricardo said. He looked sideways at me. "You know, if it's the cost...?"

"It's not," I said firmly. It was mostly a matter of time, though part of me was offended at the notion of spending a lot of money on a ship I didn't own. I was sure I could convince Monica to approve the work if I'd really wanted to. "Can you replace the control circuit or can't you?"

Ricardo shrugged. "I'll be back this afternoon to do the job," he said.

We went back out. He headed for his vehicle. I took a deep breath and walked to Monica, who was straightening the houseboat. I guess she was, anyway.

"He'll be back this afternoon to fix it," I said. "Well, he says he will. I expect the pump to take about six hours to fill the tank from what I saw of the flow rate before it jammed. With luck we'll be able to lift tomorrow morning."

"That's very good," Monica said primly. "We'll need dinner, then. I plan to go back to the same cafe to pick that up, but I'll bring something different. And I'll get fruit and bread and cheese right now, if that's all right?"

"That's great," I said, trying to sound cheery. "Ah, it wouldn't have to be quite as spicy for me as last night—though that's all right."

"All right," Monica said, nodding solemnly. She reached out and touched me on the back of my hand. "Roy, are you all right. About us?"

I put my arms around her and kissed her. "Monica, I didn't know how you'd feel and I was afraid..."

She kissed me back, holding me hard. She started crying again but she sounded happy.

I didn't know where it was going to go in a moment—well, yeah, I did know where it was going to go—but a group of men started up the quay toward us. Lal was with three other guys.

I turned Monica so that she could see them, then broke away and climbed up to the ramp.

"Good morning, Lal," I called. "You're here earlier than I expected you. The repairs are supposed to be done this afternoon, and I hope we'll lift tomorrow morning."

Lal cleared his throat and stepped out in front of his three companions. They were dressed in bright-colored tunics and loose white slacks, more clothes than I'd ever seen Lal wear. All four were slightly built, similarly dark, and barefoot, however.

"Captain," Lal said. "We are short crewed, yes?"

"Yes, certainly," I said. "Are your friends spacers?"

"The Singh brothers are my compatriots from Kashgar," Lal said stiffly. He didn't look over his shoulder at the three strangers. "They will speak to you about their requirements."

He moved to the side and continued to stare straight ahead. More was going on than I understood. The man in the middle of the three strangers stepped ahead and crossed his hands behind his back.

"I am Rajiv Singh," he said. He was about thirty. "I am a skilled astrogator. I and my brothers offer to take positions on your ship."

"We don't need a mate," I said. "We'll pay you as spacers—depending on your skill levels, on a voyage to Saguntum. I judge that to be about fourteen days, though we might make better time with a full crew."

Rajiv frowned. "You will pay us as able spacers?" he said.

"If you demonstrate that level of skill," I said. "We have close to twenty-four hours before we lift, so I'll run you through your paces here. If you perform as able spacers, we'll hire you at that rate."

I smiled slightly. I hadn't warmed to Rajiv, but we certainly did need crewmen. "And we'll pay you for the day of testing."

The money didn't really matter. Emphasizing to Rajiv that I was in charge did matter.

Rajiv moved back to his brothers. The three spoke in whispers. Rajiv returned and said, "We will accept your positions. Though I am due better."

"One moment," said Monica as she mounted the short rope ladder from the houseboat. "What was your last berth and why did you leave it?"

"I will not take orders from a woman!" Rajiv said to me in an angry voice.

"You don't have to," I said. "I'm captain of the *Alfraz*, like I'm sure Lal told you. Only—"

I smiled again. Monica, standing beside me now and

sizzling like a pot on the boil as she listened, looked just a hair less furious.

"You'd better at least be polite, because Mistress Smith is half owner of the ship and is in charge of the money. Now, answer the question or get the hell out of here."

"We complained about the food on the *Grandee*," another Singh said. "We do not eat meat and the captain put us off the ship here."

Rajiv frowned but nodded agreement. "What Rahul says is true," he said. "The captain cursed us."

"What we've got is what we could take aboard on ben Yusuf," I said. "I haven't checked it over, but I think a lot of it is meat or it's been cooked in meat fat. If that's a problem, then..."

"We can bring our own food," Rajiv said. "If you advance us our pay?"

I motioned him back, then turned to Monica and whispered, "I don't think they're going to run off if we advance them twenty thalers and I'd like some help in the rigging. But I sure won't pretend I like the snotty bastard."

"If they take the twenty thalers and disappear," Monica replied, "then it's better to learn it now than in space. I won't miss the twenty thalers when we've reached home."

I nodded and faced the Singhs. "All right," I said. "If you've got the skills you claim, you're hired at able rates and Mistress Monica will advance you money to buy food. Unless perhaps you're too proud to accept it from her hands?"

Instead of answering, Rajiv drew himself up straight. "Test us, then, and then give us our money for food."

I decided that was good enough. "All right," I said. "I'll

erect the dorsal antenna and you can show me how quick you get up it and down."

I went inside to the console.

I put the brothers in air suits and sent them up the antenna. The topsail helpfully jammed, which it had twice done since we lifted from ben Yusuf. The Singhs shook it out in approved fashion.

Sanjay wasn't really of able quality in the rigging, but he turned out to have at least as much knowledge of a fusion bottle as I did. Our unit had an integral display, but the bottle couldn't be observed from the console.

That was a terrible situation, though it hadn't been a problem for us since we were keeping the cargo hold pressurized. The main hatch sealed well enough for that to work, though I disliked going into the hold to check readings. Given that the hatch between the cabin and hold wasn't an airlock, it would have been bloody impossible under some circumstances.

I tried Rajiv on the console. His astrogation wasn't up to the standard expected of an entering-second-year cadet at the Academy, but he knew the basics.

At the end of the morning, I told the Singhs to wait for a moment and joined Monica, who'd returned from a shopping trip with Lal. "If you're willing," I said, "I recommend that we hire them. They'll save us about a day on our run to Saguntum. We'll clear rigging problems faster, and I don't have to recalibrate as often."

Monica shrugged. "If you think so," she said, "of course. Certainly getting home a day sooner appeals to me."

I called the brothers to us and hired them as able spacers while Lal watched. Monica then gave them an advance to buy food.

I hadn't been considering Saguntum except as a destination. I thought further as I watched Monica hand each brother seven thalers and noted that it was an advance.

Rejoining the *Sunray*'s complement might not be as simple as I'd been assuming. I was probably being carried on the books as *Run*, meaning I'd left without permission or explanation. My story was simple and innocent—I was surely not the first spacer to get drunk on liberty—but it sounded increasingly thin as I went over it in my mind.

It only made sense if Maeve had deliberately sold me off planet. I couldn't come up with a believable—believable to me, I mean—reason that she should have done so. I wasn't looking forward to explaining to Captain Leary, and *especially* to Lady Mundy, that it had happened.

When Monica had paid the Singhs their advance—a five thaler coin and two ones, each, they went off.

I said, "I'm going to take Lal off to pick up more stores. Ricardo may be here before we get back, but he knows what to do. All right?"

She tried a smile. Aloud she said, "I'm looking forward to getting home."

"Me too," I said, trying to sound more cheerful than I felt. "But I'll settle for getting back to Saguntum."

Lal and I headed for Trident House, carrying one of the air suits between us. When Rajiv was running up and down the rigging, his suit's hip and torso sections separated. A wrist joint I might have been willing to tape; possibly even a knee if we really needed to use the suit. Not the waist, though.

I needed Lal to help with the load, but I also wanted a chance to talk with him.

"So…" I said. I was carrying the front end of the suit so I spoke back over my shoulder. "Where did you meet the Singhs?"

"At the hostel where I'm staying," Lal said. "They were being put out of it because they hadn't paid the rent. I paid for last night, and I said that I would introduce to them to my captain."

"They're not relatives, then?" I said.

Lal laughed. "They would be very insulted to hear you say that," he said. "They are of much higher status than I."

He laughed again. "Almost everyone is of higher status than I. Not you, of course."

"Of course," I said. "And I gather the Singhs weren't too proud to accept your money?"

"That is their right," said Lal. I didn't hear any touch of emotion in his voice. "As it is my duty to offer such help as one of my class is able to offer to persons of theirs."

"They're not friends, then?" I said.

"Scarcely."

Bagnelli was in the back when we entered the shop, but the boy ran to the back and fetched him without needing to be told. He appeared, still chewing his lunch. "Roy," he called cheerfully. "You have brought me a repair job, perhaps?"

"I've brought you a trade-in," I said. "And we want two refurbed air suits along with a few other items. We lift off tomorrow, Pietro. Heaven willing and the creeks don't rise."

By the time we headed back toward the *Alfraz*, it was getting toward evening. Lal was helping Bagnelli's boy with the cart—two air suits and considerably more in the way of supplies. The boy would carry the partial hard suit back in the cart; the transaction wasn't quite a wash, but I wasn't pissing Monica's money away either.

Lal and the boy were chatting. I walked behind, thinking. Thinking about Monica, mostly.

She was obviously somebody in Saguntum, and she probably had parents with ideas about who their daughter ought to be seeing. Spacers with twenty-two Alliance thalers to their name weren't likely to be high on their list of suitors.

At least I hadn't had to spend the twenty-two thalers. I wasn't raking off any of Monica's credit chip, though. Frankly, I don't think my father would have either. Robbing the Republic wasn't the same as robbing your girlfriend.

Monica *was* my girlfriend for now. For tonight.

When we got to the *Alfraz*, the pump was already chugging and Ricardo and his boy were loading their tricycle to leave. "It's been running twenty minutes," he told me. "I turned it on and off twice from the console. I didn't touch that bloody switch on the box. I sure wish you'd have let me rewire that."

"The next time I land on Plaquemines," I said, shaking his hand. "But I don't expect that to be any time soon."

It occurred to me that I had at least a claim to the *Alfraz*. Worst case—and I didn't know how angry Captain Leary was going to be—I might be able to set up as captain of a tramp freighter. Because I wasn't in the RCN, he couldn't have me spaced as a deserter.

I smiled vaguely. Ricardo took it as a friendly expression. "Well, I'll be happy to do the work," he said. He waved as he pedaled off with his son.

Lal and Bagnelli's boy were stowing away our purchases, leaving me alone with Monica. I cleared my throat and said, "I expect our water tank to be full by midnight, though I'll check the flow in a minute to be sure. In the morning you can look over the complete bill at Trident and sign. Then we're ready to lift as soon as the Singhs board, if they haven't done already."

"I thought we'd use the houseboat again tonight," Monica said. "If that's all right with you?"

"Yes," I said. Neither of us were looking the other in the face. "Yes." I cleared my throat again and said, "I put the repairs on the bill to Trident. It's higher by Trident's profit that way, but Ricardo didn't know me from Adam. I think the whole business will run well under a thousand thalers."

"I trust you," Monica said. She smiled, but she still wasn't looking right at me.

"Yes," I said again. I prayed that I'd never give her reason not to. "Well, I'd better give the others a hand with the suits we're trading to Trident. The hard suit is pretty awkward."

I reached out and squeezed her hand. Then I went up the ramp to help Lal and the boy.

Our crewmen—the Singh brothers followed by Lal, walking two paces behind them—arrived shortly after dawn. I left the Singhs to strike down their gear—thin bindles, plus a wicker hamper of food which Sanjay and Rahul carried between them—while Lal performed a final surface check of the rigging.

Monica and I went to Trident to clear our account with Pietro. That was business, but it was also my last time alone with Monica before Saguntum and everything changing. That was how I felt about it, anyway.

I didn't say anything like that to her, of course. It was hard enough to frame the thought in my own mind. Saying it would make it real a week or so before it had to be.

The charge from Monica's credit chip was 880 thalers. I was tempted to give Pietro another fifty; but it wasn't my money, and I guess he knew what he was doing.

When we returned to the *Alfraz*, I saw that the brothers had taken the three starboard bunks. I switched on the console, checked the readouts, and turned to the crew.

"All right," I said, speaking to Rajiv but sweeping all three with my eyes. "While I prep for lift-off, the three of you remake the bunks. The bottom one"—I pointed—"is Mistress Smith's. Rajiv, since you seem to have stripped it, you'll remake it. You'll put your bedding on the top bunk in that rack. The middle one is Lal's, so you, Rahul, remake it for him. I've got the bottom bunk on the other stack, so you take either of the two that're open."

"This is not right!" Rajiv said in a furious voice.

"It bloody well is!" I said. "Or you can get off the ship right now! Do you think you're on your own piss-pot world still? Well, you're not. The *Alfraz* may not be Cinnabar, but it's going to be run like it is so long as I'm captain!"

I wouldn't generally have talked like that, but seeing the bunks unmade and the bedding tossed onto the deck had lit my fuse. I was beginning to regret hiring the Singhs.

"Your choice, Rajiv!" I said. I didn't imagine that I could take all three, but Plaquemines had police. I was pretty sure that Pietro could find me help to put things right without going the formal route, too.

"You are the captain," Rajiv said after a moment. He bowed slightly with his hands together. He and his brothers remade the bunks while I went over my course calculations. Again.

I stayed at the console while the *Alfraz* accelerated out of orbit; Lal and the Singh brothers went out on the hull. There were only four suits so I couldn't have joined them, even if I'd felt there was a reason to.

Lal returned to report after half an hour, as I'd directed. The port mainsail had only deployed partway. The Singhs were working on it.

While I waited for them to return from the hull, I inserted a chip into the console and dipped into one of my purchases from Trident: *Annotated Charts of Region 37,* Edition 12. It was the Alliance equivalent of the *Sailing Directions.* Pietro had said that the update was about five years old.

We didn't really need it for a run to Saguntum, but I remembered the horror I'd felt when I checked the console and found only cursory data on points directly between Karst and ben Yusuf. I'd been diffident when I mentioned the *Charts* as a possible expense to Monica, but she'd merely waved a hand and said, "Of course."

I located the world where we'd touched down to fill the

mass tank. The data was cursory as I'd expected regarding an uninhabited world. It mentioned dangerous sea life, though not the worms we'd had to deal with.

The Singhs came in from the hull about an hour later than I'd expected from what Lal had told me of the situation. "Problems?" I said to Rajiv as he took his suit off.

"The starboard topsail yard doesn't extend properly," he said. "The motor is burned out, I think."

Rahul added, "We hauled the yard into place, but this cannot go on. There must be repairs."

"I think I know what's wrong," I said. "Well, get the suits off. Lal and I will go out after we've inserted."

It sounded like my jury rig with the tower gear hadn't been as satisfactory as I'd hoped. I should've replaced it with a new part when we were in Plaquemines, but it'd been working fine . . . and I'd forgotten about it.

Monica got up from her bunk and bent over me at the console. "What does that mean?" she asked. She didn't sound exactly frightened, but I heard a perfectly reasonable note of concern in her voice.

"If I can't fix it," I said, "and I may not be able to . . . it means I'll have to program our course for three working antennas instead of four. That'll work, there's plenty of tramp ships doing it right now, but it'll take longer because we can't transition between universes as smoothly as we should."

I scowled and said, "Look, I screwed up. I should've got this looked at and fixed before we lifted."

Monica patted me on the shoulder. "I didn't want to spend extra time on the ground," she said. She went back to her bunk.

I checked the series of sail-plan corrections to hold the course I'd chosen. It'd be three hours before the starboard topsail had to be furled, and after that I might be able to tweak the mainsail so that we didn't lose too much agility.

Well, that was after I'd had a look at the problem. It might not be as bad as I was imagining anyway.

Monica and the Singhs were in their bunks. Lal was facing me through the display, from the striker's seat.

"Crew," I said over the PA system, "prepare for insertion into the Matrix. Inserting . . ."

I let the countdown clock actually execute the command while I watched.

"now!"

We shivered into the Matrix. The *Alfraz*, cranky as she was in too many ways, had inserted slickly every time.

Lal and I went out on the hull wearing the two refurbished air suits I'd gotten from Trident. Mine was stiffer than the trio which we'd found aboard the *Alfraz* when we took her over. I suppose that was good, though I'd have new scrapes and bruises tomorrow.

Lal paused, looking out at the Matrix. I stopped—I was on my way to the starboard antenna—and did the same. It was the usual pastel wash, rather on the cooler end of the spectrum according to what my brain was telling me: greens, blues, and even half-glimpsed violet.

I wondered if I'd ever understand the Matrix the way Captain Leary did. Probably not: It seemed to be something you felt, not something you learned. But Lal might have been able to talk to Captain Leary in terms they both understood.

I opened the cover of the drive mechanism at the base of the starboard antenna. The clamp that held the tower gear in position had become loose. My removing the spring and snapping it back into place had weakened it; now the drive gear rode over the teeth of what should have been the driven gear. There wasn't a spare on the *Alfraz*, of course.

I laid my helmet alongside Lal's and said, "Go on back in. I want to stay out for a while." I was going to have to plot a course for three antennas. I didn't expect to gain major insights on the hull, but I'd learned a bit from Captain Leary.

While Lal trudged to the airlock, I mounted to the dorsal mainyard. I didn't see the face of the divine in the color patterns, but I did get an inkling of a course. It was critical to keep as slight a change as possible in energy from each bubble universe to the next. So long as I could achieve that, our inability to dodge in and out quickly wouldn't be too big a handicap.

I came in when my oxygen tank peeped at the last half hour. I'd been out less than two hours—there must be a problem with the tank or the suit—but that was still considerably longer than I'd intended.

As usual, I took the helmet off in the lock. As I tramped in, working the catches of the suit, I said, "I think we'll be all right as-is to Saguntum, though if we're making a lot less time than I—"

I looked up without attention. Rajiv faced me with a set expression; he was holding a small pistol. Rahul was at the back of the cabin. My own pistol—the one I'd thrown into the

325

storage locker after Monica killed the consul with it—was in Rahul's hand, though he wasn't pointing it at anything.

Monica lay on her bunk, roped to an upright. She spat out a wad of cloth and snarled, "They've mutinied! They're going to murder us!"

"You will not be harmed!" Rajiv said. "Do not resist and you both will be delivered unharmed on a developed planet. We—*don't* reach for a tool! I will shoot you!"

I'd been thinking about rushing Rajiv, true, but I hadn't been reaching for a tool. I put my right hand flat on the bulkhead beside me, which was the only way I could be sure my arm wouldn't flop down toward a wrench hanging from my belt.

I was about to be enslaved again. That would be something to talk about at cocktail parties when I got back to Cinnabar. If I ever went to another cocktail party—the invitations had stopped when Dad shot himself. If I ever got back to Cinnabar . . .

"He's lying!" Monica said. "They'll kill us!"

"No, no," I said. "They'll sell us for slaves. We're worth too much money for them to kill us."

I was worth money. The lovely, blond Monica was worth a *lot* of money. I smiled warmly.

I didn't think Rajiv would deliberately shoot me, but he was so *bloody* nervous that he might twitch off a shot without meaning to. If I calmed him down, then I'd have a chance to jump him.

Rahul would certainly kill me if Rajiv didn't, but not before I managed to bang the snotty bastard's head on the deck plating. I couldn't help what happened after I was dead, but by *heaven* I was going to take Rajiv—or at least his sense—with me.

"Where are you going to sell us, Rajiv?" I said in a friendly voice. "I don't suggest ben Yusuf, because they'd be likely to hang you and us both. You *might* be all right if you landed someplace else than Salaam, but I think you'd be better to try another planet."

"Lal?" Monica said. "We can afford to replace another switch!"

I hadn't been thinking about Lal—or Sanjay, for that matter, who was watching Lal at the back end of the cabin. Lal was still wearing his suit. Rajiv must have grabbed him immediately but held him out of the way until I entered—which they'd probably expected to be only minutes later.

Lal turned and unlocked the internal hatch.

"What's he doing?" Rajiv said when he heard the mechanism clack. He risked a glance over his shoulder, which gave me a chance that I didn't take. "Sanjay, don't let the dog leave!"

Lal stepped into the cargo hold, pulling his arm away from Sanjay's halfhearted grip. Sanjay followed through the hatchway.

Rajiv shouted, "Rahul, shoot the dog! What is he doing?"

He wasn't more than half-aware of me. I lifted my gauntlet half an inch off the bulkhead, though it shouldn't have mattered.

All metal surfaces crackled blue an instant before the cabin lights went out. Rajiv fired. My right arm jerked at a drop of fire.

For a moment the only illumination was the console display, an opalescence which didn't light anything around it. The emergency circuit closed and the cabin lights flickered on. The electrocuted corpses of Rajiv and Rahul dropped stiffly to the deck. Their pistols clanged sharply.

I looked at my arm. The shot had missed me—Rajiv's muscles had clamped his finger on the trigger as he died—but

327

the iridium pellet had splashed my arm with molten droplets of itself and the bulkhead both. The metal had melted through the air suit. I could patch it easily enough, but there were undamaged suits for Lal and me now, and we were the whole crew again.

Lal came in from the hold, holding the glowing wrench with which he'd shorted the switch. He looked dazed. He flung the wrench against the deck; the heat of the steel must have finally gotten through the gauntlet.

I went over to Monica. Her hands and feet were still tied to stanchions so that she couldn't sit up.

I was wobbly myself. There were burned patches on the soles of both of Rajiv's bare feet but nothing like the extensive charring on the worm's hide from a similar jolt. It had done the job, though.

I tried to untie Monica's legs, but I couldn't manage it even after I'd taken my gauntlets off. The cable cutter was still hanging from my tool belt. It was awkward on ordinary rope, but a final jerk broke the last uncut fibers. I moved to her wrists.

"Thank you, Lal," Monica said. "I couldn't have survived that again. I would have killed myself."

"Mistress," Lal said. "You and the captain have treated me like a man, like your equal. The Singhs treated me like the dog they called me, as they would have done on Kashgar. Mistress, we were no longer on Kashgar."

I straightened as Monica shook off the tag ends of her bonds. "We're still in the Matrix, Lal," I said. "I think that's a good place to leave the Singhs. They can have a bubble universe all to themselves."

I changed my suit before I grabbed Rajiv's ankles and started dragging him to the airlock. After this, I could plot a course to a world with a repair yard.

Chapter Twenty-nine

I won't say we exactly needed the *Annotated Charts* after all, but it made my decision to set our course for Benedict easier than it would have been if I'd only had the notation BENEDICT alongside the coordinates in the console—the data on the *Alfraz* when we boarded it. I figured the course for three working antennas and the starboard rig telescoped and folded.

Lal and I could have worked the topsail, but it would have been dangerous as well as brutally hard. We were better running crippled to a port three days away where we could get parts and repairs.

If the rig were in proper form, I wouldn't have worried about not being able to refill the mass tank. I wasn't willing to trust a dicey rig and a nonworking pump to the present very short crew of the *Alfraz*. Not if I had a choice, anyway.

Monica smiled as I started to explain my reasoning to her. "Roy," she said. "I want to know what we're doing—that's simple courtesy. But I don't need to know your professional reasoning. I'm not qualified to understand it, let alone judge it."

That was true enough. As with Lal, though, I'd have felt less alone if there'd been somebody I could discuss things with.

The trouble was, there was nobody within three days' sail who *could* do that. If Monica refused to lift some of the responsibility that was mine alone, I should be thankful.

Albeit really lonely.

Lal and I went out together to check the clamps on the starboard rig. I'd given up on the notion of tweaking the mainsail to emulate the missing topsail when I considered that we were down to a crew of two again. A jammed mainsail would be a real problem if it couldn't be cleared immediately, and that job would take three spacers; or better, four.

In the airlock, before I put on my helmet, I said, "I appreciate what you did, Lal. I was about to jump Rajiv. One or the other brother would have shot me."

"Captain," Lal said, "you saved my life, and you have always treated me like a man. What the Singhs would have done was on my honor, because I brought them to you. Even such as I have honor."

The air in the lock was getting thin. We both quickly put on our helmets, which ended the conversation. I squeezed his gauntleted hand before opening the lock, though.

We made Benedict orbit in just within the three days I'd guessed. I was over a hundred thousand miles out when we got a microwave hail from a customs launch, *"Benedict One to unidentified vessel, state your business. Over."*

"Monica?" I said. She was on the striker's seat, watching an image of the planet. "I'm trying to jump us closer in. Can you handle the commo?"

I had a splitting headache, but she probably did also. We'd both feel better on the ground, so focusing on getting there was a win for everybody.

"Freighter Alfraz *out of ben Yusuf requests permission to land in Howardport for refitting,"* Monica said. *"Over."*

There were incremental jumps preset into the console, but they'd been calculated for a full rig. I doubt they'd have been much use to previous captains either, because very few tramps were operating with a full rig. Our present condition was extreme but not unheard of, even on Cinnabar,

"Benedict to Alfraz," the microwave said. *"Say again your leaving port, over?"*

"Benedict, Captain Olfetrie recaptured this ship from pirates in the port of Salaam on ben Yusuf," Monica said. I could see tension on her face, but her voice seemed as calm as ever. *"Do we have permission to land and refit, over?"*

The response took almost a minute. The control vessel was obviously checking with superiors on the ground. As I finished my calculations, the microwave said, *"Roger,* Alfraz. *You may land in the berth you will be assigned in Howardport. Benedict One, Over."*

"Crew," I said, "We're making a positioning jump before we start braking to land. Preparing to insert—*now.*"

* * *

My second extraction brought us out within twenty thousand miles, which was almost too close. Howardport Control was marginally polite when it assigned us a landing place, and I wasn't surprised to see a pair of armored cars waiting on the quay when the steam had cooled enough for me see anything through the ship's sensors.

I opened the ship as promptly as I could and stood at the end of the ramp with my arms crossed behind my back, trying to look clean-cut and harmless. A bit to my surprise, Monica came and joined me.

"I'm planning to be polite and agree with anything they say," I explained while port personnel readied an extension from the quay to our outrigger. The *Alfraz* didn't carry an extension of her own. I'd bought an inflatable boat in Plaquemines, but in this case the authorities certainly didn't want us traipsing into their city until they'd given us a thorough vetting.

"Of course," said Monica with a touch of irritation. I noticed that the barrette was back in her hair.

I didn't respond. I'd rather be accused of stating the obvious than I would of failing to give somebody necessary information that *I'd* thought was obvious.

The port authorities were three civilians and four men wearing dull-blue uniforms. Their carbines were slung, which was better than guns pointing at us, but I wondered if maybe we shouldn't have said we came from Karst.

"My name's Hobbins," said the older male civilian. He was in his fifties and reasonably fit without being in the least athletic. "We're here to inspect your vessel and its cargo."

I gave him a short bow, because from his tone I wasn't sure

he'd accept my hand if I offered it. "Of course, sir," I said. "The ship is completely open; the console is live and there are no protected sectors in it. We have no cargo, and there's only one spacer besides myself. His name's Lal and he's from Kashgar."

Hobbins nodded to his companions. The younger civilians went up the ramp, accompanied by two of the uniformed men. The other two stayed with Hobbins and us.

"Would you like us to explain how we came to be here?" Monica volunteered. I'd been waiting for Hobbins to ask his next question.

He smiled at her. "Ben Yusuf isn't a normal trading partner for Benedict," he said. "For us or for any civilized planet in this region. So yes, I would like to know."

"Roy, you'd better tell him," Monica said. "I didn't know anything about it until we escaped."

"Lal and I were spacers on the *Martinique*," I said. That was a lie, but not one that could be proved. "We were captured by pirates and taken to Salaam on ben Yusuf. I was made a slave in the Admiral's palace. I met Mistress Smith there; she was a harem slave and wanted to escape home to Saguntum. With Lal's help, we captured a ship in the harbor and are in the process of sailing to Saguntum."

I turned my hands up. "We had mechanical failures," I said. "Which is scarcely surprising. We landed on Benedict for repairs, which we're able to pay for."

"An admirably succinct account," Hobbins said. "But quite a remarkable one. You must be very resourceful people, and very lucky."

"If we make it to Saguntum," I said, "you can call us lucky."

"No," said Monica sharply. "Roy, we're *very* lucky. I couldn't have lasted much longer in that palace. At least I can die in clean air now."

Hobbins looked at Monica oddly. "Mistress Smith?" he said. "If I may ask you, how old are you?"

"I'm twenty," Monica said, meeting his eyes. Her voice was neutral, but neither of us knew where this was going. "In standard years, that is."

Hobbins nodded. "The same age as my daughter," he said. "Well, let's go aboard your ship and see what my colleagues have found."

"Nothing that will help do much for your customs receipts, I'm afraid," I said as we walked up the ramp. The two guards—armed police?—followed us without comment. "All we have is food for the voyage."

"My colleagues are from Tax and Customs," Hobbins said calmly. "I, on the other hand, am in the Directorate of External Affairs."

I stubbed my toe on the ramp and stumbled. I looked at Robbins closely. "Pretty high up, I would guess," I said.

He smiled but continued to look ahead. "I'm not a politician," he said. "A business involving the pirates of ben Yusuf was going to land on my desk eventually, so I decided I'd take a hand at once."

Aboard the *Alfraz*, Lal stood silently in a corner of the cabin while the civilians were at both positions of the console. The woman on the couch at the main display turned her head and said, "Sir, according to the log they lifted from ben Yusuf, touched on a world that's just an alphanumeric, then Plaquemines, and finally here. No indication of piracy or, for that matter, anything else."

"Logs can be doctored," said the young male civilian on the striker's seat. "And there are two guns in the locker."

"Logs can't be doctored by me!" I said. I was probably a little hotter than I should have been, but it was a nonsense claim. "And yeah, there are two pistols in the locker. Are there any tramps in this region that wouldn't be true about?"

Before the customs man could respond, Hobbins raised his hand. "I don't believe we're dealing with pirates, Rawlins," he said. "A pair of very fortunate young people, it seems to me." As an afterthought, he glanced at Lal and smiled. "And their crewman."

"Well, Darlene and I have been told that this is in your hands, sir," said the male customs man. He stepped away from the console.

"Yes," said Hobbins. "It is."

He looked at me and said, "Captain Olfetrie, what are your plans now?"

"Well, if we're free to leave the ship," I said, "I'll see about getting a replacement tower gear and an electrician to rewire the switch that I damaged in electrocuting an animal that crawled aboard while we were taking on water. Can you recommend a ship chandler?"

"*I* can't," Hobbins said, "but I believe—"

He glanced toward the other civilians. The woman said, "Sir, my brother's a partner in LaJoie and Company. They've got a good reputation."

"Yeah, they're okay," said her male colleague, possibly

trying to make up for his earlier behavior.

"Then Mistress Smith and I will check with LaJoie," I said. "Ah—are Alliance thalers good on Benedict?"

"They pass as current here," Hobbins said. "And you are free to go, yes."

"I'd like to get some food," Monica said. "Particularly fresh fruit. I can see stands on the waterfront. Roy, you don't need me to take care of the repairs."

"Then I hope your business on Benedict will be successful," Hobbins said, making a little bow. "It's been a pleasure to meet you both."

I let out a deep breath. It had certainly been a pleasure to meet him.

I probably could have found my way to LaJoie and Company myself, but Darlene said she was off duty now and guided me there. Not only did they take thalers, I thought to ask about the Karst sequins I'd brought from ben Yusuf. I was able to get rid of those as well.

I was feeling pretty pleased with life as I ambled back to the *Alfraz*, carrying the replacement tower gear. It was heavy enough to switch from one hand to the other, but not heavy enough that I regretted leaving Lal with the ship.

I'd offered him liberty until the next morning, but he'd said he'd rather stay. He was still embarrassed about the Singhs, though there was no reason. I'd been the one to hire them, and Monica had agreed.

There were two vehicles parked on the quay as I returned

from the chandlery. One was a little port-authority jitney with a saddle in front on which the driver still sat and a bench over the back wheels that would hold two if they were friends. The other was a four-wheeled gray car with an ID legend stencilled in black and the name HKS *Meduse*. The car might be armored, but the pintle in the center was empty. It was obviously meant to support an automatic impeller or a missile launcher.

People stood in the hold of the *Alfraz*, though nobody was shouting and I didn't see weapons. I stopped beside the driver dozing on the jitney and tapped him on the shoulder. "You've got commo on this," I said. "Use it to raise the Directorate of External Affairs and tell Master Hobbins that there's trouble at the *Alfraz*. I think the Karst destroyer in harbor is trying to pull something."

"What?" the driver said. "Who're you? I don't have anything to do with External Affairs!"

"I'm Captain Olfetrie of Cinnabar," I said truthfully. "And you won't have anything to do with *any* bloody government job if you don't pass the warning on to Master Hobbins before it blows up into a real crisis!"

I walked up the ramp, whistling *Don't you remember sweet Alice?* and holding the paper-wrapped gear in the crook of my left arm. I'd spoken to the driver with certainty. The only thing I was really certain about was that I was out of my depth. That was getting to be the usual thing. That realization made me smile.

"Good afternoon, gentlemen," I said as I approached the hatch.

A woman in a blue uniform stepped out of the cabin to look at me. "And madame," I said, entering the hold. "I'm

Captain Olfetrie. May I ask the purpose of your visit?"

Lal stood in the hold also, along with a man in a khaki uniform like that of the driver of the jitney. I handed the gear to Lal and said, "I want this installed soonest. I'll be along to help as soon as I get free, but on the ground it shouldn't be much of a job even for you alone."

"Captain?" Lal said. "They say we have stolen the ship."

I clapped Lal on the shoulder. "That's above your pay grade," I said, smiling. "Get to work on the rig and I'll discuss the situation with our visitors."

Two blue-uniformed men came out of the cabin, followed by Monica. Her face was still.

"You're in command?" one of the men said. The silver script of his nametag was too worn for me to read it. He turned to the port-authority man in the hold and called, "Superintendent, I want this man arrested as a pirate!"

"Sir?" I said to the superintendent. "I've just asked your driver to inform Master Hobbins of External Affairs about the situation and asked him to intervene. You might check on your man and make sure he's done that. I fear he didn't understand how much trouble he'll get your department in if you try to handle this on your own."

The other male Karst officer was older than his colleague, forty or so, but he had hollow circles in place of pips on his collar and was obviously subordinate. He looked from me to the first man and said, "I know the *Alfraz*, I was her captain until I sold her to the government and joined the navy. She's a Karst ship."

"She may well have been," I said, stepping past the Karst

officers to get into the cabin. "The ben Yusuf pirates steal from anybody, as I understand it. Mistress Smith and I captured it from the pirates at Salaam and escaped with it. I'm perfectly willing to have the matter of ownership determined in court, but"—I smiled at the Karst officers as I put my hand on the airlock controls— "on Saguntum, please. Mistress Smith is a citizen, and I'm an officer of the Republic of Cinnabar Navy, who was shanghaied off my ship there."

I didn't open the locker to get tools out—Lal had been wearing his belt when I ordered him to get to work on the antenna, which should be enough. My real concern was to get away from the *Meduse*'s officers until Hobbins or some other high-ranking local arrived. That might be hours.

Before I could move into the lock—on the surface, the only way onto the hull was up a ladder welded onto the hull—an aircar passed over the *Alfraz* moving low and slow. I heard it circle and moments later land on the quay. *Thank goodness*.

"Gentlemen and milady," I said, passing the Karst personnel in the other direction, "I believe that will be the Benedict officials we've been waiting for."

I certainly hoped so, anyway. I led Monica and our visitors to the boarding ramp. Master Hobbins was already on the extension walkway, walking briskly toward us.

"Sir!" I said, bracing myself to attention. Hobbins didn't have military rank, but I wanted to impress on the Karst officers that he was important. "Midshipman Olfetrie, acting captain of the *Alfraz*, welcomes you aboard!"

"Sir," said the *Meduse*'s captain. "The *Alfraz* is a Karst ship and this fellow, whoever he is, isn't captain of her!"

"You'd be Lieutenant Sisk of the *Meduse*, I believe?" Hobbins said. His voice was calm but not warm.

"Ah, yes, sir, I am," the Karst officer said. "My sailing master here recognizes her."

"Yessir, I do," the older officer said. The female officer hadn't said a word that I'd heard since boarding. "I was her captain, I was, sir."

"And you're saying that Captain Olfetrie did *not* capture the *Alfraz* on ben Yusuf, Lieutenant?" Hobbins said. "Because you should know that my experts have examined the ship's log and found that she did in fact lift from Salaam on ben Yusuf and proceed here with only two short intermediate stops."

"Well, that may be," said Sisk, obviously taken aback. "But she's still a Karst ship!"

"I don't doubt that," Hobbins said. "And it should be easy to prove in Admiralty Court, though there would of course be compensation to Captain Olfetrie if he's proved to have retrieved the vessel from pirates. But that is a matter for the court to decide, Lieutenant. Not for a bureaucratic flunky like the port superintendent here."

He nodded to the man in khaki, who avoided meeting Hobbins' eyes.

"Well, what do you propose to do about it?" Sisk said. "You can't try throwing your weight around with me, you know!"

"I propose," Hobbins said without emphasis on the repeated word, "to wait for a court to determine ownership issues. And to prevent breaches of the peace from occurring on Benedict. I believe the Hegemony of Karst has friendly relations with Saguntum, does it not?"

"Of course we do!" said Sisk. "But that doesn't mean that Saguntine citizens can steal our property!"

"Of course not, Lieutenant," Hobbins said, nodding. "But if I may make a suggestion? You're a naval man, used to the cut and thrust of battle. Perhaps it would be a good idea for you to confer with the Karst Advisor in the city rather than to take matters into your own hands? I think we might all avoid embarrassment if you were to take that line."

Sisk stood without moving for a long moment. Then he nodded curtly and said, "Come on Byerly, Hesketh. We're going back to the ship!"

He strode down the ramp with his subordinates in tow. I watched silently for a moment, then turned and said to Master Hobbins, "Thank you, sir. If it's all right with you, I'll go up on the hull to help Lal."

"May I ask how long will it take you to complete the task?" Hobbins said.

I shrugged. "Less than an hour," I said. "Probably a lot less. But an electrician is coming tomorrow to give us an estimate on the switch replacement."

"Is that necessary?"

"Not necessary, no," I said, "if we've got the rig complete again. But it'll be a lot safer to be able to use the pump."

"Captain Olfetrie," Hobbins said with a cold smile. "It will be *much* safer for you to be off planet immediately. The Karst Advisor would be very embarrassed if the crew of the *Meduse* were to capture the *Alfraz* by force and hang her crew, but realistically I couldn't do anything but write a stiff note if that happened. Karst is *the* power in this region."

Monica said, "Thank you, sir. I have full confidence in Captain Olfetrie's ability to reach Saguntum without taking on additional water. We'll leave as soon as the antenna is repaired and port control gives us authorization."

"You have your authorization now," Hobbins said, bowing to her. "And I'll see to it that no other ship lifts from Howardport until the *Alfraz* has entered the Matrix."

He strode briskly down the ramp. The port personnel in their jitney and the car from the *Meduse* had already pulled away.

I kissed Monica. "I'll see how Lal is coming along," I said. "Soon!"

I was really looking forward to making Saguntum.

Chapter Thirty

We made our first insertion into the Matrix when we were only three hours out from Benedict, much sooner than I'd have chosen if I hadn't needed to vanish as quickly as possible. I could only add velocity in normal space.

I could adjust that velocity relative to normal space in bubble universes where constants of time, velocity, and distance varied; when we extracted into normal space, our location could be very much farther from our point of insertion than would have been the case if we'd remained in normal space the whole time. That said, the faster we were going when we inserted, the multiplication within the Matrix was greater in absolute terms.

Master Hobbins had laid the reason for getting away quickly on the personal safety of the *Alfraz* and her crew. That was certainly real, but there was also a serious risk to Hobbins and to Benedict. From a Cinnabar viewpoint—my viewpoint—Karst was a very minor power. To independent planets in the immediate region, however, Karst was more important than Cinnabar or even than the Alliance which had a greater local presence than we did.

Master Hobbins had been very supportive. I didn't want to cause him needless problems by remaining in the vicinity.

All things considered, the rig behaved properly. That said, Lal and I spent more time on the hull than we did in the cabin. He didn't complain, and I found I was coming to like it.

Being immersed in the Matrix made it familiar to me and even welcoming. I was beginning to notice the minuscule changes in apparent color from one viewing to another. This was all in my mind because visible light didn't exist beyond the ship's individual bubble, but it did indicate relative energy states and relative changes.

I came in, feeling tired but good. Lal was asleep on his bunk. We'd been taking solo watches because there really wasn't any choice. We had enough experience with the air suits to be willing to trust them, and I'd insisted that Lal use a safety line the way I did. I think my concern puzzled him, but I was the captain.

Monica got off the couch at the console's main screen and moved around to the striker's seat. "The rig is well?" she said, an excuse to speak.

"I twitched the ventral alignment a notch and squirted some graphite in the race," I said as I took my suit off. I ached pretty generally—as I usually did now—and I knew I'd be feeling today's work in my rib muscles tomorrow morning. "It's worn but I think it'll get us to Saguntum fine."

I needed a shower, a meal, and some sleep, but first I wanted to check our position in the sidereal universe. There were two opinions on going through extraction while you were asleep. The majority feeling was that the effects stayed with you longer; that was me in spades. Some folks, one in ten or so, missed the effects completely if they were asleep. Lal was in the minority and slept through extractions unaware.

Monica and I weren't so lucky. I glanced at my course projection and said, "Prepare to extract in five seconds. Three, two, one, *now*!"

I slid down through a bath of cold water and came out the other side shivering but unharmed a few seconds later. Monica, on the other hand, gasped so loudly that she awakened Lal. She had to cling to the console to keep from falling off her seat.

I engaged the High Drive and compared our real position with the position I'd calculated when I set the course. I was sorry for Monica, but there was nothing I could do—and goodness knows, I've had miserable extractions also. Astrogation was my job, and to my delight we were remarkably close to where we should have been in the sidereal universe.

I was feeling pretty good about that. Sure, I knew it meant that my errors were cancelling one another out, but being lucky is even better than being good. Well, I've heard guys say that.

I got up from the console and said to Lal, "We're spot on for the moment. I'm going to check the fusion bottle before I calculate the sail plan for the next insertion."

I spoke loudly so that Lal could understand me over the High Drive. Monica could hear also, but I was pretty sure nothing was going to penetrate her consciousness in her present condition.

We were accelerating at 1.5 g, the best the *Alfraz* was capable of with the High Drive alone. While we weren't really short of reaction mass, we had no means of replenishing it. I wasn't going to use what we had in a wasteful fashion.

I walked heavily to the internal hatch, opened it, and stepped over the coaming with great care. I could move easily enough, but simply raising my boot higher than usual in taking a step required deliberation.

The readout was on a box at head height on the side of the fusion bottle. I tapped the switch to illuminate the readout. I was already considering how I would modify the console's "book solution" for our next insertion.

The needle was well into the red.

In the split second while I took in the fact, the needle dropped back toward the bottom of the yellow zone and quivered there.

What in hell am I going to do now?

The needle was beginning to rise again in tiny, trembling increments. I tramped back to the console.

"Oh, that was a bad one," Monica said, trying to smile at me.

"Monica," I said. "I need you to go into the hold and watch the display on the fusion bottle. Don't worry about the numbers, just the green-yellow-red readout. Tell me what the needle's doing!"

She went to the hold, taking Lal with her. I thought she needed help walking under acceleration, but I didn't ask.

I cut back the High Drive to 1 g. There hadn't been a problem until now. I hadn't been checking the bottle constantly, but I *had* checked whenever I thought about it. Maybe hourly when we'd been in sidereal space, or at least every couple or three hours.

The power usage to feed the High Drive—converting normal matter to antimatter, which provided thrust when it combined with normal matter in the motors—was the greatest draw a starship put on its fusion bottle. Running the converters at high rate shouldn't have been an overload, but it was the only thing I could change.

Lal reappeared at my shoulder, offering a note. When I realized what he was doing, I snatched it out of his hand and read IN YELLOW ONE EIGHTH INCH ABOVE GREEN. The block printing was the same as I remembered Monica using when she wrote cards for me to read through the palace cameras.

I nodded to Lal and thumbed him back toward the hold. Then I returned to my course calculations.

Rather than try to shout over the High Drive, Monica was using Lal as a messenger. RCN commo helmets would have made the job much easier, but having a real engineer—and for that matter, regular RCN maintenance— would have been better yet. Failing those things, having somebody as sharp as Monica was the best I could imagine.

I didn't have my third-year rotation on Power Room Practice at the Academy. I'm sure there'd have been a lot of information beyond the basics I'd gotten in my first-year introduction, but I was also pretty sure that fixing a bottle that fluctuated as badly as ours had was beyond anything I'd be able to handle if I'd graduated as a midshipman.

This was the sort of problem that only a long-service expert like Chief Pasternak could diagnose. And even a Pasternak might say that the answer was to shut down the fusion bottle and replace it immediately.

Lal came with another note: NEEDLE UNSTABLE BUT ON AVERAGE HAS DROPPED SLIGHTLY.

I nodded and continued to work.

We didn't have the option of shutting down and replacing the bottle. We were many light-years away from the nearest replacement.

I finished my calculations and entered the course, including the point at which we would insert. If I died this minute, the *Alfraz* would still execute my commands. When Lal came with a third note, I took it but rose from the couch and went into the hold to join Monica.

She looked up, startled. We could talk when we were this close. "Is it all right?" she said.

I nodded. "It's as good as I can make it," I said. The needle was below where it'd been when I first noticed the problem, but it hadn't dropped into the green as I'd hoped it would. "We'll insert in fourteen minutes"—probably thirteen by now—"and the bottle will basically be at stand-by until we engage the High Drive again. I'll think we'll be okay."

Intellectually, that was true. My gut didn't think it was going to be fine, but it was no smarter than the gut of any other frightened kid. Frightened young man, I suppose, but I wasn't feeling very manly.

"So we continue as we've been doing, then?" Monica said. She was just asking a question—not protesting, not complaining. She wanted to know what the situation was.

"Not exactly," I said. "There were two things different going on when I noticed the problem with the bottle. I'd raised it to maximum output to accelerate on High Drive. When I cut it back, the bottle settled down pretty well. The other thing I did, though, was to extract from the Matrix."

"What does extracting do?" Monica said.

We were both watching the needle. There were six separate windows below that; the multidigit numbers on each ran up and down in quick bursts, like startled roaches. It was going up again. Not fast, but definitely the wrong direction.

"It shouldn't do anything," I said, "but *nothing* we're doing should be a problem. This fusion bottle was intended for a bigger ship than ours. Our six motors shouldn't have stressed it. Wouldn't have stressed it if it was working the way it ought to be."

"Will we be able to get to Saguntum?" Monica said.

"We should," I said. "But we could get back to Benedict faster."

"What will happen to us if we run out of power in the Matrix," Monica said. Her voice sounded perfectly calm, but her eyes were wide open and terrified.

"That can't happen," I said, smiling brightly. "We're at risk of a high-end failure, not a shutdown. If the bottle fails, it'll convert everything inside the hull into plasma in a heartbeat. Probably most of the hull too."

Monica giggled. "Well, that's all right, then," she said. She sounded like she meant it. "I don't want to go back to Benedict."

"The other thing…" I said, leading her back into the cabin with me. We were getting close to when I'd set the console to insert, having based the course calculations on our velocity at that time. "The other thing is that we'll being trying to reach

Saguntum in a single run instead of breaking it into three as I'd planned."

"But that's good, isn't it?" Monica said as she settled onto her couch. Lal was already on the striker's seat of the console.

"It's good if my astrogation's better than I think it is," I said. "I'll have my fingers crossed. But it means we'll be in the Matrix for seven days straight because our sidereal velocity's not as high as I'd like it to be. There's stories about long insertions causing folks to see things. Nothing harmful, but, well, really odd."

People who came back into the normal universe hadn't been harmed. What might have happened to folks who hadn't extracted, well, there was nobody to say.

"It'll give us something to tell people about when we're back on Saguntum," Monica said.

I settled onto my couch. The High Drive shut off automatically as we prepared to insert. If either Monica or I was as cheerful about our prospects as we sounded, we were nuts.

"Inserting!" I said. We rippled out of the normal universe.

I can't describe the next week. Looking back on it, everything was clear and sharp for the first day or two but after that the world lost its edges.

The work on the hull was hard from the beginning. After a while it crushed me flat. I no more thought about it than I thought about breathing.

The rig ceased to be antennas, cables, and sails. It became a pattern. When something went askew with the pattern, it glowed red in my mind until I'd put it right.

I'd heard spacers talk about seeing alien ghosts during long runs in the Matrix. One night Barnes and Dasi had described things they'd seen on a twenty-day run in the corridors of Captain Leary's corvette, the *Princess Cecile*, and sometimes walking through bulkheads. I didn't see anything like that, but by the end of the week I had become part of the *Alfraz*. I was a machine working the sails while I was awake, and when I slept my dreams were still out on the hull.

I'd just come down from checking the set of the ventral top-gallant when the Matrix shimmered brightly an instant before going coldly dark. Around me were the stars of the sidereal universe.

The *Alfraz* had extracted without me being aware it was about to happen. We were in normal space again. My head didn't hurt and I felt none of the usual discomforts of the process.

I looked around for Lal and didn't see him. I couldn't remember whether I'd ever seen him during this insertion. I found the airlock and entered it. Only when the green light went on, indicating that the air pressure had reached that of the cabin, did I remember to take off my helmet and go in.

I stepped over to the console still wearing my air suit. Lal was curled up on his bunk. Monica watched me from hers with an expression I couldn't read. I said to her, "I'm going to see how close we've come to where we're supposed to be. I just hope we're close enough that the console can locate us."

"The fusion bottle has stayed in the green most of the time that we've been in the Matrix," she said. Then, not quite in the same tone, she said, "You're speaking to me again, then?"

"What?" I said, setting the console to search and identify our location. "I'm not mad at you. I've just been busy, for heaven's sake!"

My skin was rubbed raw everywhere it touched the inside of the suit, which felt by now like my whole bloody body. Her question hit me the same way.

"You haven't spoken to me for four days, Roy," Monica said. "I thought I must've done something wrong."

"You didn't," I said. "I guess I've just gone nuts."

I was too tired to care, though I was sure I'd be horrified at my behavior when I had at least two brain cells sparking together. I looked at what the console told me about our location.

Well, I'll be damned.

Monica came over and stood beside my couch. I looked up at her and said, "If this is right, we're within a light-hour of Saguntum."

"That's very good," she said. "Why are you looking so worried?"

"It's too good," I said. "I—look, you say I haven't spoken in four days. I haven't been properly conscious for four days. I can't have been responding to the semaphore prompts. In fact I don't remember looking at the towers a single time since..."

At all, but I must've done at least at the beginning of the run. What I remembered was the way the rigging glowed red if it wasn't set right, and me trudging up and down the length of the ship fixing whatever wasn't as it should be.

I felt my lips smile as I continued to enter course calculations. Without looking at Monica, I said, "I felt I was part of the ship myself there toward the end. I guess maybe that's not a bad way to be for a spacer. Though I really don't want to go back to that way again."

"What are you doing now?" Monica said.

"We need to get into Saguntum orbit," I said. "We're so close already that I'd have been sure a month ago that I could do it. That doesn't mean I can now, of course. Being nuts isn't necessarily a good thing."

I shut down the High Drive. Monica and I both grabbed the couch when we lost the acceleration that mimicked gravity—I'd forgotten to strap in when I entered the hull.

The *Alfraz* inserted into the Matrix.

Lal awakened and stretched. "Captain?" he called. "You wish that I go out alone? I have rested."

"Lal," I said. "This is a short hop and the telltales"—no electrical sensors worked on the hull while we were within the Matrix, but hydraulic lines like those of the semaphores communicated with the interior—"seem happy. Also, I seem to have a magical connection with the ship right now and it tells me that we're on course."

I grinned. Lal's expression didn't change. Monica's face became completely blank.

"So I figure we can both take a break until we extract in what I hope is orbit around Saguntum."

"Yes, Captain," Lal said, nodding in his bunk. "I am glad to remain here."

I took off my air suit. When Monica realized what I was doing, she helped me. After a moment she said, "We'll land straight at the Haven, then?"

I shrugged. "I'll ask Orbital Control," I said. "I expect that they'll put us in the civilian port, yes."

I looked at her and added, "Or you'll ask Orbital Control, if you're willing to do the commo honors here, like you've done before."

"I was counting on it," Monica said with a grin. She walked to the other side of the console and took the striker's seat. She was cheerful, but there was more in her attitude than I understood.

"The Karst destroyer knew where we were going," I said. "If they're here ahead of us, I'll have to play it by ear."

"Will they shoot at us?" Monica said.

I shrugged. "I don't know," I said. "I don't think so, but back in the Academy folks talked like on Karst they're one stage up from dancing around fires with bones through their noses. It's not like that really, but I'll be just as glad if we don't find the *Meduse* in orbit when we arrive."

"Can you land even if they do shoot?" Monica said.

That was a good question. If they used a missile, no: A missile would gut us, even if launched from so close that it had only a fraction of its maximum terminal velocity. Aloud I said, "They mount eight ten-centimeter guns. If they're in good condition and well served, they could certainly blow holes in our hull."

I gave her a lopsided smile. "It's a Karst ship," I said. "Chances are the guns *aren't* in good condition or well served. But I'll make the decision based on how I'm feeling if the situation arises. *I* will made the decision. But let's hope it doesn't come up, all right?"

Monica swallowed and nodded.

The countdown clock winked at me. I said, "Prepare to extract!"

We were back in the sidereal universe, in an elliptical orbit above Saguntum. My body had shrunk for an instant before regaining its normal dimensions. For a moment I wasn't sure where I was; then all was well again.

I engaged the High Drive and began braking at 1 g. We were currently about ninety thousand miles out but on the descending leg of the lobe.

"*Saguntum Control,*" Monica called from her side of the console, "*this is the* Alfraz, *out of ben Yusuf, Captain Roylan Olfetrie commanding and First Officer Monica Foliot. We request landing permission for the Haven at Saguntum. Further, we request that this transmission be forwarded to the Directorate of Public Safety.* Alfraz *over.*"

I adjusted the angle of the High Drive motors to brake us a hair more effectively without having to increase output. I'd like to have a proper Power Room readout on the console, but I'd like a lot of things. If the bottle failed now and we turned into a tiny second sun above Saguntum, that was the breaks.

"Alfraz, *this is Orbital Control,*" the doorkeeper responded; rather more quickly than I would have expected. "*Your request is being processed. Say again your leaving port, over.*"

I set the rig to furl and retract. If the console noted any problems, there'd be time for Lal and me to make a hands-on check before we entered the atmosphere. The display stayed green, though. I'd have liked to brake harder than I was doing, but starting from so far out, 1 g would get us in safely.

"Alfraz, *you are cleared to land in the Military Harbor,*" Orbital Control said. "*Repeat, your berth is in the Military Harbor, not the Haven. Acknowledge please. Over.*"

Monica stood up so that she could look at me directly without the distorting screen of coherent light from my display. I nodded and gave her a V sign with my two fingers.

I didn't know why we were to land in the military harbor rather than the normal civilian one. It could be as simple as the fact that we were coming from a pirate stronghold. Saguntum didn't have a real navy but the *Annotated Charts* noted that there were six "dart sloops," some of which might be unserviceable.

I didn't know what dart sloop meant. Some sort of light warship. Well, that was fine.

"*Acknowledged, Saguntum Control,*" Monica said calmly. "Alfraz *will land in the Military Harbor.* Alfraz *out.*"

When we proceeded far enough in our orbit, a pulsing point appeared on the visual image of Saguntum which I kept on the upper right quadrant of my display. It didn't matter at this point; the Military Harbor was separated by only a mole from the Haven which occupied the remainder of the bay. We would have to be much deeper into our approach before the change of a few hundred yards from the berth I'd chosen for my rough solution made any difference.

I keyed in the data which Saguntum had sent along with the image. I'd been letting the console do the landings in the past, and I certainly wasn't going to change now.

I got up from the couch and walked to the internal hatch. "I'm going to check the fusion bottle," I said, though if it were anything short of deep into the red, I was going to ride it down.

The choice would be to hang in orbit until we could be rescued from the ground. And I just wanted to be home. The needle was still in the yellow, though.

I switched to the plasma thrusters before I would've done so normally. We had plenty of reaction mass because we'd made most of the run in a single long stage, and I could actually brake harder with the thrusters than I could with the High Drive throttled back so as not to stress the fusion bottle.

I was learning things this way that I'd never have known on a well-maintained RCN warship. There was a future for me as a tramp captain on the fringes of human space.

We hit the atmosphere without any drama until we'd bucked and rattled our way down to ten thousand feet. Then the port mainyard carried away, ripped out of its clamps and I suppose dancing off in our slipstream. It didn't flick back and hit the hull, though, so I didn't care once I was sure that the console was able to handle the asymmetric buffeting. At best a starship doesn't make many concessions to streamlining, so loss of yard and furled sail was barely noticeable.

We passed over the breakwater and approached the icon of our berth on the display. The real-time image was obscured by steam. I hadn't figured out how to correct the altimeter error which caused the *Alfraz* to drop like an anvil, but I'd changed the shut-down sequence from instantaneous to having the nozzle petals flare in a thirty-second sequence. We mushed down, unpleasantly but without jolting.

I drew a deep breath. "We're down," I said. My throat was dry and I wondered how long it'd been since I'd eaten.

"I apologize for giving you a false name," Monica said. When the words penetrated, I opened my eyes and looked at her across the console.

I'd shut down my display. I was sure people were trying to

get ahold of me. They couldn't reach me except through the console until the berth cooled down enough to open the ship, and I wasn't in shape to talk to anybody.

"Sorry?" I said, trying to figure out what she was talking about.

With a hint of irritation, Monica said, "I told you my name was Smith. It's really Foliot."

"But it's still Monica?" I said. She'd announced herself as Monica Foliot to Orbital Control, now that I thought back. I'd had other things on my mind, like the fusion bottle. "Look, I don't care. We got here. I'm glad I knew Monica Smith, and I wouldn't have made it back without her."

I got up from the couch, moving carefully. Lal was standing. He looked about fifty years older than he had when we lifted from ben Yusuf, but I probably looked like my dad too. Well, Dad had run to fat as he got older, and right now I was more like a coat rack with a set of slops hung over it.

"It's just I didn't know you," Monica said, knotting her fingers together. "I thought you might take advantage of me."

And do what that we hadn't done anyway, with a great deal of mutual pleasure? I wondered. Aloud I said, "You didn't know me from Adam," I said. "I'd like to think that my good intentions stood out like a beacon, but you'd had a rough time."

I took another deep breath and said, "I think we can open her up now. Let's go do that."

The hatch controls were in the hold rather than through the console. The *Alfraz* gave the impression of having been assembled from bits of three or four separate vessels; the antennas and yards were sized for something much smaller, which had been a considerable advantage when Lal and I were working her alone.

I opened the safety lock, then threw the big lever on the outer bulkhead. The dogs withdrew and the hatch began to rotate down into a boarding ramp. The mix of steam and ozone that curled down as the opening widened made me sneeze. I shut my eyes against the sting.

I smelled Saguntum again: its garbage, at least, as incinerated in our exhaust. I wondered how Monica was feeling—to be home, really home. Her hands were knotted together. Her lips were moving in what could have been a prayer.

By the time the hatch had lowered below the height of my eyes, the air had cleared enough for me to see that there were scores of people on the quay. Many of them were uniformed, which wasn't a surprise, but standing in the center of them was a group in ordinary spacers' slops.

They weren't armed—as some of the uniformed personnel were—but there was a cart with them. When my vision cleared enough to see who the spacers were, I was pretty sure the cart contained weapons.

I heard a hoarse order from the quay. Too early, I thought; the air and water were both too hot to link to us, but a floating extension bridge began to open toward our outrigger. Instead of yard personnel unrolling it, Dasi and Barnes were doing the job while Woetjans walked along behind them as though supervising.

The steam still glittered with occasional speckles of plasma. Woetjans and her mates gave no sign of noticing it.

An aircar howled from the city at low altitude, circled out into the harbor in order to line up with the quay, and put down smoothly. The crowd waiting for the hatch to open blocked access from the harbor road, but the end of the quay was empty.

A squad in battledress formed between the remainder of the spectators and the newly arrived vehicle, their weapons ready if not quite pointed. They suddenly fell into formal at-ease posture with their weapons by their sides in patrol slings.

"What in blazes is that all about?" I said. The ramp clanged home on our outrigger at about the same time that the extension from the quay reached it.

"That's my father," Monica said.

Before I could respond—or stop her, though I'm not sure I would have tried—Monica went running down the ramp and onto the extension. A burly, middle-aged civilian had gotten out of the aircar and was trotting toward the crowd at the quay end of the extension.

Woetjans and her mates let Monica pass. They parted for Captain Leary, Lady Mundy and their servants, then faced around to stop everyone else.

Monica and the civilian met on the quay and threw their arms around one another, but I didn't have much attention to spare.

"Sir!" I said, throwing a salute that did the Academy proud. "Welcome aboard the *Alfraz*!"

Chapter Thirty-one

"Good to see you again, Officer Olfetrie," Captain Leary said. "May I ask who the"—he gestured behind himself with his thumb—"attractive blond who just passed us is?"

"Ah, sir . . ." I said. It wasn't as easy a question as it probably seemed. "That's Monica Foliot, though sometimes she goes by Monica Smith."

"I'm curious as to how you vanished from Saguntum three months ago . . ." said Lady Mundy. "And now have turned up again with the daughter of the Director of Public Safety, who hasn't been heard of since she took ship on Greenwood six months ago on her way back to Saguntum."

"Ah . . ." I repeated. "Mistress Foliot was imprisoned in the harem of the Admiral of Salaam. I was imprisoned there too and we made our way back to Saguntum. Ah, I didn't know who Mistress Foliot was, only that she was a Saguntine citizen improperly held in Salaam."

In the general pause—Leary and Mundy were digesting

what I'd said and *I* sure didn't have anything more I wanted to say—Lal said, "Captain, what do you wish of me?"

Both Captain Leary and I turned, but Lal was talking to me. I'd almost forgotten him. "You're dismissed for the day," I said, "but come back tomorrow morning and we'll see about paying you off."

Lal's full wages—and I wanted to add a fifty thaler bonus—would take help from Monica, which I hoped she'd be willing to give, but I had a little cash of my own left. I gave him a ten-thaler coin and said, "This'll get you a room and some entertainment for the night."

"A moment, please," Leary said, touching Lal's wrist with his fingertips. Then to me, "Introduce me please, Olfetrie."

"Sir!" I said, embarrassed. "Captain, this is Lal. He and I worked the ship from Plaquemines by ourselves."

Leary nodded and said, "Lal, are you looking for a berth after you've been paid off?"

Lal bowed slightly and said, "Perhaps, Captain."

"Then talk to my bosun, Woetjans, on your way past," Leary said. "She's the tall one. Tell her for me to assign you a watch tomorrow when you've gotten squared away with your captain here."

Lal bowed again, then stuck the coin in his mouth and scampered down to Woetjans at the foot of the ramp.

Captain Leary gave me a lazy grin. "Any two spacers who can work ship alone for ten days," he said, "rate able in my book, and I want them in any crew of mine."

He exchanged glances with Lady Mundy and said, "Now let's go aboard your *Alfraz* for a moment and have a discussion about some other things. All right?"

"Sir!" I said. "Yes, sir!"

I turned to lead Leary and Mundy into the cabin. Hogg and Tovera came along also, as I'm sure everybody but me expected. Well, there was plenty of room in the cabin, though the furnishings were pretty sparse.

Woetjans looked up from her discussion with Lal and called, "Six? The kid's all right. I'll back whatever you do, you know that, but he's all right."

"Understood, Bosun," Leary called back.

It didn't change anything really: I'd from the beginning planned to tell the truth and take what happened. But that exchange showed me that what might happen was even worse than I'd been afraid.

"We'll close the internal hatch," Lady Mundy said. "I think the cabin will be as clear of listening devices as anywhere else on Saguntum. Unless you've installed them, Olfetrie?"

"No, ma'am," I said. I knew it was a joke, but I gave an honest answer. "I wouldn't know how to. But I used the cameras already installed in the Admiral's palace to connect with Mistress Smith since she didn't have a terminal." I frowned. "Mistress Foliot."

Lady Mundy cocked her head as she looked at me. "How did you gain access to the palace computer?" she said.

"They put me in charge of it," I said. "Bought me to take charge of it, really. I don't have computer skills—not like we'd mean on Cinnabar—but I had more than they did."

I suddenly wondered how the chamberlain was getting on now that I'd vanished. It could even be that the Admiral had impaled him. Giorgios wasn't anything like a friend of mine, but I didn't want that to happen to anybody. And I *sure* hoped that Abram was doing all right.

Captain Leary suddenly laughed and sat down on the couch, rotating it to face into the cabin instead of toward the console display. Lady Mundy sat primly on a bunk—mine, as a matter of fact. She'd brought out her personal data unit and no longer seemed to be aware of me.

I continued to stand at ease, legs spread slightly and my wrists crossed behind my back. The servants were standing also. Neither of them seemed tense, but that didn't reassure me.

"So, Olfetrie," Leary said. "Start at the beginning."

Which beginning? But this was a test as much as it was a question. My choice of where to start told him—and certainly told Lady Mundy—how, and how well, my mind was organized.

"I went to dinner with Mistress Grimaud our first night on Saguntum," I said. "We ate in a restaurant, then went upstairs to her hotel room. I drank too much. She wanted to discuss political things that were none of my business, so I left and went downstairs to the bar."

I coughed, wondering if I ought to say the next because it was embarrassing. *If I wonder, then I should.* "We weren't intimate," I said. "We didn't have sex."

"Why not?" said the Captain.

One guy to another, I realized. "She wanted me to do things that I wasn't going to do," I said aloud. "I wasn't going to take the price and then stiff her on my part of the bargain. And I guess I was offended that she didn't want to sleep with me, she wanted me to do things for her."

"Tell us exactly what Mistress Grimaud said," Lady Mundy said. Her attention was on the display of the data unit which she controlled with a pair of wands.

I took a deep breath which also gave me a moment to frame the words. "She said you and Captain Leary were dangerous rogues, working for an organization outside the Republic's proper government," I said. I looked at the Mundy's data unit because my eyes had to be somewhere. "She said you were on Saguntum to foment a war between Karst and the Republic. She said this would bring on full-out war between Cinnabar and the Alliance, and that this would ruin us."

Lady Mundy raised her eyes to me. I met them and said, "Maeve said she was the agent of the Foreign Ministry, trying to prevent the disaster."

"What did you think, Olfetrie?" the captain said. It was a calm question, the way he might have asked a local for directions in a strange city.

"I thought it was above my pay grade, sir!" I said, louder than I should have spoken. I was shocked at my own anger. Part of me was screaming *This isn't fair!* As though the universe or the people with me in the cabin cared about that. "I thought I'd get even more drunk and forget all about it! But there were two guys in the bar and they doped me and put me on the *Martinique*. Which pirates captured and took to Salaam on ben Yusuf."

"From where you escaped," said Lady Mundy to her data unit. She looked up at me and raised an eyebrow. "In a ship which seems to be owned by the Hegemony of Karst."

"It belonged to the Karst consul at Salaam," I said. "He

wasn't, well, he was hand in glove with the Admiral, Monica should've been freed. We took the ship, but if Karst wants it back, they're welcome."

"What will the consul say if we ask him?" the captain said.

I met his eyes and said very deliberately, "Sir, you'd better ask him yourself. If you can find him."

Tovera gave a little snicker.

Lady Mundy looked at the captain. She said, "I'm satisfied."

"Then I am too, and I'll go put Woetjans' mind at rest," Captain Leary said. He got up and added, "Olfetrie, you can report aboard the *Sunray* any time you like, but you won't have any duties for twenty-four hours. I suppose you have things you want to settle here."

I started to say that I didn't, but then I thought of something. "Sir?" I said. "Could I have Chief Pasternak take a look at the fusion bottle here? I don't know who owns the *Alfraz*, but the bottle needs to be fixed or replaced before she lifts again."

And the pump control needed to be repaired, but that's a little thing. For the cost of replacing a fusion bottle, it'd be better business to sell the ship for parts.

Leary smiled. "I think the Chief's been bored with the time we've been sitting in harbor here," he said. "He'll jump at the chance."

"Thank you, sir!" I said. "I think I'll check in at the *Sunray* and figure out the next move then."

"If you're planning to discuss matters with Maeve Grimaud, Olfetrie," Lady Mundy said, "I'd rather that you didn't. Besides which, the Foreign Ministry delegation has moved into the Councillor's Residence to be closer to the seat of government."

"Ma'am," I said, "I really *don't* want to see the lady again.

367

I suppose she was doing her job and like I said, that's above my pay grade. But now that I'm back, I just want to be back to normal where I was before I got shanghaied."

Lady Mundy gave me a kind of smile that froze me to the bones. "You're right that the matter isn't your business," she said. "But it's ours and we'll deal with it. And lest you be concerned that by speaking you've harmed a woman for whom you clearly feel a gallant concern, don't worry. We were aware of the Foreign Ministry activities before we lifted from Cinnabar. It's good that you told us yourself, though."

"This is grown-up rules, kid," Tovera said. There was a metallic softness in her voice. "You get your choice of sides, but you don't get to sit in the middle."

I swallowed and nodded to her. "Yes, ma'am," I said. "I'm on Captain Leary's side. But I wish it wasn't like this."

"Yeah," said the captain. He suddenly sounded old. "I wish it wasn't too...but then I think, if it was the kind of world I wish it was, there wouldn't be any place for me."

He looked down at Lady Mundy and added, "Nor for Adele either."

She sniffed without looking up. "The universe consists of patterns of information," she said. "A good librarian can always find a place to be useful."

Lady Mundy lifted her face. It had a terrible stillness, and her eyes were focused on some distant time or thing.

"Sir," I said, nodding to Captain Leary. "I'll be off then."

Nobody followed me out of the cabin, at least before I'd gotten to the bottom of the ramp. I guess they wanted to discuss things among themselves.

I'd wanted more than anything in life for things to go back to normal, but they hadn't and I knew they never would for me again.

Chapter Thirty-two

The crew of the *Sunray* was happy to see me—remarkably happy. I wasn't sure that anybody would've noticed that I was gone, let alone be pleased that I was back.

The thing is, everybody wanted to know what'd happened to me. I told them all the same thing: "Got drunk, got shanghaied, got captured by pirates, got back."

It was all true. My worst enemy couldn't accuse me of drawing the long bow to make myself look good. And if the answer made no bloody sense to the folks asking the question, well, it hadn't made any sense to me when I was doing it.

Pasternak was pleased as could be when I asked him about looking over the *Alfraz*. The whole crew, techs as well as riggers, was getting antsy. Gamba summed it up with, "Well, I figure Six and the Mistress are doing some kinda magic like they always do, but it's pretty bloody boring for the rest of us, I can tell you."

Pasternak took me from the *Sunray* to the *Alfraz* in a

battery-powered cart that came from the customs service. The transfer—borrowed or bought—must have been aboveboard: The vehicle still had the yellow body color and red-stencilled fender and door legends instead of having been repainted.

I'd told Pasternak what the ship was doing, but when we got to the *Alfraz* I kept out of the way except to lend a hand when requested—lifting clear the cover plate to open up the machinery and similar occasional jobs. He muttered as he looked at things and took readings with a tester from a worn leather sheath.

"Oh, you're a *lucky* lad, you are," Pasternak said. I figured he meant me, but he had his nose in his work and may very well have been talking to one of the components he was dealing with.

It wasn't a question, so I didn't answer it. And anyway, I didn't disagree.

After the better part of an hour, Pasternak rose and faced me. "I need to go back to the *Sunray*, now," he said.

"Yes, sir," I said. I knew he had duties, after all. "Ah, sir? Do you think the bottle can be repaired or should the ship be sold to a wrecker?"

"A wrecker?" the chief said in horror. "A *wrecker*! Of course she can be repaired! The circulating passages have to be cleaned and we'll replace all of the electrical circuitry while we're inside anyway. I'll be back with a crew and the parts within the hour."

He turned and gestured to the pump switch. The bulkhead above it was blackened around the point where Lal's wrench had completed the circuit. There the metal was blue in the center, hazing to yellow in a ring beyond.

"We'll fix that, too, but that'll take longer," he added. "Three days, maybe."

"Chief?" I said. "Are you sure about that? Because the electrician in Plaquemines did the job in only about four hours with a boy to help him."

"We're not going to bodge the job like *that*," Pasternak said in disgust. "We'll be opening the deck to run the cabling through safely."

An aircar landed on the quay; the howl sank to a hum as the fans cycled down. I looked out the hatch and saw it looked like the same one Colonel Foliot had arrived in just after we'd landed. That was the only aircar I'd seen on Saguntum since the *Sunray* arrived, so I wasn't surprised when Foliot got out of the passenger compartment.

"Now who's that?" Pasternak said, narrowing his eyes. "Friend of yours, lad?"

"That's the Director of Public Safety," I said. The chief hadn't been in the party of Sunrays who'd greeted our arrival. "And as for friend, I don't know. I hope at least he isn't my enemy."

I remembered my concern about how Monica's parents would feel about their daughter dating a spacer with nothing but his pay to live on—and that was before I knew just who her father was. I also wondered how Monica had described our association.

"Well, I'll run back to the *Sunray* and get things together," Pasternak said.

I started to ask him to stay a moment, then decided I wasn't afraid of a man as old as my father. Colonel Foliot could certainly beat the crap out of me if he wanted to—he had fifty pounds on me and despite his age was clearly a hard man in all ways; but if that was going to happen it might as well be now.

The chief must've seen something in my face, though, because he said, "Come to think, I'll stay for a little bit."

Foliot came to the foot of the ramp. He was wearing a business suit, dark gray with stripes that were white or maybe light blue to match the tunic under the open jacket.

"I've come to see Roylan Olfetrie," he called from the quay. "My name's Foliot."

"I'm Olfetrie," I said. I decided to wait at the top of the ramp, treating this as a visit to the *Alfraz* rather than to me specifically "Welcome aboard, sir."

Pasternak looked at me, probably wondering what this was about. I wished I could tell him.

"Good to meet you, Olfetrie," Foliot said when he reached me. He'd looked fifty at a distance from the way he moved, but close up I was sure he was older. As we shook hands firmly, he said, "I want to buy your ship."

I don't know what I'd expected, but it wasn't that.

"Sir," I said, "the *Alfraz* isn't mine."

"It bloody well is!" Foliot said. "You captured her from pirates and slavers, didn't you? That gives you title on any civilized planet in the universe!"

"I think the actual owner was the Karst consul to Salaam..." I said. I planned to say something more, but I wasn't sure what.

"Monica's told me about the bloody Karst consul to Salaam," Foliot said. "I swear the worst regret I've got in this whole business is that Platt isn't still alive for *me* to shoot. But with the help of this ship"—he nodded generally toward the cargo hold—"which Monica says you fixed so the Salaam defenses won't shoot at, I'm going to take care of a few more of the bastards."

A thought struck him. "Say, the ship will work, won't it?" he added. "Monica said there was something wrong with the engines?"

"The fusion bottle," Pasternak said, startling Foliot and me both. "She'll be up and running by midnight, I figure. The pump switch"—he gestured—"that'll take longer to do right."

Foliot flicked his hands impatiently. "Just jumper it or some bloody thing," he said. "Done pretty doesn't matter."

"Done right matters," the chief said, lifting his chin. "It'll be done right, and I'll tell you when it has been."

For a moment I thought Foliot was going to press the matter, but he suddenly relaxed with a grin. "I guess you will at that," he said. "Well, it'll take a couple days to get things together at this end, if I'm honest."

"And," I said, "I need to discuss the matter with Captain Leary before I agree to do anything. I guess he's back at the *Sunray*."

"This is nothing to do with Leary or Cinnabar," Foliot said, frowning slightly. "But I can take you over to the *Sunray* right now if you like."

"If it involves me, it involves Cinnabar," I said. "And I'll discuss it with Captain Leary."

Also with Lady Mundy, but I didn't say that.

"Colonel?" Pasternak said. "If you'll run me back too, I can get started quicker. We'll need the truck to haul the crew and the tools we need."

Foliot gave him a little bow. "It will be a pleasure, Chief," he said. He led us at a quick pace back to the quay and the aircar.

* * *

Captain Leary was on the *Sunray*—at the command console, like enough, Wedell said. She was one of the pair of spacers on duty in the boarding hold, their submachine guns hung from a rack discreetly out of sight behind the bulkhead. A watch of some sort on even a tramp at anchor was normal, but heavily armed guards would arouse attention.

The bridge hatch was open; Captain Leary was indeed at the console. I paused in the hatchway, braced to attention, and said, "Sir! Officer Olfetrie reporting to Captain Leary with a visitor!"

Captain Leary turned and smiled at me. "We're civilians, Olfetrie," he said. "I don't think quite so much formality is required. And"—he was looking past me—"Colonel Foliot, it's a pleasure to see you again. We haven't really had a chance to talk since the *Alfraz* arrived."

"I'll go back to the supplementary station, sir," Lieutenant Enery said, rising from one of the flat-plate displays that had been added to the bridge when the Republic rented the *Sunray*. At any rate, I'd never seen anything like this array on a civilian ship, let alone the supplementary station in the stern—in place of a warship's Battle Direction Center.

"Guess I'll hoof it too," volunteered Sun, who'd apparently been doing gunnery practice on another display. That left me and Foliot with Captain Leary and, at another display, Lady Mundy. I'd have asked for her presence if she hadn't been here.

Tovera sat on a jump seat, watching impassively. There was a rustle from the corridor and Hogg entered, squirming between Foliot and the jamb.

"Pull the hatch closed, Colonel," Leary said. "Then take a seat and tell us what your proposition is."

"Look, Leary," Foliot said, "I'm not trying to get Cinnabar into this. Some ben Yusuf pirates captured my daughter. They'd still be holding her now except your Olfetrie here got her loose. I want to go back and teach the bastards a quick lesson, and to do that I want to buy Olfetrie's ship. That's all."

"Larger powers than Saguntum have taught the ben Yusuf pirates a lesson," Mundy said, focused on data scrolling through her little personal unit. "The pirates are still there."

"Look, I don't think I'm the Almighty," Foliot said. He seated himself, facing outward from the station Sun had vacated. "I'm not planning to wipe out piracy. But I can put paid to the Admiral of Salaam and any pirate ships that happen to be in harbor when we stop by. This boy"—he nodded to me—"buggered the control circuits of the antiship missiles in the harbor when he got out with Monica. I want to use his ship to get back in, land troops, and blow the batteries up for real. Then my sloops can land and do something more, especially at the palace."

"Sir," I said to the captain, "the lockout was general, not just for the *Alfraz*. Somebody could turn it on as quick as that if they noticed. I think if I brought the *Alfraz* down myself, they wouldn't shoot, though."

I cleared my throat and went on, "And sir? I request permission to accompany the expedition."

"Do you indeed," Captain Leary said. "Do you consider this the business of a Cinnabar citizen, Olfetrie?"

"Sir, I do," I said. "I believe it's the business of any Cinnabar citizen to redress the insult done to a trainee officer of the RCN. Sir."

Hogg laughed. "I'll bet you can sell that to Navy House, don't you think, Master?" he said.

"I probably could, if I thought it necessary to inform anybody at Navy House," the captain said with a smile. "At present I report to Director Jimenez, however; and he has no direct command responsibility over RCN personnel, of course. Any spacers under my command, let's say."

"Then you'll let Olfetrie sell me his ship?" Colonel Foliot pressed. I was satisfied myself, but I didn't blame Foliot for wanting it nailed down beyond question. He had to think like the ruler of a planet, which from what Lady Mundy had said he pretty much was.

"I think we can do better than that, Colonel," Leary said. "The *Alfraz* should have a proper RCN crew since she's owned and captained by a Cinnabar citizen. Also, I've spent some time with your naval protection force. You've got good personnel, but sinking ships in harbor will be easier for experienced people, some of which I'd be happy to provide—if that meets your approval?"

"Yes," Foliot said. "Yes, it certainly does!"

"Then I think we should get to the serious planning," said Captain Leary. "Adele, will you please project the maps you've prepared?"

At the Academy, they talked about Captain Leary as though he were a magician. It wasn't magic but from what I saw in the next three hours he and Lady Mundy thought way ahead of anybody else I'd ever met.

Chapter Thirty-three

"Freighter *Alfraz* out of Hegemony on Karst," I said, transmitting on what I knew to be the frequency of the Harbormaster's Office in Salaam. "We request permission to land in Salaam Harbor, over."

"That's three times," Gamba shouted from the striker's seat. Even with the thrusters and High Drive shut down, a starship's cabin is a noisy environment. "How often are you going to call?"

"I guess that'll do," I shouted back. Keying the transmitter again, I said, "Freighter *Alfraz* landing at Salaam Harbor, out."

I engaged the landing program, handing all decisions over to the console. We were supposed to be a civilian freighter, and there was nothing about this landing that was likely to be a problem. We were going to land just the way the *Alfraz* had when it first arrived here—before I stole it—and the way every ship captured by pirates from Salaam landed.

The High Drive kicked in, breaking us out of orbit at about 1.5 g. Gamba was watching the fusion bottle from his position: There was now a line feeding data to the console as there should have been all along. Pasternak was back in the hold with the unit, though.

The Chief Engineer had insisted that he sail with the ship himself, even though Captain Leary had assigned Gamba, who was a thoroughly qualified motorman. Pasternak said he wanted to check the quality of his repairs and modifications; which was probably true, but I'm sure nobody else had doubts. Certainly I didn't.

There were five riggers—including Lal—on the cabin bunks, and forty additional couches welded to the deck of the hold. They weren't stacked; heaven knew that we had plenty of room. The couches were for a company of the Special Police, the unit which reported directly to Saguntum's Director of Public Safety.

Colonel Foliot himself was leading the detachment.

The *Alfraz* dropped into the atmosphere. The plasma thrusters lighted more than a second before the High Drive shut off, enough to give us a real kick from the doubled braking. *Pasternak will have done something about that before we lift, I'll bet....*

The exterior sensors hadn't been upgraded, so my view of ben Yusuf was blurry at the beginning, then blocked by a rainbow veil after the thrusters lit. There wasn't much to see anyway, and my attention was on the ship diagnostics. The rigging wasn't rattling to speak of. The *Sunray* crew had given the *Alfraz* a quick rebuild at Jacquerie. Any doubtful clamps and wrappings had been replaced, and what was there now had been snugged up properly.

"Prepare for landing!" I shouted over the PA system, but nobody aboard could hear me.

The *Alfraz* had been slanting down broadside, driving against the braking effort. As our speed dropped, the console brought our underside parallel to the sea beneath us and slowly rotated our bow forward so that we would appear from the surface to be in normal flight. We were scarcely more streamlined in this attitude than we had been when we started through the atmosphere sideways.

Because we had some forward motion, our exhaust was streaming behind us as we approached the roadstead of Salaam. I could see about a dozen ships floating there, most of them cutters of a few hundred tons like the one which had captured the *Martinique*. That seemed now to have happened in another lifetime.

I picked a fairly empty stretch, more or less in the middle and close to the beach. That was farther than I'd have liked from the pier which the heavier lighters used, but it gave the squads hoofing it to the missile batteries equal distances to go.

"Touching down!" I said. That was obvious to all the spacers aboard from the doubled sound and queasy mushing, but probably at least some of the troops in the hold had never been off Saguntum. Though if they couldn't hear me, I suppose it didn't matter.

The console landed us with less fuss and bucking than if we'd been at a proper dock whose slip walls would set the ripples bouncing back and forth. We were rocking the other ships on the roadstead, but that was their problem.

The thrusters shut off. Lal got up from his bunk and did

what I hadn't remembered to do: drop the anchors in both outriggers to hold us in place, barring a serious storm. It was a separate control on the bulkhead.

The whole crew was getting up. Woetjans helped Lal open a port in the cabin so that he could thrust a flare gun through the influx of steam and ozone. I could barely hear the thump of the flare cartridge since my ears were still stunned from the landing.

Lal brought the gun back in, replaced the expended round with a fresh one, and fired again. This time I could just barely make out the *pop* of the flare bursting above the ship.

"What's all that about?" Wedell asked, looking uneasily from Lal to me.

"Mistress," Lal said. "I am summoning boats from the shore. Usually one would come, but because I have summoned two, I hope that we will get many. The boatmen will hope we are coming with many slaves aboard."

"Thanks," Wedell muttered, but she had a sour look.

I went into the hold. The police detachment seemed to have come through the landing pretty well, though one or two had tossed their cookies. If you're not used to it, a starship's landing approach is pretty uncomfortable.

The troops were pulling on long shawls to cover their battledress and equipment. The shawls were ben Yusuf countrymen's garb, unusual in Salaam itself, but they wouldn't cause remark.

I found Colonel Foliot and said, "Sir, I'm going to open the main hatch shortly. I'd like you to move your people toward the stern so that they won't be seen from the boats approaching."

"Right," said Foliot crisply. He reached down for the bullhorn resting at his feet and said, "Squad leaders, get your teams together in the back now! We're going to open the ship up and we don't want to spook our transportation."

The troops moved away in good order. I heard a few angry corrections, but there were no major screw-ups and minimal delay. With Foliot at my side, I threw the hatch switch.

As the ramp began to crank down, a huge presence joined us. Chief Woetjans stood close, wearing a shawl like the those covering the troops. Hers appeared to have been cut from tarpaulin.

Steam and plasma swirled in. Foliot and many of his people sneezed or coughed. I said, "Chief, you're not going with us. I told you I need you to take charge of the ship while I'm gone and call the sloops down with the rest of the troops."

"Yeah, I thought about that," Woetjans said. "Gamba can handle that as well as I could. Well, hell, Pasternak's senior but he doesn't want the job; it's more Gamba's style anyhow."

"Chief, it's a Saguntine job," I said. "I'm just along as a guide."

"Six wouldn't want you going alone," Woetjans said. "And I won't bloody have it. Just belt up."

"I'm not alone!" I said. Foliot was watching us; I couldn't read his expression. "There'll be forty troops with me!"

"They're with him," Woetjans said, nodding toward the colonel. "That's as should be, but they're *not* bloody with you. I am."

I wasn't going to convince her. I just wasn't. Partly, I guess, because she was right.

"Glad to have you with us, Chief Woetjans," Foliot said. His smile wasn't warm, but he sounded like he meant the words.

The ramp seated on the outrigger with the usual bang. The first two boats were nearing us; the third was close behind.

The large lighter had chugged clear of the cargo dock.

"Stay here, Chief, till the locals tie up," I said. "Colonel, you can come with me."

I walked down the ramp, waving with my left arm and smiling broadly. I was wearing ordinary spacers' slops but with a saucer hat. My belt purse was full of Alliance thalers.

In my right cargo pocket was the pistol I'd gotten from Abram, the gun Monica had used to kill the Karst consul. I didn't like carrying it, but it would have been stupid not to.

I stood at the end of the ramp. "We want all three of you," I called to the leading boats. I thought I recognized the boatman as the man who'd taken me and Giorgios to land the day I was purchased. I held out my hand, slanted just enough that the locals could see the thalers in it—but not so much that the money slid into the water.

I made a production of giving Foliot the coins and gestured him into the first boat, a battered metal one patched with structural plastic. "Stay here till we're all loaded," I ordered the boatman. I turned to the hatch and called, "Two more men!"

Until the lighter arrived, I didn't want to give the boatmen a notion of how many of us there were. Foliot had managed to get into the first boat without displaying the submachine gun under his shawl. I knew *that* boatman would stay put now, but I really wanted troops in the others as well.

Two of Foliot's people trotted down the ramp, but Ellie Woetjans was with them. I didn't object. Again I openly gave money to the troops and pointed them to the boats. They weren't as careful as the colonel had been, but it didn't matter any more.

I walked out toward the stern of the outrigger and waved

the lighter to me when its captain showed hesitation about tying up until the smaller boats had pulled away. I shouted toward the hatch, "Send the rest!" and hopped directly into the lighter's bow, bumping the boy who held the line.

I took it from him and lashed us to a cleat as Woetjans crashed to the deck like a load of iron. She took a length of pipe from under her shawl as she headed for the stern. I hoped she knew she wouldn't need the club but that was a minor problem if it was any problem at all.

When his troops started to arrive, Foliot traded places with one of them and climbed back onto the ramp to take charge of sorting them out. The smaller boats turned toward shore with six men in each as the remainder of the detachment filed onto the lighter.

When the last one—Foliot himself—was aboard, I waved toward Woetjans and loosed the line. I walked toward the stern as the diesel chugged and we backed away from the outrigger. The boatman looked terrified as I approached.

I reached into my purse, pulled out a handful of thalers—I didn't bother to count them. I pulled the throat of his tunic open and dumped the coins down it to catch at his belt. "Just do as you're told and stay quiet," I said, looking him in the eyes. "There'll be more of these, understood?"

By the time we'd returned to the pier, the smaller boats had grounded on the beach. Squads of six headed along shore toward either missile pit. They were walking briskly but weren't running. The remaining six accompanied the boatmen to the shelter where the locals waited between runs.

"Don't follow us in a mob," Foliot ordered as we headed

up toward Salaam proper. "Squads with twenty yards between each!"

I heard a *pop* to my left and turned. A green flare floated down in the sky above the western missile battery. A moment later a similar flare popped over the battery to our right. The flares might puzzle locals but I didn't think they'd alarm anybody. We had radios but we'd only use them as a last resort; neither Foliot nor I trusted radio in the thick-walled town.

"That's a relief," I muttered to Foliot as we snaked our way up the slope. To call any two streets "parallel" in a place like Salaam was stretching a point, but we were following the more or less continuous track to the right of the street at the center of the gulley. I could generally touch the buildings on both sides by stretching my arms out.

Foliot snorted. "Even if the crews were awake," he said, "and you said they wouldn't be, it wouldn't be a fight. Not with the personnel and equipment I've seen on ships from ben Yusuf."

I nodded, but what I'd said was true: I was relieved.

Most of the pedestrians we met were women out doing their shopping. The better-off ones had a maid or two to carry purchases and often an armed slave for a guard. I wouldn't have guaranteed that any of the guns I saw would function. One carbine was missing its loading tube like the pistol we'd taken from Platt's chauffeur.

I understood the colonel's contempt. He was more used to being shot at than I was, however.

I heard the sound of a ship dropping toward the harbor, coming from the south as we had. I hoped it was one of the Saguntine sloops. They were supposed to follow us down when the *Alfraz* announced that the missile batteries were in our hands. I could at least hope that was happening.

We kinked to the right at the cross street which led past the south flank of the palace and then to the west toward the prison across the valley. Instead of doing that, I took Woetjans into the alley behind the women's wing while Foliot waited at the corner to guide his troops when the time came. Though it was high morning, the narrow passage was dim.

Half a dozen men sheltered there; I didn't know what sort of transaction was going on. I took out more thalers as I approached.

"You can come back when we've finished our business," I said, not shouting but loud enough to hear. I held the coins out in my left hand. "But you leave now, *fast*."

Instead of giving the money to the nearest man, I tossed it over the heads of the whole group. The fellows closest to me had seen I was holding thalers, so they led the rush toward the other end of the alley.

I signalled to Foliot to come through. Woetjans went deeper into the alley with the pipe in her hand. A couple of the locals were taking longer than they should have to search for coins in the bad light. A swipe of the bludgeon across a man's backside sent him squealing with his fellows into the far street.

"It was just a tap, sir," Woetjans said. "If I'd hit him like he deserved, I'd've broken his hips."

"I'm not so softhearted that I cared," I muttered. I tugged at the door. It resisted for a moment. There wasn't much likelihood that in the short time I'd been gone that Giorgios—or his successor—had found somebody to engage the electronic lock through the console, but I was afraid that somebody'd drawn the bolt on the inside.

Only rust had been fighting me. The door started to move. Woetjans reached past and dragged it fully open so quickly that I had to jump out of the way.

There was room in the tunnel for the whole Saguntine detachment. I stopped at the far end and waited till I heard the alley door clank shut. As I opened my mouth to speak, Colonel Foliot said, "Remember men, we don't want to leave any survivors. Kill everyone you see!"

"No!" I shouted, hoping to be heard over the general growl of agreement. "Sir, three weeks ago that would've been Monica! I won't let you go any farther if you plan to massacre slaves and children!"

I couldn't really stop them—the only lock on the door was the little bolt on the top edge—but I had to say something. To Foliot, the palace was where his daughter had been imprisoned and raped—I assume he knew she had been raped. To me, and even I think to Monica, it had been home for several months. I had friends here.

Foliot stared at me. Several of the troops had small lanterns which provided enough light for me to see his features distorted with anger—and for him to see the horror in mine.

Foliot relaxed. "Yeah, you're right," he said quietly. He turned and roared, "Cancel that last order! If anybody resists, if anybody's got a weapon, shoot them."

He faced me again. I gave him a rueful nod and pulled the door open. The palace staff hadn't even thrown the bolt since I'd escaped with Monica.

We burst into the wives' garden. Two wives and half a

dozen attendants were there. I'd deliberately set the assault for midmorning: the palace was a maze at any time, and a night attack would be like charging into quicksand.

A maid was coming out with glasses and a carafe of sherbet on a tray. She saw us and screamed. Dropping the tray, she turned to run back inside. Somebody shot from behind me. The maid slammed into the doorjamb and slumped down. I hopped over her legs to get to the door from which she'd come.

I'd provided as good a plan as I could of the interior of the building, but I'd never expected to be coming back—let alone to be coming back through the Wives' Wing. If we'd used the main entrance, we'd have been in a battle from the first instant. I didn't doubt that Foliot's troops could mow down huge numbers of the Admiral's soldiers, but there were hundreds of them—a thousand being paid, but probably about six hundred in reality.

The places we wanted to get to were on the third and fourth floor. By entering the Wives' Wing, I was certain that we wouldn't meet serious armed opposition for maybe as much as an hour.

Inside was a tiled lobby. The maid had come from the food preparation area to the left. It wasn't exactly a kitchen, but food which had been cooked in the main kitchen was passed through the flap in an iron-bound door to the women's side. Here it was separated and carried upward to the wives' apartment.

The eunuch posted at the armored door had heard the scream and burst of shots in the garden. He was coming toward us, holding his impeller at the balance. Foliot gave him a short burst which flung his body into a preparation table.

The cook who'd started to follow him screamed and threw

herself to the floor. I was pretty sure she was unharmed.

I was sorry about the maid outside, but that was just bad luck. The shooter, one of Foliot's men, probably regretted killing her too, but everybody was on edge.

The dead eunuch was one of the pair who'd taken the lute from Monica so that Azul could break it. He died because he was carrying a gun, but I wouldn't have mourned him regardless.

To the right was a circular metal staircase which must have come out of a starship. I started upward with Woetjans pounding along behind me. Another eunuch leaned over the fourth-floor railing. Several people shot at him, blasting sparks of burning steel from the staircase. None of the shots hit the eunuch, but he dropped his carbine as he screamed and jumped back. That was just as good so far as I was concerned.

There was no doorway on the second or third floors between the wives' section and the general palace, so there were no guards either. Another companionway had been mated to the unit which served the two lower floors; it was black-enameled instead of stainless steel.

So far as Woetjans and I were concerned, the stairs were tedious but not a serious stretch of our abilities. Though older than I was, the bosun had spent her life since childhood climbing companionways and antennas. She'd still be going when I ran out of steam.

The Saguntine contingent was well below us when we reached the top landing, though. They were reasonably fit, but spiralling up scores of steel treads was unusual exercise for any landsman.

I was concentrating on each next step rather than looking

up, which I suppose was a bad idea since somebody might look down at any moment and blow my head off. I wasn't used to thinking about that sort of thing. I didn't realize how high we'd gotten until I cut my left hand on the railing and realized that I'd reached where shots at the guard had gouged it.

That eunuch had vanished. The only place he—it—could have gone was into the wives' suites.

I took the pistol out of the pocket where I'd let it ride throughout the assault. I didn't need to be running and jumping while waving a pistol I wasn't comfortable with.

The door was light, an ordinary interior panel. I measured the distance, judging where to kick with my boot heel.

Woetjans brushed past. She smashed the door to flinders with her shoulder and continued on through. She tripped on the bottom portion of the doorframe and therefore buried her head in the stomach of the eunuch who'd been waiting inside with a leveled carbine. I stepped over the eunuch's flailing legs and rapped him on the skull with the butt of my pistol.

We'd entered the wives' lounge. Furniture was overturned and various paraphernalia were scattered on the floor—cups, knitting, reading materials. The only person in sight was a maid who stood at the end of the corridor screaming her head off. Quite a lot of people were screaming. Since the doorways to the wives' rooms had curtains rather than solid panels, the voices didn't get much muffling.

To my left was another iron-strapped door, the entrance to the Admiral's private apartment. Beyond that would be a staircase down to the common part of the palace, but the door there was just as solid.

I tried to jerk it open but it didn't budge. The troops had brought a shaped charge in case we'd had to blow open the alley door—I knew where the drawbolt was and could have placed the explosive to chop it out of its hasp. I ran to the stairs to shout for somebody to bring it up soonest. Foliot—he was the third man—and his people had reached the top.

"Bring the explosives!" I shouted.

"Stay clear!" Woetjans wheezed. I spun to look back at her. Holding on edge the great marble-topped table from the lounge, the bosun stepped forward and smashed it into the center of the armored door. The stone broke into three great shards plus a spray of dust and gravel and the door burst inward.

Woetjans sat down in the rubble that she'd created, looking stunned. Even for her strength, that table must have been close to an overload.

Two Saguntines charged into the Admiral's apartments before I could get there. I heard shots, then a long burst from a submachine gun.

The Colonel and I ran in behind his men. One of the troops was clutching his bleeding left arm with his right hand. The air was sharp with ozone from the submachine gun and gray with plaster dust blasted from the ceiling and far wall.

On the vast circular bed lay the wounded Admiral, trying desperately to raise his pistol for another shot. Azul sprawled across his legs. At least three slugs had hit her in the face as she tried to shield her master.

The wounded soldier had dropped his submachine gun; the other man was trying to load a fresh tube into the weapon he'd emptied by locking on the trigger. Foliot stepped past them, aimed, and put a short burst into the base of the Admiral's throat.

Foliot turned. I think it was a moment before he recognized me.

"We've finished our business here," the colonel said. "Let's get back to the harbor and see how Leary's getting on there."

For several minutes I'd been hearing explosions that rattled ornaments. I suspected that meant Captain Leary and the naval contingent were getting on quite well.

Chapter Thirty-four

We went back down the stairs, gathering up the troops that Foliot had left behind at each stage. As I passed the second floor I sneezed at the sharpness of ozone and saw that a swatch of plaster had fallen from the wall at the far corner, exposing the bare bricks.

There were no additional bodies on the floor. If the shots had been unnecessary—or even accidental—at least the only damage was to the palace decoration.

The Saguntine troops had dropped their shawls when we entered the building. They carried their submachine guns openly, ready for trouble. I just hoped they weren't going to provoke it: Several thousand people lived in Salaam, and a lot of them had a gun of some sort. The locals weren't organized—and wouldn't have been even if the Admiral were alive—but they could overwhelm the forty-some of us if they simply got the notion to try.

The wives' garden was empty except for the men on guard.

The maid's body had been dragged to where it wouldn't be further stepped on; not that she cared any more.

At the far end of the passage, a grizzled noncom checked the troops off as they entered the alley. He looked startled at me and Woetjans, but Foliot called, "There's four more after me, Gridley."

We went back to the harbor in a ragged line. I heard several shots while we strode along as briskly as the pavement allowed. Because the path through the buildings was so irregular, we didn't look like an army. I doubt that more than half a dozen of us were visible at any one time. That shooting could have been anything; at any rate, there were no signs of it being aimed in our direction.

When I came in sight of the water, a column of water shot up from the port outrigger of one of the pirate cutters out in the bay. I heard a shudder through my boots a moment before the *bang!* of the explosion arrived through the air.

The blast lifted the outrigger. The cutter rocked upward, then rolled onto its port side as the torn metal no longer supported it. The hull continued to fill slowly as it sank. The starboard outrigger wouldn't be enough to support the whole ship, but it would settle to the bottom on its side.

I didn't see any civilians on the waterfront. Not only was there no one under Etzil's marquee, he'd drawn a grating over the front of the shop proper. Other businesses facing the harbor were closed and often shuttered.

One of the cutters I'd noticed when we landed was in water so shallow that about half the hull was still visible. Others must have sunk out of sight, but there were three sloops from

Saguntum's naval protection force that had arrived. They weren't much bigger than the pirate cutters, but each was built around a single antiship missile similar to those in the defensive batteries here and in most harbors.

Their chemical fuel made them short-range weapons with nothing like the impact of a warship's missiles at interplanetary distances. They accelerated much more quickly than High Drive motors could move the five-tonne warship projectiles, however.

Pirate cutters carried bombardment rockets to strip the rigging from prey and threaten the hulls—but not to do serious damage to the ships they were trying to capture. These sloops were armed to gut pirates and kill everyone aboard. There was a fourth sloop in orbit for protection, but these had landed when the *Alfraz* had captured the port defenses.

A large inflatable boat was making for the shore. Others were in the harbor around the remaining pirate cutters.

The inflatable ran up on the shore, near the local craft. Colonel Foliot carried his submachine gun slung right-side up under his arm with his hand on the grip—a patrol sling. He called, "We got the bastard, Leary! And you seem to be doing well yourself."

The last pirate cutter in harbor spouted water from the side, then dipped and began to fill. An inflatable boat like Captain Leary's had already left the pirate and was heading to shore, as were the two others in the harbor.

"It's been a very satisfactory morning," Leary said, hopping out of the boat. Hogg remained seated in the bow, his stocked impeller pointed skyward. His eyes scanned the buildings on the harborside, reminding me of a bird of prey on its perch.

The coxswain and the other five armed passengers were in Saguntine battledress.

"Olfetrie?" the Captain said. "All the Sissies and I will return to Saguntum with you in the *Alfraz*. Colonel, you'll load your people into the sloops like we'd planned. And we've got plenty of room"—he nodded to the west, where a line of ragged people were staggering to the shore on the other side of the town: prisoners released from the slave pen. They were guarded by troops in battledress—"for the freed slaves. We've brought along hammocks if there's too many for the couches already in the hold."

"Sir?" I said. "Will you be taking command of the *Alfraz*?"

"Goodness no, Olfetrie," the captain said with a broad grin. "She's your ship, and as far as I can tell you've been handling her quite well."

The inflatable boats would carry about thirty people apiece, but the line on the other side of the swale continued to come. The Saguntines who'd cleared that missile pit must've gone straight to the prison instead of waiting for support from the sloops as planned. Because they'd had more time, the troops had knocked in doors and taken any slaves who'd wanted to come.

That'd worked out all right—they hadn't started a full-scale battle while deep into a hostile city. I didn't like thinking about it, though. It was like somebody telling me I needn't bother with a safety line in the rigging. Most times that was true, but why take a risk when there wasn't any reason for it?

"Woetjans," I said. "Go head the freed slaves over to the lighter we came to shore with. I'll get the crew aboard and ready for you."

It occurred to me as I trotted off to the boatmen's shelter that maybe I should've checked with Captain Leary, but it was the obvious thing to do. The lighter would carry the best part of a hundred passengers. That was better than shuttling them in inflatables.

The troops guarding the boatmen looked glum about missing the action, but their prisoners were sitting on their haunches, chatting and brewing coffee much as they would have been if we hadn't arrived on ben Yusuf. I recognized the lighter's owner and his boy.

We had the motor rumbling by the time Woetjans arrived with the head of the line of freed prisoners. Thirty or forty of the slaves were women, a complication that hadn't occurred to me. The ex-slaves were from dozens of cultures and many of the individuals had been brutalized while they were held on ben Yusuf.

I said to Woetjans, "I hope we don't have any problems with prisoners thinking the women aboard are fair game. I don't assume all of those we've freed are saints, and the facilities in the hold are pretty basic."

The bosun snorted. She still carried the length of pipe. She slapped it against her right palm and said, "I guess we can teach everybody to keep RCN discipline while they're aboard. And anybody who gets notions after we've already warned him once, he doesn't have to stay on board."

Captain Leary joined me with Hogg and three motormen as the last of the freed slaves filed onto the lighter. He said, "Officer Mundy is in orbit on the *Concha*. The sloop's commo suite isn't all you might hope for, but she thought she'd be useful there if we got hostile visitors. We're ready to go off whenever you are."

"I think we're ready to board, then," I said. I checked my belt purse. It wasn't nearly as heavy as it'd been when we landed, but there were enough thalers left to make the lighter's owner happy that the Saguntines had come to town. I never expected to return to Salaam, but having the boatmen pleased if I did was worth more than ten thalers.

I gestured the RCN spacers to the rope ladder up the lighter's bow. To Captain Leary I said, "You brought our techs to set the charges that sank the pirate ships, sir?"

Leary laughed. "Well, I'm pretty sure the colonel's boys could've blown up the outriggers without specialist help," he said. "What they might not have been able to do was set the fusion bottles to fail in about six hours. I didn't want that happening while any of our people were still in harbor...but I don't think it'll prove a good idea for the locals to try raising their cutters after we've gone."

Captain Leary and I were both laughing as we climbed aboard the lighter.

I returned to the cabin following my first excursion since the *Alfraz* had inserted into the Matrix. Captain Leary, seated in the striker's seat, looked up and called, "Anything unexpected?"

The starboard watch was on duty. Three of the bunks were occupied. One of the empties was permanently mine, but two off-duty spacers must be in the hold with the passengers. I didn't object. Captain Leary and the tech crew were berthed there already, and I figured that the presence of RCN personnel kept order without need for formal measures.

"I'll adjust the course a little," I said. "I can make two of the next three transitions a trifle gentler. To tell the truth, the main thing I'm doing is getting used to wearing a hard suit on the hull. We didn't have one on the *Alfraz* when we escaped from ben Yusuf, and I got used to working the rigging in an air suit."

Leary got up from the console and walked toward me. "I've been going over your course log," he said, gesturing to the display he'd been studying when I came aboard. "There's remarkably little deviation from the stages you programmed. It would be good for a full crew, but it approaches magical when I know that you and Lal were alone on the ship. And your record actually improves as you got deeper into the stage."

I grimaced and bent my face away as though I needed to look at the torso catches I was opening. "Well, sir . . ." I said.

I looked up and met the Captain's eyes directly. "Sir," I said as calmly as I could. "I wasn't in my right mind for a lot of that time. I thought, I *felt*, that I was part of the ship myself. I wasn't eating much, and I wasn't talking at all except to Lal on the hull with hand signals."

I shook my head, smiling ruefully. "As best I can remember, I knew when something was wrong the way I knew to scratch my back if I was itching. And it worked, I guess, because we got there; but sir, I *really* don't want to get that way again."

"No, I don't suppose you would," Leary said. "There are times when I'm on the hull in the Matrix that I *know* things. . . ."

His serious expression vanished into a smile as bright and cheery as the sun coming out after a spring rainstorm. He said,

"But it's not Daniel-Leary-the-human-being who knows those things, if you see what I mean. Which I suspect you do."

Leary's expression changed again. He cocked his head and said, "Olfetrie, have you thought about staying on Saguntum? Colonel Foliot speaks very highly of you, and his daughter seemed—"

"Sir!" I said. *Does he want shut of me?* "Sir, I'm a citizen of Cinnabar and I dreamed of becoming an RCN officer. That didn't work out and maybe it can't work out, but I'll die a Cinnabar citizen!"

"Then stop taking your suit off," Leary said, smiling again. "I'll put one on myself, and you can show me the course as you see it."

He chose one of the hard suits that wasn't in use at present. Then he reached into the locker and brought out the sling with a sheath from which one of his brass communication rods hung.

Obediently, I began doing up my catches again. I didn't know what was going on, but at least it no longer seemed that the captain was looking for polite ways to get me out of his crew.

Aloud I said, "Sir? Monica Foliot and I became close during our escape from Salaam, but we haven't had any contact since we arrived on Saguntum."

The ambient noise in the cabin was considerable, even in the Matrix. In particular, the pumps and gears of the rigging set up a constant racket in the hull. I was sure that nobody any farther than me from Captain Leary could hear my words.

"Well, you weren't on Saguntum for very long before we lifted for this operation, were you?" Leary said. He'd gotten on the lower half of his suit, boots included, in a fraction of the time it would have taken me. "Which Mistress Foliot knew about, since her father was leading it. A sensible and perhaps shy girl wouldn't have bothered you."

"I guess, sir," I said, following the captain into the airlock as he did up the torso of his suit.

I didn't know what I really thought about Monica and me. I'd told myself that "we" were over as soon as she got home to her wealthy family. I still figured that was true...but I wasn't sure that I'd be able to shrug off her absence the way I'd expected to do.

The captain didn't say anything in the airlock. Getting used to the rigging suit meant developing calluses at different points than where the air suit had rubbed. I'd been looking forward to a little sack time after I tweaked our course.

I wasn't complaining, mind. Captain Leary was choosing to talk to with me in private, the only truly private place on a starship: outside the hull.

We tramped into the far bow. Two riggers were adjusting the dorsal mainyard. The sail wasn't set at the moment, but I knew from experience that the gears that rotated the yard sometimes stuck.

For a moment Leary looked up at the Matrix: the whole cosmos. Ours to sail through for as long as the *Alfraz* held together; ours to vanish into forever if she came apart.

He took out the half-meter-long brass rod. The bulbous tips were engraved with three leaping fishes; I looked at the design for a moment before putting my end firmly against my helmet.

"That's the Bantry crest," Leary said. "The tenants had a set made up for me in the shop there."

His voice was thinned but clear. I wondered what the rods were filled with. They gave better sound quality than touching helmets would have, and they were *much* handier.

"Sir?" I said. "Why doesn't the RCN make them standard equipment?"

Leary laughed. "You'd have to ask somebody else about Navy House policy," he said, "but if I had to guess I'd say that very few captains feel a need to communicate privately with members of their crews. And also that it's not a practice that our lords and masters would want to encourage if it were brought to their attention."

He cleared his throat and went on, "Most captains don't have someone like Officer Mundy in their crew, of course; which brings me to why we've come out here."

He waved his free arm in a broad gesture ahead of us.

"Besides getting a look at the most beautiful sight in the universe, of course," he said. "The universe itself. Besides that, I say. Olfetrie, you've never commented on what you were told just before you were shanghaied: that Lady Mundy and I were part of an intelligence operation to bring about a war with Karst."

I swallowed. When I was sure the Captain was waiting for me to speak, I said, "Sir, it's like I said to Maeve at the time: That's above my pay grade. I trust you and Lady Mundy to know what you're doing."

"You don't think we could make a mistake?" Leary said.

"Sure you could make a mistake!" I said. "You don't have

divine wisdom! But you've got more facts than I do, you've got a track record, and you're a hell of a lot smarter than I am."

Captain Leary burst out laughing. "Well, Olfetrie," he said, "I wouldn't bet against Adele having divine wisdom, though I'll tell you that she's not a god to get on the wrong side of. And also"—his voice changed slightly—"I haven't noticed anything wrong with your own intelligence. But we can talk about that over a drink, and maybe talk about women too. Right now, I'm going to discuss what Mistress Grimaud told you."

"Sir," I said, automatically bracing to attention.

"Lady Mundy and I *are* on Saguntum to provoke a war with Karst," he said. "What the Foreign Ministry does not know—very, very few people besides Adele and me, and now you, *do* know—is that the highest level of the Alliance has secretly given Cinnabar authorization to bring Karst into the Friendship of the Republic."

In nondiplomatic terms, to absorb Karst into our empire.

"Wow," I said. I hadn't meant to say that. I guess I had to say something.

"Now, it occurs to me that Guarantor Porra might not keep his word about accepting Cinnabar's action," the captain said. "In that case the Republic is going to need the RCN, and the RCN is going to need officers. Either way, I'd say you've made the right choice, Olfetrie."

"Sir," I said. "I kept my word with you." I swallowed. "I'd say that was always the right choice."

Captain Leary laughed again, but he also reached over with his free hand and squeezed my shoulder.

Chapter Thirty-five

The remainder of our return to Saguntum was an intensive course for me in astrogation, taught by the man acclaimed as the finest astrogator in the RCN—Captain Daniel Leary. I learned a great deal, but one of the things I learned was that Captain Leary—Six, he told me to call him, did things that couldn't be taught or learned.

Twice Six suggested changes in the course I had programmed. I made the changes, though I couldn't see any reason for them. In one case, after our second transition on the new course it became obvious that the next stage would be far easier than the course I had originally chosen. The other case was the reverse: When we had made two transitions on the new course, the different perspective on the Matrix showed me that my planned course would have been so stressful that the *Alfraz* might even have broken up.

"Sir?" I said as we stood in the bow, looking at the Matrix with the communication rod connecting us. "How did you know to avoid GC75951? It was the console's choice, and there was nothing visible to say otherwise when we viewed it two transitions ago."

"Umm," said Six. "If there'd been something I could see, I'd have pointed it out to you. I just had a feeling, I'm afraid."

"I'm glad you're on our side," I said, and that was the truth if I've ever spoken it.

The other benefit of spending time on the hull was that I didn't have to be aware of our passengers. The crew, all of them Sissies—veterans of Captain's Leary's armed yacht, the *Princess Cecile*—kept order. For the most part, the freed slaves were just glad to have gotten away from pirates who had held them, for as much as ten years in some cases.

Sanitation in the hold of the *Alfraz* was rudimentary. What had been installed for the police commando worked if the users were disciplined enough to use it properly. Cultural norms in Salaam and on some of the worlds from which the slaves had come didn't involve anything but a patch of ground on which to squat. Hoses cleared the immediate problem, but the entire hold stank like a latrine after the first day out.

When we extracted from the second long stage, the *Alfraz* was within a light-minute of Saguntum. I was proud of that, but I managed not to say anything aloud. I plotted the final jump, though my left side felt like frozen wood and my vision of my right eye blurred.

"*Mind if I announce us*?" Captain Leary said, speaking through the console. He was in the striker's seat.

"Sir, I'd appreciate it if you'd handle commo," I said. "Or if you'd like to bring us in, that'd be fine too."

"I want you to be the best astrogator you can be," he said. "You won't get that way from me doing the work for you."

Six hailed Orbital Control. We'd be about three minutes real-time reaching Saguntum orbit, so we were getting a slight edge on the formalities. I didn't expect to be boarded—and I certainly hoped not; the shorter time our passengers were in free fall, the better—but Orbital Control could assign us a landing berth in Jacquerie Haven.

This is even better than having Monica aboard! I thought. But it wasn't.

My final extraction brought us out within thirty thousand miles of the surface. Woetjans led the watch onto the hull to make sure the rig locked down properly, while Six took care of the berthing details with Control.

When we had our berth assignment, I set it up in the console. I'd thought of making a manual landing to show Captain Leary that I could do it—and rejected the thought. Now that I'd programmed the thrusters to flare as we set down, there was no reason to land manually—any more than there was reason to work in the rigging without a line.

I didn't guess Six would think better of me if I showed myself to be a boastful fool—and if I was wrong in that, he wasn't the man I thought he was. Besides, I might really muff the landing in a fashion that would be embarrassing or worse.

"We're here ahead of the *Lezo* and the *Magellanes*, Olfetrie," Captain Leary said. "*El Cano* and *Concha* are in harbor, but not their sisters. That's very good time."

That was great *time, given* Alfraz's *minimal rig!* Aloud I said, "They didn't have a crew like ours, sir!"

The riggers started coming through the airlock in groups of two. I was smiling.

The landing was a satisfactory one. Not neat, not exceptional, not something for Captain Olfetrie to preen himself with. We'd gotten safely to where we were supposed to be, and for *that* I could feel pride.

Woetjans and Pressy, another of the riggers, opened the cabin's two hatches almost immediately. The gush of steam and ions wasn't as unwelcome as it would have been under other circumstances. Even the garbage in the harbor water had been thoroughly incinerated before it entered the ship.

Hogg got up from a jump seat and stood beside Captain Leary at the console. The crew, Lal included, was getting ready to disembark. I planned to hold them until we'd handed the freed slaves over to the Saguntine officials who were waiting on the quay to process them. I was pretty sure that the arrival of over a hundred former slaves wasn't an entirely welcome event for the authorities in Jacquerie.

"Olfetrie?" Captain Leary said. "I'd like you to stay aboard for a while after everyone else has left the ship."

"Yessir," I said. "Ah—you want to talk to me?"

Six smiled. "No," he said, "though we'll talk later. Officer

407

Mundy is coming aboard to go over the business you and I discussed on the voyage back."

"Yes, sir," I said.

Discussing politics at that level with Captain Leary made me feel honored. The thought of discussing them with Lady Mundy—and Tovera—was frightening in a way that an ordinary human bully like Wellesley had not been.

I greeted Officer Mundy and her servant at the bottom of the boarding bridge instead of in the hold. They had waited on the quay until the *Alfraz* cleared; Captain Leary, the last person to disembark, spoke briefly with them as they passed.

"Welcome aboard," I said, hoping that I sounded less nervous than I was. "I apologize for the condition of the ship. We had quite a load of passengers and there hasn't been time to steam the hold out yet."

Mundy walked up the ramp beside me. Tovera was a half pace to Mundy's rear and about that much to the side.

"My parents, my mother especially, were strongly supportive of the lower classes," Mundy said. "Because of their political activity, I spent fifteen years living with the lower classes, and for a time with the lowest classes. The condition of your hold isn't going to be worse than flophouses where I slept in Bryce City."

"I was luckier than you, Lady Mundy," I said, using her title for the first time. "Captain Leary threw me a lifeline before I had to move out of my room in Xenos."

"Quite a number of people have been lucky to have met Daniel," she said. "None luckier than me."

She spoke with such calm that a fool might have believed that there was no emotion behind the words.

In the cabin, I offered Mundy the console couch. She shook her head and seated herself primly on the edge of a bunk; she brought out her data unit. Tovera, having closed and dogged the hatch, stood beside it with her back to the bulkhead. I took the couch myself, rotated into the compartment.

"Daniel has informed you that our purpose on Saguntum is to cause Karst to behave in a fashion which can be construed as an act of war against the Republic," Mundy said. She looked up from her display and met my eyes.

I took that as a question. I nodded and said, "Yes, ma'am. Technically I suppose Mistress Grimaud informed me first, but I didn't believe her."

I hadn't really *dis*believed Maeve either, to tell the truth. I just closed it out of my mind because I didn't want to think about such things. And here I was, waist deep in the whole business.

"The Foreign Ministry's information is incomplete," Mundy said, "but what you were told was accurate so far as it went. My original plan was to convince Colonel Foliot that Councillor Perez was plotting against him with the backing of the Karst Residency."

I didn't react, or I tried not to; but Colonel Foliot wasn't just a foreign politician to me. I liked and respected him as a man; and he was the father of the girl I, well, liked very much.

"I gave that up," Mundy went on, "because I became convinced that Foliot would not act against his superior even if he thought that his superior planned to have him disposed of. Foliot would leave Saguntum with his daughter rather than strike first against the man he'd sworn his oath to."

I nodded. That described the man I'd entered the Admiral's palace with.

"My replacement plan was to convince Councillor Perez that the Colonel was plotting against him with Karst help," Mundy said. "That was developing in a promising fashion, but your return with Colonel Foliot's rescued daughter provides an alternative which would be even simpler. If Colonel Foliot learned that unless he aids us we will make public his daughter's murder of a Karst official, he'll be forced to do as we say."

I swallowed. "I shot Platt myself," I said. "That doesn't put any pressure on the colonel."

"You did not shoot the consul," Mundy said. "Your crewman Lal gave a full account of what happened before you lifted from Salaam."

I didn't think Lal had seen the shooting, but I guess he might've done. Regardless, I didn't think I could convince anybody if I stuck to the lie. I was a terrible liar.

"Olfetrie," Mundy said, looking into her data display again. "We don't need your help to do this, though it has advantages. If you prefer to stay out from the business, just tell me now."

"No, ma'am," I said, shaking my head. "Look, I'll help, I'm a Cinnabar citizen. But I just want to talk to the colonel straight. He didn't swear any oath to Karst, and he's got no reason to love them, either. Let me just talk to him."

"There's a risk to Saguntum if war with Karst breaks out," Mundy said, looking up.

"Sure, Karst isn't going to beat *us*," I agreed, "but they could do quite a job on Saguntum before Cinnabar could stop them. The Colonel knows that, but I'd tell him anyway. But Karst isn't carrying out its part of the bargain with Saguntum. I don't believe that Platt was the only Karst official who was screwing"—the pun was accidental—"Saguntines instead of helping them. And I'll promise that Cinnabar will help, just maybe not much at the beginning. I *can* say that, can't I?"

If I couldn't—well, I didn't know what I'd do if I couldn't say that. If Cinnabar was just throwing Saguntum to the wolves, then I didn't stand with Cinnabar after all.

"Yes, you can say that," Mundy said, nodding crisply. "Obviously the Republic's immediate resources in the region are limited, and I won't guess at when that might change."

She stood up, shutting down her data unit. Tovera opened the hatch, glanced into the—empty—hold and stood aside for her mistress to exit.

Tovera looked back at me and grinned. She said, "I see why Six likes you, kid."

I didn't respond. I didn't know what to say.

I went over the ship at leisure, since I had it to myself. The cabin was, well, shipshape: nothing out of place, and even the bedding squared away on the bunks.

The pistol I'd bought from Abram was still in the secure locker. I stuck it into my right cargo pocket, where I'd carried it until I'd entered the Admiral's palace. It made me think of the Admiral, his legs pinioned by Azul's body. He'd flung his arms up when Colonel Foliot shot him. I grimaced, but I didn't want to leave the weapon on board.

The hold looked like a disaster area, the wrack left by a violent windstorm. Besides trash, there were dozens of items of clothing including a boot, a sandal, and a slipper—for different left feet. Now that the passengers were gone, the hold could be hosed out with steam—

But I couldn't do that alone, and at the moment I didn't even have Lal to help. For that matter, I was an officer on the *Sunray*. I hadn't reported aboard since our return from ben Yusuf.

I set off for Jacquerie Haven, walking briskly. I'd have liked to leave an anchor watch on board, but there wasn't much for prowlers to steal.

Evans, on watch in the *Sunray*'s boarding hold, called cheerfully to me as I started up the extension. A moment later Pointer, another of the techs, stepped into view. I waved at both of them.

Evans was good-natured and the strongest spacer on the ship; even Woetjans would have said that. He wasn't the man to make even simple decisions, though: They weren't simple to him.

"Lieutenant Olfetrie reporting," I said. "Who's got the duty?"

"That's Master Cory, sir," Pointer said. "He's usually in the TDC or whatever they're calling it on this cow, but I can buzz if you like."

"I'll find him, Pointer," I said. "Starting with the Supplementary Station."

I skipped up the companionway, thinking of the stairs of the Wives' Wing. I'd known what I was doing then. I didn't have a plan now. I was just doing the thing that was in front of me and wishing that somebody would give me orders to carry out.

The Supplementary Station was at the stern of the A Level corridor. It wasn't armored like a true Battle Direction Center, but the *Sunray* could be conned from it if a missile clipped off the bridge in the freighter's bow.

How that could ever happen was beyond me, but I strongly suspected the modifications had been paid for out of Foreign Ministry appropriations. I wondered if Bergen and Associates had gotten the contract? Well, the job would've been done well if they had.

Cory looked up from the compartment's console when I rapped on the open hatch. "Reporting for duty, sir," I said.

He smiled back. "Not to me," he said. "Until I'm told otherwise, half the crew's at liberty, and it may as well be all of us. I don't have a watch to put you on."

"Umm," I said. "Is Sun around? I'd like to get my paperwork straightened out. I don't know whether I'm listed as Run or if I'm due some back pay."

I'd been too busy with planning for the Salaam operation to ask about that when I'd landed after our escape. I wasn't worried, but I had literally no money of my own at the moment. The thalers I'd drawn from Colonel Foliot had all been expended.

"And also, I'd like to borrow a couple techs to clean the *Alfraz* up," I said. "If I get paid myself, I'll pay them—but it's a volunteer job regardless."

"I don't expect Sun back until 0800," Cory said, "but Pasternak's in the Power Room like you'd expect and—one moment, hey?"

He adjusted his console display to omnidirectional and

made an intercom connection. The holographic face of Chief Pasternak looked out at us from the air above the console.

"Chief?" Cory said. "Olfetrie wants to borrow some of your people to clean his ship out. I gather the civilians made a real dog's breakfast of it."

"I'll pay them, Chief," I called. "As soon as I can, anyway."

"*You bloody well will* not *pay, sir!*" Pasternak said. "*I'll have a crew over there in an hour. And glad I am to have something to do with them! Over.*"

"Thank you, Chief," I said. "I'll expect to meet you there. Over."

Cory broke the connection. I remembered the pistol and took it out of my pocket. "Say," I said. "Can I leave this with you for Sun to put into the arms locker? I don't want to leave it on the *Alfraz*."

"Sure," said Cory, reaching over the console to take it. I nodded and was turning to leave the compartment when the console alerted us to an incoming call. Cory raised an eyebrow and gestured me to stay.

"*Sunray,*" he said.

"*This is Mistress Foliot,*" said Monica's voice. Jacquerie's commo net didn't have bandwidth for visuals. "*I'm trying to locate Officer Roylan Olfetrie and I was hoping you can help me.*"

"Yes, ma'am," Cory said, grinning. "I have him with me now. Would you like to speak with him?"

"Monica?" I said, without bothering about a formal handover. "Are you all right?"

"*All right? Oh, of course,*" she said. Well, maybe it was obvious to her. "*My father and I would like to invite you to dinner at our house tonight. Is that possible?*"

"Ah..." I said. Cory nodded firmly from across the

console. "Yes, I believe it will be. At your house?"

"*Yes, at eight o'clock,*" Monica said. "*Our time, that is.*"

The *Sunray* went on local time at each port according to RCN doctrine. No reason a civilian would know that, though.

"I'll be there," I said. "Eight o'clock. Olfetrie out!"

Cory closed our end of the connection when Monica broke hers. He grinned broadly, then got up and walked to a locker.

"Two things," he said. "First, take this communicator along."

He handed me a small unit meant to be clipped to an epaulette or breast pocket. "It's netted in to the local system, but it'll also communicate directly with the ship."

"What's the range?" I asked.

"It travels through the local system if you're more than half a mile out," Cory said. "I set up the link myself."

He then reached into his pocket. "And take this," he added, handing over a fifty-florin piece as he had at our first meeting. "You're going on a date, so you shouldn't be broke."

"I don't expect to need money tonight," I said, maybe a little more stiffly than I meant.

"You're good for it," Cory said. "Hey, you own a ship, don't you?"

"Thank you, Cory," I said. "I'll meet Pasternak at the *Alfraz* and be back to change in plenty of time."

I left, whistling "*Don't you remember sweet Alice ...*"

I got back to the *Sunray* about six o'clock. The local hour was a little longer than standard, so I'd have plenty of time to shower and change.

The *Alfraz* was as clean as she had been since it came from the builders, who- or wherever they may have been. I'd insisted on working alongside the Sunrays, despite Pasternak's protests. She was my bloody ship—apparently—and the old chief engineer wasn't going to tell me how I could behave on her.

To my surprise, there were six spacers in the *Sunray*'s hold in addition to the usual pair on watch. Dasi was in charge of them. The weapons were racked out of sight, but they included two stocked impellers as well as the submachine guns I'd more often seen dismounted spacers carrying.

"What's going on, Dasi?" I said to the bosun's mate.

"Dunno, sir," he replied, looking up from the card game. "Six wanted us ready, but he didn't say what for. You've got your communicator?"

I reached into my tunic pocket and clipped the communicator to my lapel. I'd put it where it wouldn't hook the hose while I was working on the *Alfraz*.

"He hasn't cancelled liberty," Dasi said. "But everybody's supposed to be on immediate recall."

I shrugged, though it disturbed me to hear. I headed up to the bridge, hoping to find Six there—or Lady Mundy, that would've been as good. Neither of them were aboard, according to Lieutenant Enery, who'd taken over as duty officer. She used the command console, the usual station.

"There's a Karst destroyer in orbit," she said. "The *Meduse*. Maybe she has something to do with it."

"I wonder if I ought to go off to dinner?" I said.

"There hasn't been a recall," said Enery. "I'd like to think that I'd have been told if we were about to be attacked, but I can't swear to that. I'm not one of the inner circle, you know."

I cleared my throat. Enery didn't seem to have been drinking, but, well, she shouldn't have been talking that way. I'm not saying she didn't have reason, but she shouldn't have been saying those things.

Aloud I said, "I'm going to shower and change, then."

I felt better after showering in the officers' head and putting on a set of my civilian clothes. I was careful to transfer the communicator to the fresh suit, but I put it in my breast pocket again. This time I didn't want it getting in the way of me being a civilian for the evening.

I walked back to the bridge. It was still an hour till dinner and the Foliot's house—I'd checked the route after I left the *Alfraz*—was an easy fifteen minute walk.

Enery was still at the console, but to my surprise Tovera got up from a jump seat and came over to me. She said, "Can we talk for a minute in your cabin, sir?"

"Sure," I said, leading the way back down the corridor. "Does your mistress happen to be aboard?"

"Sorry," said Tovera. Pleasant as she sounded, I couldn't think of anybody I less wanted to spend time with. "She and Captain Leary had business of their own, but since Hogg was along, I thought I could take a little time for something I know more about than most people."

She closed the hatch of my compartment behind her, then set her attaché case on the small table that hinged down from the inner bulkhead. "I took a look at the pistol you turned in to the arms locker today," she said.

"I bought it when I was a slave in Salaam," I said. "I thought I might need it for the escape. As it turned out, I probably didn't."

"You carried it when you went back to ben Yusuf, though," said Tovera, opening her case. "You hadn't reloaded the two rounds you'd expended there before."

I swallowed. "I didn't need it the second time either," I said. "Well, I knocked a guard over the head with it. Look, I don't want the gun even for a souvenir. The memories I've got of it"—Platt vomiting blood and falling over—"aren't anything I'll want to refresh."

"What you had was an Alliance service pistol," Tovera said, bringing out a short, squat weapon and laying it on top of her case. "I thought of getting you a holster to carry the big one in the small of your back, but I decided this was a better choice for your tunic pocket. It's lower velocity and has only a ten-round magazine, but it'll be effective at any range you can hit things. Hogg has one just like it."

"I don't want a gun!" I said. "I've seen what they do and I don't want to do that!"

Tovera smiled, but I couldn't read the emotion behind that expression. I'm not sure there was any emotion.

"There's a Karst destroyer in orbit whose captain you personally pissed off on Benjamin," she said. "There's a Karst Residency here with nearly fifty people, many of them intelligence operatives. Now—if Karst agents knock off a Cinnabar spacer, we've got our cause of war and the rest of us can go home. But my mistress doesn't want that, and Six *really* doesn't want that. Have this gun on you any time you're not on the *Sunray*."

She smiled again. Her face suddenly looked hungry, and not for food.

"Don't worry," she said. "We'll get the war even if you don't get killed."

I put the pistol in the right-hand pocket of my tunic. "Thank you, mistress," I said.

I certainly wasn't happy about this. But Tovera was clearly acting in what she took to be my best interests.

And as she'd said, she was an expert.

Chapter Thirty-six

Barnes was in charge of the emergency squad in the hold when I left. "Good luck, sir!" he called. "You're seeing that cute blond you brought back from Salaam, right?"

"Right," I said, smiling but a bit embarrassed. "*And* seeing her father. I'm expecting a very quiet evening."

The major streets of Jacquerie ran parallel to the harbor, like contour lines along the side of the mountain. They were curvy but basically flat.

The problem was that Colonel Foliot's house was two streets higher than the waterfront. The up-and-down streets were short, but they were steep enough that several had steps in the middle and were pedestrian only.

That was fine while the sky was still bright—the steps were painted white on the edges—but it wouldn't be good in pitch darkness. I planned to come back along one of the sloping streets, and I wouldn't be drinking much at dinner. Well, that was true regardless.

Foliot's house was set behind a five-foot wall of the same dense gray limestone that the two-story house was built out of. Probably the same material as what it rested on. The gates were wrought iron and guarded from inside by two men in tailored dark-green uniforms and saucer caps. They carried carbines instead of the submachine guns I'd seen in the hands of the police commando on ben Yusuf.

"I'm Roylan Olfetrie," I announced as I approached the gate. "I'm invited for dinner with Colonel Foliot and his daughter. Ah—I may be a trifle early?"

I wondered if they were going to search me. I was very aware of the pistol in my jacket pocket, though it wasn't obvious through the loose, heavy fabric, a brown tweed.

"The Director told us to expect you, Master Olfetrie," the older guard said, drawing a gate leaf open with a squeal.

I walked up the walk to the front door. The house wasn't exactly a palace, but it was big for Jacquerie and on a prime piece of land. It was a good half acre and naturally flat, unusual here. The Councillor's Palace had been at a considerable distance west of this, the old residential area.

The door was solid, but there were narrow stained-glass sidelights to right and left with small clear sections at eye height. As I raised my hand to the knocker in the middle of the panel, the door opened inward. Instead of a servant, Monica said, "Oh, Roy! What a nice suit!"

The tweed was as close as I came to formal wear and wasn't—as I knew my mother would have said—very close at all. I looked at Monica and said, "You're lovely!"

I'd planned to say something politely bland, but seeing

Monica in a black jumpsuit with a translucent wrap over her shoulders startled the truth out of me. We'd been, well, close during our voyage here from Salaam, but she'd blossomed in a combination of freedom and proper clothes.

The harem outfits were designed to make the wives look childish and vulnerable. Monica as an adult companion in hard places was a long sight more attractive to me.

She took my hand and led me into a parlor where the colonel was rising from an upholstered chair. I'd noticed on the way past that the door's sidelights were backed by a panel of clear thermoplastic thick enough to stop a carbine slug.

"Glad you could make it, Olfetrie," Foliot said, pointing to a well-stocked sideboard. "Will you have a drink?"

"Ah, sir?" I said. "I'd happily take a beer if you had one, but I'm not a drinking man."

Foliot's face twisted with anger. "Did my daughter tell you to say that?" he snarled.

I stiffened, shocked and furious. "Colonel," I said, feeling my voice tremble, "I thought I was being asked a question. Since it appears that it was a test and I failed, I'll leave now and find my own dinner."

"Roy?" said Monica in a false tone. "Will you take me to dinner with you? Since my father doesn't seem to be in a mood to behave in a civil fashion tonight."

I didn't take my eyes off the colonel. I learned while I was a kid that you don't turn your back on somebody that angry.

Foliot's flushed face went pale. In a ragged voice he said, "Olfetrie, stress sometimes makes me an idiot. This was one of those times. Will you shake my hand?"

"I'd be honored to, sir," I said, doing so. When I leaned forward, the inertia of my tunic pocket made it swing. It wasn't a big thing, but Foliot noticed it. He didn't comment, but I saw his eyes flick down and a little *something* in his expression.

"We're still on for dinner, then?" he said with a rueful smile. "My daughter thinks I've been drinking too much—"

"You *have* been drinking too much!"

"—and she's probably right, so I'm prickly," Foliot said calmly, nodding to his daughter. "Monica, will you fetch two—"

He looked at me and said, "Ale or lager?"

"Either."

"Two lagers for me and my guest and bring them into the study for us? I'll show him some of the things there."

Monica nodded brightly and disappeared through a doorway in the back. Foliot gestured me to follow him across the hall into a room with two desks—one large, one small, and both supporting consoles. There was egg-crate shelving along the wall across from the door.

A man in his thirties stood up behind the smaller desk when we entered. He was very neatly dressed in dark gray. "Sir?" he said.

"I'm just showing Olfetrie my trophies, Samuels," Foliot said. "You can either stay or go home. Olfetrie, Samuels is my secretary."

"If you don't mind, sir," Samuels said. "I'm reconciling the accounts from the Orne property."

"Suit yourself," Foliot said, walking past the secretary's desk to get to the shelves of curios. I followed silently. The colonel clearly wasn't a man to mouth meaningless words.

If he'd meant for Samuels to get out, he would have said so; when he said he didn't care, he didn't care.

He reached into a cell and brought out an irregular, cream-colored chunk of plastic about the size of my palm. There was a threaded eight-millimeter cavity in one side.

"Know what this is?" Foliot said, plopping it into my hand.

"It's a Alliance cluster bomblet," I said. "Unfused, which is good because"—I hefted it—"from the weight, it's still got its explosive filling."

We—Dad—didn't handle cluster bombs as a regular thing, but there'd been some passing through our hands. The comparable Cinnabar munition would've been khaki. And while I wouldn't have kept a live bomb on the shelf of my office, the cast explosive was about as stable as the frangible plastic casing unless initiated by a fuse with a very high propagation rate.

"It was good for more reasons than that," Foliot said as I returned the bomblet to him. "It knocked me silly instead of blowing my head off. It was a friendly round: I commanded an Alliance light infantry company on Breisach. *I* didn't find it very bloody friendly."

Monica came in with a pair of frosted beer mugs which she set on coasters on the large desk. "I'll leave you men to talk," she said.

Foliot's eyes followed her out of the room. "She's the image of her mother," he said quietly. "Sometimes when I see her when I'm tired, and I think I'm back thirty years ago."

I coughed. "Sir," I said. "Monica is a very solid girl. Woman."

Foliot looked at me. In the same soft voice he said, "I'm not a heavy father, Olfetrie, don't worry about that. But if you ever hurt my daughter, I'll come looking for you."

"Sir," I said, nodding agreement. "I don't want to hurt anybody, certainly not Monica."

After a moment Foliot said, "Glad to hear it," and resumed describing fragments of his life from the objects on display. Not all of them had anything to do with his military career. Careers, really: with the Alliance; on Garofolo, where he'd risen to become head of state; and finally on Saguntum, where he was the Director of Public Safety, the title the guard at the gate had used.

"Sir?" I said. "The guard called you 'Director.' Do you prefer that or 'Colonel'?"

Foliot's smile was as firm as his handshake had been. "I prefer Gene," he said. "From people I like to see. Which I hope includes you, Olfetrie."

"Roy, sir," I said. "That is, Roy, Gene."

He took down a pin in the shape of a crescent moon. "I'd just been appointed a captain in the Army of Saguntum," he said. "This was my cap badge. I had some money with me from Garofolo, but I didn't like the idea of sitting around. A company command would give me something to think about besides—"

He shrugged. "Besides why I'd left Garofolo. Then the Councillor died and his son Israel succeeded him, but his younger son Pedro had his own ideas. Which failed, after quite a lot more excitement than I'd expected when I emigrated to Saguntum. When it was all over, Israel was still Councillor, I'd become a colonel, and the Councillor and advisors had created a new Department of Public Safety, into which moved the army, the Naval Protection Force, and a new Special Police

Commando. All under me, as Director."

"Those men at the gate aren't police, are they?" I asked. They didn't have the *feel* of the men who'd gone into the Admiral's palace.

"They're regular army," Foliot said. "I try to keep the police commando out of sight as much as possible. A lot of the people in it are from off planet and served with me on Garofolo."

He grimaced. "Look," he said. "Saguntum's security may require having folks like them, but I don't want to rub the civilians' noses in the fact."

"Yessir," I said. I *did* understand. Hogg and Tovera probably understood even better.

Monica came to the office door, carrying a half-full wineglass. We both saw her, so instead of tapping the doorjamb as she'd started to do, she said, "Are you ready for dinner, or would you like more beer?"

Foliot raised an eyebrow toward me. I said, "I'm ready to eat something."

"Then let's see what Augustine has for us," Foliot said.

The dining room would have held eight but was more comfortable with just us and the servant, Beechy, shuttling food from the kitchen in the next room. Monica fetched me another lager and a glass of red wine for her father.

As Beechy filled the soup plates, Foliot said, "I've been talking about myself a fair amount, Roy. What's *your* background?"

"The short version is two years at the Naval Academy before my dad shot himself ahead of a fraud indictment," I said calmly. I took another sip of oxtail soup. "The money vanished with Dad and I had trouble getting a job. Captain Leary gave me a job and I think may get me back into the Academy if I work out on the *Sunray*. Which I hope I'm doing. He doesn't seem to have held it against me that I got shanghaied."

"Mmm," said Foliot, his eyes on his soup. "Ever thought of settling somewhere else for a fresh start?"

"Sir," I said, "I belong in the RCN. It's going to be harder to get there than I thought it would be when I was a kid, but I'm not giving up."

We talked about the history of Saguntum through cutlets—I'm not sure of the animal—with potatoes and corn. The portions had been modest, but from the clattering in the kitchen, the parade of entrees was far from finished. I'd learned to pace myself at my parents' formal dinners.

Beechy came in through the hall doorway instead of from the kitchen. Foliot looked up at him and said, "A problem with the chicken?"

"Sir," Beechy said, sounding very worried. "Augustin and I noticed the guards at the rear had withdrawn, and I just checked the front. I saw Samuels leaving—"

"I gave him permission!"

"—and the guards at the front gate are gone also. I don't—"

Beechy jumped out of the way as Colonel Foliot strode through the hall door. I followed without anything in mind except to stick close to the man in charge.

Foliot ducked into his office and pulled open the top drawer of the big desk. "The gun's gone!" he said. "The front door—"

I was there a half step ahead of him, reaching for the prominent turnbolt above the latch plate. The door burst open, pushed by two men in civilian clothes. The one in front

427

was drawing a pistol from a shoulder holster.

I shot half a dozen times. The recoil punched my hand. The slug that hit the half-open door ricocheted up the staircase beside the hall. At least one round hit the leading attacker because he lost his grip on the pistol and fell to his knees. The second man dodged out of my line of sight.

Foliot jerked the wounded man out of the way so that I could slam the door. I heard Monica shout, "The phone is dead!"

As I threw the bolt left-handed, I saw Foliot scoop up the fallen pistol. An instant later there was a *Crack!* as Foliot shot the wounded man in the head. The corpse sprawled forward, voiding its bowels.

I dropped my pistol back into the side pocket and took out the communicator with my left hand. I squeezed it live and shouted, "Olfetrie to base! Emergency! Colonel Foliot's house on East Madeira, armed"—there was a crash at the back of the house, maybe a door being broken in—"attackers. Backup! Backup!"

Monica screamed from the dining room.

I reached into my pocket for my pistol and burned my fingers on the hot barrel shroud. It startled me into dropping the communicator in my other hand. I left that on the floor but got my right hand firmly around the grip of the pistol by holding the weapon steady with my left through the cloth.

Colonel Foliot ran back into the dining room with me behind him. I could see Beechy's feet under the table. A man had come through the kitchen door and was struggling with Monica. He was a big fellow and wouldn't have had much trouble if he'd had both hands free, but he was holding a pistol in his right and trying to point it toward Foliot coming in from the hall.

The stranger suddenly screamed and slammed Monica against the wall above the sideboard. A serving fork stuck out of his thigh where she'd stabbed him. Foliot shot him twice at the base of the throat. He fell backward, choking out a spray of blood.

There were men in the kitchen behind him. The colonel shot and ran to the kitchen door. I caught Monica before she slumped to the floor.

Six or eight shots crashed from the kitchen. Foliot backed away and let the connecting door swing shut.

Monica squirmed onto her feet. I let her go. Several guns within the kitchen fired, chewing pieces out of the door. The colonel had backed clear. The right shoulder of his jacket was bloody but he continued to hold his pistol out.

"Upstairs!" Monica called behind us. "We can hold them there!"

The kitchen door twitched. Foliot and I both shot into it. "Colonel, go back with Monica. I'll hold them till you're clear!"

The pistol fell from Foliot's fingers. "*Bloody hell!*" he snarled and bent. He picked the gun up with his left hand. His upper right sleeve was dark with blood.

"Olfetrie!" he rasped. "We both fire one shot and move into the hall. Got it?"

"Right," I said. My stomach was churning with the stench of ozone and blood. I was on the verge of vomiting, though I guess that wouldn't matter.

"Now!" said Foliot. We both shot at the tattered door

panel. Foliot backed through the hall door ahead of me, then fell down as he tried to turn.

Monica reached over her father and took the pistol. She began to drag him down the corridor one handed. I crouched between them and the door, pointing my pistol but suddenly wondering if it was loaded.

There was an enormous crash from the foyer. The door burst open, smashed off its hinges by a stone planter. "Coming through!" someone shouted and Cory and Barnes charged in. I squeezed myself to the side.

Barnes kicked open the dining room door. Both spacers emptied their submachine guns into the dining room and perhaps the kitchen beyond—I couldn't tell from my angle. They stepped aside, loading fresh tubes into their glowing weapons, while two more spacers entered the shattered dining room and began shooting into the kitchen.

"Help me get Dad into the medicomp!" Monica said. "There's one under the stairs."

I dropped the pistol back into my pocket. The wool had charred earlier. I wondered how I'd be able to replace the jacket.

I grabbed Foliot under the shoulders and took three shambling steps to get him to the door which Monica had opened under the stairs. Now she was removing the cover of the medicomp. I took a breath and heaved Foliot up and into the chest-style medicomp, dragging the colonel's legs over the lip because Monica couldn't get around my body in time to help me.

I felt bones grinding under my left hand when I lifted the wounded man. It was like my damaged jacket: Needs must when the devil drives.

Monica closed the medicomp over her father and began adjusting its dials. I stepped away, breathing hard. The hall was full of people carrying guns and talking in loud, angry voices.

The man standing next to me waved a hand slowly across the direction in which my face was pointing. I focused and saw Captain Leary. He held a submachine gun.

"Sorry, sir," I said. I wanted to brace to attention, but my brain couldn't seem to communicate with my body. "I was just..." I didn't know how to finish the sentence. "We were having dinner and they broke in. And they'd cut communication."

That reminded me of the communicator which had saved our lives. I looked around the room and found it squarely between my two feet. I picked it up and put it in my tunic pocket again, wondering if it still worked.

"Did they give any notion of their particular target?" Leary said.

"No, sir." The question reminded me that I'd thought I recognized the man who'd first shoved through the door. I lifted his torso so that I could see his face. Foliot had shot him through the base of the brain so that his face was still identifiable.

I straightened. "Sir, he was with the Karst official who tried to seize the *Alfraz* on Benedict," I said. "What was he doing here?"

"He was one of three personnel who landed yesterday by lighter from the *Meduse* in orbit," said Officer Mundy, who was suddenly beside us with her servant. "The remainder of the force appear to have been on planet already, at the Karst Residency."

Hogg joined us—coming from the back of the house. He carried a stocked impeller. "A couple of 'em got away," he said, including all of us. "I didn't figure a nice quiet neighborhood like this needed me shooting it up with this"—he patted the fore-end of his impeller—"since the slug's going to keep going after it exits. Ma'am"—he focused on Lady Mundy—"I guess you know where we can find them, don't you?"

"Yes," said Mundy. "That won't be a problem."

"Is it okay—" I started to say. Then I decided that if I didn't get some fresh air, I was going to throw up in front of everybody. I bolted out the front door.

Outside I bent over, placing my hands on my knees to support my torso. After a few deep breaths of air that didn't stink of gunfire and dead men, my stomach settled down.

Half the dirt from the planter which Woetjans had used to break down the door was spilled here on the stoop. The other half was in the entry hall, where at least it was soaking up blood.

Woetjans had been standing beside the front door, though I hadn't noticed her when I rushed out. I straightened and smiled at her. "Thank you, Chief," I said. "You saved time that we needed a lot."

"You all right, kid?" she said. The remaining planter stood on the right side of the stoop. How even Woetjans had been able to move its mate was beyond my imagination. She looked exhausted, and no mistake.

"I'm all right," I said. "The colonel was wounded but I think he'll come through."

I frowned. I didn't have a clear picture of what had just happened, but the timing didn't make sense. I said, "You really got here fast after I called for help. Thank heaven you did, but I don't see how."

"I think the Mistress heard something before you called,"

Woetjans said. "Anyway, it was her that got us moving. We were just a couple blocks away when I heard the shots."

Tovera had come out of the house. She nodded to the bosun, then said to me, "Do you mind if I take a look at your pistol, kid?"

I reached into my pocket and handed it to her, butt first. The barrel shroud was warm but no longer fiercely hot. I said, "It saved our lives."

"Good," said Tovera, ejecting the loading tube. She replaced it with a fresh one from a pack of five and returned the weapon to me. "Did you hit anything?"

"I wounded the first man through the door and locked it behind him," I said. I swallowed, remembering the scene. "Colonel Foliot shot him in the head then."

Tovera laughed. "Foliot's a stone pro," she said. "I knew from the first time I saw him that I'd have to shoot him in the back."

She handed me the pack of ammunition with four tubes remaining. "Here," she said. "If you carry them in the opposite pocket, they'll balance the weight of the gun."

I took the pack silently. *She'd been praising the colonel,* I realized. *This is the world I've chosen to be in.*

Monica came out the front door. She looked pale. "Roy," she said. "Dad wants to talk to you and Captain Leary. Can you come in?"

I dropped the pistol and ammunition into the right and left jacket pockets respectively, nodded to Tovera and Woetjans, and followed Monica inside.

There must have been about a dozen people clustered around the door to the medicomp facility; there was only room for two, of course. In a clear voice Monica called, "Captain Leary? Will you please let me and Roy through to pull my father out into the hall so that he can address all of us?"

I winced when I heard her, but Six was grinning as he turned and mimed forcing a path for us—which of course opened. There were several men in the battledress of Foliot's police commando. They must have arrived while I was trying to get control of my stomach. I recognized Cassidy and Briggs from the *Alfraz*.

Monica unlocked the medicomp's casters and guided the front in while I slithered around to the back and pushed. She was speaking in a low voice to her father. His complexion was yellowish, but his eyes were bright and his expression was as lively as an electric arc.

She gestured me to stop, then set the casters. "All right, Dad," she said. "Everybody can hear now."

Foliot's voice was neither firm nor loud, but I think all those standing around the cabinet could hear him. "I recognized the men who came through the back and grabbed my daughter," he said. "They're from the Karst Residency. I don't know what's going on, but it's bloody well not going to happen again. Cassidy, how many troops can we get together in two hours?"

"A hundred and twenty, give or take," Cassidy said. His skin was extremely dark, and his body was on the same design as that of Woetjans: tall, and as knobby as a length of rattan.

"Get them together," Foliot said. "Form up at the Councillor's Palace. That's close to the Karst Residency, which is where we're going, but keep that under your hat. You'll be in command, but I'll be going along. Understood?"

"Yessir," Cassidy said. "Do we kill them all?"

"No," said Lady Mundy. "I'll want prisoners and particularly I want to capture the electronic files intact. Which they won't be if killing the personnel is the priority."

Foliot looked at her hard when she interrupted, but his expression softened as he listened. He nodded and said, "Leary, that was why I wanted you. Look, my people can do the job easy enough, but you know stuff that we don't. The way you got here tonight proves that. You don't owe me anything, but I'd be glad of your help."

"A pleasure," the captain said, "and a duty. Karst is no friend of Cinnabar."

Foliot turned to me. "Roy," he said, "this isn't work you're used to, but if you want to come along you'll be welcome."

"Sir," I said. "I do want to come along."

Heaven help me, but that was the truth.

Chapter Thirty-seven

Colonel Foliot's aircar had two seats in front and six—three abreast, facing one another—in the passenger compartment. I was in the middle of the back row, between Hogg and Six. Each of them held the fore-end of a stocked impeller, the butt on the floor and the muzzle hovering close to the roof. Mundy was across from me with Tovera and Woetjans to either side of her.

I wore my tweed suit. I didn't have anything handy to change into, and I figured it would do as well as a set of spacers' slops for the current job. It had served me for one gunfight tonight, after all.

We overflew a platoon of the police commando, coming up the street in loose order. A moment later we landed at the gate of the Karst Residency. On the other side of the fence stood a squad of soldiers in the same sharp green uniforms as those who had abandoned their posts at the Foliot home earlier. They were clutching their carbines with expressions of concern.

"Hold this," Captain Leary said to me, thrusting the

impeller toward me. He got out of his door at the same time that Foliot opened the cab. Both men walked to the gate. The colonel was stiff but didn't stumble; his right arm was in a sling. Leary didn't support him, but he was obviously ready to grab the wounded man if necessary.

Foliot's driver had shut the fans down. I could easily hear the colonel say, "Canfield, I'm relieving you and your squad immediately. We've got intelligence that there's an attack planned on the Residency tonight. I'm taking over personally with the Special Police."

"But, sir," the officer said. "We haven't gotten any orders about that."

"You're getting them now from me, the Director of Public Safety," Foliot said. He didn't shout, but there was no question about the order. He pointed to the sling with his left hand and added, "Do you see what they did to me? Get out of here now, before I decide you're part of the problem!"

"Right!" said the army officer. He pulled the gate open; it had been latched but not locked. "Back to barracks, men."

As the soldiers filed out, the officer said to Foliot in a voice I could barely hear, "Sir, we could stay and help?"

The colonel squeezed his shoulder and said, "Thanks, Canfield, but I've got this covered."

The soldiers passed the police coming the other way. Captain Leary got into the aircar beside me and a noncom from the commando took the front seat where Foliot had been.

The colonel remained at the gate with the arriving platoon. He pointed toward us.

"All right, driver," Leary said. The privacy panel between

the front and the passenger compartment was down.

The aircar rose smoothly, then curved to the right to take us over the stone Residency as the troops swept into the landscaped grounds. As we banked, I saw that several pairs of Foliot's men carried frame charges between them.

The building was arranged around a courtyard. We dropped into the middle abruptly and pancaked in. The driver must have done something besides just cutting the fans, because we didn't hop upward again as I'd expected. This vehicle was a limousine with inlays and luxurious seats, but this wasn't the driver's first assault landing.

Leary, Hogg, Tovera, and Woetjans were out while the car's resilient skirt was still flexing. They'd had their doors half-open from the moment we took off.

A man was starting across the courtyard. As we swept in, he turned and ran toward a doorway in the right sidewall at its corner with the rear wing. He got the door open when a clatter from Tovera's miniature submachine gun dropped him dead on the threshold.

A door was rolling up in the opposite sidewall; I heard lift fans revving from there. Leary and Hogg leaned over the front and rear decks of our car and began shooting. Their impellers *crash*ed instead of crackling the way Tovera's weapon did.

Fan motors came apart as heavy slugs crashed through the car's body and into the motor housings. Windings shorted. Metal which had been blown from the leading motors sprayed the blades of fans farther back; unbalanced, they tore themselves out of their housings. The car tried to dive onto its nose, but the back end hit the ceiling of its stall. The vehicle bounced sideways and turned over, spilling passengers.

Colonel Foliot had said the Residency had an aircar. During the planning for the assault, I'd asked why Captain Leary was going in as one of the shooters tasked with making sure the vehicle didn't get away. "Don't the police"—I nodded to Colonel Foliot—"have marksmen?"

Hogg gave me the kind of look you do for something on your shoe and said, "Because the young master's a better snap shot than I am, which makes him plenty bloody good. Myself, I'd rather whack them when they're asleep."

Lady Mundy was running with a small pistol in her left hand. I followed, figuring my body covered hers from anybody trying to shoot her from behind. The second-floor windows all overlooked the courtyard and it wouldn't be hard for somebody to start popping shots at our backs.

I left my own pistol in my pocket. It wasn't hard to imagine myself tripping with a gun in my hand and putting a slug into the back of somebody in front of me. There were plenty of things that I couldn't control, but at least I could avoid making situations worse.

Woetjans threw open the door and turned right, bracing her left hand against the wall in front of her and brandishing the length of pipe overhead. Tovera was just behind her, keeping low and moving as fast as the long-legged bosun.

I followed Lady Mundy, jumping the dead man in the doorway. A man was coming down the hall from the direction of the commo vault. He reached under his coat but was dead before he even got his fingers around the grip of the holstered pistol.

I heard blasts from three directions. Foliot's commando was

blowing in doors and windows with charges set against the frames. An explosion shattered the door of an office farther down the hallway, slamming it in pieces against the courtyard side of the wing.

The door of the commo vault slammed closed. Woetjans gripped the loop handle and tried to jerk it open.

Do the platoons attacking from outside have any entry charges left?

I opened my mouth to volunteer to go find explosives. Two things stopped me: Lady Mundy was squatting on the hallway floor, doing something with her personal data unit. And I realized that running toward a squad which had just blown its way into an enemy base was a very good way to be shot dead by people who'd only registered *movement coming from a hostile direction.*

Something went *clink* inside the armored door. Lady Mundy said, "Don't shoot!"

Woetjans hauled the steel panel open. I stepped into the vault before the bosun could. A man my age—a boy—in a tan uniform stood behind a console, pointing a pistol at me.

I raised my hands and stepped forward, smiling. "Let's both survive this, hey?" I said. "If you let me take you out of here really slowly, nobody will touch you."

I didn't know if that was true. I hoped it was.

The pointed pistol began trembling. I stopped in the middle of the room.

"Who are you?" the clerk said.

"We're the government," I said. "Your lot tried to kill Colonel Foliot tonight. You'll be arrested and deported because you're diplomatic staff. Unless you murder me, of course."

There was some truth to that. Mostly I was just trying to sound plausible. I hoped I did.

"You really won't kill me?" the clerk whispered. From his tone, the words were a prayer. He closed his eyes and tears started to leak out. When he set the pistol beside the console, it slipped off and clanked to the floor.

I leaned over the desk and put my arms around him. He began sobbing and clutched at me with both hands. He was blubbering words, but I couldn't understand them.

Tovera walked around the desk and gently disentangled the clerk's arms. I let Woetjans lead me back to the doorway. I was so frightened I could scarcely walk. I was glad of her presence.

"You could get yourself killed that way, kid," the bosun said.

"So you're going to live forever?" I managed to say. I squeezed her arm, then stepped over to where Tovera held the clerk. The muzzle of her submachine gun was close to his ear.

"Woetjans and I will take him now, Tovera," I said. I was trying to sound firm, but my voice trembled.

Tovera grinned and gestured with her left hand. "Be my guest, kid," she said.

"Stay behind me," I said to the clerk. "We'll be going into the courtyard."

As we passed Woetjans, I said, "Would you watch our backs, Chief?"

We returned to the door the way I'd arrived. It was a much shorter distance than it'd seemed when I'd arrived a few minutes ago, tensed up against the bullet that I was sure was tear into me.

We passed the man Tovera had killed when he tried to draw a gun; realistically, she would have killed him regardless. I glanced back to see how the clerk was taking it. He stared, his throat working. I had to touch his arm and guide him through the outside door.

We were using the courtyard to gather the people we'd captured in the Residency. Among the group under guard there already was Representative McKinnon, whom I'd met during the presentation at the Councillor's Palace on our arrival.

He looked at us with dawning fury, then snarled, "Did you open the Commo Vault, Carey? You traitor, you bloody *traitor*! You'll be *shot* for this, you know!"

I started to say that we'd opened the door from outside, but I caught myself. Why did I care what the Karst spy thought, let alone want to correct him?

The clerk, Carey, looked at McKinnon, then turned deliberately to me and said in a clear voice, "That's Representative McKinnon. He gave the order to attack Foliot. The men beside him are Lestrup and Watts. Watts was in command during the attack. He's from the Central Office in Hegemony on Karst."

Carey looked around at the increasing group of prisoners. "I don't see any but Lestrup and Watts who were involved in the attack. I think you must have killed most of them."

Despite the weapons pointed at him, McKinnon lunged at Carey with his fist raised. I moved forward and blocked the punch, then hit the representative twice in the belly. He doubled over and fell to the ground.

With Cassidy beside him, Colonel Foliot entered the

courtyard. He looked better than he had when I saw him just before the attack. Another dozen prisoners followed them out, guarded by police.

Some of the commandos' submachine guns had been fired recently, judging by the sheen of the muzzles. Coil guns accelerated heavy-metal pellets down their bores, but the flux worked on the pellets' aluminum skirts which vaporized in the process. The gaseous metal recondensed on the outer surfaces of the weapon and on anything else near the muzzle.

"We've got both floors of the front wing cleared," the colonel said. "Any problems at your end, Leary?"

"Not that I've heard," Six said, "but—ah, here. Adele, were you successful?"

Lady Mundy had come out of the building. She'd put her pistol away but held her personal data unit. Tovera was walking behind her and seemed to be trying to look in all directions.

"I've transferred the data in the console to my unit on the *Sunray*," Mundy said. "It will take time to sort it, of course."

"You're Lady Mundy?" said Carey unexpectedly. He turned his head. "And you'd be Captain Leary, sir?"

"Yes," said Six. "What of it?"

"Then, sir," Carey said, "you ought to know that a Mistress Grimaud of your own Cinnabar delegation was behind the attack. She told McKinnon that you and Lady Mundy had turned Foliot and were about to help him overthrow the government. McKinnon decided that getting rid of Foliot was the quickest way to take care of that problem."

"Indeed," Captain Leary said. "And you would know that how, sir?"

"He's the code clerk," Lady Mundy said. "And just skimming the message traffic I can confirm his statements."

"I think we'd better discuss that with Mistress Grimaud, don't you, Adele?" the captain said. He smiled. He really did look amused, but he was carrying his impeller at port arms. The muzzle was bright with recent firing.

"Yes," Mundy said. "We're close to the Palace, but—"

Before she got the question out, Colonel Foliot said, "We'll go in my aircar. I need to inform Councillor Perez about the plot anyway."

He turned to Cassidy and said, "I'll leave you in charge here with thirty men or however many more you think you need. Send the rest double-time to the Councillor's Palace. I left twenty people there and the late arrivals will join them. I think the army's pretty much loyal, but McKinnon here obviously got to my own guards tonight, and I don't want to take any chances."

"I'll be able to tell you very shortly which soldiers have had dealings with Karst," Lady Mundy said. "But for now, keeping a good number of your Special Police close by is the best idea."

As we all started to get into the car, I remembered Carey. There wasn't room for him to ride with us, but—

I turned to the noncom who'd taken Foliot's seat during the assault and said, "Sergeant? This prisoner is being very helpful, and his colleagues aren't happy about it. Can you make sure that they don't harm him when I'm gone?"

The fellow looked over at Foliot who had just gotten into the cab beside the driver. "Sir?" he said.

"Absolutely right, Sergeant Peters," Foliot said, nodding.

As I got into the center of the middle bank of seats, Peters transferred his submachine gun to his left hand alone and walked over to McKinnon and his henchmen. Without warning, he punched McKinnon in the stomach much harder than I'd been able to.

We took off steeply because the courtyard didn't allow as long a run-up as we'd had on the street in front of the building. I hadn't meant for Peters to do that, but I'd left up to him the way he wanted to execute my directions. And to be honest, his choice didn't really bother me.

"Sir?" I said, speaking up to be heard over the intake rush; the windows were open. "I didn't think to ask Carey if he'd warned the orbiting Karst destroyer that we'd attacked the Residency."

"He didn't," Lady Mundy said, shouting from the seat opposite. "I did in his name, though. Remember, we're here to encourage Karst to attack Saguntum, which will shortly be a Friend of Cinnabar."

I hadn't been thinking about that. I'd just watched a number of people die. Thanks in part to me, more people were going to die.

We dropped in front of the Council House. I'd seen from the air that at least fifty Special Police formed in a block on one side of the plaza. They were easily identified by their battledress. There were also other military personnel in a variety of uniforms, and a growing number of civilians despite the late hour.

"Colonel," Lady Mundy said, speaking through the open panel to the cab when the fans shut off. "Lieutenant Cory in the *Sunray* has taken director control of the antiship missile batteries around the harbor. I don't believe the regular crews are in Karst pay, but I thought it better not to take chances."

Foliot's face went hard for an instant. Then he nodded crisply and said, "Thank you, Lady Mundy. You were thinking ahead of me."

A squad of Special Police ringed the car, giving us room to get out. The crowd wasn't hostile but their shouted questions had created a complete babble. Most questions were directed at Foliot.

He turned and shouted, "Leary, will you come with me to brief Councillor Perez?"

"In a moment, sir," Captain Leary shouted back. "We have our own business to take care of. Will you lend us an official presence in case we need to discuss the matter with the attendants at the rooms occupied by the Cinnabar delegation?"

Foliot got out and pointed to an army officer wearing a green field uniform and a worried expression. "Major Hafner?" he said. "Captain Leary and his people from Cinnabar have my authorization as Director to do anything they damned well please. Do you have any objection to helping them do that?"

"No objection at all, sir," Hafner said. He threw Foliot a salute, then said, "Captain, what do you need from me?"

"Lead us to the west wing, ground floor," Lady Mundy said. We set out.

I'd thought for a moment that Six should have asked for a larger escort to get through the crowd, but as soon as we'd passed the initial ring of Special Police, a score of spacers formed around us. They weren't carrying guns, but most had tools or batons made from a length of high-pressure tubing.

Evans carried a maul. He handled it so easily that if I

hadn't once tried to pick it up, I wouldn't have believed it was really bronze.

Our group entered the Council House alongside Foliot and his entourage, but we turned left in the central rotunda while he marched straight across into the Councillor's suite. An army sergeant wearing a Sam Brown belt of white leather with a holstered pistol stood doubtfully.

"These are Cinnabar officials, going to see their colleagues," Hafner said. That was more than he'd been told, though it was pretty much true.

The sergeant stepped aside, though he still looked doubtful.

Leary with Hogg beside him stopped at the first door to the left. "Open up, please, Mistress Grimaud," he called.

The next door down the hall opened; Director Jimenez peeked out, keeping his body concealed. I smiled toward him, but his expression looked frozen.

"I'll get it," said Woetjans, stepping forward and raising her right boot.

The door opened before the bosun could kick it in. Maeve, wearing the same slinky outfit as when she invited me to dinner, stood in the opening. "You have business with the Foreign Ministry, Captain Leary?" she said.

"*I* have business with you, Mistress Grimaud," Lady Mundy said. "You're under arrest as a traitor to the Republic. My warrant as Senate Plenipotentiary to Saguntum is sufficient authority, I believe, though you're welcome to object when you're tried in Xenos. Unless"—Mundy cocked an eye at Major Hafner—"you plan to ask asylum from the Saguntine authorities?"

"Ma'am," Hafner said to Lady Mundy. "A buddy of mine

in the police says that this woman had our boss shot, Colonel Foliot. I wouldn't be the one to grant asylum regardless; but if the story's true, then nobody else is going to do it either."

"I don't believe your claim of authority!" Maeve said, but I could see in her eyes that she did. She was beginning to grasp how badly she'd misstepped when she went up against Lady Mundy.

"Turn around and stick your wrists out," Tovera said. I thought for an instant that Maeve might refuse, but thank goodness she turned. Tovera twitched the wrists together and lashed them with something so thin I could barely see it. A bead the size of my little fingernail bound the ends of the tie.

Tovera stepped away. Maeve faced around again. Tovera smiled at her and said, "You used some local talent to shanghai the kid here. If you'd like to involve them again, I'd be happy to discuss matters."

Maeve didn't reply. She glared at Tovera, then let her glance stray toward me. She lowered her eyes.

The spacers with us had rousted the senior members of the Foreign Ministry delegation into the hallway. Banta was wearing a bathrobe and sandals. His lip was swollen and bloody; I hadn't heard it happen, but chances were that he'd protested a little too strongly for Dasi's liking and had gotten knocked down.

Dasi held a lug wrench in his right hand. He hadn't bothered to use it to make his point with Banta.

Captain Leary looked over the assemblage in the hallway lighting. "I think we're all here now," he said. "Lady Mundy, what next?"

"Now," she said, "I present my credentials to Councillor

Perez and see if Saguntum would like to enter the Friendship of Cinnabar."

We started toward the rotunda again. A pair of riggers were marching Maeve along, each holding an elbow. I hoped nobody would stumble, because I was pretty sure that Tovera's monocrystal tie would cut through bone if enough pressure were put on it.

I expected we'd have to shove our way to the Councillor's office, but as soon as our party reappeared from the west wing, a double column of Special Police did the pushing for us.

I followed Six and Lady Mundy to the door of the office, then stopped. An aide in civilian clothes waited outside the door with his hand on the knob; a special policeman stood beside him, looking uncomfortable and squeezing the grip of his submachine gun nervously. His finger wasn't inside the trigger guard, but I won't say he made me feel easier.

The aide spoke into his lapel mike. After a moment he bowed to Six and opened the office door.

Mundy turned and said, "Director Jimenez? Come in with us, please; you need to hear this also."

Her eye lit on me. I won't say that she smiled, but I thought she almost smiled. "You too, Olfetrie. You were in this at the beginning, after all."

She ushered Jimenez in, then with the captain entered also. I slipped in behind them and heard the door close like a pillow of blessed silence.

Councillor Perez was behind the big desk at the back.

Colonel Foliot sat in an armchair which he'd moved beside the desk. He looked more worn than he'd been when we entered the building. The medicomp would have dosed him with drugs; they were probably wearing off. The quicker he got back into the medicomp, the better.

"Councillor Perez," Mundy said, "I apologize for not presenting my credentials at our earlier meeting."

She handed over a large leather bifold, open. I saw seals and, to my amazement, ribbons. I guessed that the trappings were for the presumed tastes of a planet far from Cinnabar—culturally as well as physically.

"The Republic has appointed me its representative to offer the Friendship of Cinnabar to the government of Saguntum," Mundy continued. "The grant of friendship will have immediate effect—that is, without having to be confirmed by the Senate after the fact."

"I don't understand," Perez said, frowning. "*Lady* Mundy?"

He glanced over at Foliot and said, "Gene, what's going on? First you tell me that Karst agents have shot you, and now I've got a Cinnabar senator—"

"Not senator, sir," Mundy said sharply. "I am the Senate's representative, but unlike my father I am not a member of that body."

Foliot roused in his chair. "They're offering us an alliance, Israel," he said. "Oh, we'll pay for it, don't doubt that, but without Cinnabar's help we'll have Karst garrisons and a thirty percent Karst tribute inside of six months. Take the offer, because it's our only choice."

"But there must be a misunderstanding, Gene," the

Councillor protested. "We've always gotten along with the Karst representatives, and the customs duties aren't really that big a burden. Surely . . . ?"

Foliot pointed his left index finger at the bandage over his right shoulder. "Look, Israel," he said. "There's not much bloody way to misunderstand *this*, is there?"

"The contents of the Mission's own computers confirm what Colonel Foliot is telling you, sir," said Lady Mundy. "I'll transfer it to your own system so that you can see for yourself."

She laid her data unit on the desk in front of her and began twitching her control rods. The display was a blur of light to everyone but the operator, but I didn't doubt that she was streaming data into the console hidden within the Councillor's desk.

An attention signal went *bing* somewhere in the desk. Perez said, "Yes?"

A voice—I thought the aide who'd admitted us was speaking—said, "Courier from the messaging center for Director Foliot, sir. He says it's of the greatest urgency."

Perez and Foliot exchanged glances. Foliot said in a clear voice, "Send him in, then."

The door opened to admit a small man with a trim goatee. He gave a folded piece of flimsy to the colonel.

Foliot read it. Then, without speaking, he handed it to Councillor Perez.

"This says that the *Meduse* has left Saguntum orbit," Perez said, frowning in amazement.

"That was the Karst destroyer which arrived two days ago," Foliot said.

"And it says that before the *Meduse* left, it destroyed Orbital Control with plasma cannon." Perez looked up. "Whyever would it do that? Orbital Control doesn't have any weapons, does it?"

"No weapons at all," said Foliot. "It was bloody murder. And we're at war, Israel. Whether we like it or not."

"I *don't* like it," said Councillor Perez, looking older and sounding far more impressive than had been the case before. "But it's reality."

He drew a deep breath and said, "Lady Mundy, how do I go about accepting the Friendship of Cinnabar?"

Chapter Thirty-eight

I slept in my cabin on the *Sunray*. Nobody'd given me any orders. I wasn't important enough for the folks who were giving orders to think about, and the heavens knew that I needed sleep. When I got up, I dressed in slops and put on the saucer hat. I'd change if I needed to after I learned what the day required; for now I was a watchstanding officer of the transport *Sunray*, out of Xenos.

I walked onto the bridge, looking for information. Cory must have been on duty in the aft station, because Mundy was alone at the console. Well, alone except for Tovera, which was like saying that her shadow lay on the deck beside her.

"Ma'am?" I said. I didn't know how to address her now—neither Officer Mundy nor Lady Mundy reflected the whole present reality—so I'd fallen back on the form used by the Sissies, the spacers who had served for many years with her. "Can you tell me where to report?"

"There'll be a meeting in the Naval Defense building in"—

her wands twitched— "fifty-seven minutes," she said without looking up from her data. "Cory would have awakened you in half an hour. Daniel thought you should sleep in if you wanted to. And Monica Foliot has called, making sure that you were all right but emphasizing that you shouldn't be awakened."

"Ah!" I said. "I should—"

I stopped there because I didn't know what I should do. The Naval Defense Forces Building was close enough to the *Sunray*'s slip that I could probably hit it with a stone, but I didn't want to be involved with Monica when I was about to have real work to do. If I could just chat with Monica for a moment, that would be fine, but I didn't know what she had in mind.

Lady Mundy suddenly turned on her couch. She said, "Have you wondered why you were with us when we entered the Karst Residence, Olfetrie?"

"Ma'am?" I said. "Because I'd been present at the attack on Colonel Foliot's house, I supposed. In case I could identify some of the personnel."

"No," said Mundy, her eyes on her display again. "Director Foliot requested that you go in. He wanted someone whom he trusted to be at the heart of the operation."

"Ma'am!" I said. "I'm not a traitor to Cinnabar! I wouldn't act for the colonel against you and Captain Leary, and I can't imagine the colonel asking me to!"

"Daniel and I trust you also, or you wouldn't have been involved," Mundy said. "I doubt you'd have been the first pick for the open seat in the car, but there were shooters enough without you"—Tovera grinned. She reminded me of a predatory fish—"and in the event you proved to be quite useful. But I thought you ought to know."

"Thank you, ma'am," I said. "I, ah, think I'll go ashore and have something for lunch. And perhaps to return Mistress Foliot's call. Briefly."

Colonel Foliot's aircar was parked beside the Naval Defense building, and a special policeman was at the door along with what I took for the usual pair of Shore Police in black on gray pin-striped uniforms. One of the latter directed me to the briefing room, but it was a straight shot in from the lobby.

It was an auditorium, with eight arcs of seats sloping down from the entrance.

Foliot was at the table below, with Six and Lady Mundy to his right and a pair of officers—one was female, very unusual at this distance from the more developed worlds—in Naval Defense uniforms on the other side. People kept dribbling into the room, local personnel as well as officers and senior riggers from the *Sunray*.

I chatted with Lieutenant Enery, who asked me about the attack on Colonel Foliot's house. She was from an RCN family; obviously smart, obviously skilled; and completely alone on the *Sunray*. Because of my training on the run out, I'd developed a friendship with the warrant officers which an officer of Enery's background couldn't possibly have done.

I found myself feeling sorry for her, but . . . not enough that I expected to change my own behavior. I hoped to spend such free time as I had with Monica. Our chat before the meeting had been short, but very positive.

The entrance door thudded shut. Simultaneously, Colonel Foliot rose to his feet. Additional hours in the medicomp had helped his appearance considerably, though he still looked frail compared to what he'd been before he was shot.

"Most of the talking this afternoon is going to be by Captain Leary," Foliot said. "All I have to say is that he speaks for me and for Saguntum. We're in an all-out war with Karst now, and we're very bloody lucky to have Leary and his staff with us."

Foliot nodded to Six and sat down. I wondered if his reference to Leary's staff meant Lady Mundy or the entire crew of the *Sunray*. Either choice made sense.

"Fellow spacers," Leary said. His voice wasn't amplified, but it was strong and the room's acoustics were good. "Karst has attacked us. Their thugs shot Colonel Foliot and missed killing him by only a whisker, and a Karst warship destroyed Orbital Control, killing four of your colleagues. Then the warship ran back to Karst to return with a force large enough to crush Saguntum."

He looked around the room. "Before they can get it together to do that," he said, "we're going to take the war to Karst. They'll be starting to work up their ships to attack Saguntum, lifting to orbit and making short runs within their planetary system. We'll stage a light-minute out and pick our targets, then attack and run straight for home."

The muted discussion was entirely among the Saguntine personnel. Former RCN spacers—myself included—made a point of appearing unfazed by the planned operation. Possibly some of my fellows really were bored at the notion of making a catch-as-catch-can attack on a hostile fleet, but I certainly wasn't.

A Saguntine officer stood up. "Captain Leary?" he said. "When you say 'we,' exactly who do you mean?"

"The four dart sloops of the Defense force," Leary said. "The ships will largely be crewed by their current personnel, but Captain Esterhazy from the staff"—he nodded toward the female officer seated on the other side of Foliot—"will command the *Concha*, and the others will be under me and two of my officers."

This time the rush of surprise was general. After letting it go on for a moment, Leary resumed, "This is not a comment on the courage of the existing captains. Rather, it's a reflection of the six-day voyage to Karst and the need for precise astrogation. Captain Esterhazy is a graduate of Fleet Advanced Training, and my officers have RCN training. Saguntum has never before needed the expertise this mission requires."

"Sir," someone from the back called without rising to his feet. "Sloops aren't meant to take on major warships."

"Sloops are what we have," Leary said. "And for that matter, I believe that dart sloops are ideal for the hit-and-run attacks we'll be carrying out."

There was another nervous rustle, maybe louder than there'd been earlier. The officer who'd asked the question stood up. "I resign," he said loudly. "This is bloody crazy!"

He stepped into the aisle and started up toward the door. Over his shoulder, he called, "I never signed up to commit suicide!"

"Sergeant Ciano?" Foliot called to the Special Police standing at the door. "Arrest former Lieutenant Brassey. He'll be released and deported as soon as our striking force returns, but not while the operation is ongoing."

Foliot rose to his feet again. He looked around the room slowly before he said, "Is there any other member of the Saguntine defense forces who's afraid to fight?"

Nobody spoke. I glanced over my shoulder and saw that Brassey had stopped protesting. The guards were binding his wrists behind his back.

"Go on, Leary," the colonel said, sitting down again.

Six unexpectedly grinned at the audience. "Believe me," he said, "I didn't sign up to commit suicide either. I've got people waiting for me back on Cinnabar, including a very attractive wife...but I did know that my job involved fighting. I hope you all are clear on that, because there *will* be fighting—at least on our side. If we do it right, there's a good chance that the Karst lot will still have their thumbs up their arses when we've all gone back home."

I could feel the room relax, me included. Brassey was a coward, but I sure didn't think he was wrong to be concerned. I'd bet that Six would agree—but his little speech made me feel that the attack was reasonable. Which it hadn't before.

"I want the new captains and crews to get to know each other," Captain Leary said. "I'll be taking Master Brassey's place on the *Lezo*. Lieutenant Cory is going to the *Magellanes*, and Lieutenant Olfetrie is in command of *El Cano*. My first officer, Lieutenant Enery, will accompany us in the *Sunray*, which won't be attacking but will provide intelligence through a sensor suite superior to that of the dart sloops."

He grinned again. "Not coincidentally, my signals officer, Lady Mundy, will be aboard the *Sunray*. Which I'd prefer to a light cruiser if I were given a choice."

I started to say something to Lieutenant Enery. Her face looked carved out of stone, so I swallowed instead.

I needed to meet the crew of *El Cano*. My new command.

El Cano had a Saguntine crew of six, including Lieutenant Smith, who had just become my second-in-command. Six had added Barnes and Wedell. I was confident that those two and I could work the sloop to Karst by ourselves if we had to.

In fact the locals seemed to be a pretty decent material—about as good as the crew of a Xenos-registered freighter. They were certainly better than the spacers I'd served with on the *Martinique*.

The darter was named Whitlake, called Red. He wasn't much older than me. He was rated spacer, but I judged that landsman would be closer to the truth. Sun said grudgingly that Red seemed to know his job as darter, which was all that really counted. These sloops were really just minimal propulsion wrapped around a "dart"—an antistarship missile like those in the ground defenses defending most harbors, those on Cinnabar, Saguntum, and ben Yusuf among them.

Pasternak had interviewed the motorman, Moss. He hadn't formally given his approval, but I knew that he'd put Gamba in charge of the *Lezo*'s fusion bottle.

I took *El Cano* through the Matrix to the three outer planets of the Saguntum system, testing both my astrogation and the crew's skill. I did all right, though the second jump was a lot farther out—nearly two hundred thousand miles—than

I'd intended it to be. According to Barnes, the riggers were adequate, though he'd have liked to have a couple months to get them properly into shape.

We three Sunrays wore rigging suits. The Saguntines had only air suits, and I agreed with Barnes that training them in the time available to use borrowed hard suits was impossible.

The lighter garments were adequate for short hops within the system; they weren't really safe for longer voyages where exhaustion and frayed cables could be expected. But as Wedell said with a shrug, "Well, if they thought being a spacer was safe, I hope they die before they breed."

When we returned to the Military Harbor, I reported to Captain Leary that *El Cano* was ready to execute his orders. At 1000 hours the next morning, we lifted to orbit as the fourth sloop of the operation. When the *Sunray* joined us, we headed for Karst.

Chapter Thirty-nine

The rendezvous point was a light-minute from Karst. *El Cano*'s run to it was four days, with three extractions. On the first extraction I estimated us to be twelve hours short of our goal. I'd calculated we'd be ten out.

That was quite a decent piece of astrogation, given that the sloop had a minimal rig and the longest run it had made in the past was of six hours. I was calibrating the console. The star sights I took on extraction refined the console's predictions in a fashion that five years of short runs had not done.

That said, my second run of twelve hours was out by three, a much higher percentage error. That was useful for keeping me from getting too full of myself.

The crew behaved pretty well. Hammocks had been rigged again in the machinery spaces, like in the raid on Salaam, so everybody had a separate bunk. The amenities were spartan: The designers had expected the sloops to return to base every day or two at the longest. Everyone got along together well enough, and the Saguntines got a great deal of training from Barnes and Wedell.

I spent part of each watch out on the hull to observe the Matrix and also to see how the Saguntine riggers were doing. Pretty well, it seemed to me, but I checked—helmet to helmet—with Barnes or Wedell.

Lieutenant Smith was a willing rigger if not a particularly skilled one. He was only a little older than me and had gotten his place by virtue of his family's prominence in Jacquerie rather than for any obvious aptitude. His astrogation was a short step better than entering the desired destination and letting the console make all the decisions. I tried to train him, largely to keep myself occupied, but he wasn't interested.

The third run brought us to within a hundred thousand miles of the rendezvous, as confirmed by multiple star sights. I shut us down and began searching for the rest of the strike force.

El Cano's optics were quite good, though the sensor array as a whole was no better than that of the *Martinique*. The *Sunray* and one of the sloops were already at the rendezvous, within one hundred thousand miles. That pair were within ten thousand miles of one another. I was willing to bet that *El Cano* was responsible for the greater separation between us and the other ships.

I *thought* that a third sloop was in-orbit from us at about four hundred thousand miles, but I might well have been seeing an asteroid. Against the faint sunlight and without optical-sharpening software that hadn't been loaded into *El Cano*'s console, I couldn't be sure without using an active emitter. We were under orders to shut down on arrival and not to transmit anything but a minimal check-in message.

I'd warned the crew that we'd be in freefall at the rendezvous until we actually launched the attack. There weren't any real complaints, though Lieutenant Smith did comment loudly that freefall made him queasy. Barnes' even louder comment was that anybody who puked got to clean up the mess.

That probably wasn't the correct way to respond to an officer, but I didn't say—or feel like saying—anything. The run had been stressful for everybody, myself included.

I was queuing up my arrival message when I got a tight-beam microwave squirt from the *Sunray*. This consisted of WAIT FOR *Magellanes* and sharpened visuals of Karst.

Through *El Cano*'s equipment I'd been able to see that ships were orbiting the planet. The new data showed that they were four light cruisers, probably preparing for a short work-up voyage.

It was possible that they were actually about to embark for Saguntum. A squadron of light cruisers could overwhelm Saguntum's defenses, though I would have expected Karst to use destroyers and transports for their attack.

"Captain?" Red asked from the other side of the console, where he had the attack screen up. "What do we do now?"

"Crew," I said, using the PA system. There were overhead speakers in the cabin and the machinery spaces. "We're waiting for the remaining sloop to join us. I expect that when the *Magellanes* arrives, we'll attack immediately."

"Well, where is it?" Smith said. "Why aren't they here? Aren't we in danger all the time we sit here?"

"Lieutenant Smith," I said. "Take your bunk and wait there

until I order you to do something else! As for danger, no—not particularly. So long as we're drifting here, shut down except for the environmental system, it would take a better sensor pack than any Karst warship carries for anybody to notice us."

That was more true than not, though I wasn't nearly as certain as I tried to put in my voice. I didn't say anything about why the *Magellanes* hadn't arrived, because I didn't have a clue. Cory was a better astrogator than I was, and he had Dasi and Carlyle to tone up his Saguntine rigging crew.

I used the time to plot approaches to Karst, starting with the rig as it was and then modifying the sail plan variously. If I hadn't done something, I'd have gone nuts waiting for the *Magellanes* to arrive.

I was working on another attack plan when the upper-left quadrant of my display flashed to a real-time plot of another ship's arrival—close enough to the *Sunray* and *Lezo* that all three would fit within a twelve-thousand-mile-diameter sphere. I focused my optics on it and found the *Magellanes*. Her ventral antenna had carried away.

I remembered my struggles to plot a course when the *Alfraz* was running with a partial rig. Granting that he had a full crew, Cory was an even better astrogator than I'd thought.

"Crew!" I said. "Prepare for action. All riggers suit up, though I don't think you'll be going onto the hull. Captain out!"

I used the console's cancellation field to cut off the babble of my crew. I had nothing more to say to them, and I was afraid that they might distract me from the message which I expected from the *Sunray* in a few minutes.

In fact the message came within ten seconds: RESPOND WHEN

READY TO EXECUTE THIS ATTACK. The message accompanied an updated plot of the space above Karst, this time showing five cruisers in orbit and another rising from Hegemony Harbor. One of the orbiting ships pulsed red. The adjacent legend identified it as the *Forbin*; her antennas were raised, but the only sails set were the topsails of the C and D rings.

The target was suitable for my original attack plan. We would make it without any adjustment to the sails, which was why it had been my first choice. I didn't want to have people on the hull until we were in the Matrix again and outbound.

I sent my attack plan to the *Sunray* with the header READY. To the crew I announced, "Ship, prepare to insert for attack. Extraction is calculated in fourteen minutes."

Because I saw people—everybody but the two Sunrays—trying vainly to shout through my cancellation field, I added, "I will not be deploying riggers. Break. Darter, are you ready for action, over?"

"*Get us there and then get us the hell out!*" Red said. I echoed his display in my right quadrant and saw that he had a targeting screen overlaid on the predicted image of the *Forbin* when we extracted.

SQUADRON, EXECUTE! the *Sunray* ordered.

I pressed Execute. *El Cano* entered the Matrix. I shivered from reaction to what was happening, not to the insertion itself.

I set the latest target imagery from the *Sunray* to advance as the console predicted. If my astrogation was as precise as the console's mathematics, the projection now on the display would be replaced seamlessly by the real-time visuals of the *Forbin* when extracted.

After that there was nothing to do for the remainder of the fourteen minutes and five seconds of the programmed run. I rotated my couch to face the cabin. That was better than watching the image of a cruiser crawling across the image of a planet.

I had an urge to go out on the hull for no reason—*absolutely* no reason. I could almost certainly get back to the console in plenty of time, but that was like saying that someone as careful as I was didn't need a safety line while working on the hull. It was a stupid idea!

I grinned at my own foolishness. Having silly thoughts was harmless so long as I didn't try to execute them—just as in much of life.

My expression had nothing to do with the crew, but when my mind returned to the present I saw that all the eyes in the cabin were on me. From what I could tell, they'd relaxed. I smiled more broadly.

The little red warning signal pulsed in a corner of the display. I caught the reflection and had started to rotate my couch before the bell tone which followed the light.

"Ship," I announced. "Prepare for extraction. Extracting—now."

El Cano slipped back into the sidereal universe. For an instant the lower half of my body vanished. I could feel my intestines sliding onto the metal couch frame.

The predicted imagery on my display had been replaced with reality. Which was nothing like what the console had predicted.

While *El Cano* was in the Matrix, the *Forbin* had begun to accelerate outward. That was half the problem; the other half was that I'd done a really crappy job of astrogation. We were almost two hundred thousand miles from our target instead of being within thirty thousand as I'd planned.

Red was adjusting his point of aim. I shouted, "Hold off! We've got to get closer!"

"We got to get the hell out of here!" the darter shouted. He reached for the Execute key. I locked his controls and shouted, "Inserting!"

My skin prickled and we were back in the Matrix. I could feel my lower body again.

"Ship, we'll attack again in a moment!" I shouted. I left the cancellation field on. I started calculating.

I didn't have time to explain to the crew what was going on. To be that far out in a short hop I had to have reversed a couple digits, but that didn't matter now. I couldn't return to the past, but I could get us close to where the cruiser would be when we extracted.

Foss, an able spacer who'd been a welcome member of the crew during the run, decided in frustration to shout in my ear if he couldn't be heard through the cancellation field. Wedell clipped him with a wrench. Then she and Barnes stood between me and the Saguntine spacers.

Out of the corner of my eye I saw Lieutenant Smith join the two Sunrays. He just might have a future as an officer after all.

"Ship, we'll be inserting for thirty-seven seconds," I announced. I unlocked Red's controls. "Break, darter, are you ready? Over."

"*I was ready before,*" said Whitlake. Maybe he sounded sullen. I wasn't in the best shape myself.

We were back in sidereal space. Usually a short insertion meant that extraction was relatively mild for people. This time, though, I felt as though somebody had slugged me in the middle of the forehead with a hammer. My vision went fuzzy, and everything I saw pulsed between orange and violet.

We were almost on top of the *Forbin*. Red turned a vernier control and stabbed FIRE with both thumbs together. Our antiship missile ignited deafeningly and ripped down in its port-ventral channel. The chemical exhaust—boron fluoride—scoured *El Cano*'s hull and gave the ship a jolt.

"Inserting!" I shouted.

The Karst cruiser was within fifteen miles. She mounted a pair of fifteen-centimeter plasma cannon and eight ten-centimeter guns. One bolt from even the smaller weapons could breach *El Cano*'s hull.

The *Forbin* didn't fire. As we vanished into the Matrix, her turrets were still locked fore and aft so as not to shift during acceleration.

In our last visual, a bright flash cloaked the cruiser. Our hypervelocity missile had struck an extended antenna, vaporizing itself and a portion of the ship's rig.

I engaged the escape route I'd prepared before the initial attack and felt our hull groan as the rigging shifted us onto a new course. Not the correct one, because we'd jumped twice since I calculated it. I'd plot something better after I caught my mental breath, but for now the crucial thing was to get us away from the Karst system. Even a random course would do that, and what I'd loaded would be better than that.

"Starboard watch on the hull," I ordered, hearing my voice

as a croak. I needed something to drink.

"I'll go out in place of Foss," Wedell said. "Somebody watch him and make sure he doesn't have a concussion, okay?"

I started recalculating our course.

I made the first extraction at twelve hours. There was no chance that Karst pursuit could have followed us. Captain Leary had a reputation for supernatural skill at astrogation, but I don't think even he could have tracked *El Cano*.

Our insertion had been the next thing to random. I had a bad couple minutes while the console processed the star sights when we extracted, though I sure tried not to let the crew know I was worried. It's possible to get so far off course in the Matrix that you can never get back to known space.

When ships vanish, as they do every year, there's always the question of whether there was a hardware failure—the fusion bottle overloaded, a thruster burst while landing on an uninhabited world to take on reaction mass, or a thousand other mechanical problems. Or if it was an astrogation failure and the ship is stranded somewhere in the void, a coffin for the crew when supplies and life support finally give out.

We got our bearing points. I announced to the crew, "Next stop, Saguntum," and engaged the program. I knew it might not be quite that easy, but I hoped to do as well as I had in our run to the Karst system.

The crew was in a good mood. Sure, we'd been out a long time for so small a ship, but this was the run for home. *El Cano* was no longer facing an unknown but certainly overwhelming force. So far as they were concerned, we'd won our battle, and we were going home.

We *hadn't* won our battle. We'd taken an enormous risk and escaped only because our enemy was slack. Despite being at point-blank range, our dart had missed the cruiser and purely through luck had damaged its rigging. I grinned when they bragged and asked to watch the log of "our hit" over and over again. They'd done their parts after all, everybody but Red Whitlake.

And if I'd done my job better, we might not have been so far out of place on the initial attack. The darter had gotten thrown out of his course of action. If he'd been more experienced, that might not have happened; but it was still my error.

I went through our log during the run back and found exactly where I'd made the mistake: I'd transposed two digits in the course sequence. The good part was that I could tell Captain Leary where the error was. The bad part was that I had an extra three days to kick myself for it.

Halfway into the first stage, Red linked through the console, saying, "*Captain, can I talk to you on the hull, over?*"

I said yes and put my suit on, leaving Barnes at the console. Truth be told, I'd been hoping never to have to see or speak to Red after we landed on Saguntum.

When we were out on the hull, I looked at the rigging and remembered returning with Monica to Saguntum in the *Alfraz*. I'd become a machine, a part of the ship's complex mechanism. I didn't want to do that again, but I was proud to have done it once . . . and the experience was still with me.

This was where I belonged. I hoped with the RCN, but out among the stars for certain.

When I'd viewed the rig, I turned my attention to my companion. Red was watching me. The Matrix didn't provide enough light for me to read his expression. He took a step closer and leaned sideways to bring his helmet toward mine. I shifted into contact but I waited for him to begin the discussion.

"Sir," he said. "I funked it. I was too scared to take proper time to adjust the dart. You haven't reamed me out in front of the crew, but you know it too."

I cleared my throat. "I thought you'd been hasty," I said. "I'm not a darter myself. I was going to hand the log over to the Defense Force staff in Jacquerie and leave it to them."

"Look..." Red said. The helmet-to-helmet transmission made his voice sound thin, but I thought I heard desperation as well. "We were trained to hunt pirates who don't have anything much to shoot back with. Sure, we're supposed to go after big ships if somebody's trying to invade, but that's a bloody suicide run and nobody expects it. *I* bloody well didn't. And I panicked."

I didn't respond; I didn't know what to say. Red suddenly blurted, "Sir, just give me another chance. That's all I ask!"

"Whitlake," I said, "I'm only in temporary command. As soon as we land, I'll go back to my duties under Captain Leary. I don't know what they'll involve, but I don't expect command of a dart sloop to be one of them. But—"

I cleared my throat, partly to let me choose the phrasing, before I continued, "I have been planning to study dart gunnery when we reach Saguntum because I don't know anything about it. The RCN doesn't use dart sloops, so there's no training at the Academy and I'd never even spoken to someone who'd used them before now. Maybe you could find me some training materials?"

"Bloody hell, sir," Red said. "We don't have to wait for that. There's a training program on the console and I can help you with it. Ah—if you like?"

I laughed and said, "I like. Let's go back in and we can get started."

We made Saguntum in five hours and twenty-nine minutes less time than our outpassage. I could have cut several hours off our inbound time if I'd been willing to run down our reaction mass by longer acceleration in sidereal space, but I didn't like the thought of an emergency planetfall to refill the sloop's small tank.

As it turned out, we had over a quarter tank left when we arrived in Saguntum. I didn't regret playing it safe.

Orbital Control was now a dismasted freighter, probably snatched from the scrapyard. Seeing her reminded me that our raid on Karst wasn't the end of the business. We were at war.

We landed in the Military Harbor, where the *Sunray* and two of the three other sloops already floated. I wasn't surprised that Captain Leary was waiting on the quay when I opened up the ship.

"Lieutenant Smith," I said. "*El Cano* has just reverted to the control of the Naval Defense Forces of Saguntum. I'm going to see my commanding officer, and you're in charge."

I smiled at him, shouldered my bindle, and started for the ramp.

"Want me to carry that for you, sir," said Wedell.

"No thank you, fellow spacer," I said. I doubted whether that was required in the RCN for officers as junior as I was, and the *Sunray* was a civilian vessel anyway.

"But, Captain?" Smith called plaintively. "We've always just closed the ship when we land and report to the Navy Building."

I paused for a moment, then said, "Well, follow normal Defense Force protocols then. But Smith? See to it that the ship is rearmed. You know how to do that, don't you?"

"Requisition a replacement dart?" Smith said. "Oh, yes sir."

I smiled again, saluted him, and strode off to meet Captain Leary. He was waiting alone, except for Hogg. I'd hoped to see Monica....

"Sir..." I said. I didn't salute because Six didn't like them, but I paused two paces from him and braced to attention. "I screwed up the attack. I'd made an astrogation error, I caught it on the run for home but it was just"—I shrugged—"dumb. I think the darter would have been all right if I hadn't spooked him by having to go in again."

The crew of *El Cano* streamed past us, chatting happily. Even Red seemed to be in good spirits. Trying to train me had bucked him up no end. He really did know his job, and what I'd just told Six was the truth.

"Well, I wouldn't call the attack that bad a screw-up," Captain Leary said, smiling at me. "The *Forbin*'s hull has serious structural damage—you hit the Dorsal Three mast with the folded mainyard, and the transmitted shock must have warped two or three frames."

He pursed his lips and went on, "Using Saguntine darters may have been a mistake. I had to override mine or we'd have missed *Surcouf*, and neither Cory nor Lieutenant Esterhazy got a hit either, I think for the same reason. I am a little concerned about your decision to jump closer to the *Forbin* when the target had been warned, however."

"Sir?" I said, startled. "Sir, it was all pointless if we didn't press home!"

Six smiled slightly. "Weren't you afraid that the *Forbin* was going to blow you to atoms before you could escape?"

"I was bloody terrified when I had time to be, the whole fourteen minutes to extraction," I said. "They must've been bloody asleep! But sir, there wasn't any choice."

I frowned and said, "I've been studying dart gunnery on the way back. But I really think that Darter Whitlake is going to be all right the next time. Not that he's RCN business any more."

"I'll keep that in mind when I talk to Colonel Foliot," Six said. "And speaking of the Foliot family"—he looked back to where the quay jutted from the shore—"I think that somebody's waiting for you at the end of the dock. You're off-duty till 0800."

I guess my smile showed how I felt about that.

"Oh, and Olfetrie?" Six called after me.

I turned in sudden concern.

"Good work, spacer," he said, smiling as broadly as I just had.

Chapter Forty

The first thing I learned when I woke up in a guest room of the Foliot house was that the Cinnabar presence on Saguntum—including the RCN detachment—had moved into the west wing of the former Karst mission. Director Jimenez had become Cinnabar Resident on Saguntum by decision of Lady Adele Mundy, the Republic's plenipotentiary.

From my contact with Jimenez, a trade negotiator, he was only a little better suited for the position than Woetjans would have been. It was a tremendous jump in status for him, though, and he'd be thrilled at his new role.

The next important change I didn't learn until my formal briefing from Lady Mundy, still aboard the *Sunray*. I had been assigned as RCN Liaison to the Saguntine Department of Public Safety.

"Ma'am?" I said, trying to get my head around the concept. "Does Colonel Foliot know about this?"

"Colonel Foliot requested the appointment," Mundy said.

Her voice wasn't what you'd call warm, but she didn't flat out call me an idiot. "I gather he didn't inform you of it when you ate dinner together last night. As a military man, he might be too punctilious to interfere in another unit's chain of command."

Tovera grinned at me and said, "I'd have told you, but I just kill people."

Mundy looked at her servant. "You do rather more than that, Tovera," she said. "But it's a valid point. I too would have told Olfetrie."

I drove from the *Sunray* to the new Cinnabar mission in a four-wheeled ground vehicle of Karst manufacture. Tovera said that Hogg had provided it to the Sunrays. I'd formed an opinion of Hogg during the time I'd known him. I didn't worry that the police were going to pull me over for driving a stolen car, but it did cross my mind that a careful search of the interior might turn up traces of a former owner's blood and brains.

In her office as Adjutant, Lieutenant Enery debriefed me thoroughly on the Karst attack. Her only comment on my astrogation error was, "It's the kind of mistake that seems to occur only at the worst times. And you recovered from it."

After that, Captain Leary explained my duties as liaison. I was to visit all the units and facilities under the Director of Public Safety and assess them for possible inclusion in the military forces of the Republic of Cinnabar.

I was to have a local guide. I chose Lieutenant Smith for the purpose. Smith had sharply limited skills, but I trusted him within those limitations. And I asked that Woetjans accompany us. She was a spacer rather than a soldier and ground forces made up most of what we would deal with, but she could size up the quality of a unit at a glance.

We—my new team—began by visiting the barracks of the Jacquerie Battalion, which provided troops for ceremonial duties. The guards at Colonel Foliot's house the night it was attacked had come from that unit.

The major in charge was drunk and sleeping with his face on the desk when we arrived, and the battalion staff could only account for sixty percent of the personnel supposedly on duty. I thought of the Admiral's guards in Salaam and wondered how many of the troops really existed.

Lieutenant Smith was embarrassed; Woetjans was openly disgusted. It was possible that when we visited units scattered at a greater distance from the capital, we'd find more to praise. I kept an open mind about the question, though I didn't expect to be positively impressed by what we learned.

As it turned out, we didn't have a chance to continue our inspections because my world changed again. The 7th Destroyer Flotilla of the RCN arrived in Saguntum orbit, requesting permission to land.

The flotilla had arrived to pick up its newly appointed commanding officer, Captain Daniel Leary.

Captain Leary boarded the *Quilliam* to receive his orders from Commander Sansom, now his second in command. He was accompanied by Lady, now Officer, Mundy and their servants.

When they returned, they walked into the auditorium of the Navy Building where all RCN personnel had been summoned by radio.

Captain Leary faced us and crossed his wrists behind his back. "Well, fellow spacers," he said, "this may be a surprise to you, but I swear on my mother's soul that it's a bigger one to me. Still, it's good news, right?"

There was a roar of agreement. I pretended more enthusiasm than I felt. All I knew for certain was that I was in limbo again. I suppose I should've been used to that.

"My flag will be aboard the *Rotherham*," Leary said. "There would be places for all of you aboard her. The RCN is on a war footing again so of course the flotilla's short crewed— *but*, I'll be leaving five of you with an officer on Saguntum to support the civilian mission. Resident Jimenez insisted, and under the circumstances I had to agree with him."

He shrugged. "Now, some of you may have your own reasons to want to stay on Saguntum for what I expect to be a month or upward until Xenos gets the official staff sorted out," he said. "I'll take volunteers, but I tell you now that there's going to be at least one motorman and at least three riggers. Think about it."

There was a general rustle of unease. "Now," Leary said, "all the enlisted spacers are dismissed. Officers, come down here to me and I'll explain a few things more. You too, Midshipman Olfetrie."

"Execute, spacers!" Woetjans roared.

I waited until the way cleared of departing spacers before I headed down. I met Enery in the aisle. Her face, not just the reconstructed side, was stiff and white. She stood directly in front of Six and, before he could speak, said loudly—not quite shouted, "Sir! I respectfully request that I accompany you with the flotilla where I have a chance to see action. Sir!"

Lieutenant Cory was standing to the side, looking at the floor and apparently pretending that he was on some other planet. Six, looking uncomfortable, said, "Well, Lieutenant, as the senior officer remaining—"

"Sir!" Enery said. "I didn't say anything when you put me in the *Sunray* when even Olfetrie here got a combat assignment. But you're *not* going to leave me babysitting a bloody trade mission and losing the last chance I'll likely ever have to make lieutenant commander!"

"Lieutenant, what I will do is not the business of my subordinates—"

"Permission to speak, sir!" I said without thinking about it. If I had thought, I'd still have said it—if I'd had the balls. I hope I'd have had the balls.

Six closed his mouth. He looked at me and took a deep breath. From his expression, he was glad to have an excuse to cool things off. He said, "Permission granted, Olfetrie."

"Sir," I said, "she's right. She'll be more use to the flotilla than I would, especially since she's way senior to the first lieutenant of the *Rapid*, who's been acting captain since Captain Weyman's heart attack last week."

Leary's face changed. "Do you want to stay on Saguntum, Olfetrie?" he said. "I can see why—"

"No, sir, I very much want to go off where the action is," I said, stepping on the rest of what the captain was going to say. "But Lieutenant Enery has earned the slot and I haven't. Believe me, M-monica isn't as important to me as a chance to serve with Captain Leary in a battle."

Leary nodded slightly. He said, "What's this about the *Rapid*'s captain?"

"What?" I said. "Ah, well, I checked the logs of the destroyers that just landed. And I saw the entry about Captain Weyman. Ah, I didn't break into the ship's systems, sir, it was openly logged to anyone with RCN clearance."

"Weyman drank like a fish, sir," Enery said. "Even when we were in the Academy together."

Leary's smile was very faint. "That's been true of a number of us, Lieutenant," he said, "but there's no few whose hearts can't stand it. I've been fortunate in my genes, I'm glad to say."

He looked at Enery. "Lieutenant," he said. "I'm appointing you to command of the *Rapid*. After you've looked her over, you'll report to me on your impressions. Ah—the formal orders may be an hour in coming, so you may want to..."

Lieutenant Enery laughed. "Captain Leary," she said, "I haven't forgotten what happened when I boarded the *Princess Cecile* ahead of the official orders to take command. I have some things to gather up in my quarters, so I'll repair there if you don't mind."

"Dismissed, Enery," Six said. "I'm glad to have you with me."

Enery headed for the exit. Cory faced around. He too looked more relaxed than he had at the beginning of the discussion.

"And I *am* glad to have Enery," Captain Leary said softly. "But you know, Olfetrie, I could find better uses for you than what she rightly called babysitting a trade delegation. Be that as it is, you'll remain on Saguntum to support the civilian mission as required. You are not under the control of Resident Jimenez, however."

That was a relief, though Jimenez wasn't really a bad guy. He was full of himself, but he wasn't one of the sort who went off looking for ways to make the folks around him feel miserable. I'd figured to keep out of his way. That would be even easier if he wasn't in my chain of command.

"I gather the RCN detachment is on Saguntum to get the mission out if things go belly up?" I said. "Do you want me to continue surveying local units?"

"Sure, continue the survey," Six said. "People in Xenos will want it done, though I don't guess we'll be incorporating locals into the Land Forces of the Republic any time soon."

He shrugged. Then he said, "Jimenez has to know that there's a force on Saguntum ready to get him off. I'm not leaving you here to do that, I'm leaving you here to reassure the Resident that you *can* do that."

I nodded. "Yes sir," I said. "Ah—has the Resident—that is, the Foreign Ministry delegation—been informed of the secret compact between us and the Alliance?"

"Yes," said Officer Mundy, seated at the small table that acted as a podium when required; Six had stood in front of it. "I thought it was necessary to explain so that Resident Jimenez wouldn't worry. In the event"—she looked up from her data unit. I won't say she was smiling, but her expression was as positive as I'd ever seen it—"I got the impression that he hadn't understood that there might have been a problem."

"Oh, one more thing, Olfetrie?" Six said. "I won't be leaving any of the warrant officers—and certainly not Woetjans."

"Understood, sir," I said. "I suspect I'll be able to assess most units here without expert help, though I may take the rest of the detachment along just to give them something to do."

"I've never noticed that spacers had trouble finding things to do in a city," Six said, smiling again. "But it might be just as well to keep your people close if you're going to be wandering here and there. At any rate, you're dismissed until the meeting here at 1600 hours. I'll make the final assignments then. And Olfetrie?"

"Sir?"

"Thanks for helping me out of the hole I was digging for myself with Enery."

"Sir," I said. "I'm honored that you think of me as part of your team."

I saluted and went off. Mostly I was thinking of the opportunity I'd thrown away. But at the back of my mind, I knew that I'd be seeing Monica shortly.

I stood with my five spacers on the porch of the Naval Building, watching the destroyers of the 7th Flotilla rise to orbit one at a time. There'd never been more than six in the Military Harbor at the same time, but there were two more in powered orbit. There'd been an exchange every couple hours to top off reaction mass.

"Where they off to first?" Mixon asked while the echoes of the *Quail* faded as she climbed.

"Lauren," I said. Mixon didn't need to know any more than I had, but the flotilla would arrive before any Karst spy could get word there. "There's usually a Karst naval presence in the system, a couple gunboats and maybe a destroyer. And a great deal of civilian traffic."

Wedell and Gamba were the only members of my crew whom I really knew, but Mixon, Gadient, and Tyler were able spacers whom any captain would want in his crew. None of them had volunteered to stay on Saguntum, but neither had they complained about the assignment. I had no intention of being the sort of superior who concealed information just because he could.

"They going to capture the place?" Gamba asked.

"Dunno," I said. "I guess it depends on how the locals react. I don't think the flotilla's got any ground troops embarked, but if the Karst governor wants to roll on his back and kick his legs in the air—I'd guess Six would oblige him, wouldn't you?"

The *Quail* had been the last of the flotilla. I looked at my people and said, "Well, I don't think they're coming back down to ask our help, so lets get cracking. I think *that*"—I pointed to the long brick building at the westernmost cape of the harbor—"is the Naval Arsenal. I figure we can check it out before supper, right?"

We set off along the harbor road without bothering with our vehicle.

It was late afternoon when we returned to the Residency after going over the arsenal. Twelve of the fourteen staff had actually been on duty, and I didn't know that you'd do a lot better in a similar RCN facility.

I hadn't seen any sign of overbuying to please a brother-in-law or the like … "the like" in this case meaning a Saguntine Dean Olfetrie with a backhander. The most expensive items were munitions for the dart sloops; there were seven in store and the sloops hadn't been reloaded since the Karst raid. The darts were manufactured on Pantellaria and probably couldn't be replaced in under six months time.

"I wonder if ground-launched antiship missiles can be adapted to the sloops," I said to Gamba.

"Are we going to need more?" he said, frowning. He looked back over his shoulder toward the building we'd just left.

"I don't know," I said. "And it's not our job at the moment. But what's the difference besides the more energetic first-stage propellant?"

"I guess we can check the dimensions of the sloop cradles," Wedell said. "They eyeball about the same, and I'll bet we could butcher something together that'd work if we could get the use of some tools."

We paused at the entrance to the building. The crew was watching me expectantly. I grinned and said, "All right, you're all released until 0800 tomorrow."

"Sir, can we take the car?" Gadient said.

My instant reaction was, "No," but the word didn't reach my lips. These weren't young tearaways, and they weren't old lags with long histories of punishment on every ship they'd served on. Aloud I said, "Who can drive?"

"I can," said Gadient. "And I think Gamba too."

"And me," said Wedell.

"All right," I said. "But 0800, don't forget. We're going

out to the training facility at Aures."

We went inside to shower and change. I was heading to the Foliot house for dinner, though I intended to return here to sleep, given the early start I wanted tomorrow. The civilian vehicle would be cramped with six of us, and I wondered if I could borrow something bigger from the Director of Public Safety.

I had time, though. I took a deep breath and headed for the opposite wing of the building.

The Karst mission had three cells in the basement. I didn't know what they'd been intended for but now the only occupied one held Maeve Grimaud. A desk in the small lobby at the base of the elevator acted as the guardroom. The special policeman sitting there at a desktop console couldn't see the cells, which were around a corner.

"Good evening," I said. "I'm—"

"I know who you are, sir," the policeman said, smiling as he rose. His name tape read Bernotti. "I followed you and the colonel up the stairs in Salaam. You were having a lot easier time with them than I was."

I reached over the desk and shook his hand. "I can't say I remember much of that climb, Sergeant Bernotti," I said, "because I was too bloody scared to think."

I cleared my throat. "I'm here to see the prisoner," I said. "I'm the ranking RCN officer on Saguntum now."

That was edging the truth a little. I didn't think that signing on to the *Sunray* put me technically in the RCN, but it was unlikely that anybody here would argue about it.

DAVID DRAKE

"Sure," Bernotti said, slinging the submachine gun which had leaned against the desk. He took a chip key from a desk drawer and led me to the angle in the hall. "You see how they built these? The guy at the desk can't see what's going on in the cells. If you like, I won't hear nothing either till you're ready to come out."

"I won't be doing anything private," I said, smiling pleasantly at him. In fact the suggestion—I don't know whether he thought I was going to rape Maeve or torture her—made me queasy. Still, the offer was well meant.

The cells had barred fronts. Maeve was in the middle, the only one occupied. She'd risen, apparently alerted by the sound of voices. When I came into sight, she smiled and said, "Roy? I certainly didn't expect to see you."

"Do you want to go in?" Bernotti asked. "Or you can talk through the bars."

"I'll go in," I said. There was a bed, a chair—both steel stampings, much like those of a starship—and a closed chest with a padded top. There was no wardrobe.

"Sergeant?" I said. Maeve was wearing the clothes she'd been captured in. "What happened to her luggage?"

"There's stuff in the storage room out by the desk," Bernotti said. "She can have something if she wants it."

He made a face and said, "Look, sir, I guess it's up to you. But I'd sure rather you not take that gun into the cell with you."

"Sorry, Bernotti," I said. I kept my voice calm, but from the way my face felt I was blushing. I pulled the pistol from my cargo pocket and handed it over butt first. "I'd forgotten about it."

"It's good to be careful in these times," the sergeant said as he transferred the weapon to his own pocket. "And you've got more call than most. From what I hear, you saved the Old Man's ass when those scuts from Karst tried to take him out a couple weeks ago."

He opened the door. I stepped in and heard him lock it behind me.

"Welcome to my room," Maeve said. She looked more fine-drawn than she had when I'd last seen her; I wondered what she was being fed. "Have you come to tell me I'm a terrible person? Or do you just want me to apologize for trying to have you killed?"

"Well..." I said.

"I do apologize!" Maeve said. "But I swear to heaven I didn't have any idea you'd be with Foliot. I didn't even know for certain there'd be an attack! I'm sure you've read all my communications with McKinnon and you know he didn't share his plans with me."

I seated myself on the chair and adjusted it slightly to face her squarely. "I don't doubt Lady Mundy's seen everything you say and more, but"—I smiled wryly, remembering another discussion with Maeve—"that's above my pay grade. What I've really come to do is release you. But first I've got to explain some things."

Maeve sat down on the edge of her bed. "Now you've surprised me again, Roy," she said. Her face was expressionless, but I had the feeling that her nerves were quivering under the skin. "Go on, please."

"According to Lady Mundy..." I said. I believed the

487

underlying facts were true, but I was saying only what I personally knew. "There has been a secret compact between the Alliance and Cinnabar—approved by Guarantor Porra on the Alliance side and the cabinet on ours. The Alliance was permitted to absorb the Tarbell Stars; in exchange, we were granted a free hand with the Hegemony of Karst. The compact leaves in place the Treaty of Amiens—and the truce."

"If that was true..." Maeve said. She paused, then looked me straight in the eyes. "If that was true, why is it a secret?"

"You'd have to ask somebody else about that," I said. I thought it was pretty likely that the cabinet hadn't wanted to alert the Karst authorities as to what was about to happen to them, but that was a guess. "I do know that the Tarbell Stars accepted the Friendship of the Alliance last year, and that the Cinnabar Senate didn't object."

"Yes," said Maeve. "Your information is self-consistent."

There was no emotion in her voice. She leaned back slightly.

I said, "I don't know much information you've gotten"—I gestured generally around the cell—"but Cinnabar is openly at war with Karst now. It doesn't seem to me that there's any further reason for you to be locked up."

"Would Lady Mundy agree?" Maeve said, tossing her head dismissively.

"Dunno," I said. I shrugged. "For the time being, I'm the highest-ranking member of the *Sunray*'s company on Saguntum. I'm pretty sure that you've got the resources to get off planet and probably back to Cinnabar before Lady Mundy returns. If not, I can find you some help."

"I'd be better off in this cell than on Cinnabar," Maeve said.

She stood up suddenly and walked to the cell door, putting her back to me. "I'm a real embarrassment to my superiors."

"If you're worried about what I'll say at a hearing," I said, "don't be. And I really doubt that anything Lady Mundy knows is going to make it back to the Foreign Ministry. There obviously isn't a lot of information passing between the two groups."

Maeve turned with a furious expression. "It's not that!" she said. "The people who tasked me know *exactly* what they ordered me to do—and how wrongheaded they appear to have been. It's not what I did that they want to hide, it's what *they* did and they're afraid I could prove!"

"Ah," I said. I'd never regretted leaving the Foreign Ministry, but I was getting plenty more evidence to support my decision. "Well, if it's any consolation, what you did resulted in exactly the desired result. Saguntum has accepted the protection of Cinnabar, and Karst has attacked us."

Maeve smiled faintly. She said, "I doubt that will make Undersecretary Dowland any more willing to have his part in the matter become public."

Her face suddenly shifted, looking younger and softer. "Are you serious about letting me go, Roy?" she said.

"Yes."

"What will happen to you when Lady Mundy comes back?"

I shrugged. "I don't know," I said. "Look, you were following orders. The reasoning behind the orders was solid, there were just things your superiors didn't know. You were doing exactly what I'd have done, and I won't leave you locked up for that. Since for the moment it's my decision."

I wondered if I'd be saying that if Maeve Grimaud looked

like a pig instead of being the sexiest woman I'd ever met. I'm not saying she was prettier than Monica, and I'm *certainly* not saying that I could imagine wanting to spend more than maybe a half hour at a time with Maeve.

What I'd just said was true, regardless. I could look Lady Mundy in the eye and say it again; as I'd probably have to do.

"If you can get me out and get me my reticule back," Maeve said, "I won't need any other help. Even without the reticule."

"Let's see," I said. I went to the door and called, "Sergeant Bernotti? I'm ready to leave, and I'd like to release Mistress Grimaud now."

The sergeant came around the corner. He was smiling, but the patrol sling meant that his weapon was pointing at us as he approached.

"Is there something I need to sign?" I asked.

"I'll have you read the request into my console," he said as he unlocked the cell and gestured us out.

"And Mistress Grimaud wants her purse out of storage," I added as we preceded the sergeant down the hall.

"If it's there, she can have it," he said.

The purse was about big enough to hold a pair of eyeglasses. Maeve snatched it up. She didn't open it in front of me. "Am I free to go?" she asked, looking from me to the sergeant.

"Yes," I said. Sergeant Bernotti nodded.

He looked at me and said, "You can accept delivery of the purse too, sir."

Maeve nodded. "Thank you both," she said. She pressed the call button of the elevator.

I went through the formalities at the console. The elevator arrived while I did that; it rose again with Maeve aboard.

Sergeant Bernotti looked at me and said, "I hope you know what you're doing, sir." Then he grinned and added, "I guess I'd do the same if I was your age. Hell, I guess I would now."

Chapter Forty-one

Things settled into a pattern over the next few days. Our car only held four comfortably, and I came to trust my crew. Here in Jacquerie, I mean. In space, I'd trust them implicitly under any circumstances. I decided quickly that they weren't going to cause a real incident on the ground either, but that wasn't the same thing.

For small facilities that didn't require any special expertise, I took only one spacer with me when I made the inspection. Six days after the flotilla had left, Wedell and I were at the tracking and guidance station in the Genevieve Mountains.

Our arrival had doubled the number of people present. Boelke, one of the techs based there, was awake when we drove up. Our voices woke the other, Sacrisson, though he was pretty clearly hung over.

And why not? The station was a belt-and-suspenders backup for Jacquerie Control. The telemetry antennas here, on a high ridge a hundred miles north of the capital, had a broader sweep of the heavens than those in the harbor, but the harbor array was perfectly adequate for the amount of traffic that Saguntum got. There was a dedicated line from here to the harbor, and there was a microwave antenna which could be switched to any target at line of sight.

This was precisely the sort of facility I'd expected when I decided that most of the crew could have the day off. I was simply checking off boxes for my report to Captain Leary.

I plugged my portable—luggable—terminal into a socket on the local console, sending my report to the *Sunray* to be stored. Sacrisson suddenly said, "Say, that's funny."

I paused as I started to insert my personal key into the terminal. I said, "What is?"

"Well, there's three ships orbiting," Sacrisson said. Boelke came and joined him. "They're not responding to queries from Control, and their transponders are turned off—but they *are* communicating with a ground station that isn't part of our network."

I finished connecting my own terminal. The key gave me unlimited access to all government sites, a necessity for my liaison job. I called, "Wedell? Be ready to move. This doesn't look good."

"Bloody hell!" Boelke said. "One of them's dropping out of orbit, but they don't have approval to land."

I linked to the primary array at Jacquerie Harbor and tried a trick that Cory had taught me after explaining that he'd learned it from Lady Mundy. The vessel landing had switched off its identification transponder, but it was a large ship and carried a pinnace with interstellar capacity as well as a pair of lifeboats limited to normal space.

The attached vessels had their own transponders. When queried, the pinnace told me that it was aboard the *Kurfurstendamm*, which a Landing Control database told me was a twelve-thousand-tonne transport homeported on the Alliance world of Stryker.

Aloud, I said, "I believe Jacquerie is about to be attacked. And I'm very much afraid—"

Still using the Jacquerie transceiver, I checked one of the ships still in orbit. It didn't have a lesser ship on board, but it was carrying seventy-one missiles which duly reported that they were embarked on the *Erich Koellner*, a modern, powerful Alliance destroyer.

I sent a note to everybody in my electronic circle: ALLIANCE ATTACKING JACQUERIE. ESTIMATE 2000 TROOPS. That was based on the load capacity of the *Kurfurstendamm*. ESCORT TWO DESTROYERS.

I shut down my terminal and rose. "Wedell?" I said to my companion. "You and I are heading for the training facility at Gironde, where we were a few days ago."

To the technicians, I continued, "I think you guys will be fine here, or as well off as anywhere, but we spacers need to drop out of sight in Gironde. Good luck, and I hope you'll wish us the same."

"But what's happening?" Boelke said to our backs. I ignored him.

I turned the car around in a plume of dust. The access road was paved, but the parking area beside the station was not.

"Sir?" Wedell said when we were moving. "Why is it we're going to Gironde?"

"We're not," I said. "But I hope to keep the other side in the dark for a while about where we *are* going."

I thought about it and decided she had a right to know. As we got on the pavement, I said, "It appears that Saguntum is at war with the Alliance. And I'm very much afraid that *we* are at war with the Alliance also."

Despite everything that Six and Lady Mundy had assured me. Well, as I'd said before—that was above my pay grade.

Wedell and I didn't really talk until I passed the intersection with the road to Bevedere—the one we'd have taken if we'd really been going to Gironde. Then she said, "Sir? If that ship landing is attacking Jacquerie, why didn't the missiles engage it?"

"They tried," I said. My quick scan of my terminal had given me enough data to figure out the Alliance attack plan. "The batteries didn't take the commands from Jacquerie Control. Either the battery crews have been bribed, or somebody's locked out the centralized control."

I'd done just that on Salaam. It hadn't been difficult, but the batteries in Jacquerie were protected beyond *my* ability to get in—I'd tried, just for the hell of it. Even with the access key on my terminal, I couldn't enter the missile director. I was sure it could be done, probably by somebody like Cory. Certainly by Lady Mundy.

But that meant that we weren't just facing Alliance troops. The security services—probably including the 5th Bureau, reporting to Guarantor Porra himself—were involved also.

"Look, Wedell," I said. "I know Captain Leary put me in

charge, but he wasn't expecting things to blow up the way they have. I've got a pretty screwy idea that's likely to get us killed even if it works. Are you sure you want to stick with me?"

Wedell turned toward me. I kept my eyes on the road, but I could see her from the corners of them.

"Six put you in charge," she said. "What part of that do you think I don't understand? And if you're afraid I'm going to run and hide if the shooting starts, don't be; I was at Cacique."

"I don't think that," I said truthfully. "But I just thought..." I swallowed before I could think of the right word. "I thought I ought to ask."

"Well, you were bloody wrong," Wedell said, though she sounded good-humored. "That's not how the RCN works. Sir. Now, what are we going to do?"

"There's a military prison on the north side of Jacquerie," I said. "It's just off the road we're on now, and I'm hoping taking it over isn't high on the invaders' to-do list."

If Wedell had backed out, I'd have had an excuse to back out myself. Except that I wouldn't have.

I laughed out loud. "The people from the Karst Residency are held there," I said. "I'm hoping their luggage is too, because that'll make the next part a lot simpler. We'll shoot our way into the Military Harbor if we have to, but I've got something else in mind."

If I hadn't had the exact distance to the prison driveway—turn right off the North Road onto Kustis Road, 312 meters—I'd have missed it. A band of bushy local trees screened the double fences completely, and from the road the guard towers weren't visible over the vegetation. The place was obvious after we curved down the drive, but not before.

Two guards were at the gatehouse. Instead of coming out to ask my business, one of them called, "Who are you?" His partner thrust a carbine through the gatehouse window.

"I'm Colonel Foliot's aide!" I shouted. "And if your buddy doesn't point his gun somewhere else, he's going to regret it!"

The outer gate opened so that I could drive in. The fellow who'd spoken before leaned out and said, "What the hell's going on, sir?" His partner was looking over his shoulder; the carbine had vanished.

"Karst has invaded," I said, displaying the fancy document holder that Colonel Foliot had made up for me. "I'm here to help stop them."

Explaining that it was really the Alliance wouldn't help me. For that matter, Karst probably *was* involved in this.

"What are *we* supposed to do?" the other guard asked nervously.

"Your jobs, of course!" I said. "And start with letting us through to see your CO."

The inner gate slid aside. "Chantal's already left," the first guard said. "I think Sergeant Busoni's in charge."

"Then I'll see Sergeant Busoni!" I said as I drove through.

The administration building was brick and of one story. Running deeper from the back were a pair of two-story blocks of pinkish structural plastic with barred windows. They were separately fenced and wired. I didn't think the facility would hold more than a hundred or so prisoners in single-occupancy cells, but my business wasn't with the occupants anyway.

The only vehicle in front of the building was a six-wheeled bus painted light tan with the stencilled legend ARMY OF SAGUNTUM. Though there were half a dozen other spaces, I deliberately parked in the one marked COMMANDANT and got out.

"Do I come with you?" Wedell asked.

"Yes," I said, simply to make a decision. I didn't care where she was, but I didn't want to discuss it.

A heavy man—hell, he was fat—had risen behind the counter as we walked to the glass doors. I held out my identification in my left hand and said, "Sergeant, Colonel Foliot has sent me to get some items from the personalty of the Karst prisoners. Take us to the storage area, please."

"I can't do that," the sergeant said. I suppose he was the Busoni the guard at the gate had mentioned. He didn't move.

"Then take us to somebody who can," I said. I was letting my voice be sharp but I didn't raise it.

"The only guy who can do that is Commandant Chantal," the sergeant said. His eyes were glazed and he was sweating. "He left—"

"Look, you dickhead!" Wedell shouted, leaning across the counter. "You may want to be shot for a bloody traitor after Karst gets sorted, but we don't! We're going get what the colonel sent us for, with you or without! Which is it going to be?"

"I don't have a key t' the padlock!" the sergeant said. I was afraid he was going to start crying.

"Well, you've got a tool chest, don't you?" I said. "Or your maintenance people do. Take us there *now*. We're okay for the moment, but I don't know how long that'll last."

The sergeant led us down the hall to his right to a door marked MAINTENANCE. It was locked, but I kicked it open while Busoni fished for a key. I'd hoped for bolt cutters but settled for a large screwdriver to use as a pry bar. I noticed as we followed the sergeant through the door at the end of the hall that Wedell had brought a short-hafted cross-peen hammer.

A heavy metal shipping container stood against the side of the building, overlooked by one of the confinement blocks. A solid-looking padlock closed the outer double doors. I was looking for the best way to use my screwdriver when Wedell said, "Let me take a shot at it, sir."

"All right," I said and stepped out of the way. I didn't see how she could knock the lock off, but she seemed confident.

Wedell measured the distance with her eyes, then brought the back of the hammer around in a sudden blow. The narrow peen hit the top of the lock barrel squarely, without touching either the hasp or the rings which it locked. There was a loud crash from the container itself. The lock sprang open.

Wedell grinned as I pulled open the outer doors and then the single inner panel. She said, "A rigger gets used to quick and dirty ways of doing things, sir."

Thank heaven I didn't tell her to stay in the car, I thought.

In the steel container were a score of fiberboard boxes, a meter long and about half that wide and deep. They were numbered in red, but there were no names on the outside.

"Are all of these from the Karst prisoners?" I asked Busoni.

"Yeah," he said. "Normally prisoners don't have anything outside the cells, but these're prisoners of war. They hauled the container in and filled it with the boxes they took from where they were captured."

"Then let's start opening," I said, hauling a box onto the ground and thrusting my screwdriver between the top and the side before twisting. Staples gave way and allowed me to pry the top up.

Wedell had a sturdy folding knife and got to work beside me. The sergeant watched us, bemused.

On my third box I found what I was looking for: the contents of Director McKinnon's closets. As I expected, there was a full military dress uniform in bright blue fabric, complete with saucer hat. If I remembered what I'd heard about Karst insignia, the silver triangles marked him as a full colonel. I'd have to wear my own footgear—soft black boots, suitable for wear within a vacuum suit—but they would pass.

"Sergeant," I said as I straightened. "We've got what we came for. If you put the clothes back into the container and close it, you shouldn't have any trouble with the troops who arrive—unless you mention our visit. If you tell them about us, you'll have a *lot* of questions to answer—and they won't be best pleased that you don't have answers for them."

Wedell and I headed back to the car. Behind us, Busoni meeped, "Hey, it's not right you leaving this mess for me!"

"You drive," I said to Wedell. "I'll change in the back seat."

"How about my clothes?" she asked. She was wearing RCN utilities, mottled gray and loose.

"You'll pass for my driver," I said as we got into the vehicle. "You don't look Saguntine. Remember, we're dealing with Alliance Army, not Fleet personnel."

We headed off toward the harbor facilities. McKinnon and I were similar height, but he was heavier from thirty years of office work.

I wondered if I'd live another thirty years.

Wedell wasn't a good driver, but there were fewer people than usual on the streets of Jacquerie and very, very few cars. I wondered if the invaders had ordered people to stay inside or if folks had just decided it was good sense to do so.

I could see people watching past skewed shutters, but nobody called to us. We didn't run into any patrols—police or military—either.

Instead of going directly to the naval barracks, I had Wedell drive us to a Public Works motor pool which was more or less on the way. A frightened-looking watchman let us in, but the regular staff had fled. A dozen small tractors and scores of wheeled garbage hoppers were parked within a wire-fenced yard. The only permanent improvement was a small shed, but it had a connection to the government system.

I connected my terminal while Wedell and the watchman fidgeted nearby. The barracks didn't have active imagery, but the dart sloops floating in the harbor adjacent had sensor packs on their spines.

The naval buildings and the frontage of the Military Harbor had always been fenced off from the rest of Jacquerie. The Alliance forces were reinforcing the woven-wire barrier with rolls of concertina wire at the base. Judging from the preparations going on, they planned to add more on top of the original fence.

Instead of a single member of the Shore Police, a squad of Alliance troops in battledress guarded the gate. Teams of four were stationed at front and back of the naval barracks while Alliance engineers fenced it off from the rest of the enclosure. The invaders were apparently using the barracks as a prison, at least for the time being.

"Well," I said to Wedell, "it isn't going to get easier. There's room to park on Water Street near the gate. Let's go do that."

The watchman stared as we went back to the car. It was a half mile to drive from the lot down to the harbor entrance; we could have walked the two short steep blocks more quickly. I preferred the look of arriving by vehicle, however.

It would have been better yet if we'd had a limousine instead of a cramped little beater, though I figured we'd be all right. Maybe next time I could ask Hogg for an upgrade in case we had to do something like this again.

We pulled up just short of the gateway. I'd been riding beside Wedell in the front; the back seats were all right for legroom, but the roof there brushed the top of my head even though I wasn't much above average height—five foot ten inches if I got the benefit of the doubt.

The guards watching us through the wire wore a uniform pattern I'd never seen before—green on green on green, all the shades dull—and carried stocked impellers of an unfamiliar pattern. These threw lighter projectiles than the standard-issue weapons I was used to. Dad had handled small arms, though it was a minor part of his business.

"I'm Colonel McKinnon of the Karst security service," I said to the officer on the other side of the wire. "We're here to pick up one of my agents who was caught with the unit he was observing."

I held up the bifold from McKinnon's effects, with text and photo on one side and a hexagonal platinum badge on the other. The picture looked as much like me as these ever do, and the text—which indicated I was fifty-three—was unreadable without concentration or a magnifier.

"I haven't had any orders about this," the officer said. He frowned. His cap badge was an R on crossed lightning bolts. These must be local auxiliaries, the sort of unit Saguntum might provide if my survey was satisfactory.

"Well, get them!" I said. "I don't know who you report to. I talked to an aide to Major Wittgenstein of the 5th Bureau, and believe me, you *don't* want him to have to sort this!"

I pulled Wittgenstein's name out of my arse; I didn't figure a low-ranking reserve officer would have any better idea of who commanded the Alliance security detachment than I did. The threat was perfectly believable, though.

"Just tell them that Colonel McKinnon wants to remove an agent from the general captured population before his fellows realize that he's a traitor who's been helping us," I said.

The officer had a portable phone the size of a shoe box. He dutifully began making calls, trying to get somebody to take responsibility for something he didn't understand well enough to explain. He had no more luck than you'd expect.

The other guards were staring at the man, which probably bothered him as much as Wedell and I did. After two minutes, which I'm sure seemed like more to the officer, I said, "Bloody hell, man! One wog more or less doesn't matter, but if you get an agent killed and he's working for the 5th Bureau, you might as well eat your gun now. It'll be quicker and a *lot* less painful."

I'm pretty sure that a real Karst security official would be less overbearing with Alliance troops, but it seemed to me what the job required here. If this fellow had been a long-service regular, I wouldn't have tried it with him...and I suspect I'd have been coughing up my teeth if I had.

"Oh, go get him, then!" the officer said petulantly, breaking his connection. He seemed to have been on hold anyway. Then, to one of his men, "Let them in."

Wedell and I sauntered through the pedestrian door. The way the barbed wire had been laid meant that they couldn't have opened the vehicular gate if they'd wanted to.

The quartet of guards at the front of the barracks watched us come. I said to the oldest, "We're here to pick up a prisoner—Whitlake, goes by Red. The lieutenant"—I nodded toward the man who'd let us in. He was probably a lieutenant—"cleared it with your headquarters."

"We got a Whitlake?" the man I'd spoken to asked the fellow beside him who'd taken out a data unit.

"Yeah, room three, ground floor," that man said.

Rather than go inside, the older soldier walked closer to the building and shouted, "Whitlake! Get your ass out here now!"

The windows were open, but I still wasn't sure how well that was going to work until the front door suddenly opened. Whitlake stepped out, looking worried and glancing over his shoulder.

"This way, spacer!" I said. "And get moving!"

"Sir?" Whitlake said, gaping.

"No talking now," I ordered bruskly. "We'll discuss your assignment aboard *El Cano*."

I nodded to the guards. "Thank you, men," I said. "I hadn't counted on being in time."

With the Saguntine darter between us, Wedell and I walked down the quay to where *El Cano* was berthed. Some of the Alliance troops may have wondered about what was going on, but they didn't say anything aloud.

Chapter Forty-two

Whitlake started to say something as we strode along, but I snapped, "Don't talk till we're in the ship." Nobody was nearby and I wasn't sure there was even a parabolic microphone on the planet, but I wanted to have my discussion with the darter in a controlled—confined—space.

The sloop's boarding ramp felt solid after the quivering nervousness of the extension. As soon as we were in the hold, I used the local switch to start the hatch closing. On the bridge I brought the console up, glanced at the read-outs—reaction mass had been topped off; another mark in Lieutenant Smith's favor—and started the internal pumps cycling.

Then I rotated the couch inward and grinned up at Whitlake, who stood nervously beside Wedell. "Red," I said, "you asked me for another chance when you funked it on Karst. This is your chance if—"

"Yessir," Whitlake said.

"Red, you really do have a choice here," I said. "I'll put you off and act as my own darter unless you're sure you can do it."

"Sir, I'm better than you'll ever be," Whitlake said, leaning forward. "I can *do* this. You said you were giving me a chance, so stop talking and let's get bloody on with it."

"Yes, all right," I said. "Take your stations. We'll lift off, insert, and then extract to make our attack. We'll all be in suits, but Red? You won't be going out on the hull. Wedell and I will take care of the rig. And I'll say right now: If there's a bad problem with the rig, I'll reprogram and keep trying till I'm happy about where we're going to extract. We're not in a rush to do this, but we're only going to get one chance. Understood?"

Wedell shrugged; Whitlake said, "Yessir."

"Then let's get our suits on," I said. We all went to the locker. The three rigging suits that Captain Leary had sent to *El Cano*—from commercial suppliers, I'd noticed—were still aboard. Wedell and I each donned one, but I was pleased to agree when Red asked if he could wear an air suit. He might be marginally less safe, but he'd certainly be more effective as a darter in less uncomfortable gear.

I wasn't ruthless enough to order Red to wear the lighter suit, but I didn't try to argue him out of it. In all truth, I didn't think any of us were likely to survive.

El Cano had only four plasma thrusters. I tested them in diagonal pairs, bringing each set up to half power with the sphincter petals flared. The sloop rocked unpleasantly and the external view fogged to sparkling gray as the steam rose to blanket the sensors on the spine.

"*El Cano* to Control," I called on the local VHF frequency. "*El Cano* lifting to test new High Drive installation as scheduled. Over. Break. Ship, prepare for lift-off."

I ran the thrusters at full, then reduced the sphincters to minimum aperture. The sloop paused in a ball of steam, then began to lift in her leisurely fashion. The six High Drive motors gave the sloops considerable agility in vacuum, but their thrusters were the minimum necessary to get them to orbit.

I wondered whether the personnel in Saguntum Control were all from the Alliance or if the regular Saguntine crew was on duty with Alliance guards, The only ships in orbit at present were the two destroyers, so I wasn't worried about an ordinary movement problem.

It *was* possible that the missile batteries had been restored to function—I'd been afraid to check in case I called attention to them and to me. I hoped that if we sounded normal, nobody would panic and gut us on the way up.

"El Cano, *you are clear to lift,*" Control responded through the RF hash from the thrusters. "*Out.*"

We were already lifting, but that was good to know. So far, so good.

I'd timed the ascent to avoid as much as possible the destroyers already above the planet. I hoped they would ignore us so long as we appeared to be ignoring them, but the *Meduse* hailed us as we rose through one hundred thousand feet, "*Saguntine ship, this is Hegemony vessel* Meduse. *Return to Jacquerie Haven at once. No vessels are permitted to leave Saguntum during the present emergency. Acknowledge, over.*"

Instead of switching propulsion modes as I normally would at that height, I engaged the High Drive but left the thrusters running at maximum output. We had plenty of reaction mass for this operation. What we might *not* have was time.

As our acceleration more than doubled, I switched to tight-beam microwave and said, "*Meduse*, this is sloop *El Cano*, now under Alliance control. We are cleared to test our High Drive motors which have been recently replaced. Repeat, we have clearance from Jacquerie Control. *El Cano* over."

Although *El Cano* was a naval vessel, its plot-position indicator was rudimentary compared to what I'd trained on at the Academy. The *Koellner* and *Meduse* were red and orange beads respectively at the head of thin tracks of the same color; but the console didn't automatically predict those tracks in the future. We were higher than the *Meduse* and continued to rise, but her orbital course continued to close the distance.

"El Cano, *you must land immediately or you will be destroyed!*" the *Meduse* ordered. "*Respond and obey immediately! Over.*"

I focused my optical sensors on the Karst destroyer. She was under way, starting to lift out of orbit to pursue us. That was alarming enough, but even worse her dorsal turrets were rising out of their locked position. The *Meduse* had been prepared to land; now she was coming to action stations.

"Roger, *Meduse*," I said, ignoring the way Whitlake moved in his seat to stare at me past my holographic screen. "We are shutting down to return to Jacquerie Haven. *El Cano* out."

"*You mean we're not going to attack?*" Whitlake asked through the console.

Instead of replying directly, I said, "Ship, prepare to insert."

I shut down the thrusters and the High Drive. Both means of propulsion released ions which made it impossible to balance the ship's charge to enter the Matrix.

"Inserting!" I said as I executed.

We made a smooth transition. I gave a great sigh of relief and set the rig to deploy. Heaven knew how much of it really would rise without human help.

"Wedell," I said, "you'll need to go out by yourself for the time being. I sketched out a course while we were on the ground, but the *Meduse* forced us to insert way early, out of place, and with less sidereal velocity than I'd planned for."

"Roger," she said, getting up from the bunk. She walked to the airlock with her helmet in her hand.

"Red," I said, "we're going to attack just like we planned. I lied to the *Meduse* so they wouldn't start shooting at us. Even a near miss would change our surface charge enough that we wouldn't be able to insert until we'd rebalanced it. We're safe as long as we stay in the Matrix."

I shrugged. "Now," I said, "we won't be able to move very far when we've started out at such a low speed. On the other hand, we don't need to move very far. We'll be extracting very close to where we inserted—but we'll be coming back from a vector I hope they don't expect. Right?"

The Saguntine darter nodded to me. "Right," he said. "I'll be ready!"

He was making an effort to sound enthusiastic. That was good enough. Certainly it was as good as I could manage myself right now.

El Cano rang as Wedell closed the outer hatch of the airlock. I got to work plotting our new course through the Matrix.

The sloop's limited rig—four antennas, with only main

and foresails—meant there was less to go wrong than a more maneuverable ship would have, but the dorsal antenna wasn't fully vertical and the port mainyard hadn't even begun to rotate into place. I considered joining Wedell despite what I'd said, but then the telltale indicated that dorsal had locked. The hydromechanical indicators were touchy; the antenna itself may have been fine all along.

I resumed work on the course. I'd planned to attack the *Meduse*, but I couldn't predict her location. The likelihood was that when *El Cano* disappeared, the *Meduse* had stopped accelerating outward. She might be anywhere in a sphere of too large a volume for me to plot an attack.

That left the *Erich Koellner*. There was a reasonable chance that she would hold her orbit, in which case putting *El Cano* in an attack position would be just a question of my skill.

Though the *Koellner* was the only option as a target, there were several downsides. The Alliance destroyer mounted heavier plasma cannon—quite heavy, in fact, 12.5 centimeter weapons. In addition and probably worse, the Alliance crew would show a higher state of training than that of the Karst crew, and they were more likely to be alert.

There wasn't any choice. I worked on my course.

We shunted through four separate bubble universes. At each transition I rechecked the course according to the actual sail plan as it varied from the intended plan. The rig seemed to be loosening up with use. There were no serious misalignments after we made the final shift, so the attack should go in as I planned it.

If my calculations were right. And if the *Koellner* had held its same orbit.

I called Wedell in from the hull. I felt bad about not having gotten out to help her, though she clearly was capable of handling the job. My calculations had been more complex than I'd expected, both because of the initial problems with the rig and because I was so very aware of the fact that I had to get it right this time.

Rechecking wouldn't necessarily catch my errors; it hadn't when we attacked Karst. It was the only thing I knew to do, however, so that's what I did.

Wedell reentered the cabin, holding her helmet under her arm. "It's all solid, sir," she called. "I was worried about the port mainspar, but it only hung up the first time. It's been right as rain since."

"Ship," I said, using the PA system though with the propulsion systems shut down in the Matrix I wouldn't have had to. "We'll extract in three minutes. Red, launch when you bear. Over."

Wedell nodded and settled onto her bunk. Whitlake, running the console's simulation of the *Erich Koellner*, nodded but didn't speak.

For want of anything better to do, I began plotting a course to Benedict. Succeed or fail, *El Cano* couldn't very well land again on Saguntum. It made very little sense to plot so distant an escape course, but I preferred doing that rather than watching a clock read down.

When my screen pulsed pink to alert me, I switched the console to current sensor data—there was none, so the display was an opalescent cloud—and said, "Ship, prepare for extraction in five seconds. Extracting—*now*."

We extracted into normal space. I felt my bones freezing as the display came into sharp focus: The *Koellner* was exactly where the console had predicted it would be if I'd done my astrogation correctly.

I was reaching to engage the High Drive motors when a plasma bolt hit the starboard antenna. The mainsail diffused it slightly, but the heavy steel tubing caught most of the energy and slammed *El Cano*. We lurched; the second bolt hit the ventral topsail and yard.

The *Koellner* had registered the disruption to sidereal space caused by a ship extracting from the Matrix. She'd begun firing before *El Cano* even existed in the normal universe. Four of her heavy cannon could be brought to bear on our predicted location, and the last two bolts met us when we appeared.

My display fogged; vaporized metal from the rig had recondensed on the sensor pick-ups. If the first bolt hadn't jerked us out of our original alignment, the second would have struck us straight on in the bow.

A jolt and a roar, not another plasma bolt but *El Cano*'s weapon launching. "Dart away!" Whitlake shouted. "We got the bastard!"

The third bolt hit the underside of our port outrigger and spun the sloop like a flipped coin. The *Koellner*'s big guns were slower firing than the four-inch weapons which the RCN standardized for destroyers, but she got in that one additional round.

Our hull was leaking. Whipping when the outrigger was ripped away had started seams. My helmet was clipped onto the couch fitting intended for the purpose. I donned and latched it before the pressure had dropped to the level where riggers in the airlock going out would bother.

My first job after getting the helmet on was to correct our spin. The third hit had vaporized most of the outrigger. The bubble of gaseous steel had acted like a sudden rocket burn driving us clockwise. I engaged the motors on the starboard outrigger, giving them a five-second burn.

I was afraid to overcorrect because I had no way to deal with a counterclockwise rotation. The portside motors had vanished with the outrigger on which they'd been mounted.

The *Koellner* fired twice more while we spun. The plasma bolts appeared as glowing tracks in the glimpses I got of the screen. Neither of them came close; the damage we'd taken had flung us out of any predictable path.

My finger poised to try another tiny burn. I wondered if the destroyer would continue firing at us when the captain realized that *El Cano* was harmless junk. I guessed they would: Gunners don't get much chance to use their weapons, and the sloop was a real live-fire exercise.

I tapped the MANUAL EXECUTE icon. As I did so, the *Erich Koellner* turned inside out, scattering bits of itself and its crew like a slow-motion piñata. Our dart—Whitlake's dart—had gutted it like a fish.

"*Sir! Sir!*" Whitlake was shouting. "*I did it! I really did it!*"

I heard the words—he was shouting them into a two-way link formed by the word "Sir"—but I wasn't really connecting them with the wreck of the Alliance destroyer. Some of the *Koellner*'s crew must have survived—riggers suited to go out on the hull, damage crews standing by to glue sheeting over torn seams and to pinch off ruptured hydraulic lines.

Many of those drifting figures must be shouting in hope and terror, but I couldn't hear them; I couldn't hear anything from outside our cabin, not even static.

I brought up the communications screen. There was nothing, zero, on any of the media: long wave to microwave radio, modulated laser, *anything*. We were cut off from all forms of communication.

I stared at the debris spreading from what had been the *Erich Koellner*. They at least could call for help.

"Come on, Wedell," I said. "Let's go out and fix what's wrong with our commo suite."

Wedell and I went out together, leaving Whitlake at the console viewing over and over again the logged moment when the dart struck the *Koellner* just starboard of her central axis and quartered through the ship. The fusion bottle didn't vent, but that honestly couldn't have increased the damage much beyond what the dart had done to her as it was. Red had every right to be proud.

So did the *Koellner*'s gunners, as I saw even before I stepped out onto our hull. The airlock was on the port side. We had to push the outer hatch open with our shoulders, not because of warping as I'd first thought but because a mist of gaseous steel had cooled over everything facing what had been the port outrigger. The coating was as smooth and even as the layers of a pearl.

I supposed that steel similarly coated the commo suite, a blister on the port bow, but the problem there was even

DAVID DRAKE

simpler: A chunk of outrigger, still solid, had shaved off the blister and a six-by-three-foot patch of *El Cano*'s outer hull. If the angle had been slightly different, it would have come through the bridge and carried most of both me and the console out the other side.

There was nothing to fix about the commo suite. It was just gone. I took a look at the plasma thrusters. The starboard pair was apparently all right. The portside thrusters were problematic. The sphincter petals were bright with redeposited steel, which would keep them from opening and closing initially, but during use the stellite leaves should burn clean in seconds or at worst a minute or two.

Wedell had been looking over the rig. I signalled her to join me back in the cabin. We still had to keep our helmets on, but it was marginally more comfortable. The proper leads would have permitted us to speak through the console, but *El Cano* didn't have them; we were helmet to helmet inside as well, but without the risk of colliding with drifting debris.

"How's the rig?" I asked Wedell.

"Starboard may retract," she said. I'm sure she was shrugging in her rigging suit. "What's left of dorsal ought to be easy to cut away. Port is torn bad but'll be a bitch to cut the rest of the way, maybe as bad at if it was still as-installed. And Ventral, I'd say we're screwed. All the joints are plated. It'll take days to cut. Explosive'd be better, but we don't have any aboard. Do we?"

"No explosives that I know about," I said—also shrugging. "I'm going to see if I can angle the thrusters to counterbalance the surviving High Drive motors. I'll retract the outrigger if I can—that'll help."

516

Whitlake leaned forward from the striker's seat to tap me on the leg for attention. He pointed enthusiastically to the display, then settled back to continue watching on his own reduced screen. Wedell and I shifted to see what was happening on the main display.

Default on a military display was to caret movement, so even with degraded optics I could pick up not only the ship nearing orbit but the one that was rising through the atmosphere. I touched a control and a legend appeared next to either ship in a contrasting color: They were the *Magellanes* and the *Lezo*, respectively.

Whitlake shouted something I couldn't hear; I didn't need the words to understand his delight. As he spoke, a third caret appeared when our surviving sensors could distinguish the ship from the Military Harbor from which it rose. The legend CONCHA confirmed my expectation.

I shouted and slapped my thigh; the gauntlet cracked sharply on the stiffened plate of the rigging suit. "By heavens!" I shouted—to myself. "If they know what they're doing, they'll handle the *Meduse* even though she's on the alert!"

The trouble was—as I saw at once—the sloops' crews *didn't* know what they were doing. They weren't extending their antennas to enter the Matrix and come at the destroyer from unpredictable directions.

A destroyer with skilled crew, knowing what to look for, could pick up the disruption of sidereal space for up to ten seconds before a ship extracts from the Matrix. The *Erich Koellner* had done that, and we'd been lucky that her plasma bolts hadn't detonated our dart's fuel before Whitlake was able to launch.

The *Meduse*'s crew probably wasn't that good and the Karst vessel might not even have had sufficient sensor discrimination to do that. The sloops were surrendering their greatest advantage by coming straight in. In addition, the sails protected the target's hull from gunfire—once. Plasma bolts loosed all their energy on the first object they hit.

All the *Meduse* had to do was to keep at a distance and to fire at the sloops until the darts exploded or the darters launched them beyond burn-out range. When a dart's fuel was expended in vacuum, it no longer had any homing ability.

The *Meduse* was accelerating. I think the Karst captain initially planned to engage the *Magellanes*. When a second sloop joined her with a third rising behind them, the plan must have changed. The *Meduse* was accelerating not only at the best rate her High Drive could manage, but for over a minute, with the plasma thrusters burning also.

Her drives shut down. "I swear..." my lips said, but what my mind was really thinking was, "Pray heaven..."

The destroyer faded from our display as she inserted into the Matrix. The *Meduse*'s captain had watched one dart sloop destroy an Alliance vessel that was more powerful and better crewed than his own. Here were three more sloops.

The *Meduse* was running rather than face them.

I hugged Wedell, and Whitlake sprang up to join us. Space above Saguntum was now firmly in the control of the Saguntum Naval Defense Force.

I looked at the display again to see whether any of the sloops were shaping toward us. We had no way to communicate with anybody.

Whitlake slapped me on the shoulder and pointed into the holographic display, disrupting it until he took his hand away. I looked at the planet again instead of toward the sloops.

A fourth vessel was rising from the Military Harbor.

She was the *Alfraz*. I cheered myself hoarse.

Chapter Forty-three

After the first rush of relief—*I'm not going to die when the air runs out!*—I realized that I had more work to do. Using the thrusters with the petals flared open, I managed to kill our spin completely. I'd gotten close enough with the High Drive that there was no discomfort to the crew, but if we were going to transfer to another ship it'd be a lot better if we were dead still.

I had another concern that I wouldn't have spoken aloud even if it'd been easier to communicate while wearing suits: I didn't trust the shiphandling skills of whoever was crewing the *Alfraz*. It was possible that somebody in the Saguntine force was expert, but there was no reason any of them should be. As for the Sunrays, Gamba *might* have played with shiphandling, but ordinary riggers wouldn't have. Generally warrant officers had some experience conning small boats, but they'd all gone off with Captain Leary.

Wedell attached a full air bottle and went back out on the hull. I stuck at the console in case there was something I could do. I could maneuver *El Cano* to a degree, but I didn't intend to do so since I had no means of communication with our rescuers.

The *Alfraz* swelled slowly on my display. I half expected her to collide with us, but tiny blooms from her thrusters damped her motion perfectly. She hung alongside us, so close that we'd have touched if our dorsal antenna had been full length.

I could see three spacers on the hull. There was a *clang*—felt through my boots, not heard in the vacuum—as a magnetic grapple locked on. Wedell moved into the field of my optics and proceeded up the line arm after arm.

I tapped Whitlake on the shoulder and pointed to the airlock. It was time for us to be going also.

I put Whitlake on the line ahead of me and waited till his magnetic boots were on the hull of the *Alfraz* before I followed him. Mixon gripped me and motioned our helmets together.

"Anybody else?" he asked.

"Just the three of us," I said.

He gestured the three of us to the airlock and with his fellow Sunrays began coiling up the grapnel after cutting the power to release it. Three people—two of them in rigging suits—was about capacity for the *Alfraz*'s lock, so I didn't argue the point.

We had our helmets off when we stepped onto the bridge. The people greeting us were clinging to whatever each one could, since they weren't wearing boots with magnetic soles. I'd hoped Monica would be here, but I had to call, "Watch it!" when she would've thrown herself into my arms. "There's metal fittings on this suit and they're cold!"

It hadn't even crossed my mind that Maeve Grimaud might be aboard. She stood against the rear bulkhead, gripping the vertical support of a stack of bunks. She was smiling coolly and trying to look as though holding herself in place that way wasn't a strain.

I was almost as surprised to see Lal seated at the console. "I have done this before, sir," he said, nodding politely. "I am glad to see you well."

And of course he'd maneuvered ships together in the past. It was a rare skill among honest spacers, but fairly common among pirates.

"Lal!" I said. "Where did *you* come from?"

"It was kind of your Captain Leary to offer me a place," he said. "It seemed that such an excellent organization as the RCN, however, was not a suitable place for so humble a person as me."

The Sunrays came in from the hull, laughing about how well the operation had gone. "Hey, good to see you, sir!" Gadient called. "When we heard what you'd done, we figured that was all she wrote for you."

"And pretty bloody close from the way the ship looks!" Mixon said.

"The *Koellner* looks worse," I said. "Say, can we get under way now? Unless there's a problem, Lal, just bring us up to one gee. We'll worry about the course later."

I finished getting my suit off a moment after the High Drive kicked in to provide the equivalent of gravity. I turned to find Monica, but she was already beside me. The Sunrays cheered as we kissed.

Then she stepped back and with an unexpectedly serious look said, "Roy, you asked where Lal came from. Mistress Grimaud located him and convinced him to join us. And she really planned this whole operation. Except what you did yourself."

Maeve hadn't moved from where she stood, though her nonchalant appearance seemed a trifle more genuine now that she no longer had to grip the stanchion. She said, "I thought it was possible that my loyalty to Cinnabar might have been in doubt. I've tried to allay those doubts."

"I didn't realize the two of you had met," I said, smiling brightly and really wishing I weren't in the middle of this conversation. "Ah, Maeve"—I thought of calling her *Mistress Grimaud* but didn't—"I'm pretty sure that when this story gets back to Xenos, you'll find your superiors lining up to take credit for sending you to Saguntum."

"One can only hope," Maeve said with a cold expression.

"Ah, sir?" said Cassidy, the big man in battledress whom I'd met as Colonel Foliot's second-in-command. "I've got some wounded men and I'd appreciate if we could get them to help sooner rather than later. Ah—if you could?"

"The temporary capital is at Borodin," Monica said. "It's on the other side of the Genevieves and you can land starships there. The *Kurfurstendamm* brought armored vehicles as well as men, but Dad says he can block the passes if they try to move on Borodin."

"Sure, let's set down there," I said. "But—wounded? Who?"

"Mistress Grimaud got the roadblock on Holywell Street moved before we arrived," Monica said, "but Major Cassidy and a platoon of Special Police hidden in a furniture van were necessary to get us into the Military Harbor. They're on the couches in the hold—it was the best way to escape."

"Ah," I said.

I was trying to decide what next to say when Lal got up from the console. "Captain?" he said. "Since you're here, would you care to land us? I would rather that you did."

I settled behind the console. I had a lot of questions to ask and I'd get around to them. Right now, though, I was glad to have a moderately challenging job to do that would prevent anybody from talking to me for an hour or so.

Borodin was at a river mouth. It wasn't much of a place by itself, but the *Annotated Charts* said the river system drained most of the plain to the east of the Genevieve Mountains. The agricultural products—mostly grain—were taken to Jacquerie by sea on bulk carriers and loaded on starships there for export. Though Borodin wasn't a starport, it had plenty of sheltered water to land on, and better facilities than Salaam to serve any ships that did land.

I'd figured to set down without landing control, but in fact the signal from Borodin was sharp and professional. That puzzled me as I started braking us in. Then I remembered the station and microwave link in the mountains above us. Boelke and Sacrisson were earning their pay, possibly for the first time. A fire department isn't a waste of tax money, even if those assigned to it spend most of the time washing their cars.

Harbor Control brought us down on a spot not far from the surface docks. I let the console make the landing. I grinned as I recalled that the facilities here were a considerable step up from what we'd found when we first stopped to take on water after our escape from Salaam. To begin with, we weren't going to have a giant slug—or whatever the devil it'd been—crawl aboard through the pump intake.

We landed more smoothly than if we'd been in a proper harbor; here the waves our thrusters raised could expand at will across the broad estuary. Surface vessels and other starships—if there'd been any; there weren't at the moment, though I supposed the dart sloops would operate from here—would rock and pitch, but the *Alfraz* didn't dance in her own violence reflected by the walls of a slip confining her.

I shut down the thrusters. Lal went through the hatch to the hold—to drop our anchor, I supposed, though I'd have to send somebody else if I didn't hear the rattle of the chain shortly.

The Sunrays began opening the bridge hatches. I saw Wedell and Mixon start toward the hold and called, "Sunrays? Not yet. The police aren't used to the fog and crap, and we'd none of us be here if it wasn't for them helping."

I sneezed violently. I'd slitted my eyes, but they were watering anyway. Frankly, I'd have been just as happy if my crew hadn't been so quick to prove how tough they were by letting in the steam and ions that would hang over the *Alfraz* for another ten minutes.

The sparkling fog thinned as it cooled, so I switched my display to real-time visuals. I could see people waiting on the seawall which ran for a half mile along the river frontage, but I wondered why they'd brought us down here instead of closer to the grain docks. Then a barge and a second barge following pulled slowly between us and the seawall. Even before they dropped anchor, I saw teams on their decks readying walkways to link all of us in a chain to the shore.

"Ship," I called, "I'm opening the main hatch. Everybody remain aboard until I get direction from Harbor Control."

The hatch began to grind down, filling the ship with fog rather than steam with just a tang of ozone. Because our anchorage wasn't enclosed, landing didn't involve the usual stink of burned garbage.

"Alfraz," the console said. "*You are free to disembark. Control out.*"

I'd decided not to bother with an anchor watch. I keyed the PA system and said, "All personnel! Saguntum is proud of you, and by heaven, so am I! You are all free to disembark. Captain out!"

The Sunrays on the bridge with me paused for the police contingent—some pairs using couches as stretchers—to clear the boarding ramp; then they followed. I started after them, holding Monica closely.

Maeve Grimaud, standing beside the hatch, said, "Mistress Foliot? You probably want to greet your father. Roy will be along in just a moment."

Monica looked at her, then smiled with her lips and said, "Yes, Dad's probably been worried. Roy, I'll see you soon."

She turned to me and lifted to give me a quick peck. "Don't forget me, please," she said as she slipped out the hatch.

"Ah, Maeve," I said, liking this situation only slightly more than I had finding her and Monica both waiting when I entered the *Alfraz*. "I plan to tell anybody who'll listen that you're the reason Saguntum owns its orbital space. And that you saved my life besides."

"I guessed you'd think that," Maeve said, "and I'm sure nobody else will tell you different, so I will. The only reason those three sloops lifted to join you is that Monica Foliot gave a speech to the crews that made them ashamed to do anything else. Believe me, they'd planned to stay in barracks whether or not there were Alliance guards. Many of them aren't even from Saguntum, remember?"

She grinned in a fashion that I remembered. "They're men, though," she said. "And she made them believe they wouldn't be if they didn't go up to help you. And this ship"—she rapped her knuckles on the bulkhead—"wouldn't have been much use if there was still a Karst destroyer in orbit." Her face settled slightly. "Though we'd have tried. Your Sunrays were clear on that, and Monica and I were going to tag along."

I swallowed. "Thank you, Maeve," I said. She was probably right that nobody else would've told me.

"That's all I had to say," she said. She turned toward the hatch.

"Maeve?" I said. "If I can ask? How did you get the roadblock to withdraw for the commando to enter?"

"An order from the Alliance communications center directed the troops at Holywell Street to reinforce the roadblock on the next street to the east," she said. "A signals lieutenant thought he was allowing my fiancé to escape. And if you wonder how he was bribed to do that"—Maeve's smile was as hard and cold as a scimitar blade—"let's just say that not every young officer is as iron-willed as you are, Lieutenant Olfetrie."

I bowed to her. Maeve left the bridge, and a moment later I followed.

"Your alert saved us," Colonel Foliot said as he grasped my hand on the pier. "I knew we couldn't hold them in Jacquerie and I didn't want the kind of bloodbath that'd mean anyway, but I was able to get most of my people and even some of the Jacquerie Regiment out of the city."

Borodin had looked like a tent camp as *Alfraz* thundered down for a landing. At sea level it wasn't much different. The original buildings, mostly stabilized earth and structural plastic, were surrounded by and interspersed with structures whose walls were flattened cans and packing crates with tarpaulin roofs.

Foliot followed my eyes. "Sanitation's a problem," he said, "and we're bloody lucky they didn't invade in fall when the rains start. We're trucking in water from upstream but there's no way to purify it besides boiling."

I could see that many of the barges drawn up along both banks were being converted into accommodations also. They couldn't all have come from Jacquerie. I asked, "Do you have a government?"

"I'm ruling in the name of President Perez," Foliot said. "I tried to warn him, but I couldn't get through his *bloody* staff. General Meyerberg, he's the Alliance CO. He's tried to get Perez to welcome Alliance help, but Israel's got balls enough for two, so that isn't going anywhere. What we've got for now is a stalemate."

He made a sweep of his arm. "Folks are coming in from all the farms," he said. "There's three thousand militia here or on the way. And I've got about a thousand with training, my Commando and army. What we *don't* have is guns, but even if Meyerberg could get his people over the mountains there's no way they can take Borodin. He's got about twelve hundred troops, but there's fifty armored personnel carriers with automatic impellers. I can't push that out of Jacquerie with what I've got."

"Ah, sir?" I said. "How are we going to proceed?"

"We're going to sit on our hands," the colonel said. "The future of Saguntum is going to be decided by whoever gets reinforced. If an Alliance squadron shows up, I'll capitulate. It's that simple. If it's Cinnabar, then Meyerberg will if he's got any sense."

Foliot gave me the sort of smile you might expect from a man on the gallows. "I've killed plenty of people in my time," he said. "I don't need to kill more, for no bloody reason. So we'll hold what we've got and wait for the odds to change— one way or the other."

I took a deep breath. "Then with your approval, sir..." I said. "I'll set up a training and patrol schedule for the sloops. After they come in, of course. There's obviously nothing wrong with the courage of the crews, but we can work on more effective tactics. And I'll integrate the Sunrays into the local personnel, just to have the experience available if needed."

Foliot smiled sadly. "I used to have energy," he said. *The man who'd just created a functioning state a matter of days after the old one was destroyed.* "But given that the sloops are still in orbit, I suggest you take the rest of the day off."

He looked away, cleared his throat, and added, "And Olfetrie? Thank you for bringing my daughter back from ben Yusuf. And, well, thank you."

"Yes, *sir*," I said. Monica was waiting ten feet down the pier, seeming to view the landscape of transformed Borodin.

It was good to have her in my life.

I expected arguments from my new command—at least from some of the Saguntine spacers. Instead they acted like I'd been sent from the heavens to guide them. Part of it may have been Red, who made it sound like I'd put *El Cano* close enough to our target to reach out and touch it. We'd been close enough in all truth, but some of that was luck.

And nobody seemed put off by the hammering *El Cano* had gotten. The wreckage was still drifting away from Saguntum; maybe out of sight really was out of mind.

A portion of the *Koellner* near the stern continued to orbit: the Battle Direction Center and compartments immediately forward and below. Using that as a target, I demonstrated to each crew how to slip into the Matrix, then extract to launch attacks. Only Esterhazy of the Saguntine captains could really astrogate so cleanly, but it was good exercise for the others and they might get lucky.

At worst, it was better than lining up in normal space the way they'd done with the *Meduse*. If they'd been facing the *Koellner* instead, she'd have knocked all three of them down before they got into dart range.

I kept one sloop in space at all times, trading off every four hours. I took a tour daily, moving from one sloop to the next. I got to know the crews better that way and showed myself to them besides. They were a good bunch, a lot better than I'd given them credit for being when I first met them.

I'd gone up in *Magellanes* with Gadient added to the Saguntine crew and Smith as captain. Smith had made the insertion on the command screen while I was shadowing him from the striker's seat. My calculations showed that Smith's course would put us about a hundred thousand miles out from the drifting target, too far for effective use of a dart, but I'd go over it with him in private after we landed.

In fact we were within fifty thousand miles—still too far, but ten times better than Smith could have managed at the start—but I wasn't paying attention to the exercise. We'd extracted to find a fleet orbiting Saguntum.

"*Saguntine ship* Magellanes," announced my console. "*Lay to and prepare to be boarded. Do not make any hostile move by orders of Commodore Leary, commanding Combined Force Harbinger. Over.*"

I'm good on voices. Despite being distorted by transmission, I recognized Lady Mundy speaking.

"*Sir!*" Captain Smith said through the link. "*Has Cinnabar rescued us then?*"

"A lot of the ships are from the 7th Destroyer Flotilla," I said. "The *Ariadne*'s an Alliance cruiser, though, and there's at least two Fleet destroyers besides."

But we had more important business than figuring out what was going on. "*Magellanes* to *Rotherham*," I said. "We understand your instructions and are obeying. Our dart firing circuits are locked at the console."

"Sir, what's happening?" Gadient asked, leaning toward me. He didn't sound worried, exactly, but spacers don't like surprises.

"Ship, we're waiting for Captain Leary to send somebody to board us," I said. "That's all I know, but"—I smiled around the cabin—"I'm happier now than I was a little bit ago!"

A pinnace pulled away from the *Rotherham*. That was a bit of a surprise because it was larger than I'd thought any RCN destroyer carried—even destroyer leaders like the *Rotherham* and *Quilliam* in the 7th Flotilla. Because we had time, I queried the pinnace's embedded data—and learned it was assigned to the light cruiser *Ariadne*.

"Ship," I said, because I thought it was a good idea that everybody on *El Cano* was aware of the situation before people came aboard. "The boat arriving to search us is from the Alliance. This isn't a problem. Captain Leary sent it to us. Captain out."

I certainly hoped it wasn't a problem.

"Smith," I said, linking with the Saguntine captain, "I'll take over now, if I may."

Smith didn't just agree, he thanked me.

"Ship, cutting power," I said. Then I set the sails to furl; Gadient took the riggers out to guide the process. When the sticks were bare, I retracted and clamped the rig. I didn't know what Captain Leary had in mind for us, but I didn't think it would involve maneuvering through the Matrix. Lowering the rig would make it easier to come aboard.

The pinnace came alongside expertly. The boat had steam jets for extremely low-impulse movements, but this coxswain didn't need them. They joined faster than I thought was safe, but it braked alongside with precise enthusiasm. The airlock rotated open and two spacers in rigging suits came out on the hull. One cast a magnetic grapnel toward our hull; Gadient caught it and manually slapped it down.

The next surprise was that three more figures got out wearing air suits. The riggers actually walked them to the line and crossed before and behind what must be a group of laymen.

I'd hoped—it didn't make any sense, but I had—that Six himself would be boarding us. I wanted somebody to take over so that I could stop thinking.

Our airlock opened. The man who entered first with his helmet off was unfamiliar to me. He said, "I'm Colonel Grozhinski of the Forces." The Alliance military. "Captain Leary suggested that the safest way to get me down to Borodin would be for you to take me, Captain Olfetrie. We realized you that you might have doubts"—that was putting it mildly! —"but Lady Mundy is here to vouch for what I've told you."

And there she was when he stepped aside; and Tovera smirking beside her. "Yes," Mundy said. "We will announce ourselves after we land, but it appeared to all parties—"

She paused and I could almost see her mind revisiting to what she had just said.

"—all the principals to the decision, that is, that it will be safest if we land as part of the existing order of business rather than arousing particular attention. Do you see any problem with that?"

"No, ma'am," I said. "As soon as the rest of the crew is aboard, we'll do just that."

The airlock was cycling behind our passengers, bringing in Gadient and the remaining Saguntines. I manually keyed commo and said, "Borodin Control, this is sloop *Magellanes*. We're coming in as scheduled."

I'd tweaked the automatic landing system of the *Lezo*, much the way that I'd done with the *Alfraz*, but I hadn't gotten around to *Magellanes* or *Concha* yet. Regardless, I let the console land us. The thrusters had a nasty lateral wobble in final approach, but it never became dangerous.

Watching the pinnace match velocity with us had made me very well aware of how much I had to learn about shiphandling. I'd keep on training, but not while carrying Lady Mundy and an Alliance envoy—who didn't want to be put down in Alliance-held Jacquerie.

Though I'd said that we were making a scheduled landing, Control knew better and so did Colonel Foliot, judging from the fact that he and half a dozen aides were waiting on the pier for me to open up the *Magellanes*. I didn't let the situation rush me.

Well, rush me very much. *Magellanes* had only four thrusters and we were anchored on an estuary flushed by the river and by the regular winds up and down the channel. I shaved two minutes off our cooling time.

"Ship, opening up!" I said and pressed Execute. "Crew, stay on board until our passengers have gotten off!"

Mundy turned to me. "Officer Olfetrie," she said. "I suggest you join us when we meet Director Foliot."

"Yes, ma'am," I said, same as I'd have done if she told me to jump into the harbor.

I followed Tovera, who in turn followed her mistress and the envoy, across the walkway. When they'd all reached the six steps to the pier, I turned and waved back to the *Magellanes*. My crew, waiting for release in the boarding hold, poured out.

"Director Foliot," Lady Mundy said as joined her, "this is Colonel Grozhinski. He's here to end the fighting."

Foliot was in battledress and carried a pistol in a shoulder holster. Grozhinski had been wearing a dress uniform under his air suit and he'd brought a saucer hat as well. It must have been designed to compress, because he'd been holding nothing when he crossed from the pinnace.

The two colonels shook hands. Foliot straightened and said, "I don't recognize your branch of service, Colonel?"

"We wear the same ranks and uniforms as the Army," Grozhinski said, tapping his lapel insignia. "But our chain of command in the 5th Bureau is separate."

"Ah," said Foliot. "Shall we go into my office where we can discuss your terms in private?"

"There are no terms, Director," Grozhinski said. "A colleague—in a different diocese—exceeded his authority by committing the Alliance to warlike actions without clearing them with the Guarantor. I'm here to correct his mistake as quickly and completely as possible."

"Bloody hell," Foliot said in a quiet voice. I hadn't realized how tense he'd been until that moment; his flesh suddenly hung on the bones like a snapped elastic.

"Lady Mundy said that you might have an aircar," Grozhinski said. "If that's true and you're willing to lend it for this purpose, I believe we can take care of the business very quickly."

He smiled. "I thought we could inform General Meyerberg that you're sending peace envoys," he added. "Our first concern was that your forces not shoot us down when we landed, which is why we used one of your own ships. The second concern is the reverse of that, but we believe Meyerberg will take good care of anyone whom he believes can get him out of the hole into which he's dug himself."

"The car and a driver are at your disposal," Foliot said. Then he repeated, "Bloody hell."

Epilogue

I'd planned that the Naval Strike Force would end the march with a jog for the last half mile back to barracks, but after the ninth mile I radioed Mixon, who was in the lead, and told him to bag the notion. As it was, two of the Saguntines were clinging to me as we staggered the last hundred yards and each of my Sunrays helped support another.

Besides, Wedell had three who'd collapsed in the cart she was hauling behind a farm tractor. I think the only reason the Sunrays and I were doing so well was that we were embarrassed at the thought of giving up in front of the Saguntines.

"Catch you in the showers," I wheezed to the spacers I'd been helping. I moved over to where Wedell had pulled up to help her with the people who'd gotten a lift in the cart.

They were actually in better shape than I was after having a few miles rest. Lieutenant Smith was among them. "Sir," he said. "My right calf cramped. I'll do better next time, I swear I will."

"We all will," I said. "And I'll know better the next time than to start the program with a ten-mile hike."

"Need a hand, sir?" Wedell said. From the worry on her face, I wonder what I looked like.

"No, just park the tractor and show up at 0800," I said. Before we started off I'd told my people they were automatically dismissed for the day when we got back. A shower would feel good. Especially if there was still something left of the water that the sun had been warming in the rack of drums while we were gone.

I was so tired that I only noticed the men who'd been waiting on the bench in front of the barracks when they got to their feet. The figures could have been bushes for all the impression they'd made on me but my eyes registered the motion.

"Good afternoon, Olfetrie," Captain Leary said. The man beside him was Hogg.

"Sir!" I said and tried to straighten to attention. I started to topple; Hogg's left hand steadied me. He didn't say anything but he smiled.

"Let's sit down on this very comfortable bench for a moment," the captain said. He was smiling too.

"I'm sorry, sir," I said as I thumped down. "I'm trying to get the Strike Force into shape, but I started out with too ambitious a program. Bloody near too ambitious for me, obviously."

The army engineer company had put in the bench in front when they built us the barracks. Most troops and all the militia were in tents or shelters they'd built themselves, but I'd asked Director Foliot to jump the Strike Force to the head of the line. Somebody had to be first, after all, and my boys had seen real action.

"I watched you coming in," Captain Leary said. "I'd say you were doing pretty well. But you said, 'Strike Force'?"

"Well, I changed the name for, well..." I said. "Anyway, I changed the name to reflect what we really do. That attack on Karst wasn't defense, after all, and we cleared hostile vessels out of the system pretty actively!"

"Indeed," Leary said. "Exercising together should help build team spirit, too." Without changing his mildly positive tone, he went on, "Are you planning to build a career here?"

"Sir!" I said. I'd have jumped to my feet except I was pretty sure my legs would dump me back on my arse, looking like a fool. "Sir, I've just been doing this until you gave me orders to do something else."

"You've clearly done very well," Leary said, "but you're technically a civilian and wouldn't have to answer to anybody if you wanted to take a position on Saguntum. And before you answer, you should know that Resident Jimenez has made a strong request that I transfer you to the diplomatic service at the rank of Counsellor of Mission."

"What?" I said.

"Indeed," Leary said, bobbing his head. "I gather the status of the position varies depending on the importance of the world involved, but even on Saguntum you'd be the equivalent of a lieutenant commander in the RCN."

"Why in heaven's name would Jimenez recommend *that*?" I said. I hadn't seen the Foreign Ministry delegation since before the invasion. They'd been captured along with Perez and the civil government when the *Kurfurstendamm* landed.

"I gather he's convinced that you held Saguntum to its Friendship with the Republic while he and his staff were incarcerated," Leary said. "And from what I've seen, he may have been right."

"No, sir," I said. "Colonel Foliot *was* Saguntum until you came back and freed the civil government. He could be that now if he wanted to be. And he wasn't going to cut a deal with the Alliance."

I wondered how much Maeve had to do with the Foreign Ministry offer. I wondered a lot of things about Maeve.

Taking a deep breath, I got carefully to my feet. Leary and Hogg stood also.

I said, "Sir, what I want to be is an officer of the RCN. If you can arrange it for me to reenter the Academy, I'll be eternally grateful. I think this—"

I waved sort of generally, indicating the harbor and the *Rotherham* now floating there. We'd heard the destroyer descending halfway through the hike, but it hadn't occurred to me that it meant anything in particular for me.

"—has been enough to make people forget my dad. I hope so, anyway."

Captain Leary pursed his lips over a thought.

"Sir," I said, "you don't have to do that, do *anything* more for me to be eternally thankful. I'll enlist as a common spacer if I have to and work my way into a commission that way."

"That's not easy," Leary said, "but you know, I think you might be able to pull it off. Still, I don't think third-year cadet is really the best use of you. You're aware that my current post makes me a commodore?"

"Yessir," I said. He was the captain in charge of a squadron; or in this case, flotilla, because they were destroyers.

"The rank permits me to appoint a flag lieutenant," Captain Leary said. "That's a dogsbody, really, an aide who might have to do any bloody thing that might come up."

Hogg snorted. "And he means *any* bloody thing," he said. "Except for women—them he can take care of himself."

Leary's smile wasn't directed at me; I'm not sure it was directed at anybody. "A range of duties, at any rate," he said. "The choice out here is slimmer than it would be on Cinnabar, but even on Cinnabar I don't think I could find a better man for the position than you've proven to be in the time I've known you. Do you want the job, Olfetrie?"

"Sir," I said. I was afraid I was going to cry, but that wouldn't be the first time I'd embarrassed myself. "Sir, there's some things I need to take care of here"—I wanted Monica in my life; forever, if that was possible. But if she wanted me as I hoped she did, she was getting an RCN officer—"but sir, *yes*. If you'll have me."

I *did* start crying. I tried to salute when I remembered to, but as my hand rose. Captain Leary gripped and shook it.

ACKNOWLEDGMENTS

Dan Breen continues as my first reader, thank goodness, and archives my texts; as does my webmaster, Karen Zimmerman. Dorothy Day, who was the West-Coast member of my distributed archive, died while I was writing this one.

I regret this a lot. Dorothy was a good person.

My printer and computers behaved well during the writing until Microsoft, in its infinite wisdom, forced a software update, at the end of which my three computers didn't talk to one another and only one of them recognized my printer. Fortunately, my son Jonathan was able to fix things.

What do people do if their kids aren't geeks? But perhaps there aren't such people nowadays.

I eat well and the house stays clean and neat, which is wholly due to my wife Jo.

I thank all of you for making it possible for me to write.

—Dave Drake
Chatham County, NC

ABOUT THE AUTHOR

David Drake was attending Duke University Law School when he was drafted. He served the next two years in the Army, spending 1970 as an enlisted interrogator with the 11th Armored Cavalry in Vietnam and Cambodia. Upon return he completed his law degree at Duke and was for eight years Assistant Town Attorney for Chapel Hill, North Carolina. He has been a full-time freelance writer since 1981. His books include the genre-defining and bestselling *Hammer's Slammers* series, and the nationally bestselling RCN series including *In the Stormy Red Sky*, *The Road of Danger*, and *The Sea without a Shore*.